A DAY IN THE LIFE OF ANCIENT ROME

Alberto Angela

A DAY IN THE LIFE OF ANCIENT ROME

*Translated from the Italian
by Gregory Conti*

Europa
editions

Europa Editions
116 East 16th Street
New York, N.Y. 10003
www.europaeditions.com
info@europaeditions.com

Translation by Gregory Conti
Original title: *Una giornata nell'antica Roma*
Translation copyright © 2009 by Europa Editions

Library of Congress Cataloging in Publication Data is available
ISBN 978-1-933372-71-6

Angela, Alberto
A Day in the Life of Ancient Rome

Book design by Emanuele Ragnisco
www.mekkanografici.com

Illustrations by Luca Tarlazzi © 3ntini Service
Virtual imaging appearing in cover art by Altair4 Multimedia, Rome
(www.altair4.it)

Prepress by Plan.ed – Rome

Printed in Canada

CONTENTS

To Monica,
Riccardo, Edoardo, and Alessandro.
And to the light they have brought
to my life.

INTRODUCTION

What was life like for the ancient Romans? What went on every day on the streets of Rome? These are questions that all of us, at one time or another, have asked ourselves. And my guess is that it's precisely this kind of curiosity that led you to open this book.

No doubt about it, ancient Rome holds an indescribable magic for all of us. We feel it every time we visit an archaeological site from the Roman era. Unfortunately, more often than not, the guidebooks and site exhibits provide only generic notions about daily life as it was actually lived in the places that you are exploring, while focusing almost exclusively on architectural styles or dates.

But actually there is a trick to acquiring a real understanding of everyday life in these sites. Pay attention to the details: the signs of wear on the steps, the graffiti inscribed on the plaster walls (Pompeii is full of it), the grooves left in the pavement by cart wheels or the scratches on the marble doorsill of a house, caused by the movement of the (long since vanished) front door.

If you concentrate on these particulars, any ruin you visit will suddenly come back to life and you'll be able to "see" the people of that bygone age. That's the spirit behind this book: rediscovering one of the greatest eras in human history as it comes down to us in countless little stories.

During my many years of shooting television shows among the ruins of ancient Rome and Roman archaeological sites throughout the Mediterranean, I've happened upon an extraordinary number of stories and details, forgotten for centuries and rediscovered by archaeologists, about life in the time of imperial Rome. These site visits have put me in touch with the habits and practices of everyday life; with the customs and social rules of a world that no longer exists. I've had the same experience when I've talked to the archaeologists working on the excavations or read their books and publications.

I have come to understand that this precious information about the Roman world is almost never made accessible to people and is generally kept prisoner in specialized scientific journals or cordoned-off archaeological digs. So I have tried to tell you about it here.

The objective of these pages is to make the ruins of ancient Rome live again through an account of everyday life that tries to answer some very simple questions. What did it feel like to walk down the city streets? What kinds of people would you see? What could you see from the balconies? How was the food? What brand of Latin did people speak? How were the temples on the Capitoline Hill illuminated by the first light of dawn?

In a certain sense, what I have tried to do is turn on a television camera and explore the various parts of the city as they must have looked two thousand years ago, giving the reader the sensation of being on the streets of Rome, smelling its odors and the fragrances, observing the facial expressions of the people, going into a shop, a house, or the Colosseum. This is the only way to understand what it really meant to live in the capital of the Empire.

Living in Rome myself, it was fairly easy for me to describe the varying slants of sunlight shining on the streets and monuments throughout the day, or to visit archaeological sites to take note of the many small details to be added to those gathered in years of television programs and onsite inspections.

Naturally, the scenes that you will be looking at during this visit to ancient Rome are not imaginary. On the contrary, they are the direct result of scientific research and archaeological discoveries, laboratory analyses of specimens or skeletons, and examinations of ancient documents and texts.

It seemed to me that the best way to present all of this information in an orderly fashion was to follow the gradual unfolding of a day in the city. Each hour of the day has its corresponding place in the Eternal City with its own special activities. And so, hour by hour, we will discover a day in the life of ancient Rome.

There's just one more question. Why a book on Rome? Because our own way of life is the child of Rome. If ancient Rome had never existed, we would not be the way we are today. Think about it. Usually, Roman civilization is identified with the images of its emperors, with the legions marching off to war, and the long colonnades of Roman temples. But the real power of Roman civilization lay elsewhere. It was something that allowed Rome to survive for an unimaginably long time: over one thousand years in the West and, in the East, though the imperial capital was moved from Constantinople to Byzantium, even longer, over two thousand years, right up to the dawn of the Renaissance. No number of legions, no political or ideological system, is capable of ensuring such longevity. The secret of Rome was its everyday *modus vivendi*, its way of life: its way of building houses, dressing, eating, and interacting with others, both in and out of the family; all framed by a precise system of laws and social rules. Although it experienced some gradual evolution, this Roman way of life remained essentially unchanged for centuries, and it is what allowed Roman civilization to survive for such a long time.

But are we really sure that the Roman era is totally extinct? Actually, our legacy from the Roman Empire does not consist only of extraordinary statues and monuments. Rome also left us a lot of software that we use every day to live our lives. The alphabet that we use, even on the Internet, is Roman. The Italian language, like Spanish, French, Portuguese, and Romanian, derives from Latin. And much of the English language does too. Not to mention the Roman foundations of our legal system, road building, urban planning, architecture, painting, and sculpture. None of these would be the same without the Romans.

Indeed, when you really think about it, many of the most basic elements of Western civilization are nothing more than the modern evolution of the Roman way of life. That is, exactly what we would have seen every day on the streets and in the houses of imperial Rome.

I have tried to write the book that I've always wanted to find in a bookstore: a book that would satisfy my own curiosity about the world of ancient Rome. I hope it will also satisfy yours.

It all begins on a Roman side street in 115 CE, during the reign of the emperor Trajan, at the moment in which, in my opinion, Rome reached the height of its power and, perhaps, when it achieved the greatest expression of its beauty. It's the beginning of an ordinary day. Not long before daybreak . . .

Alberto Angela

The World Back Then

In 115 CE, under Trajan, the Roman Empire had achieved its greatest geographical expansion. The perimeter of its borders was over six thousand miles long, almost a quarter of the Earth's circumference. The Empire stretched from Scotland to the edge of Iran, from the Sahara to the North Sea.

Its inhabitants were drawn from the most diverse populations. From the blonds of northern Europe to the dark-haired peoples of the Middle East, from Asians to North Africans.

Imagine, today, trying to bring together the populations of China, Russia, and the United States. Relative to the world's population at the time, the population of the Roman Empire was even larger than that.

And above all, the Empire ruled over a vast variety of environments. Walking from one end to the other, we would have encountered icy seas with seals and sea lions, immense forests of fir trees, prairies, snow-capped mountains, huge glaciers, and then lakes and rivers leading us down to the warm beaches of the Mediterranean and the volcanoes of the Italian peninsula. Continuing on to the opposite bank of what the Romans called the *Mare Nostrum* (Our Sea), we would have found ourselves before the dunes of a boundless desert (the Sahara) and then the coral reefs of the Red Sea.

No empire in all of history has included such a variety of natural environments. Everywhere, the official language was Latin. Everywhere, payments were made in sestertii. Everywhere, there was only one law: Roman law.

Curiously, the population of this vast empire was small: barely fifty million; a little less than the population of Italy today. It was dispersed in a constellation of villages, boroughs, isolated agricultural villas, distributed throughout an immense territory, like crumbs on a tablecloth, with great cities suddenly rising up out of nowhere.

All the major cities were connected by an efficient network of roads, which extended over somewhere between fifty thousand and sixty thousand miles, and which we still use today, in our cars and trucks. This network of roads may be the greatest and most enduring monument left to us by the Romans. But immediately beyond these roads, there were still enormous expanses of untouched wilderness, with wolves, bear, deer, and wild boar. To us, accustomed to landscapes of cultivated fields and industrial warehouses, all of this wilderness would have seemed like an endless series of national parks.

The defense of this world was entrusted to the legions, stationed in forts, the famous *limes,* in the most delicate points of the Empire, almost always along its frontiers. Under Trajan, the army consisted of one hundred and fifty thousand men, grouped into thirty or so legions with historic names, like the Thirtieth Ulpia Victrix on the Rhine, the Second Adiutrix on the Danube, or the Sixteenth Flavia Firma on the Euphrates, not far from the border of present-day Iraq.

The legionnaires were supplemented by auxiliaries, soldiers provided by the peoples of the provinces, who doubled the size of the effective armed forces, bringing them to a total of three hundred to four hundred thousand armed men under the emperor's command.

The heart of it all was Rome. It stood at the exact center of the Empire.

Of course, Rome was a power center, but it was also a city rich in art and culture—writers, philosophers, and legal scholars. And above all it was a cosmopolitan city, not unlike New

York or London today, a city where you could meet people from all over the world. Among the crowds thronging its streets you would have encountered rich matrons reclining on their litters, Greek doctors, cavalry officers from Gaul, Italian senators, Spanish sailors, Egyptian priests, Cypriot prostitutes, Middle Eastern merchants, German slaves . . .

Rome had become the most highly populated city on the planet: almost a million and half people. The world had seen nothing like it since the appearance of *Homo sapiens*. How did they all manage to live together? Our visit to the Eternal City will help us uncover what everyday life was like in imperial Rome, at the time of the Empire's maximum expansion and dominion over the ancient world.

The lives of tens of millions of people throughout the Empire depended on what was decided in Rome. But, in turn, what did life in Rome depend on? It was the product of an intricate web of social relationships. A surprising universe, unique in history, which we will get to know by exploring an ordinary day, let's say a Tuesday, 1,894 years ago.

A Few Hours Before Dawn

H er eyes are staring off into the distance, like those of someone lost in contemplation. The pale moonlight reveals a soft countenance, milky white, with just a hint of a smile. She has a ribbon around her forehead and her hair is up, but a few disobedient strands have broken loose and lie on her shoulders. A sudden puff of wind raises a cloud of dust around her, but her hair doesn't move. Nor could it; it's made of marble. Just as her bare arms are made of marble, as well as the hundreds of folds in her gown. The sculptor who crafted her used one of the world's most precious marbles, fixing in stone the likeness of one of the Romans' most revered deities: *Mater Matuta* (the Great Mother), "the mother of good auspices," goddess of fertility, of the "beginning," and of dawn. And the statue has been here for many years now, on its imposing marble pedestal, presiding over a neighborhood intersection. She is surrounded by darkness, but the diffuse pallor of the moonlight reveals the presence, beyond her marble arms, of a wide street lined with shops on both sides. At this hour of the night they are shut with sturdy bolt locks and heavy wooden boards inserted in the pavement. They are on the bottom floor of immense unlit buildings. These huge black profiles are all around us, as though we were on the bottom of a canyon looking up at the star-filled canopy overhead. The buildings are *insulae*, housing for the lower classes, or plebeians, similar to our apartment buildings, only a lot less comfortable.

The lack of lighting in these buildings, and generally on the streets of Rome, is surprising. But maybe that's because we've grown too used to the bright lights of our modern cities. For centuries, when night fell, the cities of the world were engulfed in darkness, apart from the rare lanterns of some inn or the lamps illuminating some sacred images, usually placed in strategic places, like street corners or intersections, to assist those who were out and about at night. And that's the way it is in imperial Rome. It's only possible to make out the "geography" of places in the city thanks to these few "night-lights," or the glow of lanterns left burning in some of the houses.

Another striking thing is the quiet. As we walk down the street there is an unreal silence. A silence broken only by the cascading water of a neighborhood fountain, a few yards down the street. It has a very simple design: four thick slabs of travertine marble form a square tub topped by a short, squat column. The moonlight, struggling to break through to the street between two buildings, reveals that the column has the face of a deity carved on it. It's Mercury with his winged helmet, a stream of water flowing from his mouth. During the daylight hours, women, children, and slaves take turns here, filling wooden buckets with water to carry back to their homes. But now the place is deserted and the sound of the falling water is our only company.

It's curious, this silence. More than curious, it's rare. This is a city of a million and a half people, and we are right in the middle of it. Usually, nighttime is delivery time in the shops, with the metallic clamor of iron wagon wheels turning on the stone pavement, men shouting, horses neighing, the inevitable imprecations. And those are the noises we can hear now, off in the distance, coming from another street. Echoed by a barking dog. Rome never sleeps.

Ahead of us the street widens out a bit, creating what seems like an oasis of light. The moon illuminates the network of basalt slabs that make up the pavement. It looks like the petri-fied shell of a gigantic turtle.

A little further on, at the end of the street, something is moving. It's a human figure that stops, walks forward a little more and then, staggering, leans up against a wall. He must be drunk. He mumbles something incomprehensible and sways back and forth toward an alleyway. Who knows if he'll make it home? Actually, at night the streets of Rome are as terrifying as a nocturnal predator: there are thieves, criminals, and plenty of hooligans who wouldn't hesitate to stick a dagger in someone's belly in exchange for a little money. If tomorrow morning someone finds a body on the street, robbed and stabbed to death, it certainly won't be easy to find the murderers in such a densely populated and chaotic city.

Before making his way into the alleyway, the drunk trips over a bump at the corner of the street. He curses it, har-rumphing a few words, and then continues on his improbable itinerary. The bump moves. It's alive. It's one of many home-less people in the capital, searching desperately for some place to sleep in peace. He's been living on the street since his land-lord kicked him out of his modest rented room a few days ago. He's not the only one; beside him is an entire family seeking shelter as best they can, huddled together with the few things they were able to bring with them. Rome fills up with people like this, every six months, when leases expire. There are always people who, from one day to the next, find themselves camped out on the street, looking for a new place to live and sleep.

Suddenly our attention is attracted by a rhythmic sound. Indistinct at first, but then much clearer. It echoes off the façades of the buildings, making it hard to tell where it's com-ing from. The sudden sound of a bolt lock and the glow of a bunch of lanterns solves the mystery; it's a patrol of *vigiles*. Who are they? In theory they are firefighters, but because they constantly have to conduct inspections to prevent fires, they also have responsibility for maintaining public order.

The *vigiles* are a military corps, and you can tell. There are nine of them: eight new recruits and a drill sergeant. They come scrambling down the stairs of a large portico. They have the authority to enter almost any building in order to check for fires, risky conditions, or negligence likely to cause tragedy. They have just completed an inspection and the sergeant is saying something to them. He holds his lantern high so the recruits can see him; he's got the strong build and hard, chiseled features that go well with his gravelly voice. Once he finishes his explanation, he takes one last look at the other *vigiles,* transfixing them with his dark eyes under his leather helmet. Then he barks an order and they all start marching. A march step that is almost too cadenced, typical of new recruits. The sergeant watches them march off, shakes his head, and follows them. The sound of their stamping feet gradually fades away, until it's finally drowned out by the splashing of the fountain.

A glance to the east shows us the sky has changed. It's still black, but now you can't see the stars. It's as though an invisible, impalpable veil were slowly spreading over the city, almost trying to separate it from the starry black dome. In a few hours a new day will begin. But it will be a morning different from all the others, in the capital of the most powerful empire of the ancient world.

CURIOSITY—Rome in Numbers, the Eternal City

In the second century CE, Rome is at the height of its splendor. It really is the best time to visit the city. Keeping pace with the growth of the Empire, the city has reached its greatest territorial expansion, covering an area of 4450 acres, with a perimeter of about fourteen miles. And that's not all. It has a population of between a million and a million and a half (and according to some estimates as many as two million, almost as many as live in modern Rome!). It's the most populous city of the entire classical period.

Actually, this population growth and building boom should not surprise us: Rome has been developing steadily for generations. Each succeeding emperor has embellished it with new buildings and monuments, gradually changing the face of the city. Sometimes, however, its face has been changed radically and suddenly by fires, an all too frequent occurrence. This constant transformation of Rome will go on for centuries, turning the city, even in ancient times, into a gigantic open-air museum of art and architecture.

In this regard, it is astounding to run down a list of the city's buildings and monuments compiled under the emperor Constantine. We won't cite the entire list, of course, but even a look at the highlights makes your jaw drop, especially if you keep in mind that the city was much smaller then than it is today.

40 triumphal arches
12 forums
28 libraries
12 basilicas
11 large bath complexes and 1000 public baths
100 temples
3500 bronze statues of illustrious men and 160 gold and ivory statues of deities

25 equestrian statues

15 Egyptian obelisks

46 brothels

11 aqueducts and 1352 street fountains

2 hippodromes for chariot races (the larger one, the Circus Maximus, holds almost 400,000 spectators)

2 amphitheaters for gladiator matches (the larger one, the Colosseum, has between 50,000 and 70,000 seats)

4 theaters (the largest, the Theater of Pompey, has 25,000 seats)

2 large *naumachiae* (artificial lakes for aquatic and naval battles)

1 stadium for track and field events (the Stadium of Domitian, with 30,000 seats)

And so on.

And what about green areas? It is truly incredible to discover that in this city, so densely occupied by monuments and residential buildings, there was plenty of green. Between private gardens and public parks, sacred woods, peristyles of noble houses, etc., vegetation covered approximately one fourth of the city's surface area, something over one thousand acres.

A curiosity. What was the real "color" of Rome? What hues would have captured our attention as we observed the city from a distance? Probably there were two dominant colors: the red of the terra-cotta rooftops and the bright white of house façades and the marble colonnades of temples. Here and there, in this expanse of red roof tiles, we would also have noted roofs of a green-gold color, glittering in the sunlight. These were the gilded bronze tiles of temples and some imperial buildings. Over time they oxidized and often took on a greenish tint. We would also have been struck by the gilded statues on top of columns or temples, standing out above the city skyline. White, red, green, and gold: these were the colors of Rome.

THE *DOMUS*: HOME FOR THE WEALTHY

Where do the Romans live? And what do their houses look like? We are accustomed, in movies and television dramas, to seeing them in brightly lit houses, with columns, courtyard gardens, frescoed rooms, little fountains, and *triclinia* (formal dining rooms with couches). But the reality is much different. Only the rich and the nobles can afford to live in villas with servants. And there aren't many of them. The vast majority of the residents of Rome live amassed in large apartment buildings, often in conditions of hardship, which in some cases might remind us of houses in the poor neighborhoods of Mumbai.

But let's take things in order, starting with the homes of the Roman elite, the so-called *domus*. Under Constantine, the authorities recorded 1790 such houses in Rome, certainly a sizable number. But they were not all alike. Some were quite large but others were small, suited to the chronic lack of space in Trajan's Rome. The one we're about to visit, however, has the classic old style structure, which makes its owner very proud.

The most striking thing about this house is its exterior; it's shut in on itself like an oyster. Practically speaking, you have to imagine the typical Roman *domus* as something resembling a small fortress of the foreign legion. It has almost no windows, and if there are any they are always the rare and small exceptions placed high up on the walls. There are no balconies and its perimeter wall isolates it from the outside world. It actually reflects the archaic structure of the family farms from the dawn of Roman and Latin culture, with a defensive perimeter wall.

This detachment from the chaos of the city street is made immediately evident by the modest front door that faces the road almost anonymously. On either side of it are a number of shops, still closed at this hour. The main entrance is constituted of a high wooden double door with big bronze doorknobs. In the center of each side of the double door there is a bronze wolf's head, holding a big ring in its mouth to be used as a knocker.

Beyond the door, there is a short hallway. Our first steps take us over a mosaic with the figure of a menacing dog and the inscription *Cave canem,* "beware of dog." Many residents of ancient Rome have chosen the same mosaic, which we know from the villas in Pompeii. Already in Roman times, burglars and door-to-door solicitors were a problem.

A short way down one side of the hallway we notice a small room, with a man snoozing on a chair. He's the "doorman," the slave who guards the entrance. Beside him, on the floor like a dog, sleeps a young boy, who must surely be his assistant. Inside the house everyone is still asleep, and we can explore the villa without being disturbed.

A few more steps and the hallway opens on to a grandiose space: the atrium. It's a rectangular room, large, painted with bright frescoes already illuminated by the early light of dawn. But where does this light come from if there are no windows? A glance upward gives us the answer: in the center of the ceiling an entire piece of the roof is missing. There is a big square opening where the light shines through, as in a courtyard. A cascade of light penetrates vertically through the roof before spreading horizontally throughout the various rooms opening onto the atrium.

But this opening was not planned just to let light in. It also allows something else to come in from above: water. When it rains, the large surface of the roof above the atrium collects the single drops and channels them toward the opening, just like a funnel. With a spectacular leap into the void, streams of water flow out of the mouths of a number of terra-cotta figures placed along the edges of the roof and come splashing down into the atrium. During a thunderstorm the noise can be deafening.

All this water is not wasted, however. With great precision it falls into a large square pool in the middle of the room. This is the *impluvium*, or rainwater collector, a very old and very rational idea. It collects rainwater and transports it to an underground cistern. The cistern is the house's reservoir. A small marble well makes the collected rainwater accessible for the house's daily needs. This well has been in use for generations. Its edges in fact, are worn with grooves left by the ropes that lift the buckets up from the cistern.

The *impluvium* also has a decorative purpose: it's an indoor pool that reflects the blue sky and the clouds. It looks almost like a painting sitting on the floor. For all those who enter the house, guest or visitor, it makes a very striking and pleasant first impression.

But the *impluvium* that we're looking at now has something more: there are flowers floating on the surface of the water. They're what's left of the banquet that was held in this house last night.

Like a mirror, the water in the pool reflects the morning light throughout the house. The little ripples generated by a light breeze reverberate on the walls of the living room in waves of light that seem to chase each other across the surface of the frescoes. On closer inspection, there's not a wall in the whole room that's been left uncolored. All around there are paintings of mythological figures, imaginary landscapes, and geometric decorations. The colors are intense: azure, red, ochre.

All of this leads us to an important consideration: the

Roman world is a colorful one, much more so than our own. Vivid colors adorn the interiors of houses, monuments; even the clothes people wear for big occasions are a true triumph of varied hues and tones. While we, more often than not, believe that the height of elegance is a black or dark gray suit or dress. It's a shame we've lost all those colors, especially in our houses, which are dominated by white walls. A Roman would think of them as blank canvases with frames.

We continue our exploration. Some rooms open onto the sides of the atrium. These are the bedrooms, known as *cubicula*, or cubicles. Compared to where we sleep they are extremely small and dark, much more like cells than bedrooms. None of us would be very happy in them; there are no windows, and the only light comes from the weak glow of a lantern. It is striking, therefore, how hard it is to see the magnificent frescoes and mosaics that so often decorate these rooms and that can be seen today in museums, exalted by the clever use of lighting. The Romans never saw them like that. But once their eyes had adapted to the semi-darkness of the *cubiculum*, the flickering flame of the lantern made these paintings very suggestive, bringing out the contours of the landscapes or the features of the faces represented in them.

In a corner of the atrium we can see some stairs. They lead up to the floor above, where the servants live, along with some of the women of the family. The ground floor, the "noble floor," is the men's territory, especially that of the head of the family, the *pater familias*.

We continue, moving beyond the pool to the wall on the other side. For the most part it's closed by a large wood panel which opens like a folding door. We open it, and there it is, the *tablinium*, the office of the man of the house. This is where he receives his clients. A large throne-like desk and an imposing chair sit in the middle of the room, while some stools are placed along the sides. All of them have turned legs and are decorated with inlaid bone, ivory, and bronze. There are also some lanterns on tall candelabras, a brazier of burning coals on the floor (for heat), and precious silver objects on the desk (undoubtedly prestigious gifts or souvenirs) and writing implements.

On the far side of the room is a large curtain. Opening it, we enter what we might call the more intimate part of the *domus*. Until now, we have seen the public part of the house, what can be seen even by unknown visitors. But beyond this curtain is the private part of the house. This is the peristyle, or the *domus*'s large interior garden, the house's green area. It's surrounded by a beautiful colonnade, with marble disks hanging from the ceiling, between one column and another. They represent mythological figures, are painted or sculpted, and they have an odd name, *oscilla*, like oscillate, the reason for which is not hard to figure out. When the wind blows they swing gently back and forth, lending a sense of movement to the rigidity of the colonnade.

At this hour of the morning, the peristyle has an enchanting atmosphere. We are enveloped by an extraordinary number of fragrances coming from the ornamental, aromatic, and medicinal plants cultivated in the garden.

In these gardens, in fact, depending on the *domus*, we might find myrtle, boxwood, laurel, oleander, ivy, acanthus, and even large trees, such as cypresses and plane trees. And then flowers, such as violets, narcissus, iris, or lilies, planted in flower beds. Often there is also a grape arbor. The peristyle is truly an oasis of peace inside the *domus*. An oasis with its own works of art: the plants are not arranged by chance but geometrically, with footpaths, flower beds, sometimes a small labyrinth. Quite often, the gardeners prune the bushes and trees, shaping them to look like animals. And it is not unusual to see real animals in the garden, such as pheasants, doves, or peacocks.

In the pale light of dawn we can see two motionless human figures: little bronze statues decorating the corners of the garden. Two *putti*, chubby baby boys, each holding a duck. We move over closer to them. One of the two is making a strange noise, like a gurgle. Suddenly, after two noisy spurts of spray, a thin stream of water comes gushing out of one of the ducks' beaks. These are fountain-statues. Their streams of water fall right into the center of a circular tub, creating an amusing play of water. It's not the only one. We turn around: three more small fountains start spurting.

It's obvious that in this *domus* the *impluvium* is not the only source of water. For some time now the house has been supplied with water from another source: the aqueducts. The owner, thanks to his contacts and connections, has managed to obtain his own private water main. In fact, his is one of the few lucky families to have running water in the house. Something quite rare in Rome. And he also uses it to delight his guests with these little fountain games.

Now a bony hand shuts the spigot hidden among the bushes. It's the hand of a slave who has been checking to see that the water pipes are in working order. He's tall, lanky, dark-skinned, with black, curly hair. He's almost certainly Middle Eastern or North African. Now he's going around picking up fallen leaves and dead flowers. He must be the gardener.

Some other noises are coming from a little room that looks out onto the colonnade. It sounds like someone is sweeping. We walk toward the sound. It's coming from the *triclinium*, or dining room. This is where the banquet was held last night. The couches where the guests reclined have already been tidied up, the food-stained covers have been replaced. Another slave is cleaning up the last remains of the night's festivities. Among them is a lobster claw. It's the custom, in fact, during a banquet, to throw food scraps on the floor rather than keep them on your plate.

Someone's already at work in the kitchen. It's a woman, another slave. She has short hair, hidden under a scarf made of rags, but you can see that she's blond; some blond curls are hanging down around her neck. Maybe she comes from Germany or from Dacia (Romania), one of Trajan's recent conquests. The kitchen is very small. Strangely enough, the Romans, famous for their banquets, don't seem to give the kitchen much importance. They consider it a secondary room that has a role similar to a kitchenette in a modern studio apartment, so it doesn't have a standard location in the *domus*. Sometimes it is at the end of a short hallway, sometimes under a stairway. Strange certainly, but it shouldn't really be so surprising. In the houses of the wealthy there is no one with the role of "housewife." The only ones who work in the kitchen are the slaves. It is exclusively a service area, so no one worries about decorations, amenities, or space. In the homes of more humble Romans, on the other hand, it's the woman of the house who cooks, but her role in the family, compared to today, is much more like that of a domestic servant than a wife.

But one aspect of Roman kitchens that is familiar to us is the display of copper (or bronze) pots and pans and casserole dishes on the walls. There are also some colanders whose holes form such elaborate designs they seem like embroidery. And then there are marble mortars and pestles, skewers, and clay pots, as well as roasting pans shaped like fish or rabbits, to be filled with favorite recipes. Observing the shapes of these objects is the equivalent of perusing the menu of the era.

The food is heated on a cooking surface comprised of a masonry counter where embers are spread out as on an outdoor grill. When the embers are hot, burners, or metal tripods, are placed over them, and the pots and pans are set on the burners.

Very often these brick counters are supported and embellished by elegant arches, whose underlying spaces also serve as small wood-storage areas. Here, a supply of wood is kept on hand, the ancient equivalent of the gas cylinders used in many Italian kitchens today.

Now the slave is lighting the fire. But how exactly do Romans light a fire? We move closer to look over her shoulder and discover that she's using a piece of steel. It's shaped like a small horseshoe and she holds it in her hand as though she were holding a jug handle. She strikes it against a piece of quartz that she holds in her other hand. Some sparks fly up and one of them lands on a thin slice of a mushroom that serves as tinder (it's from the genus *Fomus*, the wood-like mushrooms that grow on tree trunks). The girl blows on it lightly and holes start to form on the surface of the mushroom from the incandescence. At this point she touches it to some straw, to "infect" it with the heat of the mushroom. She blows some more. First a puff of smoke billows up from the straw and then, suddenly, a flashing flame. The deed is done. Now she can burn some wood and prepare the embers.

Let's stop here for a minute. This visit to the *domus* has helped us understand some things about noble Roman houses. To be sure, they are beautiful, but not nearly as comfortable as our own. In winter it's cold, with drafts everywhere, and you have to warm yourself with braziers (the equivalent of our electric heaters) set on the floor of each room. In addition, the houses are poorly lit, with semi-darkness reigning in every room. In the rare cases where there are windows, they are usually very small and less transparent than ours. In the homes of the wealthy the window panes are made of sheets of talc, mica, or even glass, while the poor use translucent animal skins, or more usually, nothing but wooden shutters.

All things considered, in order to understand the atmosphere inside the houses of the Romans, even the houses of the wealthy like this *domus,* what you have to do is imagine an old farmhouse with overstuffed beds and thick blankets, light gleaming through the cracks under the doors, the smell of wood burning in the fireplace, dust and spiders.

INTERIOR DECORATION, A PECULIAR ROMAN TASTE

As we have seen, the daily activities in the house have already begun. As on every other day, the first to get up are the slaves. There are eleven of them, and together they make up what is called the *familia*, or the entire group of slaves possessed by the homeowner. Eleven might seem like a lot for just one house, but that's about average. Every wealthy Roman family, in fact, owns somewhere between five and twelve slaves.

So where do they sleep? After all, it's like putting up a whole soccer team . . . The slaves don't have their own rooms. They sleep in the halls, the kitchen, or all together in the same room. One in particular, the most trusted, sleeps on the floor in front of the bedroom of the *dominus* (the master). Exactly like a dog and its master.

We'll have a chance, later this morning, to get to know the world of the slaves, who they are, how they were bound into slavery, and how they are treated by their masters. For now, let's continue with our tour of the house as it's waking up.

A slave girl pulls back a heavy purple drape and walks over to a big marble table with dolphin-shaped legs. It stands right along the edge of the pool of the *impluvium*. It is clearly a table meant for receiving guests, as indicated by the beautiful silver pitcher sitting on it, which the slave girl delicately picks up to dust. We walk around the table. So where's the rest of the furniture?

The most striking thing about Roman houses is the contrast between the abundance of decoration on the walls (frescoes) or on the floors (mosaics) and the scarcity of the furniture. Basically, it's the exact opposite of our modern houses.

The couches, armchairs, carpets, and bookshelves that fill up our living rooms are all missing. It feels as though all the rooms are bare and that everything has been reduced to the essentials.

But there's a reason for this. The Romans have a completely different approach to interior decoration than we do. Instead of focusing attention on the furniture and the room décor, they usually try to hide them or camouflage them. Beds and chairs sometimes disappear under cushions or drapes. While at the same time the frescoes on the walls frequently reproduce false doors, fake curtains, even fake landscapes— which might even alternate with real openings in the wall with views of the garden. (One of the great examples of this technique is the famous Villa Oplontis, in Torre Annunziata, which may have belonged to Poppaea, Nero's mistress and second wife.)

So, a lot of noble houses display this strange predilection of the Romans: to play hide and seek between reality and illusion, making some objects disappear and creating replicas of others, at times even painting entire landscapes on the walls. Considering the time, the Romans had extremely refined and modern taste.

But even though there was little of it, the furniture on view in Roman houses was nevertheless quite precious. Tables were probably the most common element. There were many types; the favorite one seems to be a round table with three legs, carved to look like the feet of a feline, a goat, or a horse. (The three legs are not a coincidence; it's the easiest way to ensure that a table doesn't wobble.)

We may be surprised to discover that the Romans were the first to come up with what seem to us like modern inventions, such as, for example, folding tables or semicircular tables to stand against walls.

Roman chairs, on the other hand, are no great shakes. They are not at all comfortable. The Romans knew nothing about the upholstery that we commonly use today for couches and armchairs, and they tried to compensate for this shortcoming by using cushions. They really are everywhere: on beds, couches, chairs.

In this *domus,* the sight of a wardrobe in the corner may seem normal, but in reality it is a recent invention of the ancient world. The Romans, in fact, were the first to use them. They were unknown to the Greeks and Etruscans. Oddly, however, the Romans do not use them as we do, to hold their clothes. Instead they use them to store delicate or precious objects, such as wine glasses and goblets, toiletries, ink wells, or scales.

Clothes and linens are actually kept in special chests called *arcae vestiariae*, very much like a modern bench chest. They stand on little lion's feet and open from the top. This is a furniture item that will be used for centuries, throughout the entire medieval period and the Renaissance.

Naturally, the interior décor of wealthy Romans' houses always includes the ample use of curtains and drapes. They protect the rooms from the sun and wind, create an island of warmth in the winter and coolness in the summer, and keep dust, flies, and indiscreet eyes at a safe distance. In this regard, archaeologists have recently made some interesting discoveries among the ruins of a *domus* in the Roman city of Ephesus, in present-day Turkey, which was destroyed by an earthquake and buried for centuries. During their excavations, the archaeologists uncovered a wealth of minor curiosities of Roman décor. In the colonnade surrounding the garden or peristyle of this aristocratic house, it was still possible to see the remains of a system of bronze poles that were used to support a series of curtains hung between the columns. In effect, the colonnade could be closed with a barrier of curtains, thus creating a cool, shady portico where the residents could walk during the torrid summers in Ephesus. More bronze poles, placed above the door frames, confirm the additional use of curtains to block passageways, just as they are used today in bars and shops in Mediterranean countries. (And it can't be ruled out that some of these Roman curtains, like ours, were made of colored strips of cloth or long cords with hundreds of little knots.)

We should also add that the Roman *domus* were also often decorated with very lovely tapestries, floor mats and even rugs, a fashion brought to Rome from the Middle East.

Silverware, strongboxes, and antiques

Some of the decorative items in the *domus* of the wealthy were meant to serve as status symbols. These included such things as marble busts and statues and, obviously, silver cups, bowls, and other objects, which were always kept on display. Entire sets of silver pitchers and goblets are displayed on special exhibition tables or sideboards, so that guests or clients can admire them.

Those who can't afford silverware make do with bronze, glass, or precious ceramics. But in any event, something has to be put on display; it's a social rule. Actually, this custom has survived right down to our own time in the widespread practice of displaying "the good tableware" in glass-doored credenzas kept in the living room.

Another symbolic item for well-to-do families is the strongbox. While we tend to hide the safe in our houses, the Romans did just the opposite. The strongbox is often kept in a place, such as the atrium, where everyone can admire it.

It's a clear sign of opulence and wealth. Naturally, it is well fixed to the floor or walls and there is even a special slave, the *atriensis*, or butler, who, like a security guard, monitors the movements of people in and out of the atrium, especially when unknown visitors arrive to talk business with the master of the house, or on nights when parties or banquets are held.

The strongbox is not really a safe in the proper sense; it's more like a big chest that's armored with studs and iron strips. But there are some ingenious systems for opening it, worthy of James Bond: fake bronze heads to be pulled, levers to push or rings to turn. And once it's open what's to be seen on the inside? Certainly, the family's most precious gold and silver objects, but also important documents, such as wills and testaments, contracts, deeds—all inscribed on wooden tablets or papyrus scrolls with the ever-present seal bearing the emblem from the owner's ring.

A curiosity. Even in ancient times the Romans had a passion for antiques, objects and masterpieces from the past which they displayed in their homes. But since we're in the middle of the classical period, what objects can be considered antiques? Archaeologists have given us the answer. Their digs among Roman ruins have brought to light Etruscan statuettes, mirrors, and goblets that the Romans considered precious antiques. Archaeologists have also found objects from ancient Egypt. And actually, for a Roman during the reign of Trajan, the civilization of ancient Egypt could truly be considered as antiquity. The Pharaoh Ramses II, for example, lived one thousand four hundred years before Trajan! An interval of time not much different from the one that separates us from the Rome that we've been talking about.

The Origins of Our Apartment Buildings

One last observation. The *domus* that we have just visited has a classic floor plan, similar to the one tourists can admire in many archeological sites, and especially in Pompeii. But in a city like Rome, where urban overdevelopment has put a premium on space, not all *domus* have enough room to use the classic plan. Some surprising discoveries have been made by archaeologists working in Ostia Antica—the ancient port of Rome—where houses (built during an urban redevelopment project in the Trajan era, the period that we have been exploring) are still very visible, contrary to Rome, where everything has been buried by now under centuries of new construction.

In Ostia Antica it's possible to see many "mutilated" *domus*, that is, without an atrium, the big room with the pool to collect rain water. The chronic lack of space and the presence of aqueducts in the city (and the consequent lack of need to have a well in the house) often led home, owners to eliminate the atrium.

Elsewhere, as in Pompeii, the *domus* often had a third floor with an independent entrance. Apparently wealthy families had no qualms about having tenants on the floor above them. Maybe they lost a bit of their privacy, but they had the benefit of being able to collect hefty rents.

At a certain point these houses were no longer inhabited by the wealthy and were occupied by people from the lower middle class. City life, in other words, had, for several generations by now, begun to see a fundamental evolution in urban housing, which would lead to higher and higher buildings with more independent apartments inhabited by more families, ending with the construction of outright apartment buildings or condominiums.

The apartment buildings of today, where many of us city dwellers live, have their roots in this transformation, which happened in Rome and the other major cities of the Empire about two thousand years ago.

6:30 AM

The Master Awakes

Outside the bedroom of the *dominus*, the master of the house, we can hear the sound of deep snoring. We slowly open the door and a blade of light crosses the room and shines on the bed, tucked into a sort of niche carved out of the wall. There's the *dominus*, wrapped in embroidered blankets with purple, blue, and yellow stripes that cascade down to the floor, creating sumptuous folds.

We're surprised by the size of the bed. In keeping with tradition, it is very high and you even need to use a stool to climb into it. We can catch a glimpse of the stool, almost buried under the covers, with the sandals on it that the *dominus* took off before slipping under the covers.

It's a bed with an old style triple head board, which reminds us of a sofa. Its wooden legs are turned and decorated with ivory inlays and gilded bronze plaques. The corners are embellished with the heads of felines and satyrs, sculpted by the slanted sunlight. There are no springs; the mattress rests on leather strips, which complete the bed frame. Roman beds are decidedly less comfortable than our own.

But what material are Roman mattresses made of? As far as we can tell today, some mattresses were stuffed with straw. Others, like this one, with wool.

There are some exceptions, like the crib found miraculously intact in Herculaneum, still bearing the skeleton of a baby killed in the eruption of Vesuvius. The mattress was stuffed with leaves (it could also be that the leaves had a protective purpose for the baby's health or that they were used to keep away parasites).

The *dominus* is alone in his room. Where is his wife? In our society, husband and wife traditionally sleep in the same bed. In the Roman era that is not always the case. In fact, although newlyweds normally sleep in double beds, for a well-to-do couple it is considered tasteful to sleep in separate rooms. So the wife of the *dominus* (the so-called *domina*, or mistress) sleeps in her own personal *cubiculum*.

It's time to get up. The Romans get up early, with the first light of dawn, and go to bed early, following the natural rhythm of the sun. And that's the way it will be for centuries; it's we who are the exception.

The master is awakened, with great delicacy, by his most trusted slave. A few minutes later, the *dominus* leaves his room, still a little sleepy. He is tall, robust, with white hair and blue eyes. His prominent nose accentuates the nobility of his face.

Wrapped in tasteful blue robes, he slowly makes his way toward a small wooden structure, built against a wall. It looks like a small temple, with a triangular drum supported by two columns. And it really is the sacred place of the house: the Lararium. It is a shrine to the Lares, the domestic spirits who protect the family. They are represented by the two statuettes at the center of the "temple." They look like a couple of long-haired young people dancing. Beside them are statues of two other deities, Mercury and Venus. The slave hands the master a small plate containing offerings. The *dominus*, moving solemnly and reciting ritual phrases, places them in the Lararium inside a goblet in front of the statuettes. Then he burns some essence.

The day begins with this ritual every morning. And the same thing is happening in thousands of other houses. Never underestimate the powers of these little deities. They are the ones responsible for looking after daily life in Roman houses. The ritual is the equivalent of an insurance policy against theft, fire, or ill fortune for the members of the family.

7:00 AM

Roman Dress

It's time to get dressed. How do Romans dress? We're used to seeing them, in movies and on TV shows, wrapped in colorful togas that look like long sheets. But do they dress like that all the time? It's true that on first glance these clothes do look uncomfortable; they make it difficult to move, impossible to run, climb stairs, or even sit down without getting tangled up somewhere or other. But in reality, they're comfortable. Even in the modern era there are people who dress this way. If you go to India and many other Asian or Arab countries, you'll find a traditional way of dressing not very much different from the way the Romans dressed, based on long robes, tunics, cloaks, and sandals. It's just a question of habit.

Let's start with underwear. Do Romans wear underpants? The answer is yes. Actually, what they wear are not really underpants but a sort of girdle made of wool, called a *subligar*, or loincloth, which is tied around the waist and wraps around the intimate parts.

You might be surprised to know that it's not always the first thing that people put on in the morning. In fact, it's quite usual for Romans not to get undressed before going to bed, but to go to bed half-dressed. They take off their cloak, throw it over a chair (or use it as a cover), and slip under the covers wearing their loincloth and tunic, which during the night take the place of pajamas. This might not seem very hygienic to us, but it remained the common practice in rural areas right up through the nineteenth century. With one difference: the Romans are very clean because they go to the baths every day. So, just a few hours before going to bed they have had a good washing. The only problem is their clothes are still dirty.

The basic garment in Roman fashion is the famous tunic. There is a good way to understand its practicality. Imagine stepping into a T-shirt that goes down to your knees (let's say an XXXL), that you can then fasten around your waist with a belt. Well, despite some minor differences, the tunic is pretty much the same. It is truly surprising to see how we still continue to use (especially in summer) a way of dressing born in the ancient world. We just call it something else: a T-shirt.

Naturally, the tunic is not made of the same material. While we use cotton, the Romans mostly use linen, or wool. The linen is not dyed and has an intense beige tone; it's the perfect color for masking stains and dirt.

For the most part, linen is grown and woven in Egypt, where it is then exported to the rest of the Empire. So the Romans, like most of us, wear clothing produced in faraway countries, a phenomenon that is the result of the first large-scale "globalization" in history, brought about by the Romans in the Mediterranean basin. We'll have more to say about this subject, especially when we visit the markets of the imperial capital.

Tunics are the right clothing for all occasions. They can be used as night shirts, as an undergarment for togas, or as a proper garment for the lower classes. All a poor man has to do, once he has his tunic on, is slip into his sandals and leave the house. Not so for the wealthy, because before leaving the house they have to put on the most important garment of all for citizens of Rome, the toga.

We could define the toga as the sport coat and tie of the era clothing to be worn to make a good public impression, above all on important occasions.

The toga has been in use since ancient times, and has gone

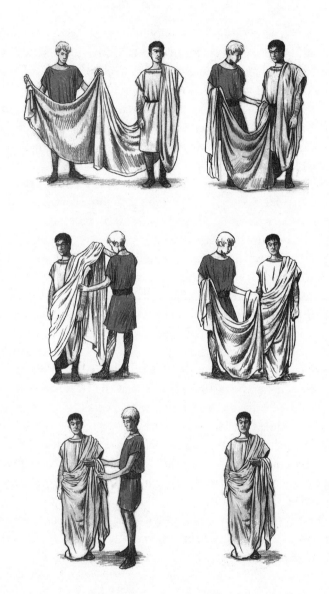

No wealthy Roman would leave the house without a toga. It is so long (up to six yards) that they often need the help of a slave to put it on. Elegance demands that the folds be just right.

through a true evolution. Initially, its dimensions were quite small, and then kept getting bigger and bigger. Stretched out on the floor, it has the shape of a semi-circle (of wool or linen), with a diameter of six yards!

It is no wonder, then, that it is often necessary to have the help of a slave to put it on. Just what's happening now in our *domus*. And this will enable us to see just how the tunic has to be worn.

The master is standing, motionless, staring off into the distance. The slave lays the toga over his shoulders, almost as though it were a blanket, being careful, however, not to center it exactly, but to leave one end of it much longer, hanging all the way down to the floor. Very delicately, he gathers up this end and passes it under one armpit, wrapping it around the chest under the neck, like a bandolier. Then he wraps it, like a scarf, in a wide circle around the neck and fixes it with a pin above the collarbone. But we're not done yet. The long end is still so long that it has to be wrapped one more time around the body, sticking it under the previous layers. At the end, the slave takes a step back to take a look at the overall effect. He is satisfied. His master is very elegant, especially because of the lay of the folds that lend his figure nobility. One arm is free, while the other is semi-covered in drapery, and the *dominus* has to constantly keep it raised a little to make sure it doesn't drag on the ground and get dirty. It's a little awkward, but you get used to it pretty easily.

The toga is truly a symbol of Roman culture and civilization. Only Roman citizens are allowed to wear them, and they are forbidden to foreigners, slaves, or *liberti* (freed slaves). And togas, almost like uniforms, follow a true social code. They have different names depending on who wears them and for what purpose. For example, white togas with a purple border have a protective meaning (*toga praetexta*) and are worn by Senators and young boys under fourteen or sixteen. Upon reaching that age, the boy gives up the protective toga in an important ceremony. It's a rite of passage symbolizing the end of adolescence. From this moment on, the boy is "officially" an adult, that is, ready to take up arms and enter public life.

And what about pants? You don't see too many around. Pants are not actually a part of Roman and Mediterranean dress. At the time of Trajan, the only ones to wear pants are legionnaires. But the pants they wear are short and tight-fitting, and go down to just below the knees. Actually, pants do exist but they are worn only by the enemies of Rome, the "barbarians," who invented them. These are the Celtic and Germanic peoples, in the north, and the Persians, in the east, in present-day Iran. But it won't always be that way. Over the next hundred and fifty years, pants will conquer Rome because of their convenience and will become an integral part of Roman fashion.

Now the *dominus* is sitting down and the slave is slipping some shoes on his feet. Curiously, the Romans don't wear socks (except in the northern reaches of the Empire, where the rigid climate makes it necessary to protect their feet), so when they take their shoes off they remain in bare feet.

There are many kinds of shoes: closed like boots, open like sandals, with many leather strips or else with a lot of little cleats, nails on the soles, for better traction (these are the famous *caligae*, worn by legionnaires), and so on.

For life in Rome, the *calcei*, soft leather moccasins, are certainly the favorite of many wealthy Romans, but they usually don't wear them in the house. Do you know why? Because good manners require that you take your street shoes off when you enter the house. So, inside the *domus*, people wear simple sandals with leather or cork soles. When they go to visit friends, they take their sandals with them because, obviously, the same rules apply at their friends' houses . . .

7:10 AM

Feminine Fashion

Contrary to modern times, in ancient Rome male and female clothing are very similar. Women also wear garments that are similar to tunics (*stolae*), but go down to their feet. Their look is decidedly more elegant, flowing, quite similar to the Greek chiton. Their special feature is that they are held fast not by one but two belts. In addition to a belt around the waist, there is another around the chest, just below the breasts, to highlight shape and volume.

In theory, a Roman woman could also wear a toga, but you'll hardly ever see one do so. In fact, togas worn by women are a sign of having been condemned as an adulteress, or of being a prostitute. So, over the tunic, or *stola*, feminine fashion calls for a long, rectangular shawl that goes down to the knees, forming elegant folds. It's called a *palla* and it's so big that women often use it to cover their heads when they're walking down the street. Think about it—this is something you've seen many times without really noticing it. In every representation of the life of Christ, from movies to religious paintings, from manger scenes to crucifixions, Mary and the other women generally have their heads covered with this same type of shawl.

In contrast to men's clothes, women's clothes are more colorful and almost always embroidered. The colors are vivid and make it so that women are noticed immediately on the street, even when it's crowded. Sometimes women are also noticed for their shoes, which are elegant and fine compared to men's, and often white.

There is one curiosity with regard to the intimate clothing of Roman women. What do they wear under their *stola*? They wear a rather scanty undergarment, similar to the male loin-cloth, but more elegant. And they also wear a bra, a soft band of fabric or leather, the *strophium* or *mamillare*. The name varies, but the substance is the same: its purpose is to support and lift the breasts. In his writings, Ovid suggests that women stuff the band should their breasts not be sufficiently developed.

Archaeologists have found many images of these bras, such as the famous erotic paintings in the brothel in Pompeii. But the most impressive one is the mosaic in the Roman villa of the Casale, in Piazza Amerina in Sicily. The picture shows several girls wearing surprisingly modern two-piece bathing suits. This is the way Roman women dressed to bathe in a pool or to do gymnastic exercises. There is no doubt about it: the bikini is a Roman invention. The clothes of the women you meet on the streets of Rome are usually made of linen or wool. But wealthy women also have other, very exclusive, options: fine cottons and silk. Both have become true status symbols, to be displayed on special occasions.

As is well known, for a long time silk was a monopoly of the Chinese, who preserved the secret of its origin, the silk-worm. Silk came to Rome thanks to incredibly long journeys by caravans, after crossing the steppes of Mongolia, the deserts of Asia, to arrive finally at the Mediterranean. So the price of silk was sky high, and a lot of aristocrats spent fortunes in order to wear it or use it to decorate their houses. So many, in fact, that more than one emperor tried, futilely, to introduce legislation to regulate the silk trade in order to limit the immense quantity of money that ended up in the pockets of the sworn enemies of Rome, the Persians. The silk caravans had to pass through their territory, between Iraq and Iran. But it was all useless. In reality, the Romans later went on to dis-

Following the dictates of Roman fashion, women wear a large rectangular shawl, called a palla, which goes down to their knees, forming elaborate folds. Often, in public, they use it to cover their heads. Her hairstyle, gold jewelry, and elegant carriage are the marks of this matron's (left) aristocratic status.

All the women of Rome wear long tunics. They are light and brightly colored and go down to the ground. A belt worn around the chest highlights the curves of the body, as can be seen on this common woman (right).

cover the secret of silk, and silkworms were imported to Constantinople. But it was too late. Rome and the Roman Empire of the West had by now fallen under the barbarian invasions. All the benefits of the new silk production went to the Roman Empire of the East, the newly born Byzantium, ruled by the emperor Justinian.

THE WELL-GROOMED ROMAN MAN

As the day begins, we discover yet another curiosity about Roman domestic life: almost no one washes in the morning. At most they might rinse their face a little, using water from a basin held by a slave, more to wake up than anything else. What's more, the use of soap is yet to be discovered (the word *sapo* refers to a dye!).

If we look more carefully around a Roman house, we also discover that there are no showers (they haven't been invented yet), and bathtubs are a rarity. Yet, as we know, Roman society was the most dedicated to hygiene of any society in the ancient world. It wasn't until the modern era that mankind achieved a comparable level of water use for washing. How is this possible? The answer to this paradox, as we might guess, is that Roman bathrooms are located outside of the house, a few blocks down the street: the great public baths. That's where people wash, quite abundantly, and where they get massages and other treatments for their bodies. But all of this usually takes place after lunch. That's why nobody washes in the morning.

To be sure, some wealthy people have small private baths in their homes, but we're talking about a small elite, an elite to which our *dominus* doesn't belong. His house has no private baths, and he, too, will have to go to the public baths later on, as we shall see.

Right now, he's sitting in a comfortable chair with cushions, and a slave is shaving him with a sharp razor. This slave is the in-house barber, something that only the wealthy can afford. It hurts. Shaving cream doesn't exist yet, nor do double-edge razors. The barber uses only water and razors shaped like half-moons, made of bronze or tempered iron, sharpened on simple grindstones. But this is just the beginning of what the *dominus* considers a true torture: when he's done shaving him, the slave will use tweezers to pluck out, one by one, the "superfluous" hairs around his eyebrows and all around his neck.

It might come as a surprise that men would subject themselves to such a meticulous cosmetic ritual. But the Romans really did pay a lot of attention to the care of their bodies. The use of organic-base body waxes, for example, was fairly widespread among men (for shaving too). We know from the historian Suetonius that Julius Caesar had himself depilated and that Augustus, in order to grow softer hair on his legs, used to rub them with scalding-hot walnut shells.

And even in these early times, the most worrisome problem for many men is their hair. When their hair starts turning white, a lot of men have it dyed black. And when baldness sets in, for some it's a real tragedy. But there are a lot of remedies.

The first is a comb-over that hides the areas where hair is scarce. Julius Caesar, for example, combed his hair to the front to cover up a noticeable bald spot.

When things grow worse and the head is completely bald, covered only by thin strands, a lot of men resort to lamp-black to color the skin on their head and give the impression, from a distance, of black hair.

When baldness finally wipes out any trace of hair, the most stubborn victims resort to wigs, hairpieces, and toupees, which already exist in a variety of colors.

And, just like today, lotions promising the miraculous regrowth of hair were to be found everywhere, even though, obviously, they didn't work.

Beauty Secrets of Two Thousand Years Ago

Inside the "torture chamber," the *dominus* emits a stifled scream with each plucked hair. One scream is so grotesque that the faces of two slaves light up with a fleeting smile, immediately concealed. To further hide their amusement, they bend down even lower and rub the floor more vigorously. They seem like two sailors scrubbing the deck of a ship, but actually, they are polishing a beautiful mosaic using little blocks of pumice. It's the best way to keep these stone masterpieces clean and shiny.

By now the morning's activities are in full swing. In one room in particular there is a continual coming and going of women, all slaves. It's the room of the master's wife, the *domina*. A slave pulls back the curtain and a very special scene opens up before our eyes: three maidservants are putting makeup on the mistress of the house.

She's sitting on a high-backed wicker armchair. The operation is in a delicate phase. One slave is "lengthening" the *domina*'s eyelashes with a stick made of coal. She'll shade them with the help of a bit of ash. She works with infinite care. Opposite her, another slave holds up a bronze mirror so the *domina* can follow each step in the progress of her makeup. There's as much tension as you'd expect to find in an operating room.

We take a look around the room. Off to the side, on a little lion-footed table, sits an open beauty case. It's an elegant wood box decorated with carved ivory inlays. Inside the box we get a glimpse of creams, perfumes, and oils, contained in small amphorettes, made of glass, clay, and alabaster. We also notice two combs made of very fine bone, carved ivory hairpins, tweezers, and then some small silver brushes for applying creams and beauty masks. All around the beauty case, open jars of various other essences are scattered about.

The gestures and tools used for making up are actually very similar to those we know today: eyelashes are enhanced, eye shadow is spread on the eyelids, etc. The ingredients, however, are a little different. For example, the substances used on the eyes, which are the object of particular attention. Kohl already exists, but to bring out the contours of the eyes Roman women also use squid ink, antimony, or lamp-black made from roasted dates. In the case of our *domina*, the slave girls are using something else, truly surprising. On the table, there's a valve of a seashell used as a plate which still holds a bit of dark paste. The main ingredient of this paste is toasted ants!

Now the makeup artist is preparing the final touch: she's about to color the *domina*'s lips. According to Ovid, Roman matrons can choose from a wide range of colors, but the favorite, as in the modern area, is bright red. It is made from a base of minium (red lead) or cinnabar (red mercuric sulfide), unfortunately, both toxic.

Now the *domina* purses her lips and peers into the mirror. Her gaze is penetrating and her skin is luminous. The job has been done well; that's confirmed by a glance at the slave girl, who, intimidated, bows her head.

Actually, we've only seen the final phase of the morning makeup session. If we had entered the room a few minutes earlier, we would have seen the preparation of a special foundation cream.

The objective was simple but subtle: make the matron of the house, who is approaching forty (a respectable age for the time), look younger. How? The slave girl has prepared a thin layer of honey, adding some fatty substances and a little ceruse, a white pigment that makes the skin more luminous. In order to give it a more youthful pink tone, she has added some red pigments. Then, after applying it delicately to her face, she has rubbed her cheeks with hematite powder, giving the skin a noticeable sheen.

The morning makeup regimen of a wealthy Roman woman is a complex affair, and not unlike the preparation of a complicated recipe.

Sometimes even the rest of the body is colored: red for the soles of the feet and the palms of the hands and gold powder for the tips of the breasts. For those who can afford it, obviously.

Finally, one particularly surprising aspect of this ritual is the use of moles. Already in Roman times, women applied fake moles to their faces, using a precise code: the moles sent a different message depending on their position (corner of the mouth, cheek, and so on).

Beauty Masks

Before moving on, it may be worth dedicating a brief note to beauty masks and skin creams. They were very fashionable in the Roman era and were recommended by a number of writers, from Ovid to Galen and Pliny the Elder. There are various kinds. What's surprising are the ingredients and their virtues, especially those for women with skin problems. For example: cow placentas were used to cure skin ulcers; bull bile was used for face stains (and lentils for stains on skin in other areas); butter for boils; narcissus bulbs as emollients and whiteners; bicarbonate of soda for cuts; cantaloupe root and cumin as whiteners; and for dermatitis the recommendation was an extract of calf genitals . . .

Hair Like an Egyptian

The *domina*'s most trusted maidservant claps her hands. The makeup girl leaves the room and two more girls come in.

During this time period, women's hairstyles have reached pharaonic dimensions. Some are so grandiose and pointed (left) they recall the papal tiara.

The matron's hair styles are very complex: the bun of rolled braids and the crest that rises above the forehead are made of hair pieces of imported hair. New hairstyles are often launched by the wives of the emperors (right).

They'll be doing the *domina*'s hair. One of them, the caretaker of her wigs, goes over to a small cabinet, takes out three wigs and puts them on the table. Each is a different color: blond red, and black.

We shouldn't be surprised that wigs were used in the Roman era. They were actually very fashionable for women. They are made of real hair; the red and blond wigs come from Germany, the black ones from the Middle East and from India. Wigs are a luxury item on which heavy customs duties have to be paid.

The *domina* chooses the red one; she'll have to wear it tonight at a banquet. The slave's job for the next few hours will be to see that it's in order and make sure it's in perfect condition for the evening. Not an easy task, given that it's enormous and full of curls to be put in order.

The *domina* won't wear a wig during the day, she'll be showing her own hair, and so it will have to be combed and styled. That's why she has called the second girl, the comber. She has brought with her a whole series of ivory combs, hairpins, ribbons, and barrettes. She's got a lot of work to do, starting with curling the *domina*'s hair, whose natural wave is very slight. So, she'll use a technique which is still in use today. She has had another slave bring in a small brazier whose embers are already hot. She'll use it to heat two hollow iron rods (the *calamistra*) that she'll then use to curl the *domina*'s locks.

It must be said that under Trajan the fashion in women's hairstyles reached a remarkable complexity, the result of a gradual evolution.

You have to imagine something similar to our own fashion trends; depending on the period, hairstyles can change radically. And often the one who launches a new style is the First Lady, that is, the wife of the emperor, or a woman in the emperor's family. Throughout the Empire, all the members of the fairer sex, seeing the statues of these women of power on display in public places or their faces engraved on coins, try to imitate them. The great "fashion designers" of the Roman world are actually the women who inhabit the corridors of power.

And so, with the passing into and out of power of the dynasties, hairstyles became ever more complex. For example, Octavia, sister of Augustus, lent her name to the so-called "Octavia look." It called for wavy hair around the temples and a little curl on the forehead, which was the starting point for a braid which ran around the top of the head in the form of a crest until coming together, on the back of the neck, with a bun (which was made up of more rolled braids).

If you think this hairdo is complex, listen to what happened later under Nero and, even better, under the Flavians (Vespasian, Titus, and Domitian).

It became a custom to frame the woman's face in wreaths of curls. And people started exaggerating. Women's own hair was no longer sufficient and so they resorted to hairpieces stacked on top of one another, like the rows of seats in a theater. These hairpieces were mounted so high they made the woman's hair look like an enormous fountain of curls. These hairdos were rather showy, similar to styles popular during the Renaissance and the Baroque period, culminating in the inevitable bun of rolled braids on the back of the neck. It's easy to imagine the endless hours of work put in by the slaves responsible for hair styling, the *ornatrices*, every time they had to fix the *domina*'s hair. Like a pastry chef who has to construct a wedding cake.

It seems that these monumental hairdos were often exhibited by women of short stature in order to increase their own visibility. And in the Roman era, as we shall see, women generally were not very tall.

In the period we're describing, the hairstyles of wealthy Roman women have reached their evolutionary peak, with hairdos of unprecedented shape and height. They create a vertical fan of hair that runs from one ear to the other, terminating in elegant curls made to look like earrings. Some women look like they're wearing the back of a chair on their head. With others the hairdo is so imposing and pointed that it recalls the papal tiara. The woman responsible for this new fashion is Trajan's wife, Plotina. That's why the style is named "alla Plotina."

We'll stop here. But it may be helpful to know that this is only one phase in the evolution of Roman hairstyles. In subsequent generations, new and famous hairstyles will emerge, such as the "melon," the "turtle," and the "elm tree."

One last curiosity. Roman women obviously love to color their hair; special mixtures allow them to have blond and red hair. To have jet-black hair you have to mix lamb fat and antimony. There are also blue and yellow dyes, but they are typically used by prostitutes and women of dubious virtue. It's evident that in the long-run dyes end up ruining one's hair. That's another reason why there is such wide use of colored wigs, which allow you, from one day to the next, to have a new hair color and a very different style.

ROMAN BREAKFAST

What does a Roman eat first thing in the morning? Roman breakfast is abundant and high in calories; today we'd probably call it an "American breakfast." Naturally, not all Roman tables are decked out with the foods that we'll be describing. A poor family eats what it can, and not always enough. An aristocrat, on the other hand, has a much wider choice. For the Romans, breakfast has a precise name: *ientaculum*.

The table always has some *focacce* (buns), bread, some bowls of honey and, obviously, milk. It's not hard to guess that these are the ancestors of the croissants and toast and jam that we are accustomed to dipping in milk and/or coffee. And it doesn't end there. There is also fruit, cheese, bread dipped in wine, and even meat. And breakfast often includes leftovers from yesterday's lunch and dinner. So for the Romans, breakfast is one of the big meals of the day, while lunch, on the other hand, will be meager.

But the Roman breakfast table lacks two fundamental ingredients typical of our breakfast: coffee and hot chocolate. The Romans had no knowledge of them. At this time, in fact, coffee is still growing wild in Ethiopia and will not be discovered for several centuries by, we are told, hermits who will appreciate its capacity to keep them awake during prayers and their long nocturnal meditations. It will not become widely used until the Middle Ages and the Renaissance, and even then it will be confined primarily to the Islamic world. For a long time, one of the ports for the export of coffee will be Mokha, on the Red Sea, a name that is still heard in our kitchens and often comes up during breakfast.

As for chocolate, that's a different story. The Romans don't know it because the cacao plant grows in the New World, which will be discovered by Christopher Columbus in about thirteen hundred years. At the time of Trajan, cacao is known by the populations of Mesoamerica. But the drink they make from its seeds has such a bitter taste that the Romans probably wouldn't like it (nor would we). It will be necessary to wait for several centuries before somebody comes up with the idea of mixing cacao with sugar (adding at times various types of aromas) in order to obtain what we call chocolate.

After breakfast every wealthy Roman is ready to start the day. It will be a day filled with meetings and discussions. So it will behoove him to take care of another important aspect of personal hygiene: teeth and breath.

To ensure good breath, aromatic lozenges are already available, a real life saver if you have eaten a heavy meal the night before. For teeth, things are more complicated.

The Romans take good care of their teeth. At table they use toothpicks. The ones on display at patrician banquets are often made of silver and are the size of dinner forks. On one end they have a long flat and curved point, to be used to clean your teeth. At the other end is a spoon—to be used to clean your ears (in front of everybody).

In Roman times there are already various kinds of "toothpaste" made from a base of bicarbonate of soda, which a slave rubs on the master's teeth. Nevertheless, some prefer another way of cleaning their teeth that is more than a little disconcerting: washing them with urine. It's a technique that appears to have been quite widespread in Spain and North Africa.

OPEN THE DOORS!

The master's most trusted slave takes a look around. The atrium is in order, the bedrooms are closed, nothing is out of place. He nods to the door slave, who nods back and heads into the hallway that leads to the front door. Outside, a small, quiet crowd of people has already gathered. Many of them are seated on two masonry benches on either side of the door. Others are standing around. Who are they? From their clothes we can imagine that they are humble people, from a much lower class than that of the *dominus*.

All of these people are the so-called clients of the *dominus*. But not what we mean by clients today. To use a contemporary example, imagine the faces of the people you might see in the waiting room of some politician's office or the office of some other prominent figure.

They have come to ask for a favor, some advice, a job for a relative, a show of support for an acquaintance, a recommendation. And there are obviously some people who work for the *dominus* and some small businessmen. Actually, two young men in elegant togas seem to have come to talk business, and they stand off to one side. But in this little crowd there are also some very modest people who have come to ask for small sums of money in order to live. It's a sort of donation that the *dominus* gives them at each visit, sometimes in coins, sometimes in the form of food baskets. It's the so-called *sportula* or dole.

What does the *domius* have to gain by receiving these humble people with problems to be solved? Certainly, he may ask them in exchange to carry out some small tasks, or that they look after the successful completion of some business deal. But his real aim: power. By being generous he creates his own base of supporters and sympathizers, and he becomes an important figure for some key social groups or for the common people in his part of the city, who will vote for him if he becomes a candidate for office.

The word "clientele" is a pretty good definition of what the *dominus* hopes to create. And the thick network of clients spreads throughout the entire city, and constitutes an important part of its social fabric. Because in Rome almost every free man has a bond of respect and at times obedience toward someone wealthier or more powerful than he, his *patronus* or patron, as he is called.

These meetings are repeated every morning. It's the so-called morning *salutation* or greeting, where homage is paid to the powerful. The front door shakes, you can hear the sound of the heavy bolt sliding through the bronze rings. The crowd hushes and draws nearer. Then one side of the door opens and reveals the face of the door slave who peers into the crowd, scrutinizing their faces. He knows them all. He steps aside and in a few seconds the little crowd is swallowed up by the darkness of the entryway.

Inside the atrium everyone takes their proper place in a disciplined manner. Then, one by one, they are called by the right hand slave to be received by the patron in his office, the *tablinium*. The scene that opens up before their eyes is quite impressive. The *dominus* is in the center of the room. He is sitting on what looks like a small throne; it has a high back, carved legs, and is finely decorated. It is partially covered by cushions and a drape. The patron's feet rest on a lion-pawed footstool. The impression is that you have just entered a temple and you are standing in front of the statue of a deity. And, after all, that's the way it is: that man is very wealthy, he is an influential aristocrat, but first of all he is the *pater familias*, the master of the house. And you are now in the heart of his territory.

The *dominus* sits there staring at you with his chin held high to accentuate his position of dominance. And this certainly does not make you feel at ease. This is how his day begins. Yours, probably, will begin with you clearing your throat to ease your embarrassment.

Flying Over Rome in the Morning Mist

Outside, Rome is starting to wake up in an atmosphere that seems unreal. The city is enveloped by unusually dense and cold air. What's more, the air is becoming decidedly more humid and penetrates deep into your lungs with every breath. Maybe that's why the first passersby, wrapped up in heavy clothes, quicken their step under the porticoes. The city is immersed in a thick morning fog, as sometimes happens in modern Rome too. You can't see all the way to the end of the great boulevards, nor make out last colonnades of the Forum. Everything seems to fade into the fog.

Now, imagine yourself lifting off the ground, rising gradually upward, until you are finally above this blanket of fog. Up there, just a few hundred yards above the ground, the air is fresh and crystalline, and the capital of the Roman Empire offers you an extraordinary view.

In front of you, in this vaporous expanse, all you can see are the seven hills, almost as though they were islands in a stormy sea. Here and there, isolated groups of taller buildings and monuments break through. Without the sunlight, their sharp, dark profiles stand out perfectly against the diffuse whiteness of the fog. Entire portions of the eternal city seem to have vanished, together with all of their inhabitants. In total solitude, the giant dome of the Pantheon emerges from the mist and, just beyond it, the colossal obelisk of the Pharaoh Psammetichus II, brought to Rome from Heliopolis in Egypt, and used to indicate the time in the enormous sun dial built by Augustus.

Compared to today, ancient Rome was more "polluted" with humidity. In fact, the city was surrounded by much more farmland and forests. Plus, the Tiber flooded much more frequently. In the very heart of Rome there were areas that were former marshes, like the area where the Colosseum was built. Even today, under the feet of the almost four million tourists who visit the monument every year, there is so much water that some of its deepest passageways can only be explored by scuba divers. Elsewhere, the situation is no better. In the Forum of Augustus, just a few yards from the boulevard where today's Italy celebrates the birth of the Republic with a parade every June 2, the ravines are populated by a colony of crabs! All this helps us to understand how humid the terrain and air of Rome were, in the age of the empire, especially in the low-lying areas of the city. And the humidity had a number of consequences: from the morning mists (occasional) to the mosquitoes and unhealthy atmosphere (perpetual).

The morning fog seems to spare only the most important areas of Rome, allowing us to make a rapid tour of the imperial capital from above, moving from one to another of the seven hills. Suddenly, the first rays of sunlight cut through the air and inundate the gilded monuments of Rome with light, pulling them out of the fog. It is only a brief moment, but indescribably magic. In that brief instant some of the most symbolic places of the Eternal City are bathed in light, the foundations which gave rise to Rome's origins and its power.

Among the first to be illuminated is the Capitoline Hill. Like a beacon shining over the city, the temple of Jupiter, whose shape recalls the Parthenon in Athens, gleams brilliantly. Its rows of white columns glow in the sunlight and the gilded bronzes mythological figures of its pediment are emitting incandescent flashes, as though it were on fire. It's a spectacular sight.

Next, on the second summit of the Capitoline, another temple lights up, the smaller temple of Juno Moneta ("Juno Who Warns"). Nearby was the mint of Rome, which was habitually indicated with the phrase "*ad Monetum*" or "near the temple of Juno Moneta." This expression gave rise to the habit of referring to currency by using the term "moneta." A term that has been handed down to the Italian of our own time and has also spread to other languages: *moneda* (Spanish), *money* (English), *monnaie* (French), etc.

Flanking the Capitoline Hill is a steep, vertical slope that looks almost like the prow of a ship cutting through the fog. Down through the centuries, this cliff has had a very precise role and meaning in the daily life of the Romans. It's the Tarpeian Rock. From the earliest days of Rome, citizens convicted of high treason have been thrown to their death from its heights. It is a symbol of Roman law, but above all a symbol of its ancient traditions.

On this very special morning, the other "promontories" of Rome, one after another, are lit up by the sun. They are hills with famous names: the Quirinal, and next to it the Viminal, whose name apparently derives from the willow trees that grew there in ancient times.

Like the hump of a whale, the top of another hill breaks through the fog; the Esquiline with its roofs and its beautiful villas with their gorgeous gardens and peristyles. A lot of important Romans had their homes here, such as Mecenate, the great patron of the arts. Next to it is the Caelian hill, another famous residential area.

Finally, off on its own a little to the south, there's the Aventine, once a popular neighborhood, but later gentrified into an aristocratic area and famous in history because the plebeians seceded here in 494 BCE.

We're missing the Palatine. We've all heard it talked about but today not many people remember why it was important. What is on the Palatine that's so special?

The Palatine is the emperor's hill. It's here that he resides and commands the Empire from his great palaces. For the ancient Romans, if you will, it is the equivalent of modern Rome's Quirinal, home to the President of the Italian Republic, or Washington's famous ellipse, where the White House stands. And that's not all. A Roman would tell you that it's the hill at the foot of which the Wolf suckled Romulus and Remus, the brothers who were the founders of the Eternal City.

This is obviously a myth. But archaeologists have discovered traces of ancient cabins here, dating back to the Iron Age, that prove that this hill was actually among the first sites in the area of Rome to be permanently settled. The holes made in the ground by the poles supporting these cabins are still visible today, among the ruins of the buildings from the imperial age.

This hill, in short, is a concentrate of history, tradition, and power. Decisions that played a decisive role in the history of Europe, the Mediterranean, and part of Asia were made here. Yet today there are very few tourists who understand its importance and who go to visit the extraordinary ruins of its palaces. All you have to do is climb the stairs next to the Roman Forum, a place mobbed with tourists, and you immediately find yourself in a beautiful, quiet, enormous natural space, immersed in vegetation; exactly as it must have been back then, in the time of the emperors.

Exactly as it is now, during our visit to Trajan's Rome. The Palatine, in fact, rises out of the morning fog like a fortress. It looks like a separate city. In the oblique light of dawn, we can make out palaces that are still asleep, their interior courts black and dark, several levels of colonnades, long porticoes . . . We imagine, still wrapped in silence, the splendid corridors, lined with precious marbles coming from the four corners of the Empire and extraordinary statues that we will never see because they will be lost over the centuries. The march-step of the praetorian guards echoes through the colonnades. The palaces are ready to start their day.

A curiosity. The Italian words "*palazzo*" and "*palazzina*" (and their equivalents in other languages: palace, *palais*, etc.) are derived from the name of this hill, which in Latin was called *Palatium*. For centuries in the lives of Romans, this hill was synonymous with the luxurious residence of the emperor. It was not a very big step, then, to coin a new word to indicate a princely home. And so the *Palatium* gave rise to all of the words for "palace" in languages descendent from Latin.

In this early morning overture of the Eternal City, however, we haven't seen its most famous monument: the Colosseum. Where is it? We can't see it. It's semi-submerged in the mist, anchored in a low-lying, wet area in the central part of the city. Only its uppermost level pokes through the blanket: the attic, above the last level of arcades, is topped by a crown of 240 enormous poles that delineate a perfect oval. These poles serve to support the *velarium*, a combination of awnings that protect the spectators from the sun. Dozens of slaves are already at work on the final organizational touches of the show that will be held there during the day. And that we will be going to see. Naturally, gladiator fights will be one of the highlights. Along with plenty of surprises.

By now, the sun's rays are stretched out over the city, the fog and its vapors can't hold them back any longer. Rome begins to take shape before our eyes. Slowly, whole neighborhoods materialize, with their colors, their sounds, their lives. The fog begins to thin out and gradually opens up, like a theater curtain, signaling the start of a performance with a cast of a million and a half actors and extras; a day in the life of Trajan's Rome. It's 115 CE.

W hat time is it in Rome right now? If you ask people on the street each of them will give you a different answer. To hear Seneca tell it, it's not possible to know the exact time in Rome. On the contrary, it's easier to get philosophers to agree among themselves than it is to synchronize people's watches.

In fact, Roman methods for telling time aren't very precise. The most common is the sundial. They come in all shapes and sizes. The biggest sundial in Rome was commissioned by Augustus and placed in the Campus Martius. It's the size of a large piazza (200 by 525 feet) and the gnomon, the shadow-casting edge, consists of an obelisk brought to Rome from the Egyptian city of Heliopolis—an obelisk that stands today in front of the Italian parliament. Two thousand years ago, the obelisk projected its shadow onto a large piazza paved in white travertine marble. Graded lines of bronze in the pavement made it possible to tell the hour and the date. The aim of the designer of this immense solar clock was to make it so the Ara Pacis, the altar of peace, was in line with the autumn equinox, September, when nighttime and daytime are equal. September 23, in fact, was Emperor Augustus's birthday. So on that date the shadow of the obelisk pointed toward the altar, symbolically uniting the emperor, the movement of the sun, and the *pax Romana*.

In Trajan's Rome, however, there are lots of "normal" sundials. You can see them attached to public buildings, in the courtyard gardens of wealthy people's homes, and even on the wrists of people on the street. These minuscule watch faces, just over an inch in diameter and called *solaria*, are the equivalent of our pocket watches. They are concave and look a bit like little egg cups. They have a tiny hole on one side for the sunlight to pass through and project a luminous dot onto a series of marks and lines etched into the concave surface to indicate the time. The problem is they only work in Rome; their lines and marks are made for the latitude of Rome. If you change latitude they don't work anymore. So it's useless to take them on a trip.

Another system for telling the time involves special water clocks. They work like hourglasses and are made of glass vases that collect drops of water falling from an overhead container. Marks etched into the side of the vase indicate the hour, even at night and on rainy days. In Trajan's time they are easily found in the houses of wealthy Romans as emblems of their lofty status. And in certain cases they can even "sound the hour" like our cuckoo or grandfather clocks. According to Vitruvius, the great architect of the Augustan age, some of these water clocks are equipped with floats connected to special mechanisms that emit sharp whistles or toss stones—or eggs—into the air. In his famous novel *Satyricon*, on the other hand, Petronius describes a much simpler method. The main character, Trimalcione (a nouveau riche man with very poor taste), has a clock in his house that sounds the hour by blowing air through a bull's horn . . .

Fine, but how many hours are there in a Roman day? Twelve daytime hours and twelve nighttime hours. The day begins at dawn with the *hora prima* (first hour), *hora secunda, hora tertia*, etc, until sunset, when the *hora duodecima* (twelfth hour) sounds. From that moment, night begins with twelve more *horae*, until dawn. And the cycle starts again.

So are Roman hours the same as ours? Not exactly, first of

all because in the Roman era, for lack of precise clocks, there is no mention of minutes or seconds. And then because the hours are not always the same; their duration depends on the season!

In effect, the Romans' main point of reference is noon, when the sun is at its highest point. At that moment, the day is at its halfway point; six hours have passed since dawn and six more will pass before sunset. But it is evident that the days are longer in summer and shorter in winter. So summer hours last longer than winter hours. And not just by a little. To give you an example, in the summertime the "hour" between twelve noon and one o'clock lasts seventy-five minutes, while in winter it lasts only forty-four minutes.

The same thing happens, in reverse, for nighttime hours, which, however, are referred to as "vigils," *vigilae*; literally, "watches," or shifts of guard duty (from military terminology). So each night is divided into four vigils of three hours each.

It's clear that with such elastic hours and without precise clocks, daily appointment schedules are much less rigid and there is a certain tolerance for latecomers. But there is also a way to be punctual. For example, you can make an appointment at the Forum for when it's filled to half capacity; if we checked every day with a watch we'd notice that this description always corresponds, more or less, to the same time. But the real clocks that regulate Roman time are the activities that follow one another in the course of the day.

For practical reasons, however, our journey through ancient Rome will continue to use the hours of the modern age—the ones we're used to.

BARBERS AND THE MORNING RUSH HOUR

Meanwhile, outside, the street is coming to life. There's a constant flow of foot traffic, particularly of men. Or more specifically, of slaves; you can tell them by their raw-cloth tunics, in many cases fraying and stained. Some of them have their heads shaved too. None of them are strolling, they all move with a determined stride. It's clear they've got things to do, the first tasks of the day. This time in the morning, in other words, is a little rush hour of slaves. It seems odd not to hear the sound of clacking heels, but just the soft sound, often a swish, of sandals. And in fact, in Roman times, shoes don't have heels, but only a flat sole. One exception to this is the legionnaires, whose sandals, or *caligae*, have a lot of small iron cleats to give them better traction, sort of like soccer shoes. Actually, heels do exist, but only on particular kinds of shoes and especially for women.

A slave passes right by us with a big bundle of clothes wrapped in a sheet. He is undoubtedly taking some togas, or perhaps some table cloths, to be washed. But how do the Romans do their laundry? You have to take it to the "cleaners," or the *fullonica*. Once there, the clothes undergo a series of treatments that would make us grimace. What happens is that tunics, togas, sheets, and tablecloths are thrown into tubs filled with a mixture of water and alkaline substances such as soda, or smectic clay or human urine! On a lot of street corners, in fact, especially near the *fullonicae*, there are large, wide-mouthed clay jars (*amphorae*) into which passersby can relieve themselves of their impelling need. Some slaves will come by on a regular basis to collect the urine for use in the *fullonicae*. If this task strikes you as unpleasant, think of those slaves who will have to spend hours squishing the clothes in the tubs of urine, doing the work of our washing machines, engulfed in disgusting odors. The clothes are then rinsed, beaten, and treated with other substances (such as *creta fullonica*, a softening clay) to make them more compact. After they've been wrung out they'll be hung to dry in the courtyards, as we hang our wet clothes to dry on the balconies of our apartments (in Roman times you could even hang clothes out on the street), and then ironed with specially made presses.

A curiosity: there is already a kind of bleaching process. Once washed, in fact, white items are hung over a domed structure made of wooden arches, less than three feet high. This dome stands over a brazier in which some sulfur has been heated. This sulferizing is the Roman version of "the whitest white you've ever seen." Afterwards, a slave will take the washed and ironed clothes back to the house.

The slave with the bundle of clothes continues rapidly on his way, but he suddenly disappears behind a litter emerging from a side street. For a minute this human carriage blocks our view. It's impossible to tell who's inside; the interior is hidden by veils. Then, as quickly as it appeared, the litter vanishes down an alleyway, preceded by a slave whose job is to make way for his master (or mistress).

We continue down the street. Our ears perk up at an explosion of laughter coming from an already open shop. A few more steps and a typical early-morning scene opens up before us: a barber, or *tonsor*, as he is commonly called, at work on a customer. The cheery sound of chatting and bantering inside the shops is another characteristic of the early-morning hours in the capital, as it is in all the other cities of the Empire.

Apart from the few fortunate men with a house slave who

shaves them in the morning, like the *dominus* whom we met earlier, everybody else has to go to one of these barber shops to get a shave and have his hair cut.

And so the *tonstrinae*, or barber shops, are meeting places, where men gather to tell jokes and stories but also to share the latest news and especially the latest gossip and rumors.

Actually, these shops have a lot of the same features of modern barber shops. Waiting customers sit on benches lined up against the mirror-covered walls. The customer whose turn it is sits on a stool in the middle of the room, a large towel covering his shoulders and chest.

Fortunately, the current fashion in men's hairstyles is fairly simple. Emperor Trajan, who is the most imitated model, wears his hair combed forward and cut rather short on his forehead.

A man is looking at himself in the mirror checking out his just finished haircut; each cut of the scissors has left its mark, creating an uneven, terraced effect. Is that because the barber was in a hurry to serve all those waiting customers, or is it the scissors, still fairly rough compared to modern scissors? In any event, it's something rather common among the Romans, it seems even Nero's hair had this layered look.

The customer in the next chair is getting shaved by an assistant. Shaving cream doesn't exist yet, and the only lotion that's rubbed on his face before applying the razor is water! After the first few customers the *tonsor* has to spend a fair amount of time and energy to re-sharpen the razor blade. To do this, he uses a grindstone moistened with saliva.

Delicately, he holds the razor up to his customer's neck and starts pulling it slowly over his skin. The real dangers are nicks and cuts; all it takes is a tic or a sudden jerk. Unfortunately, it's such a frequent occurrence that since the time of Augustus judges have imposed *ad hoc* fines and penalties. And what does the barber do in case of a cut? To stop the bleeding, Pliny the Elder suggested the application of spiderwebs soaked in olive oil and vinegar.

But at this point isn't it better to let your beard grow? After all, in earlier times the Greeks and Romans both had beards. Nowadays, however, unless you're a philosopher or a soldier, being clean shaven is pretty much an obligation. But it won't last long. Obviously, nobody knows this right now, but when Trajan dies, in a couple of years, the old fashion of beards will make a comeback. The new trend will be launched by the new emperor, Hadrian (maybe to cover up a scar), and everybody will imitate him. It will be a relief for a lot of men to be able to avoid the daily torture of the razor, except maybe for the *tonsor* who will see a sharp drop in his earnings . . .

Now we've come to the end of the street, where it intersects with a long boulevard. It's known as Clivus Suburanus, and it's not far from Trajan's baths. At the end of it there's a fork in the road with a fountain in the middle, the fountain of Orpheus. It's a boulevard lined with lots of apartment buildings with myriads of windows looking out like box seats on the spectacle of life. A street that's already starting to fill up with people and deafening noises, like the hammer blows of the coppersmiths.

A few yards away we can hear the sound of water splashing down on the pavement; a bucket of urine has just been emptied onto the street. But where did it come from? As we raise our eyes we can make out, in all its grandeur, a tall building with countless balconies and windows. It's a real giant of the construction industry. The Romans call these buildings *insulae*. It's a world all its own, ready to be explored.

The *Insulae*, a World Apart

T he *insulae* are the Romans' houses, or better, their apartment buildings. The word *insula* is the root word of a term modern Italian city dwellers use very often, *isolato* or *city block*. And this gives you an idea of the size of the *insulae*. If you go by the number of people who live in them, they could be defined as vertical villages or boroughs. They are truly the skyscrapers of the ancient world. It's not easy to judge the height of the *insula* that's standing over us right now. Emperor Augustus had established that residential buildings could not be taller than twenty-one meters (almost seventy feet), which in modern terms would mean buildings no higher than seven stories, even now a pretty considerable height). At the time of Trajan, the law is even more severe: the maximum height is now eighteen meters (fifty-nine feet). That means a six-story building plus an attic, a real penthouse as we'll see. But it's evident that this limit is not always respected, with the inevitable accompanying structural defects and building collapses. And the *insula* that we're about to visit is much taller than the legal limit. On first glance, it has the look of a Soviet-style block, because of its square shape and the evenly spaced windows right up to the roof. But on second glance, we can notice a lot of details which actually lend it a certain elegance. First of all, the color. It's a brick building, but the bricks are totally covered in a protective cream-colored plaster that's very pleasing to the eye. The choice of this color is also quite practical because it is very luminous and its reflected light brightens the surrounding narrow streets and porticoes.

Running along the base of the building is an elegant stripe of Pompeian red, about five feet high. What could it be for? It's both esthetic and practical. Its purpose is not so much decorative as protective; it serves to mask mud stains, hand marks, the signs left by merchandise or bodies that have leaned against the wall. It's not the only touch of elegance; above every window, there's a line of bricks emerging from the plaster in the shape of a small arch. From below, it almost seems that the windows have red eyebrows. And that's not all. There is also a narrow balcony that runs all along the second floor of the *insula*, connecting the various apartments. The Romans call it the *Maenianum*, and it is truly a small luxury for its owners, something comparable to a little garden or a terrace. Above all, it's something that the others don't have and that makes it possible to go outside to get a bit of air, or some sun, and you can even keep some plants out there in vases.

Actually, the Romans, just like us, love to keep houseplants; on the balconies and in the windows of the *insulae* you can see a multitude of flower vases, exactly as on the balconies of our apartment buildings. Some people with a passion for gardening even cultivate small hanging gardens, as we learn from Pliny the Elder.

This love of greenery is something that ancient Rome shares with modern Rome; countless *insulae* are covered with climbing plants that wrap themselves around balcony railings and serve as frames for windows. On the streets there are lots of tall trees that grow up to caress the façades of the *insulae* and sometimes even lean on them for support. Imperial Rome, in short, is a green city. A characteristic that seems unchanged in present-day Rome, almost as though twenty centuries had not gone by. These are small things, but they help us understand how similar the Romans of today are to the Romans of yester-

The streets of Rome are dominated by very tall apartment buildings, the insulae. There are some forty-six thousand of them! Unauthorized construction is quite common.

day (and vice-versa). Especially in their everyday lives, modern Romans are, in a certain sense, the modern version of the ancient Romans, filtered through the centuries of history that separate them.

As has been underlined by Jérome Carcopino, one of the greatest students of ancient Rome, comparing an apartment building in Via dei Capellari in Rome, or Via dei Tribunali in Naples with an *insula* in Ostia Antica reveals not only deep similarities but sometimes even perfect correspondences, right down to the floor plans. A Roman from ancient times, observing our apartment buildings in the historic center of modern Rome or Naples, would probably feel right at home.

The long balcony on the second floor is not the only one. There are other, smaller ones, in wood, on the upper floors. They are small privileges for the fortunate few, as are the carved wood loggias sticking out from the building. The Romans call them *pergulae*. We are used to seeing them in medieval cities, in the Middle East, or in distant places such as India or Katmandu. Yet they are already part of the "postcards" of imperial Rome. The purpose is simple: to enlarge an apartment and bring in a little more light. And also to spy down on the street without being seen.

CURIOSITY—The "Skyscrapers" of Ancient Rome

In their time, the *insulae* were the tallest residential buildings on the planet, yet their height would not seem all that impressive to us; they were about as tall as one of our average apartment buildings. With some exceptions. We know, in fact, that between 100 and 200 CE, a real monster construction was built in the center of Rome. We don't know, however, exactly how tall it was, although its size was certainly shocking to people at the time. It was said that it rose above the roofs of Rome like a skyscraper. Its impact on the city skyline and on the minds of the people of Rome must have been truly remarkable since its name, *Insula Felicles*, went from mouth to mouth until it reached the four corners of the Empire. Nevertheless, it was an isolated case. With the exception of this little Empire State Building, buildings in Rome were rarely more than six stories high.

It is extraordinary that, even today, after so many centuries, we can still admire the remains of some *insulae* that are still standing. Sometimes they emerge like relics in the midst of the traffic in the capital, but only a few people stop to admire them. One well-known *insula* is located right beside the immense monument to King Victor Emanuel in piazza Venezia. On the right side of the monument, just before the stairway that goes up to the Ara Coeli, you can see the anonymous remains of dilapidated brick building, several stories high. Unfortunately, it doesn't get the attention it deserves. There is a constant flow of passersby. Busloads of tourists deposited on the sidewalk stop for just a moment, listen to a few words of explanation from their guide, and then move on, always in a hurry, amid the ever-present souvenir vendors.

But if you stop and lean against the railing, a piece of imperial Rome materializes right before your eyes: shops, rooms, windows. And, with a little imagination, your mind can furnish those abandoned rooms and put some people in them too. Who lived there? What faces would we have seen inside them, illuminated by the lanterns? From that window over there a mother called down to her son who was playing on the street, maybe together with the son of the guy who owned the shop on the corner. And who knows what scenes took place inside those shops.

That is what is so magical about archaeology. For an instant you can relive forgotten worlds; it lets you meet people who no longer exist, and it puts you into the middle of daily life as it was lived centuries ago. No special effect could give us such a strong emotional experience.

Perhaps even more impressive is the *insula* in Trajan's forum, just a short walk from the traffic in Via Nazionale. You can see it rise up all the way to the roof, and it gives you an idea of the imposing size of these buildings. But it is out in Ostia, the old port of Rome, which has the ruins of several ancient *insulae*, including the one dedicated to Diana, where we can really get an understanding of what it meant to live inside one of these buildings. They are partially explorable, and it is truly moving to climb the stairs, find yourself on the landing of a Roman-era apartment building, and then go into the rooms of a second-or third-floor apartment. You really get an idea of how the Romans lived. Yes, because most of the inhabitants of Rome lived in *insulae*.

So how many *insulae* were there in Rome? We know their exact number thanks to precious archaeological discoveries of the city's land records. In the second century CE, under emperor Septimius Severus, there were exactly 46,602 *insulae*. A huge number. Especially if you consider that the number of *domus*, that is, the typical elegant Roman houses (like the ones in Pompeii) came to just 1,797. That means that there were twenty-six big apartment buildings for every traditional house. Why this amazing disproportion?

Carcopino once made this interesting observation: since Rome, at the time of its greatest splendor, covered between 4500 and 5000 acres with a population of 1.2 million residents, it is evident that space was in short supply. Even more so if we adjust for those areas where it was prohibited to build housing (the entire Palatine Hill, where the emperor lived, or the five hundred acres of the Campus Martius, which hosted temples, porticoes, gymnasiums, and tombs). Then we have to add forty or so parks and public gardens and all of the huge public buildings that occupied enormous surface areas, such as the Colosseum, the theaters, the basilicas, the baths, the Forums, the various temples, and all the administrative buildings.

The solution to the shortage of space was simple and effective: new space was created by building upward, by constructing multi-story buildings. When most of the city's residents got home in the evening, in other words, their feet no longer touched the ground and they "slept in the air."

The number of above-ground floors in the entire city must have really been enormous if even back then, a rhetorician named Elius Aristides could exclaim that if all the city's houses had been built at ground level, Rome would have stretched all the way to the Adriatic coast (a distance of some 120 miles!).

Today, no one is amazed by big apartment buildings and skyscrapers, but in ancient times, in a world dominated by a myriad of small villages, with just a few urban centers whose buildings were seldom more than two or three stories high, seeing a city occupied by "monsters" of the construction industry like the *insulae* must have been something like what one feels walking around New York today, tormented by two questions: How do such tall buildings keep from falling down? and How do people live all squeezed together in these colossal buildings?

THE HUMAN FACE OF THE *INSULAE*

I f you go out for a walk in one of our cities, what do you see? A lot of stores. That's the way it is in ancient Rome too. The ground floor of the *insulae* is made up of a long line of shops and stores. Between one and the next are the anonymous front doors of the *insulae* themselves, with the ramps of stairs that lead to the upper floors. And that's where we're headed now.

As we approach the entrance, a man looks us over from a distance: he's one of the doormen. He's short and fat, with a dirty tunic and a double chin covered with bristly stubble. He's sitting on a simple stool and his hands are slowly twirling a knotty cane made of olive wood. That cane gives away not only his role but also his origins. It's identical to the ones used to give orders in the legions. Evidently he's an ex-legionnaire, maybe a centurion fallen into disgrace, who is now making do with this new job, which demands a direct and decisive ability to intervene and put a stop to fights and arguments between tenants. After staring at us for a long time, he turns his gaze back to the street and the faces of the passersby. Impassive and inscrutable. He even ignores us as we cross the threshold.

Our first steps are into a dark hallway; the only thing we can perceive is a growing volume of shouting. What we are about to enter, in effect, is a world apart, a small universe with its own logic, its own equilibrium, and its own inhabitants. A zoo-like collection of people and personalities.

The first scene that appears before our eyes, at the end of

the hallway, is a young girl standing next to an enormous jar, a *dolium*, placed under the first flight of a large stairway. Standing with one foot on a wooden stool, she's emptying the contents of some terra-cotta vases into the mouth of a wineskin. What is it? A few more steps, we come out into the open, and we're hit by a wave of foul-smelling air . . . it's urine. The girl is evidently a slave and she's emptying her masters' chamber pots. She doesn't seem the slightest pit perturbed by the strong odor. By now she's gotten used to it since it has been, for years, one of her first morning duties. Later on, someone will pass by to collect this liquid, which is so precious for the cleaners.

A look around reveals the squalor of the environment: the walls are chipped and peeling, covered with water and oil stains, and even traces of hand marks. There's also some writing. One piece of graffiti is particularly striking. Two gladiators in combat: a *secutor* armed with a helmet, a short spear, and a rectangular shield, and a *retiarius*, with a net and a trident. Their features are infantile; it's clearly the work of a child. He's also written their names: Sedulus and Thelonicus, evidently two crowd-pleasers who inflame children's imaginations, as happens today with football players and cartoon heroes. Next to this is another bit of rather more allusive writing: "Many women have often been deceived by Restitutus" (*Restitutus multas decepit saepe puellas*), probably a warning for all of the women of the *insula* written by a girl seduced and abandoned by one of the tenants. There are also some more, let's say, daring graffiti, similar to what we might see today in a public bathroom. Nevertheless, in the midst of a lot of obscenity, we also get a glimpse of a flowering adolescent love (*Marcus amat Domitiam*)immediately counterbalanced by "Greek Eutichide, very refined manners, gives herself away for two asses" (*Eutychis graeca assibus II moribus bellis*). The as is a coin of very little value; the price is, shall we say, extremely affordable.

Sex, love, invective, athletics: that's what archaeologists

have found engraved on Roman walls. Not much has changed in two thousand years!

The girl now starts climbing wearily back up the stairs. We follow her. She's no more than twelve or thirteen years old; her golden-blond hair belies her Nordic origins. Who knows what part of Germany she comes from? Despite her young age, there's undoubtedly some tragedy in her past. Maybe her tribe lost a battle with Roman troops and all the inhabitants of her village were sent off into slavery. More likely, however, she was captured by some other Germans from a neighboring tribe and sold to slave traders, a disturbing practice, but very common. What's certain is that in just a few seconds her life changed forever.

Now she's on the second-floor landing and she's opening an impressive door, with two elegant bright bronze rings. We enter the apartment. On first glance we can see that it belongs to a very wealthy family.

What were apartments like in imperial Rome? Our imaginary reconstruction will be based mainly on what has been discovered in Ostia Antica, the old port of Rome. The layout and architecture of Ostia Antica is actually quite typical of the era that we are exploring and it will enable us to discover a lot of details about daily life; curiosities gathered and analyzed by Professor Carlo Pavolini after years of study and excavations at this extraordinary site.

The Romans call them *cenacula*, but aside from this difference, they are very similar to our own, especially the floor plan. Today's apartments are actually the modern evolution of the Roman *cenacula*.

The first room is a receiving room. In the center is a feline-footed round marble table, with a statue of Venus on it. We are welcomed, in other words, by a work of art, a sign that the owner is a cultivated person (or wants us to think so). The apartment is not enormous and we can take it all in with a single glance. To our right is the sitting room (*tablinium*), and on the left is the dining room (*triclinium*). Behind us are the doors to the three bedrooms. The difference between this apartment and the *domus* of the wealthy Roman that we visited earlier this morning is striking. That was a house shut in on itself, with no windows, and all the rooms facing on to the atrium, with its pool of rain water. Here it is exactly the opposite: all of the main rooms "shoot off" from the center of the house, almost as though they were subjected to some centrifugal force. Why? The reason is simple. They want light and so they line up along the façade of the building where the windows are.

It's clear that the glass window panes are essential for these apartments. Glass is a costly and precious material, but still within the means of the well-to-do tenants of these luxurious *cenacula*. On the upper floors, as we will see, it's a very different story.

The furniture is scant: a few chairs, some bench chests, some folding stools and various shaped tables. Moving from one room to the next we can see some ordinary objects on these tables: a comb, a series of waxed wooden tablets for writing, a terra-cotta piggy bank (just like ours!), a bronze lantern, a small jewelry box, a bunch of keys attached to a curious key ring; a minuscule key fused to a ring, to be worn on your finger . . .

We cross a threshold. We're struck by two large vases of flowers placed in the center of the room. Flowers in the house are not a modern idea; they were already common in the Roman era. This floral composition stands out in a triumph of colored petals. And not by chance it's sitting on the most beautiful table in the apartment; it's made of exotic wood with undulating ribbing that sends off glimmers of reflected light.

These aren't the only colors in this home. As in the *domus* of the wealthy, the walls in this home are also painted with vivid colors, further evidence of the Romans' love for brightly colored homes.

The apartment is a sequence of walls dominated by bright orange, azure, or Pompeian red, applied to the plaster when it's still wet. The rest of the painting was done later, once the plaster was dry. The background colors have been enriched with the addition of slender columns or gracious architectural trompe-l'oeils in the shape of window frames, imaginary "openings" onto invented landscapes and panoramas. Sometimes there are also figures in the center; in one room we can see the famous nine muses of Apollo. These figures are the equivalents of our framed paintings.

Suddenly we feel heat against our right legs. It's a brazier, and the coals are still burning. We hadn't noticed but now we realize that in the entire apartment we haven't seen a fireplace or even a radiator. The only form of heating in this era is braziers. This one in particular has little wheels, and it can be moved to where it's needed, a little like our portable electric heaters.

There's a strong smell spreading through the entire house. It's the smell of burning wood. Where is it coming from? We walk back through the atrium with the statue of Venus. As we pass by, we also notice two lovely silver plates and a nicely engraved carafe; more of the family's status symbols. We go into the *triclinium*. Now we can even see the smoke, it's invading the whole room and it seems to be coming from a corner, under a window. The girl we saw on he stairs is standing there. She's bending over what looks like a large square brazier and she has just lit the fire. We suddenly realize what we're looking at. We haven't seen the kitchen in this house and here it is: it's that bronze stove. In effect, the kitchen in these small apartments is reduced to the minimum, almost a camp stove! And above all it's portable; you can put it wherever you want, but common sense dictates that it be placed near a window, because of the smoke. Still, it's inevitable that in the morning and at mealtimes the whole apartment fills up with various smells, whether it's burning wood or the smell of cooking food. But it's not that way for everybody. A lot of people order food from the nearest tavern, thus avoiding the problem (and the dangers) of these "camp stoves" while also varying their diet.

One myth we need to debunk is the way people eat at home. They lie on couches only when a banquet has been organized, or during holidays. On ordinary days they eat just like we do, sitting down at a table.

We head toward the exit. For the first time we look down at the floor and discover a small wonder, the floors are covered with elegant mosaics, in black and white. The designs are simple: rhombuses, stars, squares combined in all different ways. We see more mosaics in the adjoining rooms. Why are they in black and white and not colored? The explanation is simple: it's a way to save money. These mosaics, in fact, are almost always on the second floor of the *insulae*, which are usually occupied by well-to-do renters. People who are well off, certainly, but not rich. The black and white mosaics give the apartment a touch of elegance without the exorbitant costs of a villa.

Color mosaics often feature human or animal figures and require highly skilled craftsmen. For a builder of *insulae* the cost would truly be considerable. Black and white mosaics, on the other hand, are executed by simple decorators who are much more accessible economically, not least because they limit themselves to reproducing geometric figures in various combinations. Beyond that, the raw materials, limestone (white) and basalt (black) are easy to find and relatively cheap, in contrast to the colored glass-pastes and polychrome marbles used for mosaic inlays.

Basically, choosing a black and white mosaic for the house is similar to our choosing a parquet floor: it's elegant and stylish without the high costs of the marble floors in a villa. But it's better in any case not to go overboard: mosaics are only found in the living quarters of the master. In service areas or servants' quarters the floors are covered with simple slabs of terra cotta ("two footers," about two feet square), by bricks laid in a fish-bone pattern, or by floor coverings in *coccio pesto*—a blend of crushed brick, sand, and lime (when you visit an archaeological site these differences will help you identify the different rooms in a house).

THE INHUMAN FACE OF THE *INSULAE*

We're back out on the landing and we start to climb the stairs. On second thought, there's something out of synch in what we've just seen. It's surprising that a wealthy tenant would choose to live on the second floor of the building and not on one of the top floors, where there is more privacy, less noise, and most of all, an extraordinary view of the rooftops of Rome.

Yet that's the way it is throughout the Empire. The people who live in penthouse apartments are poor, while the wealthy live on the second floor. The exact opposite of today. Why?

The reasons are simple. First of all, and obviously, there's the fatigue factor. There are no elevators and so the higher up you live, the more stairs you have to climb. But there is also a safety problem. The construction industry is run by speculators with little or no scruples. The higher the building, the weaker the structure and the higher the risk of collapse (not to mention the drafts and the rain coming through the windows and roof). Finally, because of the widespread use of braziers and lanterns, fires are frequent, and people who live on the lower floors have a better chance of getting safely out of the burning building. The tenant who lives under the roof with the pigeons will be the last to notice the flames and will die a terrible death. This is how the poet Juvenal describes it: "the third floor is already burning and you don't know anything. There's chaos from the ground floor up, but the last one to roast is the miserable tenant whose only protection from the rain are the roof tiles, where pigeons come to lay their eggs."

Actually, this vertical division of residential buildings continued right up through the nineteenth century. Aristocrats and the well-to-do lived on the *piano nobile* or noble floor, but as you went up, each subsequent floor was occupied by poorer families than the one below. What today is a social division by neighborhood used to be by floor.

We keep climbing higher, flight after flight. Suddenly, just a few yards above us, what seemed like talking degenerates into a screaming match. The shouts attract the attention of other tenants who look out onto the stairs. In the middle of the landing there's a robust woman, unkempt raven black hair down to her shoulders, who's standing in the way of three men. Her eyes are flashing with anger. In one arm she's holding a baby, just a few months old, while her other arm cuts the air with powerful gestures in time with her loud voice. With every move, her large breasts jumble around under her tunic. She's clearly a working-class woman, used to dealing with people brusquely and directly.

Through the crack of the half-open door to her apartment, in the shadows, we catch a glimpse of the frightened eyes of her other children. The three men are motionless, dumbstruck. She's won the first round, there's no doubt about it. Two of the men, you can tell, are simple doormen acting as bodyguards. The third, the one in the middle, must be the cause of it all. He's tall, thin, an aquiline nose, sunken cheeks, and dressed in a dark red mantle, wrapped twice around his shoulders. What makes him so disturbing is his impassive, glacial stare. It's the look of a predator, of someone who knows, no matter how things go, he's going to come out the winner. The reason for this raucous exchange is something quite familiar to us today: a rent hike.

A house in Rome costs four times as much as anywhere else

in Italy, as has been pointed out by Professor Romolo Augusto Staccioli. We'll have a chance later on to discuss the "modernity" of the urban problems in the capital city.

What's easy to see is that for people without much money, the situation is dramatic. Things can get really ugly. To convince a tenant to pay up, the landlord might even wall up the door to his apartment, or remove the wooden stair that is the tenant's only access to his apartment, keeping him in isolation inside the apartment until the money shows up. These are obviously extreme cases, but they demonstrate that when it's time to collect the rent landlords don't play around.

Leases expire on precise dates at certain times of the year and have to be renegotiated. The streets of Rome fill up with crowds of evicted families, searching for a new apartment. A real social emergency that no emperor has ever really managed to solve.

Why is housing in Rome so expensive?

A chain of sublets

In Rome, every *insula* has one owner. But you'll probably never see him coming around to collect the rent. Someone else does the dirty work. A professional administrator. The two have an agreement: the owner rents all the upper floors to the administrator for five years and in exchange he asks "only" for the rent from the apartment on the ground floor, which often has the look and cost of a true patrician *domus*. The administrator, for his part, will have to maintain the decorum of the building, see after its upkeep, resolve any arguments between the tenants and, finally, collect the rent.

The administrator's job is not much fun, certainly, but the profits are considerable. If the owner leases him an entire *insula* for 30,000 sestertii, he can take in 40,000 from his subleases. This explains why apartments in Rome are so expensive. But it also explains why the Roman *insulae* are so big: the taller they are, the more apartments they have, and the more money can be made.

According to Jérome Carcopino, at the time of Julius Caesar, about 170 years earlier than the period we are describing, a simple apartment cost some 2,000 sestertii, a figure that you could have used to buy, under Trajan, an entire estate in Frosinone, just fifty miles south of Rome.

So it's pretty easy to imagine the profits. The philosopher and statesman Cicero, for example, earned as much as 80,000 sestertii a year just from rents collected on the apartments in his *insulae.*

All of this, however, provoked something terrible in Rome. The difficulty of paying such high rents, as Professor Carlo Pavolini has observed, forced many tenants to sublet any rooms in their apartments that were not absolutely necessary, creating chains of subleases on every floor; the higher the floor, the longer the chain.

In the case of our *insula,* all of this is very clear. The same room gets sublet to whole families or several individuals, dividing it with simple partitions. This generates the following perverse mechanism: the higher you go, the poorer the tenants, the more numerous the sublets, the greater the overcrowding and the promiscuity, the dirt, the squalor and the bugs. By the time you get to the top floor it's become a Kasbah where cohabitation is a struggle for survival.

To keep order, the building has its own surveillance corps made up of slaves and doormen under the command of a head slave. And we've now encountered some of them on the stairs. They're racing down the steps toward the landing a couple of floors below us where the argument was. The women's shrieks have now been joined by protests from other tenants. The shouting match is about to deteriorate into a rent riot.

The Third World on the Upper Floors

We keep on climbing. The steps are made of unfinished bricks, lined up on their edges, like books; it almost seems like we're walking across the bookshelves of a library. The higher we climbs the thicker and dirtier and more chipped they are. It's been a long time since any maintenance has been done around here. The walls are dirtier and dirtier, with stains and scratches. Even the air we're breathing is different; there's an odor of stuffiness, of charred wood, of food cooked hours and hours ago, all mixed together in the acrid stench of filth. It feels like we've ended up in one of the lower rings of Dante's Inferno.

There's such a shortage of space that even the landing is occupied. The entire area is crisscrossed by lines of clothes hanging on ropes and beams. The floor is cluttered with unlit braziers, broken pitchers, rags, lemon rinds, and banana peels, squashed and covered with flies. These landings look like a bazaar of human life; in the semi-darkness a lantern illuminates the profile of a naked boy, sitting on the floor in silence, his coal-black eyes staring at us, or the wrinkled face of an old man, asleep amid the folds of a soiled blanket. In the short span of a few feet the beginning of one life and the end of another intersect, united by the stench of misery.

With every step we take, the voices we hear are different. The doors are made of wood so cheap we can overhear nearly all the sounds of the lives being lived inside each apartment. And so, in the space of just a few feet, we go from a man's laughter to the constant wailing of a small baby, from a loud argument between two women to the intimacy of sex; the rhythmic moaning coming from behind one of the doors is unmistakable. A husband and wife? A man and his slave girl? What is so striking about these upper floors is the total lack of privacy.

We push on a half-open door. Its creaking is a curtain of sound that, as the door swings open, gradually reveals to us a bare and modest room, without the slightest decoration. The walls are painted in a uniform ochre color and there is just one table with a few stools scattered here and there. Nothing remotely related to the apartment on the second floor; this looks more like the inside of a hut. There are two bench chests with some terra-cotta pitchers on them. A small cabinet serves as a credenza, with some bread and a chunk of cheese wrapped in a piece of cloth. The original floor plan of this apartment has been radically altered by partitions and curtains, in order to create a lot of small spaces to sublet. Pulling open a curtain, we discover a single room with a straw pallet on the floor and an unlit lantern. The wardrobe consists of some nails planted in the wall holding a straw hat and a couple of tunics. Two clay pitchers and a canvas bag of food are hanging from other nails, almost certainly to keep them out of the reach of mice and insects. We'd be tempted to call this the kitchenette of this minuscule room.

In another cell a woman is sitting on the bed, nursing her baby. Next to her is a shabby wicker crib with a mattress made out of dried leaves.

Here there are no panes in the windows. Only the second-floor tenants can afford them. On these upper floors they use translucent animal skins, canvas, or wooden shutters. This means that in order to have a little light you have to open the shutters and let in the wind and cold. Rainy days are the worst because you're forced to keep them shut, and spend your day in semi-darkness. What little light there is on those days comes from a lot of terra-cotta lanterns, or tallow candles. The result is that all the rooms are filled with their smell and filmy grime. As the years go by the walls and other surfaces are coated by a thin dark patina that no one bothers to clean and that makes the poor hygiene of these rooms even poorer.

Who lives on the upper floors of the *insulae*? Basically, the "muscles" of Rome, that is, the people who make the city work every day: servants, manual laborers, bricklayers, deliverymen of supplies to shops and markets. They live in very modest conditions, together with their families. And then there are teachers and artisans.

Some better-off Romans, like employees in government offices or private companies, live a little further down.

The ground floor, on the other hand, is occupied only by people with a lot of money: businessmen, merchants, builders, members of the municipal government, or people who work closely with the imperial or senatorial authorities. A small urban aristocracy that certainly doesn't command the Empire but does wield real power on the streets and in the buildings of the capital.

To this ground-floor elite we have to add the shopkeepers who, for many practical reasons, often live in small apartments or cramped lofts behind or above their shops.

This, in a nutshell, is the social scale of the Roman *insulae*.

We have now arrived at the last flight of stairs, which goes up to the attic. Here, everything is made of wood, and the stairs let out a worrisome creaking sound with every step. We can feel the extreme precariousness of the structures that surround us. This level of the *insula* was not planned by the architects and was added later, with a long series of add-ons whose purpose, obviously, was to increase the number of lodgings in order to increase profits. In modern terms we might say that we are going up to a level of pure unauthorized construction.

We run into a young guy who's probably around twenty-five. He's holding a terra-cotta vase that he nimbly keeps from spilling. He's got bright eyes and a friendly air about him and as he passes by he smiles at us and we discover that he's missing more than a few teeth, probably from malnutrition. Life isn't easy for the tenants on the upper floors of the *insulae*. You've got to be clever and grab any opportunity that comes your way. Even the simplest ones. Quick on his feet, he scurries down a few flights, takes a look around, and darts into the room of another tenant who's momentarily absent. Once inside he throws open a little dormer window and flings the vase's contents out the window. It is his chamber pot.

Taking two steps at a time, he scrambles back up the stairs, winking at us as he goes by. He's managed to avoid going down all the stairs to the entryway to empty the pot into the big *dolium*. If anyone complains, it'll be the other tenant who takes the blame. The consequences could be pretty severe. There is actually a specific statute in Rome that prohibits throwing urine and excrement from buildings. And it's harsh. The penalty depends on the outcome of this bombardment from above, and whether some clothes get soiled or someone suffers some physical harm (even indirectly).So it's pretty clear that in imperial Rome the threat of being struck by falling excrement and urine was present everywhere and spared no one.

The lack of toilets on the upper floors is due mainly to the fact that there is no water up there. At most, water reaches the ground floor or maybe second floor, and usually after its first use (gardens, bathtubs, food preparation, etc.) it is also used for flushing toilets. The disconcerting thing, for us, is that this means that the toilet and the kitchen are generally in the same room, as archaeologists have verified at many sites. As unhygienic as it seems, the Romans take care of their bodily needs just a few steps away from where they prepare their food. But in the Roman era nobody knew about the existence of bacteria.

The lack of water on the upper floors of the *insulae* explains another feature of these buildings: dirt. It is so laborious to carry water home from the neighborhood fountain, or even from the courtyard on the ground floor up all those flights of stairs, that very few people "waste" it for washing floors. Consequently, the upper floors are encrusted with years', and sometimes decades', worth of dirt and grime.

Nevertheless, in many cases water manages to get up the stairs for at least a few floors, thanks largely to the labor of the slaves. We can read about this in a play by Plautus that recounts how a master would check to see that his slaves had carried out their daily chore of filling eight large terra-cotta jars with water. Houses are obliged by law to have a reserve of water. After the great fire in Rome, under Nero, every house has to have enough water to put out fires before they can spread to other buildings.

The *insulae* are also served by water porters, or *aquarii*. In theory they are supposed to carry water everywhere in the building but in reality they only serve wealthy families or those with a decent standard of living. These porters occupy one of the lowest rungs on the social ladder, among the "least of the slaves." Indeed, their work is really hard. Along with the doormen (*ostiarii*) and the street sweepers (*scoparii)* they are considered to be so tied to the functioning of the residential buildings of imperial Rome that, when buildings change hands, they are sold in block together with the building.

We're now opening the last door, the highest door in the *insula*. Inside, the room is dark and the heat, even though it's still morning, is already suffocating. We are right under the roof tiles and we have to bend over to walk. Here and there little openings in the poorly connected tiles let in the slanted rays of sunlight, which create a strikingly luminous colonnade. But when it rains these columns of light are replaced by as many streams of water. The occupant of this space is really the most uncomfortable tenant in the entire *insula*. All we can see are a few rags on the floor, a broken lantern, and some junk.

Suddenly, a noise fills the room; it's a pigeon batting its wings. He has joined his companion in their nest located in an opening between two tiles and they've both started cooing. Pigeons are a common sight in imperial Rome. Flocks of them glide through the skies over the temples and piazzas putting on the same shows that residents of modern Rome still enjoy. The person who lives here hasn't chased them away, probably because they keep him company.

We don't know what the tenant of this penthouse does for a living. Maybe he's a manual laborer. But he's certainly the poorest tenant in the building, and yet he has something that no one else has: a beautiful view of Rome. Through the hole where the doves are nesting, we can see the capital of the Empire in all of its vastness. The red roofs of the *insulae*, the columns of smoke from the public baths, just now opening for business, the statues of gilded bronze that stand out among the buildings, the temples with their bright white columns, and the wreath of green forests all around the city offer us a vista for which any real estate agency would charge a fortune. It is a city in full swing, pulsing with life. And that's exactly where we're headed now, down to the streets, among the people.

CURIOSITY—Rome as one Big Campground?

Our exploration of the imperial age apartment building has been very instructive because it makes it easier for us to understand a lot of things about the life that's going on around us, here at street level. For example, why are the streets so crowded now and where are all these people going?

Actually, the best way to get a handle on life in Rome may be to think of the city as an enormous campground. As we all know, when you're camping, your tent is used only for sleeping or changing clothes. It's small, there's only enough room for something to sleep in or on (a sleeping bag or a foam mattress) and a corner where you can put your backpack or duffel bag full of clothes. To get washed you have to go to the common showers, for bodily needs you use the common toilets, and for food, either you prepare something on the fly on the barbecue near your tent or you go to a bar or a restaurant somewhere near the campground. There are some tents equipped with showers, toilets, and kitchenettes, but they are very rare, big, and expensive. Most people who stay at a campground use their tent only for sleeping.

Well, that's exactly how the ancient Romans use their dwellings. They are small and dark, with no showers or toilets, water, or kitchens (and if they have a kitchen they are as rudimentary as a barbecue). Only a few wealthy Romans in their *domus* or ground-floor apartments in the *insulae* have these facilities in their own homes, but they are few, just like the large fully equipped tents in modern campgrounds.

So the vast majority of Rome's residents are obliged to leave home to use collective public services, exactly like in a campground. To get washed, they go to the public baths, for bodily needs they use the latrines located on the streets, and for food they sit down in a *thermopolium* or in a *popina*, the ancient equivalents of our coffee bars and taverns. It should come as no surprise that a lot of people try to scrounge a free meal by getting someone to invite them to lunch or dinner.

That's why the streets of Rome are so crowded. Everybody takes to the streets for all these reasons, adding their numbers to those who have to go out every day to work, to do errands, or to go shopping in the markets.

To get a better understanding of life in the capital of the Empire, however, we could also refer to another analogy. When you come right down to it, Rome is very much like a big house. Your bedroom is in the *insula* on one street, the toilets (public latrines) are on another, the showers (the public baths) are in another neighborhood, the kitchen (the *thermopolium*) in still another part of town, etc.

There is also a parlor in this imaginary house: the Forum. But really, there are so many opportunities to meet people in the city that we could say that the parlor is pretty much everywhere.

Generally, even people who have nothing to do don't stay at home in their small, dark lodgings. They go out on the streets too, overcrowding them. As a consequence the streets are always full of loafers.

We can conclude, therefore, that all the city's residents use Rome exactly as we use our houses. And Rome *is* their house. And the same thing goes for all the great urban centers of the Roman Empire. It is a concept, a way of living in a city, which is no longer part of our culture.

THE STREETS OF ROME

We're back down on the street, in the middle of the crowd, which in the meantime has grown considerably. We feel like we're still immersed in the smells and strong sensations of the lost world of the upper floors of these enormous buildings. We have the impression that we have been breathing in the atmosphere of some ancient *Blade Runner*. One surprising thing about walking on the streets of Rome is the great variety of itineraries. Just like a living organism, Rome has a linear circulation system composed of a few main arteries, all leading to the Forum, fed and complemented by a vast network of capillaries.

Consequently, the pattern of the streets in imperial Rome reminds us of the historic centers in most of our older modern cities: a lot of narrow, winding streets. The reason is simple: don't take up too much room that could be occupied by buildings.

The name *via* (way) is only given to the wider streets, between 16 feet 9 inches and 21 feet 4 inches wide, enough to allow two wagons to overtake or pass one another without touching. It's striking that in the heart of Rome there are only two streets this wide. The rest of the imperial capital is crossed by a network of lanes (*vici*), still narrower streets (*angiportus*), and finally by a web of outright urban footpaths (*semitae*). The ancients recount with a pinch of irony that people living across the street from one another can shake hands.

Another striking thing about Rome is the steep climbs. In a

city of seven hills there are inevitably a lot of ramps, as sinuous as mountain mule trails, which the Romans call *clivi* (Clivus Suburanus, Clivus Capitolinus, etc.). Julius Caesar ordered them to be paved but it was never actually done. Consequently, they are dusty in the summer and muddy in the winter, besides being covered with all kinds of trash, giving rise to easily imagined miasmic fogs like the ones we might see today in third world countries.

These narrow, winding streets and the close proximity of the buildings makes the city vulnerable to fires, which spread very easily from one building to the next.

After the devastating fire of 64 CE, Nero tried to rebuild Rome with a new urban plan. In order to prevent the spread of fires he had the streets widened and buildings spaced farther apart, and he created covered walkways to allow rescue teams to move through the city in greater safety.

Since then, in fact, the sun has come back to shine in a lot streets that were previously kept in darkness by the proximity of the tall buildings. But the situation is only partially better. A lot of areas have been re-infested with unplanned development, at the hands of speculators and unscrupulous real estate barons, who in the span of just forty years have taken Rome back to its age-old chaos.

We continue walking down the street among the crowd. Anyone visiting Rome for the first time, is surprised by various contrasts. The look of the imperial capital changes constantly, and we've got proof of that right in front of us. We now find ourselves in a surprisingly modern rectilinear avenue, lined with tall, luminous buildings, sidewalks, and shops. But all we have to do is turn the corner and we're immediately inside a labyrinth of dark alleys, with a chaotic hodgepodge of run-down, seedy *insulae*.

It's as though someone had brought together in the same

city the glorious, linear vistas of New York and the small, winding alleys of a middle-eastern bazaar. You feel like you've gone from the modern era to the Middle Ages simply by turning your head or going around a corner.

We start down an alley. Laundry is hanging out to dry between the buildings. The clothes are of all different colors and look like so many Tibetan flags. A heavyset woman appears on one of the wooden loggias overlooking the street and lowers a basket. Waiting for it down below is a man, a street vendor, ready to fill it with fava beans that he carries in a sack. From the way he's dressed we can see that he lives in the country and has come into the city to sell the fruits of his vegetable garden. It's clear that he and the woman know each other well; you can tell by the exchange of jokes and one-liners and the way they laugh.

It's a scene from daily life in Rome that hasn't changed over the centuries. This is really what Rome is: a network of daily rituals that unites all of its inhabitants. We move on, passing by the street vendor who's now talking to another woman looking down from a window.

Exploring these little lanes and alleys feels a lot like walking through the *calli* of Venice, where quiet little piazzas open up at the end of the tiny streets. Here too, after we encounter a fat man who doesn't even bother to say hello, the narrow alley that we're walking down ends up in a little oasis: a tiny piazza with a fountain at the center flanked by two trees which have grown up beside it, nurtured by the water spilled on the ground in the constant traffic of buckets filled and carried away by the neighborhood residents. On one side of the piazza there is a bright colonnade of white marble. It's a temple, whose doors are still closed. Two beggars are sitting on the steps, dressed in tattered rags of an indefinite color. We stay here for a few minutes, savoring this unexpected island of peace, lifting our faces to soak up the warmth of the morning sunlight.

A very narrow, dark alley runs down one side of the temple, and we start down it. The sudden semi-darkness forces us to feel our way along. Actually, it's not only light that's lacking but air. This alley is used by a lot of people as a public toilet. Holding our noses we pick up the pace toward the light at the end of the alley, now very close. Just a few yards away. Here we are. Completely unawares, we trip over something in our path. It looks like a sack filled with rags and sticks. What can it be? Who threw it here in the middle of the road? We bend down to get a better look, holding our tunics over our noses against the stench, which by now has become nauseating, but also sweetish.

Our eyes are getting used to the semi-darkness and slowly a face emerges from the dark: wooden, its eyes deeply sunken, the color unnatural . . . It's a dead body! It's been here for at least a day. Who is it? One of the countless beggars? Not very likely. None of them would choose a filthy place like this to spend the night. Now, we can make out the body a little better and, gathering our strength for one last effort, we reach out and touch his arm. His tunic is well made, a sign that he was well off, maybe not wealthy but a man of means. He's missing a finger; they cut it off to steal a gold ring. It probably happened at night. We can almost visualize the scene. This man may have been heading back home after a banquet, from a romantic tryst, or maybe he was drunk. But that wasn't what he did wrong. His truly fatal error was to walk home alone. In the unlighted street, he was attacked, stabbed, and dragged to this spot, where calmly and out of sight, his murderer finished him off and stripped him of his possessions. We stand back up and keep on walking toward the light, where we can see people walking by. We hurry out of the alley to take a deep breath of fresh air—after which we notice that we're right in the middle of a broad street, surrounded by a crowd of people that carries us away like a river at flood tide. In just a few seconds, the darkness of the alley, its stench, have disappeared, we no longer feel the weight of its atmosphere of violence and death. Now there is nothing around us but life, colors, fragrances, human faces, and the cool morning air. In a few seconds we have gone from one world to another. Rome is this awkard, too.

Stores and Shops

T he shopkeepers have started the new day. Some are already doing business; others still haven't finished putting their goods on display for sale. Still others, running late because of deliveries that were made during the night, have lost hours of sleep and are just now taking down the heavy boards that protect their goods when they are closed.

The system for shutting the *tabernae* (as the Romans call stores and shops) applies a formula that is practically universal throughout the Empire, analogous to the way modern Italian shopkeepers almost all use rolling metal shutters. The store owners use heavy wooden boards, narrow and long, placed one next to the other. They insert them into deep grooves in the marble sill (still clearly visible today in all the archaeological sites, particularly in Pompeii). One of the boards, the one that's sideways, also functions as a door and can be opened when the others are closed.

The whole thing is held shut by long iron bars that slide through rings on the boards and are lodged in an indentation in the walls. Their movement is blocked by a bolt lock or a by a lock remarkably similar to the ones we use; only the keys, made of bronze, are a little different and look like little bent forks.

While in today's cities the day begins with the metallic rumor of the rolling shutters of stores and bars, in imperial Rome what you hear is the rasping sound of bolt locks, the sound of the iron bars sliding open and being stored away in the back of the shop. This system is still in use in some

Mediterranean countries, for example in the Tunisian city of Sfax.

But that's not the only difference. We're now standing in front of a store that is opening for business. The boards move, the sideways door opens and out comes a man with bleary, swollen eyes. He's still holding the lantern that he used to see while he was opening the bolt lock from inside. It's obvious that he has spent the night in the shop. A boy comes out too. His aquiline nose is just like the man's. He's clearly his son. The man swears. During the night somebody carved some insulting phrases into one of the boards. While the two of them are removing the boards, a diminutive woman comes out of the door, her face covered by a veil. She's the man's wife. She looks at the writing, winces in disgust and, walking off, shouts out the name of the likely offender: a customer who had asked them for credit yesterday and been denied. The woman is holding two big pitchers and she's heading toward a nearby fountain. But she only takes a few steps before a feeble voice calls out to her. She stops, looks up at the sky, and turns around. A little boy, not more than three, emerges from the doorway, his face dirty and his tunic stained, and runs out to meet her.

What's striking is that an entire family lives inside this little store. They are not an exception; that's pretty much the way it is everywhere in Rome and throughout the Empire. Who are these people? Sometimes they are the store owners themselves or the managers. But how do they all manage to live together in a store no bigger than 300 or 400 square feet?

Now that the *taberna* is open, we can get a look at the inside. There aren't any window displays. Glass, as we have mentioned, is very expensive and anyway in this era no one is capable of producing such large panes of glass. So the store front is completely open to the street, as is the case today for fish stores or small grocery stores. The opening is marked by a small masonry counter, which is used to display the goods. Various regional specialties are hanging overhead, along a bar that runs the entire width of the entrance, and wrapped in bags or pitchers sealed with red labels.

Father and son start putting out baskets filled with dates, walnuts, prunes, and dried figs. This store sells food items, especially dried foods, which are easier to conserve and are good all year round.

Amid the baskets, safe from clumsy customers and thieves, there are some lovely small, elongated amphorae containing the famous *garum*, a fish sauce that the Romans really love. These amphorae hold a low-quality version of the sauce, but the way they are displayed and the exaggerated prominence they have been given allow us to understand that they are lying in wait for some lamb-like customer ready to be fleeced.

A look inside a store reveals to us that beyond the masonry counter, way in the back, amid the sacks, the amphoras, and the merchandise, there is a wooden stair leading up to the loft where the whole family lives. It's a small room no larger than few square feet, right above the customers' heads. The only source of light is a small square window above the door to the store.

The loft's interior is marked by the same disorder, promiscuity, and poverty that we saw on the middle floors of the *insulae*: a bed for the couple, a smaller one for the two children, clothes hanging from a nail, a brazier for cooking and heating, a small case, which probably holds the woman's makeup. But there is another case sticking out from under the bed, and which holds something very important: the sales proceeds from the store. The key is in the custody of the woman, now at the fountain, hanging from a chain compressed between her breasts. As in almost every human society (from semi-nomadic Himba of Africa, to the Celts, the Vikings, and so on) although it's the men who are in command, it's always the women who keep the keys to the family possessions.

What we have seen here is repeated in all of the shops, stores, and warehouses of Rome. These lofts (or else the backrooms) are home to, depending on the case, artisans, shopkeepers, night watchmen, clerks, and even prostitutes, as in the case of bars, where negotiations with customers take place on the lower floor and consumption on the upper floor, in the loft.

Now the shopkeeper is walking across the street, holding a plate with his breakfast on it: bread, dried figs, and cheese that he is chewing avidly. There is something he really wants to do, even before he's finished his breakfast. He reaches the corner of the street and looks up toward a niche in the wall that contains an enormous plaster cast of a human phallus, colored bright red. He runs his hand over it as he mumbles something. Every morning, this is how his day begins, with this superstitious ritual.

For the Romans, the erect penis is a good-luck charm. They are all over Rome: carved into the enormous slabs that pave the streets, on the walls of the avenues and store entrances. There are even clusters of swinging bronze penises, hanging from chains over the entrances to houses and stores, with little bells that ring. The Romans call them *tintinnabula* ("rattles" or "chimes") because it is good luck to touch them and make them ring each time you pass under them.

This may come as a surprise, but this custom of the phallic good-luck charm has even come down to us, albeit in a masked form. At some time in the past, the erect penis got transformed into the famous red coral or ivory horn that a lot of people still carry in their pocket or purse, or wear on bracelets or necklaces. Not to mention the more voluminous horns that we often see hanging from the rearview mirror of trucks on the highway. They are a true archaeological find in the field of superstitions.

We can hear the sound of a pounding hammer coming from the shop next door. We lean out the door and discover that the neighbor of the shopkeeper that we've just visited is a coppersmith. He's very skinny, with a black beard and olive skin, clearly from the Middle East. He's sitting with his legs crossed and striking hammer blows against the base of a cauldron. He works with remarkable precision and speed: in the fraction of a second between one blow and the next, he turns the object slightly in order to hit a new spot. It is spellbinding to see how the caldron seems to be turning on its own, almost as though it were suspended in air between the coppersmith's hand.

The man looks up for a few seconds, smiles at us, and then goes back to his hammering. To be sure, this noise must be a real annoyance for his neighbors. And in fact we know from reading the ancients that coppersmiths, and their deafening racket, were a "note of color" (and of noise) characteristic of the streets of Rome.

Who knows, maybe the object he is hammering out, with its elegant decorations, will be found by archaeologists eighteen hundred years from now and will end up in a collection. It is a common object, one of those objects that museum-goers don't pay much attention to, but to see it being made and admiring the expertise and the care being exercised by this artisan, it seems like a small masterpiece. We tend to forget, but this human dimension is part of every object exhibited in our museums, even the simplest and humblest ones. If we only would reflect on how they were created, or on the commitment of their creators, we would take much greater interest in them sitting there on the other side of the glass.

Behind the artisan, among the piles of pots and pans, pitchers, and molds for cakes and pies, we can see the usual stair leading up to the loft.

There is one unusual detail, however: the first four or five steps are made of brick and the rest of the stair is made of wood. It's a way to save money and it might also be a fire prevention measure to prevent flames from a fallen lantern from spreading to the upper floors. Or perhaps, as someone has proposed, it is a stratagem invented by landlords to enable them to "cut off" the stairs of renters who got behind in their rent, just as we saw in the *insulae*.

If that were true, then the lives of these artisans and shopkeepers would also be rather precarious and unstable. The lives of their whole family are hanging in the balance between their small income and their ability to pay the rent. Uncertainty is one of the most widespread features of life on the streets of Rome.

We are not in the middle of the street anymore, but under a long covered walkway that reminds us of the porticoes in Italy's northern cities like Bologna and Padua and Verona, which are often of Roman origin. A long line of *tabernae* opens up under its arches. It's a dazzling view. The objects on display change every fifteen feet, and so do the colors of the *tabernae*, according to their merchandise. From the hanging objects framing the entrance to each *taberna* and from the ones hanging from the cords dangling from the ceiling of the portico along its entire length, we can tell the nature of the commerce that's conducted in each one. The different amphorae and baskets are like so many storefront signs. It's as though we were leafing through a list of occupations in Rome.

The first is a lupine or bluebonnet vendor (*lupinarius*), then comes a bronzesmith with his workshop (*aerarius*), followed by a baker (*dulciarius*), a cloth merchant who can also make tunics (*vestiarius*), the entrance to a small shrine inside the building dedicated to Isis, a florist specializing in funeral wreathes (*coronarius*), a mirror maker (*specularius*), a greengrocer (*pomarius*), a men's shoemaker (*baxearius*), a pearl merchant (*margaritarius*), and, next door, the shop of his brother, who specialize in the working of ivory tusks from Africa (*eborarius*). Last is the obligatory bar (*popina*) where a lot of customers are now consuming a modest breakfast.

The constant movement of people is striking. A little like bees in a pasture, flying about incessantly from one flower to the next, under the portico there is a coming and going of customers into and out of the shops. This is the typical choreography of a morning in Rome.

The real plague of the capital of the Empire (like modern Rome) is the occupation of public space, under the porticoes, by stands with goods of all kinds and varieties. Often it is the *taberna* itself, which has extended out onto the sidewalk, provoking the protests of passersby and even of some emperors, like Domitian, who complained that Rome had turned into one giant shop. Domitian actually tried to outlaw this "invasion of the streets by barbers, shopkeepers, cooks, and butchers." But the results were temporary at best.

In Rome there are no occupational neighborhoods, with the exception of the general warehouses near the Tiber or on the Aventine Hill. But there are specialized streets, like the street of booksellers in the Argiletum area, near the Suburra. And then there is the street of the perfume shops (*vicus unguentarius*), or the street where you can buy shoes or get them repaired (*vicus sandalarius*). There is even a bankers' street and one for the money changers (*vicus* and *clivus argentarius*).

Usually, however, stores and businesses are mixed and spread about throughout the capital. A decidedly modern characteristic.

There is another striking piece of information. The line of *tabernae* covers the entire length of the building. The shops are located in the former ground floor rooms of an *insula* or a *domus* where wealthy families usually live. The owner has separated them from the rest of the house by a dividing wall. Then he opened them out onto the street in order to rent them to shopkeepers and so to increase his income from the property. There is nothing strange about this; the word "earnings" is used very widely in the Roman world. Nobody is ashamed of earning money; on the contrary, it is totally natural that real property should provide an income.

Sometimes, as has been discovered in the ruins of Ostia, the entire ground floor of an *insula* was sacrificed, creating shops on the outside and some important services on the inside (cleaners, mechanics, shrines). That is how property owners diversified (and increased) their sources of earnings—by renting not only the apartments on the upper floors but also street level stores and courtyard workshops.

But how much do these shopkeepers and artisans work? More or less than we do? The surprise is that they work less than we do today. By making a few calculations and comparing the data from ancient sources, Jérome Carcopino has concluded that a Roman workday lasts about six hours: practically speaking, from dawn to lunchtime. During the rest of the day, people didn't work; they went to the baths or did other things. Naturally, there are a lot of exceptions. Barbers and antique dealers, for example, worked much longer hours, because a large number of their customers could only come after working hours.

ENCOUNTER WITH A DEITY

S till absorbed in these thoughts, we are distracted by a strange smell. It is light but penetrating, neither good nor bad. And it's very familiar; it's the smell of incense. And so we realize that we have stopped on the threshold of a minuscule open space, a widening of the road. In the middle of it is a marble altar and, right behind it, a small temple with its stairway. It rises on one side of the street, as happens with those little parish churches you might see on the side of a busy street in the center of town. There are no beggars on the stairway, ready to pull at your clothes. Strange. But we immediately see why not; services have already ended. On closer look, we can see on the altar (a finely decorated block of marble with garlands hanging from its edges) the signs of the recently completed ritual: streaks of blood, a brazier with some dying embers, and the charred remains of the offerings, undoubtedly food.

Some workmen are cleaning the stairs. They will also remove the brazier and put the altar back in order. We approach the temple and go up the stairs. It is in the classical style, with a roof and a colonnade around the cell (the inner sanctum) with the statue of the deity. Often the statue is made of gold or ivory, or precious marble. Only priests can enter the inner sanctum. The faithful must remain outside and public ceremonies take place on the outside altar.

Now we are standing amid the columns that constitute the front of the temple. They're made of pink Egyptian granite.

For some strange reason, whenever you go near granite you can feel a cool sensation, but maybe it's just the morning shadows. While they are cleaning the stairs, the inside of the colonnade and the cell, the workmen have left the great bronze door ajar. This is a good chance to take a look inside. We go in. The smell of incense grows stronger, like an invisible mist of holiness coming out of the half-open door. Our eyes have a tough time adjusting to the semi-darkness. We notice some lanterns hanging on the walls, and there are also candelabras all around us (no torches like you see in films). As our eyes gradually adjust, we begin to make out a figure on the far side of the cell. It must be the deity. In the feeble light of the lanterns his body looks muscular; you'd almost say it was Hercules. It's made of gilded bronze. But we notice something odd: this statue has two faces! It's as though a second face had emerged from the back of the head. It must be Janus, the two-faced god. He is the deity that presides over any kind of change and transition, and in general, over the beginning and the end of all things.

This deity has also left his traces in modern daily life. Although not very many of us are aware of it, we all invoke his name constantly at a particular time of the year.

The name Janus, in fact, gives us January, the month with a year behind and a year ahead. That's why it's dedicated to the god with two faces.

In this regard, it is interesting to note that the names we use today for all the months are Roman. Here are their meanings:

January (in Latin *Ianuarius*) is the month of *Ianus* or Janus.
February (*Febrarius*) is the month of purification (*februare*).
March (*Martius*) is the month dedicated to Mars, the god of war.
April (*Aprilis*) is the month in honor of Aphrodite (from *Apru*, the Etruscan name for the goddess of love).
May (*Maius*) is the month of the goddess Maia, mother of

Mercury, who presides over the growth of all living beings, including the plants in gardens and fields.

June (*Iunius*) is the month dedicated to Juno.

July (*Iulius*) is the month in honor of Julius Caesar.

August (*Augustus*) is the month in honor of Augustus, the first emperor of Rome.

September, October, November, and December (whose names in English are the same as in Latin), as we can intuit, are connected to numbers and not to deities.

Actually, there was a time prior to 153 BCE, when the year began in the month of March and not in January, so the months from September to December were the seventh, eighth, ninth, and tenth months of the year, and they were named after their number in ascending order—a tradition that is still with us today.

One last curiosity about the Roman calendar: holidays. During the Republic, there are some 235 "auspicious" days, equivalent to our working days, on which all of the public administration functions, and 109 "inauspicious" days, when everything shuts down, the equivalent of our holidays. During the second century CE, the period in which our day in ancient Rome is taking place, the number of holidays has increased to the point that almost every other day is a holiday. Obviously, at this point in the Roman era, a holiday is no longer a day of rest but actually a *holy* day, on which regular activities are not interrupted.

Perhaps the feast days that we find most striking are the *Saturnalia*. They celebrate the end of the planting season and are held in the second half of December. Not only an occasion for carefree celebrations, for these few days household roles are reversed. The masters serve at table and the slaves are free to enjoy some liberty. How much this "liberty" is actually implemented or whether it means real freedom of movement and action for the slaves, we don't know.

Our reflections are suddenly interrupted by a severe reprimand from one of the attendants of the cult of Janus who has come into the temple and brusquely chases us out. We haven't entered the cell, and so we haven't corrupted anything sacred. But he will still have to conduct a purification ritual.

The violent closure of the temple door creates a strong puff of incense that engulfs us. Why do the Romans use incense in their temples just like we do in church? And why has it continued to be used for centuries, right down to our own time, and not just in Europe? The reason is curious and not well known.

Incense would seem to have a mild decontaminating effect on pathogenic agents. That is why, for centuries, it has been used to "disinfect" temples. Actually, the area immediately outside of the inner sanctum is a gathering place for the faithful, many of whom are sick and have come before the deity to ask for grace and healing. So the temples are often grimy places, full of bacteria, and the air tends to be unhealthy. Using incense amounts to purifying these places by way of fumigation.

Religion and Superstition

We come away from the temple. How much of a presence does religion have in the daily lives of the Romans?

For the Romans, the gods are everywhere, even though they are invisible, and they intervene in people's lives on a daily basis, sending them signs, helping them or hurting them. It is a dimension that escapes us on this journey of ours through ancient Rome, because we are blind to many messages that are clearly evident to the Romans.

For example, for a Roman an owl signals an imminent misadventure. He was sent by the gods to warn him and impede him from finishing whatever he may be doing at the time. Analogously, an eagle signals the arrival of a thunderstorm.

Seeing a bee, for example, is a normal thing for us. For a Roman, on the contrary, it's a good omen, because bees are considered messengers of the gods and therefore carriers of good luck. And then there's the flight of birds; they bring good luck or bad depending on which direction they are going. If they are flying east, where the sun rises, they are a good omen; if they are flying west, where the sun sets, they are a bad omen. This is not lost on the Roman generals, who before a battle, after the customary ritual sacrifices, are very careful to observe what is flying in the sky above them.

The high priest of the future is the haruspex, who examines the innards of sacrificed animals. The Etruscan priests were long considered the masters of this art. The liver, in particular, is thought to be a good barometer of fate. The idea is that the gods express their opinion through the liver's appearance. The priests examine its shape, color, and any abnormalities, almost as though the liver's surface were a map of the future. Then they announce their verdict.

It may seem like an archaic practice, but some peoples still use it in the modern era. In Laos, for example, in order to understand whether the rice harvest will be good or bad, the peasants sacrifice a young pig and examine its liver with the same care as the Roman haruspex.

What do the Romans believe in? They have lots of gods, too many for us to recall here. Let's just say they are divided into two major groups. The ones that deal with the small aspects of everyday domestic life, such as the Lares (the ancestral spirits of the family) and the Penati, who preside over household supplies. These gods are worshipped in small homemade temples, small shrines with daily rituals, as we have seen in the *domus* of the wealthy Roman gentleman.

The second group is made up of all the big names of the Roman pantheon. These are the official deities, so to speak, many of whom are the Roman translations of the Greek gods.

The most important, obviously, is Jove (god of the sky, of lightning and thunder, protector of the Roman people whom he has destined to rule the world). Juno (the goddess of women, who presides over childbirth) is his wife. Then there is Minerva (goddess of the arts, of war, and wisdom). These three deities are the most important for the Romans and they make up the so-called "Capitoline Triad," venerated in all Roman cities with a single temple (with three cells) located in the center of the Forum (the one on the Capitoline Hill in Rome is the prototype).

Then come all of the other deities: Mars (god of war), Venus (goddess of love, sex, and beauty), Diana (goddess of the hunt and the moon), Bacchus (god of wine), Mercury, Vulcan, and so on.

Foreign Cults

Our thoughts are interrupted by a rhythmic chant accompanied by some musical instruments, very much like the singing that accompanies many of our religious processions on important feast days. We turn around to look. Just a little ways off, we see a small procession of religious forging an opening in the crowd. The women have long, straight hair while the men have shaved heads, and some of them wear a ribbon around their forehead. The people on the street move out of the way, showing an amount of unusual respect; nobody pushes or shoves. It's a little like watching a line of bonzes going through a market in the Far East.

The way they are dressed is also odd: they are wearing long white robes, very light, tied at the waist. The head priest, at the center of the procession, is holding a pot-bellied amphora, clearly connected to the ritual. Also striking are two women who, respectively, lead and end the procession. The one at the tail end has a *sistrum*, a bronze instrument in the form of a lasso, with little metal strips. When she shakes it the metal strips make a sound similar to a jingling sack of coins. In Egypt, where it has been in use for centuries, it has a name that replicates the sound it makes: *she shesh*.

This instrument is still used in modern times for religious processions in Ethiopia. It is a true living fossil of religious ritual.

The woman leading the procession, on the other hand, has a live instrument. She advances with one of her arms outstretched, as though she wished to give her hand to the people. But nobody dares touch her; she has a snake wrapped around her forearm. It's a cobra that aims its threatening arched body toward the bystanders. It must certainly have a role in the rituals but it is also a good way to make your way through a crowd. We see several people who don't notice the snake until the last minute and jump back, unable to believe their eyes.

What religion does this procession belong to? To the cult of Isis, an Egyptian goddess. Actually, among the religious beliefs of the Romans there are also some significant imported deities from conquered lands, for example, Isis and Serapis, who also have their own temples, priests, and Roman followers.

Isis is not the only foreign goddess. The first to arrive in Rome was Sybil (or Magna Mater, the Great Mother), who came from present-day Turkey.

The rituals performed in her honor often include bloody sacrifices of bulls. The initiate is made to lie down in a trench dug out of the ground and covered with a board with holes in it. The bull is sacrificed on top of the board and its blood streams down abundantly on the new member of the faithful, exactly like the water of Christian baptism.

Originally, this ritual was meant to help the initiate acquire the strength of the bull, but in the Rome that we are now visiting its purpose is primarily purification, and it has to be repeated regularly.

Another notable imported god is Mithras. He comes from far away Persia and was brought to Rome by legionnaires who fought in the easternmost territories of the Empire. Bulls have an essential role in this religion too. Mithras is almost always represented as he is killing a bull whose blood will become the lifeblood of the universe. Mithraism was to become so rooted in Roman society that it would be the primary competitor of Christianity.

What is surprising is that Mithras and Christ have a few things in common. Both preach universal brotherhood, and both were born in a cave during the night of December 24th and 25th!

It's even more surprising to learn that Horun, the falcon-god of the Egyptians, Dionysus, the Greek god of wine, and Buddha (Siddhartha) were also born in that exact same moment of the year.

How is it that all these important divinities have the same birthday?

The reason has to do with astronomy. The winter solstice, the shortest and darkest day of the year, falls on December 21. After that, the days start to have more and more light.

Having the birth of a divinity coincide with the return of light has had a great symbolic meaning for many religions and civilizations. Not coincidentally, for the Romans December 25 is the *dies Solis*, the birthday of the Sun.

There are also some Christians in Trajan's Rome. The Christian community is still small compared to subsequent generations, and for the most part it is rooted in the more popular and peripheral neighborhoods of the city.

Under Trajan, the Christian religion, though on the rise, is a minority cult, still mindful of the fierce persecution inflicted on Christians by Nero, about fifty years ago. More flourishing, on the other hand, is Judaism. There are already some synagogues, like the one in Ostia, and the presence of Jews in Rome also has a historical basis. After the destruction of Jerusalem at the hand of Titus in 70 CE, the Jewish Diaspora brought a great influx of Jews to Rome, enlarging the community here (whose origins date back to the second and first century BCE).

Christians, Jews, worshippers of Mithras, Isis, Sybil, venerators of Jove, Juno, and Minerva . . . All of this indicates that in the Rome that we are visiting, as in the rest of the Empire, there is freedom of religion. No one is discriminated against for their religion or faith.

Naturally, it has not always been that way in the history of Rome. Nor will it be in the future. Under Constantine, the Christian religion will have priority over all the others, with frequent episodes of intolerance, which will relegate other creeds to the margins.

In Trajan's Rome, on the other hand, there is a substantial religious balance. Why?

First of all, because freedom of religion is an important strategy for the stability of the Empire. By granting freedom of worship, dangerous tensions and revolts are avoided. Everyone, therefore, can believe in whatever he wants, on the condition that he also makes sacrifice to the emperor, in recognition of his absolute power. The persecution of the Christians was provoked by their refusal to recognize the emperor as a god (and to participate in the imperial cult).

This is something that also and primarily regards the subject peoples, amounting almost to a loyalty oath to Rome. It must be recalled that there also exists an imperial cult, or the veneration of dead and divinized emperors with Augustus at the top (and before him Julius Caesar), with their own temples and priests.

There is also another, more theoretical explanation for Rome's great religious tolerance. The pragmatic Romans don't want to make enemies of foreign gods by refusing them hospitality.

We still have one more question about religion and the Romans.

Why is it that foreign cults are so successful among the Romans and spread through so many levels of the population? The explanation is really intriguing and brings to mind some typical aspects of the modern era.

Many of these foreign religions offer a vision of a goal, a future of happiness. The need to believe in a better future, felt instinctively by many Romans especially during bleak moments in the history of Rome, as in the dying days of the Republic, facilitated the spread of these new religions.

Beyond that, once they have completed an almost secret initiation, new followers find that the priests of the new religion are very different from what they are used to. They dedicate their entire lives to the divinity and have a close relationship with the faithful, listen to them, and guide them. Exactly the opposite of the official Roman religion, too rigid, cold, and detached from the spiritual needs of individuals, and most of all administered by priests that seem more like functionaries than men of faith.

Finally, another ace up the sleeve for the success of the new religions is their openness to women. The official Roman religion, with rare exceptions, is mostly a men's activity which tends to exclude women.

The new religions, therefore, have discovered an entire segment of the population to which they can direct their message but, perhaps even more important, they are able to reach out to families, finding a new audience and new recruits thanks to the educative role of women.

WHY DO THE ROMANS HAVE SUCH LONG NAMES?

While we're concluding our thoughts about all this, the man in front of us turns his head and blows his nose with his fingers, just like some football players do in the middle of a game. To clean his fingers, he simply shakes them in the air and then continues on his way as though nothing had happened. In ancient Rome handkerchiefs don't exist.

Ahead of us, in the middle of the crowd, we see a man on horseback, slowly coming towards us. He has a lance in his hand. He's dressed in a short tunic, a very light color, and a purple cape, held fast by a beautiful, shiny bronze pin. He's undoubtedly a soldier, as indicated too by his short hair, military style, and confident gaze.

He's an *eques speculator*. Up until about twenty years ago, under Domitian, these soldiers made up a special corps of mounted guards, under the command of the emperor. Now, with the change in commander in chief, they have been incorporated into Trajan's praetorian guard.

Now that he is up close, we can get a better look at him. He's about twenty-five and his features are more Celtic than Mediterranean; he has blue eyes and chestnut blond hair. A long scar on his neck suggests that he's been involved in some fierce combat. Probably, at the beginning of his career, this knight was part of a legion, then later on he was transferred here.

We hear a shout, "Peregrinus! Peregrinus!" And then well enunciated, "Publius Sulpicius Peregrinus!" The young mounted guard turns and looks our way. We don't understand. The man who shouted is right behind us and the knight is actually looking at him. The man pushes us aside now as he comes forward smiling broadly, his arms outstretched toward the knight. The knight recognizes him and jumps nimbley down to the ground (allowing us to discover that the Romans don't have stirrups on their saddles: they'll be introduced to Europe in the Middle Ages). This is followed by a long embrace between the two men. They are brothers who haven't seen each other for a long time. Now they walk on together holding the horse by his bridle. They're probably going to get a glass of wine in some little tavern. There's one at the end of the street. With every step the praetorian's purple cape swings elegantly back and forth over his calf muscles. In just a few seconds they get swallowed up by the crowd.

Fate will not be nice to the praetorian. In three years' time, he will die. We don't know exactly how. What we do know is that his brother and his father will cremate his remains on a big funeral pyre. They will have it written on his gravestone that Publius Sulpicius Peregrinus was born in the city of Mediolanum (Milan) and at the moment of his death he was twenty-eight and had been a soldier for nine years. They will also have his figure sculpted on his tomb, standing as he holds his horse, raring to go into battle.

His gravestone will be found by archaeologists in Anzio in 1979, together with the urn containing his ashes, which is now on exhibition in Rome in the collection of the national Roman museum in the baths of Diocletian.

What impresses us most about this scene are the names of the Romans: Publius Sulpicius Peregrinus. Why are they always so long?

The reason is that they are composed of three parts: *praenomen*, *nomen gentilicum, cognomen*.

CURIOSITY—Roman Names

The *praenomen* corresponds to our first name: Marcus, Caius, Lucius, etc.

The *nomen gentilicum* indicates the person's clan. It's the equivalent, if you will, of a sort of enlarged surname, common to many families and that sometimes includes thousands of people (the *gens*).

The *cognomen*, finally, is an appellative, almost an adjective, that indicates a moral or physical trait. Rufus (the red), Cincinnatus (curly), Brutus (stupid), Calvus (bald), Caecus (blind), Cicero (chickpea), Nascia (big nose), Dentatus (big teeth).

The three name formula became widespread under Silla. The problem is that from that time on, all descendants had to retain their long line of names (including the characteristic of an ancestor that they no longer had: baldness, a long nose, etc.). Other times a new *cognomen* was added to the end of the already long line of names. And that's how Publius Cornelius Scipio also became Africanus, after his great victory over the Carthaginians.

The interesting thing is that the Romans, over the course of centuries and generations, gradually changed their way of referring to one another in public.

While in the age of the Republic it was enough to cite only the first and third parts of the name (similar to what we do, when we identify a person by name and surname: Caius Caesar), later it became the fashion to use all three names. With the dawn of the imperial age it was decided that just the third name was sufficient. That's why today we speak simply of Trajan (and not Marcus Ulpius Traianus) or of Hadrian (Publius Aelius Hadrianus).

ROMAN GAMES

Kids' Games
There are some kids playing between two columns of a portico.
What games do Roman children play? Marbles! Obviously they
don't use balls made of glass or ceramics; that would be too
costly. The raw material for the game is provided by nature:
walnuts. The game we're looking at now is fairly simple. The
kids take turns from a distance trying to hit some little walnut
pyramids. It requires a good aim! Every shot is greeted with
shouts by the group of urchins who have turned this street into
their playground. In fact, some other kids are playing blind
man's bluff, a game that gets pretty wild on a crowded street as
the blindfolded kid constantly grabs hold of strangers by mistake, soliciting a wave of laughter from his playmates. A little
further on, two kids are pretending to be knights, using bamboo canes for horses.

All this confirms what the philosopher Horace had to say
about children's games: riding a bamboo cane is one of the
most popular games for children, on a par with tying small animals (such as mice or chickens) to minuscule wagons or building little houses.

We know, however, that the selection of games for Roman
children also included tops sent spinning by a thin cord, the
vaulting horse, the seesaw, and hide-and-seek. Is that it? Maybe
not. From the balcony on the second floor of the *insula* right
above us, a little girl is looking down at the boys playing in the
street. She wants to go down but her mother doesn't want her

out there on her own in the crowded street. So she stays home by herself and plays with her doll.

Dolls are an ancient invention that date back to the prehistoric era. But this kind of doll is special. It's made of terra-cotta and has arms and legs that move. It's amazing to see that even Roman children had their own Barbies (*pupae*).

Toys of this kind have been found on a number of occasions by archaeologists, especially in the tombs of small or teenage girls. Some are made of ivory, others of wood, and some are articulated in complex ways, along the lines of Pinocchio. In any event, they always have a carved version of the hairstyle in vogue, which provides in itself an indication of its age and the epoch in which it was used.

Adult Games

We continue on our walk and go by a locale that has all the trappings of a neighborhood bar, where two old guys are involved in a strange activity. Their animated gestures make it look like they're arguing. We get a little closer and discover that in reality the atmosphere is much more relaxed. This impression is confirmed by the smiles of the other customers gathered around them. The two old guys are playing at a game called morra (the real name is *micatio*). They raise their forearms and pull them violently downward, shouting out a number while showing just a few fingers at a time. The aim, as most modern Italians know, is to guess in advance the sum of the fingers shown by both players. Still, it's striking to see such a familiar game being played in such a faraway epoch. It's a true archaeological find, as ancient as the objects that we see in the glass display cases in museums. And it's not the only one. On the streets of Rome, people also play and bet on "heads or tails." Actually, they say *navia aut capita*, or "ship or heads," because coins have the head of two-faced Janus on one side and the prow of a galley on the other. Over time the images were changed but not the expression, which has come down to our own time with billions of flipped coins.

Another typical Roman game that has come down to us is odds or evens (here they call it *par impar*). Actually, it's a little different than our version of the game because it consists of guessing the number of stones that your adversary is holding in his hand.

We go into the bar, passing by the two old guys who continue playing. The shorter one, with no hair, no teeth, and a very pronounced nose, is really agitated. With every number he shouts he emits a spray of spit. The other, on the contrary, is impassive. He's got a wooden face lined by a thousand wrinkles and his hair stands straight up in a brush cut. His eyes are half-closed and he moves his hand rhythmically, calling out a different number every time.

There is a really nice expression that derives from this game. In Trajan's Rome, people will say, "that guy is so honest you can play morra with him in the dark."

Inside the bar, we notice there's a curtain; behind it must be the back room. But then why is there so much shouting and hollering coming from back there? We go over to the curtain and pull it aside, making our way into a small room. It's a gambling den! There's a table in the middle of the room with some men rolling dice. It must be a high-stakes game. After every pass the owner records the winnings by hacking a nick in the wall.

But isn't gambling illegal? Yes, it is. And so is betting (except for the Colosseum and the Circus Maximus). The law is clear: violators are punished with fines up to four times the stakes of the bet. Furthermore, Roman law does not recognize gambling debts and so no lawyer will ever be able to help you recover money lost on gambling.

Yet everyone gambles. Even though the law prohibits betting and gambling, the authorities close their eyes and nobody enforces the law. All you have to do is refrain from committing an open violation—that is, keep the gambling in the back room. This place is identical to the ones you see in films with people playing poker. Obviously, playing cards won't be around for a few more centuries, but dice (*tesserae*) are a more than adequate substitute.

Huge fortunes have been squandered on this game. A lot of players have gone to their deaths. There are even loaded dice. One of them is nailed to the wall as a warning. As if to say, cheating will not be tolerated. Our curiosity has been piqued and we move in closer to get a better look. The die is hollow inside and it has two plugs to mask the trick. Outside it must have looked perfect. But a small piece of lead has been fixed to the inside face of one of the sides so the die would land more often on that side. The bar owner and his friends must have picked up on the trick. Who knows what happened to the cheater. Some small stains and some imperfectly washed brown spots in one corner of the room give us an idea of how things ended up.

We make our way discreetly over to the table. The men shout and curse at every throw. The dice are thrown two, three, or four at a time, depending on the game, using a terra-cotta tumbler (*fritillus*) which has a curious short stem; it looks like a sawed-off wine glass. It's very hard to keep it standing upright and it falls over at the slightest touch. Maybe it's a way of making sure no one slips in a loaded die without being seen.

The rules are the universal ones. You add up the number of dots on the upturned faces of the dice. The only differences are the names of the various tosses. When all the dice show the number one, a really unlucky roll, it's called the "dog point." But, on the contrary, if all the dice are showing sixes, it's called the "Venus point."

Around the edge of the table are little piles of bronze *ses-*

tertii and silver *denarii*. There is some heavy betting going on, a good reflection of the gaming fever that has infected the Romans. It is truly surprising how much everybody in Rome gambles and bets. And we're not just talking about the lower classes. Augustus himself was a well-known gambler, capable of losing as much as 200,000 *sestertii* (580,000 dollars) in a single day. If he had lived in modern times, this great figure in Roman history would have been placed in treatment. Augustus really had an addiction; when he invited guests to his house, he gave each of them a little sack with twenty-five silver *denarii* so they could gamble (and often redistributed his own winnings so the game could go on!).

We exit the gaming room. The tension and the shouting have reached a fever pitch, and the situation could degenerate.

As we come out we run into the two old guys again still noisily playing at morra. A little further on we notice two soldiers sitting at a table who have just started playing a game of the twelve writings (*duodecim scripta,* very similar to our backgammon). Another game much loved by the Romans.

LATIN ON THE STREETS OF ROME

C ould we get by on the streets of Rome with the Latin we learned in school? This is something we've been carrying around with us since our day began. So we decide to do an experiment and we walk over to join, under the portico, a couple of women who are assessing the quality of some silk on display in a shop. They are women of stature and shouldn't be out among the crowds of plebeians shopping on the streets. But we have the impression that they are here for some special reason; they are choosing some material for a wedding. They are mother and daughter. Here is what they are saying:

Placetne tibi, mater, pannus hic, ut meam nuptialem pallam conficiam? (Mother, do you like this material for my wedding dress?)

Paulum nimium speciosus est. Tamquam meretrix ornata nubere non potes, filia. (It's a little too showy. You can't go to your wedding dressed like a prostitute, my daughter.) *Certe, matrimonium hoc primum tibi non erit, sed maiorum mores servandi sunt.* (Of course, this will not be your first wedding, but we have to respect tradition.)

Mater, festìna. Nam cena parandest, musici conducendi, eligendique, nuptiarum testes. (Mom, hurry up, because we have to decide the menu for the banquet, hire the musicians and choose the witnesses.)

The two women enter the shop and continue chatting. But we can't follow them; a tall servant, huge and head-shaven, has planted himself right in front of us and he's staring at us menacingly. The message is clear; he wants us to be on our way. But anyway, their words have been very useful. We learned that the daughter is getting remarried, something that is not scandalous (divorces are common in Roman society, exactly as they are in modern times).

The other interesting aspect is the language. For example, *cena* with a soft "c." This is an important detail, because many scholars believe that at the beginning of Roman history, and maybe even up to the time of Julius Caesar, the Latin was different than the Latin we learned at school.

The word *ancillae*, which we read "anchille," was actually pronounced "ankilla-e." In short, their "c"s were hard, like "k"s, and the "a"s and "e"s were pronounced separately. This may be how Julius Caesar spoke, who didn't pronounce his name "Cesar" but "Kaesar."

So the conversation we have just overheard between the two women would have been fairly different a hundred and fifty years earlier.

Latin, in other words, has been softened and modified over time, to the point of giving rise to the pronunciation of sounds and words that many European languages—Italian, Spanish, Portuguese, French, Romanian, and English—have in common.

In the Rome that we are exploring, the transformation is well underway, allowing us to recognize a lot of the words we hear. The process will continue during the entire Roman era and through the Middle Ages (which will leave their own fundamental mark on our current European languages). What makes the Latin on the streets of Rome so different from the Latin we learned in school, on the other hand, is the way in which it is spoken. The tone of the sentences follows cadences that deform the words, and often we can't understand them.

This is something that also happens in modern times; all

you have to do is move from one city to another or from one region to another to hear the same language spoken in a different way. You can imagine the difficulties faced by a tourist who knows only rudimentary Italian trying to figure out a Venetian, Florentine, or Neapolitan accent and cadence.

The same thing happens on the streets of Rome. Here among the crowd we can pick out a host of different inflections, tied not only to the various regions of the peninsula but also to the various corners of the Empire.

That's why the hard sound of the Latin spoken by two tall, blond soldiers who walk by us betrays their Northern European origins. Exactly as in modern times.

GOING TO SCHOOL . . . IN THE STREETS

We stop for a minute and off in the distance we can hear a chorus of children's voices struggling to make its way through the shouts of the street vendors and the noises coming from the craftsmen's workshops.

We try to figure out where it's coming from. We turn down an alley and the chorus gets progressively louder. We pick up our pace, passing two slaves carrying overloaded baskets on their heads.

The alley opens out onto a side street, less crowded, with a long portico. Here's where the chorus was coming from. At the point where the portico turns the corner, thirty or so young children are sitting on as many plain stools, reciting a text from memory. The sunlight caresses their little heads, transforming their hair into luminous halos. We can see flies buzzing around in the rays of light and a lot of dust particles in the air. The sun also lights up a stick swaying rhythmically in the air, setting the tempo for the chorus. It's the teacher's stick and he's a mature, thin, bald man with a beard. Next to him is a rudimentary blackboard. People walk by and around him, totally ignoring the lesson in progress, except for a few who have stopped and, leaning up against a column, try to take in some of the basic concepts, eavesdropping on the class.

The children have finished chanting the twenty-three letters of the alphabet and now they are reciting in chorus the laws of the Twelve Tables, the first written laws of Rome. Not everyone is paying attention. Suddenly the stick comes down violently on a shoulder. Even the flies whiz out of there. For a second, a truncated shout interrupts the chorus, which then continues on as if nothing had happened . . .

Schooling in Roman times allowed corporal punishment. Juvenal and Horace remember it well. Horace always had with him the image of his old teacher whom he called *plagosus* (the one who hit us). This is what elementary schools look like in Rome and throughout the Empire. Sometimes the lessons take place in shabby rooms, former *tabernae*, but more often than not they are held outside, under the porticoes.

Most Romans don't go beyond this basic education. They learn the three "r"s and then they go to work; child labor is not a crime in ancient Rome.

Children of wealthy families, who don't need to go to work, go on with their education in part because their parents know that a good scholastic preparation is very important for their careers and their social standing. And so these teenagers, from twelve up, attend private schools to study Greek and Latin grammar and literature. Actually, in aristocratic families, knowing Greek is a symbol of noble status.

What is studied in these lessons? The *grammaticus*, that is, the teacher, begins with poetic texts from the past—what we would call the classics. In explaining these works, he has to be able to delve into subjects as diverse as astronomy, the metrics of music, mathematics, and geography. By organizing the lessons in this way the *grammaticus* manages to give his students a very broad liberal education.

It is interesting to note, however, that the Roman "middle schools" primarily adopt a classical approach, as we would call it today, neglecting scientific and technical subjects. And they also teach a subject that pretty much doesn't exist anymore: mythology.

A curiosity. The selection of texts to be studied has a direct impact on the publishing market. Booksellers stock their shops with a handful of classics (the works of Homer, or Ennius, the father of Roman poetry, and later on those of Virgil, Cicero, Horace, etc.), while the works of many other writers disappear from circulation. And it may be thanks to the selections of these unknown school teachers that works have come down to us that otherwise might have been eliminated from history. Once they have finished with the middle school, at the age of fifteen or sixteen, the children of the well-to-do change teachers. Now they have a *rhetor*, who teaches them the golden rules of eloquence to prepare them for a career in public life.

And so his students practice both written and oral expression. They have to deliver monologues in which they analyze the pros and cons of a certain proposition by supporting the position of some famous personality from the past. This is an extremely useful exercise because it refines their rhetorical skills in a key sector of Roman public life: politics. A second type of exercise matches up two students who have to expound and defend opposing views. This skill will serve them well in the field of law. The Romans call these two kinds of exercises *suasoriae* and *controversiae*, respectively.

It is evident that middle school and high school are not located outdoors amid the dust of the streets but are held in the students' homes or in special classrooms, such as the one Trajan has made available in his great Forum, in the heart of Rome.

Neither the *grammaticus* nor the *rhetor*, despite their being in contact with the cream of Roman society, enjoys any special privileges. Except in rare cases, they are given the same consideration as a bookshop or a computer. But the ones who are really poorly treated are elementary school teachers. The man that we saw waving his stick as he directed the chorus of chanting children occupies a very low rung in Roman society. The Romans call these teachers of elementary street schools *ludimagistri* or *litteratores*, and they are held in very low esteem. They are paid directly by the parents of their pupils, but they earn so little that they have to do other odd jobs to make a living. A lot of them are scribes. Like the man on the other side of the street, sitting next to a column. He's writing a letter for an elderly man who is dictating it to him. The man is well dressed. He's probably a former slave who has made a fortune as a merchant but has never learned to read and write. What we're looking at is a scene that could have been immortalized in modern times on a street in India or in a country in Southeast Asia, where street scribes are a common sight.

How Many Romans Can Read and Write?

We just now notice that the children's chorus has gone silent. The *cathedra,* or teacher's desk, is empty. The teacher has gotten to his feet and is limping among his pupils who are bent over to write on their wax tablets. What we might call the penmanship hour has begun. The teacher has written the first ten letters of the alphabet on the blackboard and on the top line of each tablet, and the children are copying them with great care.

Some of the kids overdo it, sinking their pen point into the wax until it scrapes against the wood base of the tablet, while others can't manage to make two letters the same size. Observing the children sitting in rows we can see intense concentration, tongues sticking out, faces exaggeratedly close to the surface of the tablet (eyeglasses still don't exist), but also some noses pointed up in the air following thoughts that are flying off to other places. A crisp blow of the stick on his back brings the dreamer back to reality.

One little boy seems to be having more difficulty than the others. His letters are more awkward and less harmonious. He's left-handed. But nobody takes that into account. Everybody has to write with their right hand. Walking up and down the rows, the teacher inspects the work of his pupils, and in many cases he stops to help them trace the shapes of the letters, putting his hand over theirs to guide them.

We discover that one row of children doesn't have wax tablets, but simple tablets of wood, into which the letters of the alphabet have been engraved. Patiently, the children trace over the shapes, using a wooden pen. This is an exercise to help them learn the right movements and to learn by heart the shapes of the letters. Exactly as they would do if their hand were guided by the teacher. This wooden tablet is a sort of robot that takes the place of the teacher—a primordial form of classroom technology.

One last curiosity is the way they read. In Roman times, reading is done aloud, even if you're alone. In the best of cases there is an undertone of whispering accompanied by the movement of the lips. Silent reading will make its first appearance in monasteries, as a way of internalizing the sacred texts and not disturbing the others who are praying.

We take our leave of this class under the portico, and almost by chance we notice some writing on a wall. It's an announcement about an upcoming chariot race at the Circus Maximus. The letters are painted in red with great precision. These signs are true works of art, executed on commission by artists specialized in writing.

But how many people can really read these writings? And in general, how many people in Roman times know how to read and write? Many fewer than today, obviously, but many more than in the past. Actually, Roman civilization was the first to democratize the alphabet. Never before in antiquity have there been so many people, at all levels of society, who know how to read, write, and count—men and women, old and young, rich and poor.

Among the Egyptians, for example, only scribes knew how to write. In the Middle Ages, only monks will have these skills. The rest of the population will live in ignorance. Including the dominant classes. Charlemagne knew how to read but couldn't write. If this seems strange, think about painting. We can all appreciate a painting, but not very many of us know how to paint. Something very similar happens when it comes to reading and writing.

Illiteracy was widespread for centuries. In 1875, some 66 percent of Italians—two out of three—still didn't know how to read and write. A large part of this illiteracy was concentrated in rural areas, while in the cities there had always been a greater number of people capable of reading and writing. And this is also true for Trajan's Rome.

This also explains the diffuse presence of writings in Roman cities; from the writings on temples to the prices in the shops, from the names written on slaves' collars to the labels on amphorae, from gravestones (even in slave cemeteries) right up to the writings on the walls and in the brothels.

Even the dominant class is different than in other epochs. Many of the aristocrats are bilingual; they know how to speak both Greek and Latin in an era, it should be recalled, when one of the two languages was all you needed.

These thoughts have occupied us as we have passed through a long series of porticoes that have led us to an important place on Roman mornings: the market.

10:20 AM

THE BOARIAN FORUM: THE CATTLE MARKET

For centuries, Rome has had two famous markets: the Olitorian Forum (for vegetables) and the Boarian Forum (for cattle). Both are intimately tied to the origins of Rome. Rome was founded in a strategic location, near the first ford that made it possible to cross the Tiber, below the Tiberine Island. Naturally, there was no talk at that time of the Eternal City, nor of legions. There were just primitive settlements high up on the Palatine, inhabited by a heterogeneous population, the Latins, who were able to control all of the traffic of goods and people going north and south on the river. It was a lot like controlling the Suez Canal of the time. We shouldn't be surprised, then, that this veritable funnel of commerce and transport is the place where the big markets grew up to sell the products of farms and cattle raisers. The origins of the Olitorian Forum and the Boarian Forum go back to that time.

The one we are now crossing is the second one, the cattle market. It is truly enormous. A large piazza opens up in front of us, bordered by colonnades. We can also see some shelters with columns and tiled roofs, for the protection of the cattle and the vendors. But, on the whole, this market has maintained its traditional look: the piazza is covered by a huge expanse of stands, corrals, shacks, and tents that stretch out as far as the eye can see. At the center is a big bronze statue of a bull that a lot of people use as a reference point when they are moving around the labyrinth of the stands. And that's what we'll do too.

We try to make our way in. The initial sensation is almost

one of fear; we'll almost certainly get lost in this immense crowd. We'll be pushed, bumped—who knows, maybe even robbed . . . People move through the market with a great sense of purpose, like ants scurrying to and from their anthill.

The most impressive thing is the noise; just a few steps in and we're engulfed in a sea of voices, with shouts, laughter, people calling out to a friend, but also mooing, snorting, and grunting. Keep moving if you want to avoid somebody ramming into you. We have to move aside to let a man pass who is holding a horse by the bridle or another who's holding up two bundle of chickens by their feet, their heads hanging down and their eyes wide open, as they flap their wings in desperation.

We can smell the stalls or the hen houses, depending which area we're going through. The market is divided up into specialized sectors. Now we're walking through the ovine sector. Behind the fences, in the midst of a deafening bleating, tangles of goat horns come into view. Their eyes follow the constant movement of the tunics of the passersby. They are also frightened by the smell of blood. The stand after their corral is the beginning of the butchers' sector.

The first impression is amazing: a counter covered with the amputated heads of goats with their fixed stares and their tongues hanging out of the sides of their mouths. A swarm of flies hovers above these macabre trophies, seemingly undecided whether to land on the heads or on the rest of the body, skinned, which is swinging back and forth right above them, hanging from some sharpened hooks.

There are also two red deer. Unlike today, Rome's markets are marked by an abundance of wild animals killed by hunters: boar, hare, roe deer, and an enormous variety of birds, captured in nets.

A dull thud attracts our attention. A heavy meat-ax is cutting another corpse into sections. This one is not a goat but a much larger animal: an ox. With every blow the axe opens a breach in the vertebrae, almost as though it were a huge zipper. The arms of the slave who's wielding the axe are muscular. His semi-nude body is splattered with blood. Two more slaves are holding the quarters that are starting to separate. We walk away.

Now the stands are different; the hanging bodies belong to defeathered chickens, suspended by their feet. Underneath them, arranged to form a counter, are some wooden cages with the black noses of little rabbits sticking out between the slats. The woman who runs this stand has her hair pulled back in a bun. She's an unusual sight. In fact, as we look around, all we see are men. Unlike the situation in the modern era, the markets (and the stores) are male places. The vendors are men and the customers are men. Women are rare and they pass by on the edges, wrapped in their robes, maybe pushing an adolescent son. Purchases and food shopping are men's business; you'll never see a woman negotiating or making a purchase. It's always the husband who does it, or a servant, a slave. In the best of cases, the woman stands off to the side and lets her husband handle it. In this sense the atmosphere in the markets of imperial Rome is the same as the atmosphere in the markets and back streets of many Islamic countries.

Women's liberation is typical of the upper classes, in which women devote themselves to music, letters, sport, and sometimes even to law and commerce. But on the street, the women of the people have to follow the rules of tradition.

Naturally, there are a lot of exceptions, when necessity demands them. The woman behind this counter is probably a widow, or maybe she's filling in for her sick husband. Not coincidentally, however, she has a slave with her, well-built and bearded, almost as though he's stepping into the man's shoes at the store, strengthening the position of the woman.

Right now she's negotiating the sale of a basket of eggs. She adopts an aggressive posture so she won't allow herself to be bullied by the man in front of her. As we observe the negotiation, we discover something that's extraordinarily strange: the Roman way of counting. It's totally different from ours.

The Roman Way to Count
The woman makes the horns sign with her thumb, index, and little finger. But the customer doesn't get flustered; evidently it's not an insult. What does it mean? Our curiosity piqued, we walk over to get closer. "Four," she says. The horn sign must mean four. Calmly, the woman starts counting for the customer, undoubtedly a foreigner. For us it's an opportunity to discover how the Romans count that can't be missed. The woman shows the customer the palm of her hand with all of her fingers outstretched. Then she closes her little finger and says, "one." Then she closes her ring finger as well and says, "two." Now she closes her middle finger and says, "three." We would expect her to close her index finger, too, and say, "four," but instead she makes the horn sign; that is, she re-opens her little finger. She says "five" as she re-opens her middle finger, and so on.

We won't get into the details of counting, but let's just say that the pistol gesture means nine, and another gesture very similar to our "okay" but with the index finger touching the inside middle of the thumb means ten. In short, there is a numerical code depending on the position of the fingers.

The amazing fact is that the Romans use one hand to indicate the numbers under a hundred and the other hand for the numbers in the hundreds and thousands. So, the same horn sign means four if it's done with one hand and four hundred if it's done with the other hand. In this way, by combining the left and right hands, you can sign up to ten thousand numbers! Something we are not able to do in modern times. According to Pliny the Elder, even statues were able to count. The statue

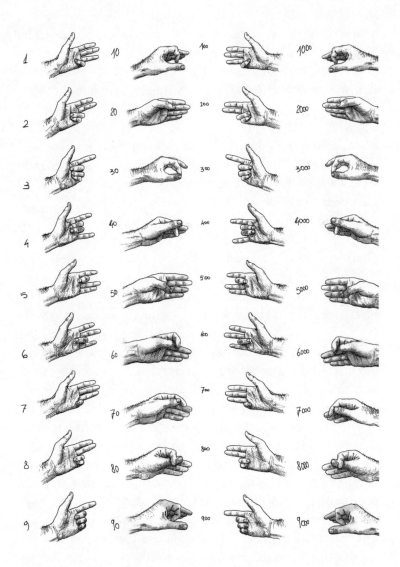

1		10		100	
2		20		200	
3		30		300	
4		40		400	
5		50		500	
6		60		600	
7		70		700	
8		80		800	
9		90		900	

1000		1000	
2000			
3000			
4000			
5000			
6000			
7000			
8000			
9000			

This is how the Romans count. There is a code based on the position of the fingers. One hand is used to indicate numbers up to a hundred and the other indicates the hundreds and thousands. By combining the two hands, it's possible to count up to ten thousand.

of Janus used both hands to indicate the number of days in the year, 365.

Unfortunately, the statue was lost; it really is a shame. It would have helped us understand which numbers were indicated with the left hand and which with the right. In effect, today we don't know how they were combined. If we take Juvenal's word for it, the left was used to count from zero to a hundred while the right indicated the hundreds and thousands. The exact opposite explanation appears in a writing by the Venerable Bede, a Benedictine monk from the early Middle Ages, who handed down to us a precious list of Roman signs by recopying them from ancient texts.

We also learn from Bede that once the number 10,000 was reached (indicated with a wide open hand held up as if to say, "enough"), other parts of the body were used: touching the heart (300,000), the belly (500,000), the hip (600,000), the thigh (800,000), the waist (900,000). Finally, the figure one million is indicated by touching the fingertips together over the head, like a ballerina.

All we can say is that there are traces of this practical Roman counting system even today in some marketplaces (souks) in the Arab world.

The woman behind the counter in the butcher shop is really losing her patience now. "Let's get our hands on some stones," she says. She calls her slave and asks him for the abacus, the Roman calculator. It's a pocket abacus made of a bronze plate with grooves cut in it where little balls slide back and forth on metal rods. The balls are called *calculi*, that is, stones (because children learned to count by using stones), and that's why today we use the words calculus and calculator. With lightning-fast gestures the saleswoman moves the balls into place and puts the abacus an inch away from the customer's face. "No matter how you cut it, the total you owe me is four sestertii!"

*

We continue on our way under the tent tops of the Boarian Forum. Now we're in the most important part: the sector where they sell cattle. In front of us, the tents have disappeared, as though there were a piazza in the piazza. There is just an expanse of horns and mooing. We walk across the main boulevard surrounded by throngs of men and slaves involved in sales negotiations. The air is pervaded with the acrid stench of the animals, and it's hard to avoid stepping on something squishy (cow pies are all over the place). We lean up against a post and rail fence; the bulls and cows that we see aren't exactly identical to ours. They are all built lower to the ground and they're smaller. And it's that way all over the Empire. If an ancient Roman could visit one of our cattle ranches, he'd be amazed at the size of the animals. The cows would seem immense to him, as would the pigs (endowed, even, with more nipples than in his day, as a result of selection processes introduced by the modern livestock industry so sows can suckle more little pigs at one time). Even the horses would seem gigantic. The Romans rode horses much smaller than ours, which would look to us like large ponies. They have more stamina and are ideal for rough terrain where our larger horses would get worn out faster and would much more likely come up lame.

On the other hand, however, they have some animals that we would appreciate immediately. Pigs, for example, are often allowed to run free in nearby woods, where they mate with boar. The result is a hybrid whose meat is a rare delicacy.

Some excited voices catch our attention. The tension is palpable. By tradition, animals are bought and sold in an open negotiation. The buyer and seller are thus inevitably surrounded by a small crowd of curiosity seekers and specialists. But the gathering that's happening here right now is rather unusual. At this very minute, in fact, negotiations are being concluded for the sale of a powerful bull. He's being held still by two slaves, pulling steadily on the ring in his nose. What we're seeing is a transaction that no longer exists today: this animal will be killed in a sacrifice in honor of a deity; the eastern god, Mithras.

The buyer is a prominent patrician, whose landed estate has a mithreum, the cavern-shaped temple where the faithful meet regularly. The sacrifice of a bull is usually something special that you see only in solemn imperial and state ceremonies, but the killing of a bull is also one of the bases of Mithraism, and on some rare occasions, we can imagine, it is symbolically re-enacted.

For obvious reasons, the patrician doesn't want to be present. It's his personal freedman who is negotiating the purchase and everyone knows how able he is in these transactions. So a small crowd of curiosity seekers has gathered around. The seller declaims the qualities of his animals, their rare features, his work as a cattle raiser, the long journey to bring them to market. However, he's dealing with a real expert in the art of rhetoric, a snake in the eyes of many, able to poke holes in his adversary's position and betray him into contradicting himself. And that's what he does now. The tone of the exchange rises and the gestures become almost theatrical in accordance with the custom imposed by tradition. In the end, it's the seller who gives in; he knows he's dealing with someone who represents a powerful client. But in his heart he knows he'll be able to exploit this generosity in the future, when he goes to the patrician's *domus* as a client to ask him for a favor. It all ends in a handshake and fake smiles. They have both won.

The crowd breaks up and we follow them. They lead us to the extreme opposite end of the market. Along the way, we see counters with animals on display that we would never have expected to see here. Porcupines, peacocks, goldfinches, turtles, parrots, flamingos.

A different kind of stand attracts our attention: no quarters hanging overhead, no cages with animals, just some terra-cotta pots lined up in a row. What do they contain? The vendor invites us to open one of them. Cautiously we lift the lid. Inside it's dark; it seems empty. Then we notice something moving on the bottom; they seem like mice. They are dormice. The Romans raise them and fatten them in these special amphorae, with holes for them to breathe and a curious little curved gutter modeled on the inside face of the amphora that climbs like a spiral staircase. It serves to give the animal some exercise (something like the wheels in hamster cages). Now one of the dormice has climbed up to the top and he's looking at us with his bright, black eyes and his little snout. It's tough to imagine him ending up roasted. Yet the Romans consider him a true delicacy.

But that's not the only surprise in this market. On the next counter there are two monkeys. They've been brought here from Africa. A leash tied around their necks, they walk back and forth on the countertop, trying to bite some kids who are bothering them. They'll probably end up in the garden of some wealthy Roman who wants to astound his guests. But it's not out of the question that he'll decide to astound them in another way: by serving the monkeys cooked during a banquet.

Now outside of the market, our attention is attracted by a vortex of colors and smells. It's a spice store, very much like you might see today in Yemen or Pakistan. Inside the store there is no room to move around; everywhere you look there are terra-cotta vases and bags with all kinds of spices. In the middle of the store a series of plates and goblets display an array of brightly colored powders arranged in cones of yellows, blacks, and reds. It is truly surprising to find that already in this era it's possible to find a store with spices of all kinds, even ones that come from far away through a long chain of transactions.

And here is some aloe wood that has arrived here from far-away Malaysia and Southeast Asia, to be used as a medicine and a cosmetic. Camphor comes from those same places. Those goblets of cinnamon tell us of a long journey that goes all the way to China. The cloves, on the other hand, come all the way from the Molucca islands, and pepper, ginger, and nutmeg come from India. Another spice from Southeast Asia is curcuma, excellent for adding aroma and color to foods.

But how did they get here? The answer is not far away from where we are now. Our visit to the market has taken us very close to a bridge; the bridge of Probus, the southernmost of the eight bridges of Rome (the ninth bridge of present-day Rome was way out in the open countryside in imperial times). We walk up the slope of the bridge and when we get to its highpoint we look out. There, right before our eyes, is the

Tiber. The blond Tiber, as the Romans call it. Actually, it's yellow because of the sediment that flows into it from the Aniene river, just outside of Rome. As we look out toward the horizon we can see people on the riverbank fishing, young boys diving, boaters mooring their boats. The red roofs of the capital are less visible from this angle; from here Rome looks white, with its temples, its long colonnades, and its *insulae*.

Down river, both banks seem to be covered by structures with a strange shape; not houses or temples but buildings that are long and low. The area almost looks like an industrial park. These are the *horrea*, the great warehouses of the capital. This is the city's "layer of fat," where it accumulates its reserves: amphorae of wine, olive oil, grain, marble. Every kind of raw material ends up in these buildings, hundreds of yards long and composed of several levels, some below ground. Behind the warehouses, we can make out a small rise, the nub of a hill just a bit higher than the surrounding river valley. Over the course of the next few centuries, that rise will grow enormously, towering over the roofs of the buildings. Today it is known as Mount Testaccio. It's not the eighth hill of Rome. In reality it's . . . a dump! Its modern profile is impressive: 120 feet high (170 feet above sea level) and a surface area of 200,000 square feet. It is composed solely of broken shards of amphorae (*testaceus*, from which the modern Testaccio derives, means "made of pottery shards"). It has been calculated that the hill is made of more than 40 million pieces of broken amphorae!

THE INDIAN ATMOSPHERE OF THE STREETS OF ROME

There are modern countries that can still give us an idea of that atmosphere that one breathed on a street in ancient Rome. India is a good example. There too, one meets people wrapped in robes with drapes and veils, wearing sandals or barefoot.

As in India, the streets of Rome are often unpaved, bands of little kids run all over the place, and on many street corners you can see small altars with offerings to the gods. And in India too, one is surprised by the brilliant colors of the clothes and the goods on display in stores and street stands.

In imperial Rome, like India, you pass from one extreme to the other in the space of a few yards: from the exotic fragrances of the women to the acrid, penetrating odors of back alleys and the greasy smell of cooking food. Another constant in this alternation of extremes on the streets is the precious ornaments and gold jewelry surrounded by the most desperate poverty. Many things on view in the daily life of Rome, in short, still exist in the modern era, spread throughout a lot of different countries: the bazaars of the Middle East, certain North African social customs, and even in the urban neighborhoods of India or the villages of Asia. It would be very interesting one day to be able to go hunting for these various sights, now on their way to extinction, in order to document them and use them in the study of antiquity.

But let's return to our walk through ancient Rome.

A woman passes by, casting a glance at us from under her

veil. Her eyes are pitch-black, lined with black makeup, her gaze deep and intense. It's over in an instant. We also notice the flash of her gold earrings and their hanging pearls. Then it all vanishes among the crowd, leaving nothing but a dazzling haze of perfume. We stop to try to come to our senses.

But we don't really have time to get ourselves together. More people, more faces, are appearing and disappearing all around us. We're amazed by the extraordinary variety of the faces brushing by us. The Roman poet Martial has left us with a good description of the charm of the streets of Rome. You meet people from all corners of the ancient world: the Sarmatians of the Russian steppes, accustomed to drinking the blood of their own horses; inhabitants of Cilicia in Asia Minor, imbued with the smell of saffron; peasants from Thrace (that corresponds more or less to present-day Bulgaria and Turkey); Egyptians who have swum in the Nile; Arabs and Sicambri (from German lands), many of whom wear their hair gathered in a lateral knot; Ethiopians with their coal-black skin and braided hair.

At certain points, the street we're walking down is so dense with people that it's hard to walk. The only comparison we can make with the modern world is exiting a movie theater or walking through a subway tunnel at rush hour. We imagine that the same scene is being repeated on almost all the streets around us. Trajan's Rome never fails to surprise us. In effect, it is truly incredible that these teeming crowds manage every day to eat, sleep, and satisfy their own needs and necessities.

Walking straight down the street is well nigh impossible. We have to avoid the vendors and their stands that crop up in the middle of the crowd and we keep bumping into passersby and bystanders. As is the case today in Asia and the Orient, the concept of distance between people is non-existent. Those of us who come from Western countries always have the sensation that everybody is on top of us.

Suddenly the crowd opens up and we see a juggler entertaining the passersby with some clever routines. We stop for just a few seconds. Just ahead a monotone melody attracts our attention. We open a breach in the crowd and discover a snake charmer standing against a wall. A cobra emerges from a basket and curves back and forth, pointing toward the end of the charmer's long flute that has a clump of colored feathers sticking out of it. As we know, it's not the music that hypnotizes the reptile but the movement of the instrument and the feathers. But the curiosity seekers who have stopped to look on don't know this, and every so often they throw money to express their appreciation for the musical talent of the charmer.

All at once the crowd moves aside to make room for a man on horseback, who is shouting and cursing to make way for himself. The horse's hooves splash into big stinky puddle that everyone had avoided, spraying the putrid water onto the robes of two men in togas, who stop the horseman. A shouting match ensues. It's probably better to be on our way.

We step up on the sidewalk to get away from the fray but we move into the street again right away. A patrol of legionnaires is passing by, evidently visiting Rome on leave. They're marching forward with an arrogant attitude, stepping on the feet of people who don't get out of their way. And it hurts: their sandals, *caligae*, as we have mentioned, have metal cleats on the soles (like the boots we used to wear some time ago) so they can get better traction in battle.

A hand stops us from behind, pulling on our tunics. We turn around. It's a beggar with deformed legs who asks us for a donation. Two coins bring a smile to his face.

But it doesn't end there. As we get back on our way, a street vendor blocks our path; he wants to sell us some of his lanterns. He has a friendly face, red hair, and a contagious smile. We struggle to free ourselves from the sales pitch even though he keeps insisting that they are rare lanterns from the Orient which "last longer than the others.

Tired of fighting to get through the crowd, we lean up against a wall to watch the people passing by. Now we can see that not everybody moves around on foot. Some people are riding mules. And you can tell the ones that have rented them; along with the animal they have also been provided with a "driver," a Numidian slave who is leading the mule by the bridle.

But there are other systems for traveling the streets without even touching the ground. As we know, daytime use of carriages in Rome is prohibited, with rare exceptions: the ancient equivalent of "official government" vehicles, carriages for the vestal virgins, and for those of a few people with connections. So some alternative ways have been invented. Typical of Roman women of a certain social standing who pay visits to their friends is the *sella*, or sedan chair. There's one now swaying through the crowd just like the one described by Juvenal. On board is a veiled woman intent on reading, or faking it to look nonchalant despite constantly being tossed back and forth as the chair swerves through the congested pedestrian traffic.

The ride is much smoother in a large *lectica*, or litter, which advances majestically above the crowd carried on the shoulders by eight Syrian slaves. It looks like a Greek galley with three banks of oars, fending its way through the sea. It's white and adorned with sculptures, paintings, and garlands of colorful flowers. And lots of veils. It's a true Rolls Royce on the streets of Rome. We look on fascinated, like everyone else, as it goes by. Two muscular slaves open a breach in the crowd, violently pushing people aside and swinging clubs over their heads—a couple of human ice-breakers. The litter passes in front of us, slowly. The porters walk with a long, cadenced stride, like soldiers engaged in the changing of the guard, lending the moment a solemn tone. We try to see who's on the inside. Unfortunately, it's not possible. Beyond the veils, there is also an arrangement of mirrors that lets the person on the

Amid the crowd on the streets of Rome, women stand out instantly, with their brightly colored clothes and the wake of perfume that follows them as they pass by . . .

inside see out without being seen. The mirrors are the equivalent of tinted windows on our limousines.

In the wake of this "city yacht" comes another vehicle, trying to take advantage of the breach in the crowd. It's a *chiramaxium*, a hand-pushed carriage, similar to a rickshaw, whose passenger is a white-haired man. The scene is exhilarating, not so much for the comparison of the two vehicles as for this very serious man, his aquiline nose pointing upward, putting on even more airs than the passenger in the litter. He is being pushed by a thin, pale slave, who seems to have arrived at the last few yards of his career as a human engine from hand to mouth. The two of them vanish into the crowd, together with the rhythmical creaking of the wheel. Not long afterward, we hear the sound of water in the middle of the crowd. If we've gauged the distance correctly, they must have made a direct hit on that stinky puddle we saw earlier. With what result we can guess: judging from the eruption of laughter, the vehicle turning on its head and the master flying into the water must have been a spectacular sight. Even the snake charmer has stopped playing his flute.

Rome Like New York or London
Let's try to sum up what we've seen so far. What's so striking about Rome is its uniqueness in the Empire and the ancient world in general. The comparison with New York or London is a natural. Those who visit the city for the first time are astounded by the size of its buildings, the density of the crowds, the stores where you can find anything you want from anyplace in the Empire. Something that's unthinkable in the smaller cities on the Italian peninsula, where the range of available products is much narrower (some products never even get there) and where goods take much longer to arrive.

It's the city of opportunity, with so many ethnic and religious groups who live all mixed up together (the first real melting pot, a term we are so used to hearing about New York); the city of fashion and eccentric dress, frenetic rhythms, and enormous waste. Characteristics that are unknown in the laid-back cities of the rest of Italy, or the provinces of the Empire, much less in rural areas.

Indeed, those who are accustomed to hard labor in the fields and the rigid rules of tradition often have the impression on the streets of Rome that they have come to a place where values have disappeared, surrounded by people who live on superficiality, often, and who wouldn't be capable of surviving anywhere else or simply of doing an honest day's work. The feeling is that everything turns on profit and power; you have to have guile and think fast, be a skilled social networker who makes friends, and clients, easily, not least because con artists and con games are everywhere you look, and so is violence.

On the other hand, for those who have been living in Rome for a long time, or who were born here (the equivalent of the classic New Yorker), this corrupt and noisy world is seen in a completely different light. Years of life experience have outfitted them with the right antibodies for walking its streets and entering its *tabernae.* To these people, the city and its world seem to be, as Martial put it, "pulsing with joy and vitality."

A Brief Pause in an Oasis of Peace and Art

Where can we go to get away from the hustle and bustle of Rome? Are there any quieter parts of the city? The answer is yes. There are oases of peace where the Romans go to take a stroll: the imperial gardens, the Campus Martius (Field of Mars), with its piazzas, temples, and sacred areas, with no shops or *insulae*; ideal, therefore, for a relaxing pause away from the chaos.

But there is one place so extraordinary for its beauty, that it was cited even by the naturalist and philosopher Pliny the Elder: the Portico of Octavia, where we're heading right now. The entrance is truly monumental, and reminds us of a grand temple. A few yards after entering, we stop, amazed. In front of us an enormous courtyard opens up, over one hundred yards per side, with a fantastic portico running all around the perimeter. Twin temples rise in the middle, dedicated to Jove and Juno.

The atmosphere is unreal. Everything is wrapped in silence, almost as though it were the cloister of a monastery. Sure, there are people talking and laughing, children running to and fro. But just the fact that their footsteps echo in the grand piazza and are not swallowed up by crowd noise has something miraculous about it. We are surrounded by a city of over a million people at full rhythm, yet that all seems to have been left behind us, just a few yards away.

We enter the portico, brilliantly decorated with frescoes and figures in stucco. And we immediately understand why

Pliny considered it a wonderland. Between the columns, inside niches, or even in small side rooms, there are statues. But they're not ordinary statues.

They are works by great Greek sculptors such as Polyclitus or his student Dionysius. Statues of the gods most loved by the Romans, like Jove and Juno.

These places (and there are others like them in Rome), are true art museums with masterpieces on display that would be the envy of any of the modern world's great classical art museums. Astounded, we continue on our way. We stop again in front of an extraordinary series of thirty-four bronze statues of soldiers on horseback. At the center is Alexander the Great; he's young, with his hair blowing in the wind. The others are his officers, killed in the Battle of the Granicus, in 334 BCE.

This sculpture group is a squadron engaged in a timeless cavalcade, on their way to glory. A work of the Greek sculptor Lysippus.

As we observe these masterpieces, we come to understand that Rome is a magnet, not only for goods but also for works of art. These breathtaking statues, all from Greece, conquered by the Romans in their first expansion, are the spoils of war.

To speak of them in terms of plunder and depredation is fair, but only in part. In the ancient world, plunder was a customary part of conquest, the devastating consequence of defeat. But unlike many other conquerors, the Romans did not systematically destroy all the masterpieces they pillaged, as did, for example, the Spanish conquistadores in Latin America. On the contrary, they often brought them back to Rome to admire them, almost venerate them, because the Romans thought that Greece was the true cultural fatherland of the ancient world and that they themselves were the heirs of that great civilization.

That's why today, the depths of the Mediterranean often yield up some extraordinary statues, such as the Riace bronzes, the statue of Poseidon (or Zeus), now conserved in Athens, or the dancing Satyr recently discovered in the waters off Sicily. They were Greek works of art being transported to Italy but that sank in shipwrecks during the voyage. And who knows how many other great works of art are still down there at the bottom of the sea?

The Roman's attitude was much different from Napoleon's. His foreign conquests were nothing but anachronistic sackings, pure and simple, in obvious contradiction with the principles of "liberty, equality, and fraternity" espoused by the culture that had generated him, and light years away from the *Declaration of the Rights of Man*, proclaimed just a few years before he rose to power. Many of these plundered works of art, especially those stolen from Italy and never returned, are on exhibit today in the Louvre Museum in Paris, as though they belonged there.

In the shade of the portico we encounter lots of people out for a stroll and little groups of people chatting. People don't come here just to do errands or go shopping. A lot of them are observing, with sideward glances, the other people passing by. It's an atmosphere very much like the Saturday evening stroll along the avenues and streets of our modern cities. In effect, the people-watching stroll of imperial Rome happens in places like this. And there are lots of them. Besides the Portico of Octavia, there are the Porticoes of the Argonauts, Livia, Pompey, the Hundred Columns. In short, it's tough to choose.

Some children are having fun climbing up on the statue of a dying buck. The trick is to climb up as far as the horns so you can stick your hand into his open mouth. You can tell that it's a popular thing to do; the back of the bronze statue is smooth and shiny. A young boy is waiting for his turn. Like most teenagers, he has a *bolla* or locket around his neck where he keeps all of his good-luck charms. But just as he's about to start his climb, his mother grabs him by the arm and reprimands him—not so much out of respect for the work of art as for the risk of putting his hand into someplace he doesn't know. Now his father comes over and tells him the story of the boy named Hylas, who (as he was represented in the Portico of the Hundred Columns) was having fun putting his hand into the mouth of a bronze bear. There was a snake in the bear's throat and it bit him. The bite was fatal and the boy died. We don't know if this really happened, but it was a story that made the rounds in the capital and that struck a lot of people, including the poet Martial, who wrote about it in his description of the porticoes of Rome.

Among the people strolling through the Portico of Octavia, we notice a fiery-red umbrella bobbing up and down with its owner's every step. It's identical to the ones carried by Victorian ladies in the eighteen-hundreds. Really? We move in closer, overtaking some fellow walkers, until we are right behind the woman who is elegantly making her way forward amid two friends, perhaps ladies-in-waiting. The umbrella's dome is made of silk, but the ribbing is made of bone and displays the same mechanism that we know today, with spokes that slide until they are fully extended. That shouldn't surprise us; the umbrella is a very ancient invention. The Etruscans were already using them some 2,600 years ago. But the purpose of this one is different.

It is not used to shelter oneself from the rain, but from the sun, exactly as ladies did in the eighteenth and nineteenth centuries. In the Roman Empire they are used primarily by women from the upper middle class, who use them to avoid getting a suntan, the exact opposite of what most women do today.

So we can see that the Roman approach to suntanning is different from ours. If you look at a few frescoes you see that men are always portrayed with a tan, with a dark, reddish complexion, while women are painted with a fair complexion verging on white. The message is clear: men have darker skin because they spend more time in the open air, engaged in various kinds of activities (work, travel, meetings, hunting, war). But not women; the pallor of their skin is synonymous with a life spent indoors, at home, doing "feminine" activities in accordance with the canons of tradition: looking after children, homemaking, overseeing the preparation of meals, receptions, and banquets, none of which require them to go out. Their fair complexion, then, is part of the charm of Roman women, as much as their hairstyle and makeup. Especially for women from the upper echelons; it is the proof that they do not have to leave the house and mix with the plebeians on the streets, a clear sign of economic ease and nobility. In short, a light complexion is a status symbol, and that's where umbrellas come in.

But as we observe the three women, we are struck by another detail. Although their faces are different, their eyes different colors, their bodies shaped differently, all three of them are almost exactly the same height; a height that just barely comes up to our shoulder.

Actually, the Romans are all very short compared to people today. You can see that when you walk the streets. The only ones who really stand out above the crowd are Celtic or German slaves or Roman citizens from Gaul. But there is also another thing that surprises us: there are lots of young people out on the streets and very few old people.

A short-statured population and a lot of young people. Exactly what we see today in the Third World. Is Trajan's Rome, therefore, a Third World city?

Rome, a City of Immigrants?

What was the physiognomy of the inhabitants of Rome? Were their faces like the ones we see there today or were they different? Obviously, as a city of a million and a half, on the streets of Rome you run into people of all different types: blonds, brunets, redheads . . . Often, however, as we noted in the shops, on the back streets, or among the slaves in the *domus*, we have encountered people with Mediterranean or Middle Eastern features.

Actually, a large portion of the inhabitants of imperial Rome would be categorized today as immigrants or aliens, because they came mostly from the eastern provinces of the Empire; places located in present-day Turkey, lands that the Romans referred to with the catchall term, Greek (Asia, Galatia, Cilicia, Cappadocia, Bithynia), or from places throughout the Middle East, with Syria in the lead.

Considerable numbers of Rome's inhabitants also had North African origins: families from Egypt or from the fertile provinces of Cyrenaica and pro-consular Africa (Libya and Tunisia). Not to mention immigrants from Mauretania (Algeria, Morocco).

The population of immigrants or descendants of immigrants was not restricted to the merchants who established themselves in Rome for business or to the multitudes that came to the capital for work and countless other reasons, very much like what is happening today in all of Italy's major cities. In reality, the overwhelming majority of them had been brought to Rome by force, as slaves. Some were still slaves, others had been freed (*liberti*), still others were descendants of slaves freed several generations ago and who now peacefully ran their own businesses.

One statistical survey has found that 60 percent of the names of Rome's inhabitants were of Greek, and not Latin, origin! Some scholars suggest that the percentage was even greater; maybe as high as 80 percent. Not that all of these people really came from Greece; for the Romans, as we have seen, "Greece" referred to an enormous geographical area that extended all the way to the Middle East. Plus, it was a very widespread practice to give Greek names to slaves, regardless of their country of origin. What these data suggest, however— that at least six of every ten inhabitants of the capital (if not more) were not from Rome or from the Italian peninsula—is astounding.

This provides further evidence of the fact that Rome was and would remain for centuries an immense genetic melting pot that combined and mixed populations and DNA of extremely different origins, as had never before happened in the ancient world. To define oneself as "Roman since forever," therefore, as one sometimes hears people say today, really doesn't make much sense, given that ever since antiquity the city has hosted a variety of people similar to that of a modern international airport.

CURIOSITY—The Population of Ancient Rome

What do the medical, anthropological, and demographic data tell us about the population of Rome? Let's get away for a moment from the porticoes and streets of Rome in 115 CE and go into the laboratories where anthropologists and archaeologists study this distant era.

At first glance, it looks like a daunting task. Some nineteen centuries have gone by. Yet thanks to a number of techniques, researchers have been able to get a fairly precise idea of the people we have been meeting up to now on the streets of the capital of the Roman Empire.

Imagine that you are at the scene of a crime, observing the forensic investigation team at work. The techniques for studying the ancient Romans are quite similar. A great deal of information, much of it truly surprising, has been brought to light by bones and skeletons found in graves and by archaeological excavations in general.

The average height of the population in the era that we are exploring, at the turn of the first and second century CE, is 5 feet 4 1/2 inches for men and 5 feet 1 inch for women! The average weight, calculated using various methods, is 143 pounds for men and 108 pounds for women.

That may seem low, but it remained the average stature of the European population for centuries. In 1930, the average height for men was still 5 feet 6 inches, and only after WWII (more precisely in the 1960s and 70s) did it go above 5 feet 7 inches. Today the average height of the European population is 5 feet 9 inches for men and 5 feet 4 1/2 for women; the average for the Italian population is a little less, 5 feet 8 and 5 feet 4, respectively.

Skeletons have given us some additional surprises. Anthropologists have x-rayed a lot of the longer bones, such as the tibia, for example, not to look for fractures, but to study the childhood of Romans. They have noted some thin white lines in the thickness of the bones (Harris lines) which show a slowing or cessation of growth during the first years of life or during adolescence, as a result of an illness, famine, or simply malnutrition. Evident signs of a difficult childhood.

Similar findings have been made from teeth. Research examining the surface of teeth grooves have found in the enamel, parallel to the gums. These too are an indication that the growth of the tooth was slowed or blocked for a period of time.

Contrary to what we might expect, those who suffered most were not the rural poor but urban Romans, even the well-to-do. And this reveals a feature of ancient Rome that is hardly ever highlighted.

As is the case in times of war, for example, in the country-side food was never lacking altogether. In the city, however, some food items were often hard to find. Even in the best of times, nutrition was not complete and well-balanced. The poorer classes were always on the edge of malnutrition, when not of outright denutrition. Beyond that, living in a large city meant being continuously exposed to various kinds of disease and contagions. All of this explains the suffering that we can read in the skeletons and short stature of the Romans.

But it doesn't end there. The Romans didn't live long. If they survived childhood illnesses, life expectancy for a man was forty-one years, and for a woman it was twenty-nine. The low life expectancy for women was caused by deaths in child-birth. Naturally, these are statistical averages; Roman men who made it to their forty-first birthday did not suddenly fall dead and even then there were those who reached an advanced age, but they were really very few.

So few as to make the news even today. The writing on a recently discovered gravestone in the slave and freed slave necropolis of Santa Rosa in the Vatican speaks of a freed slave, a certain Lucius Sutorius Abascantus, who died when he was ninety: "*qui vixit annis LXXXX.*" The epigraph surprised even its discoverers. In his time he must have been considered a real Methuselah.

There is another interesting study in this regard of funereal monuments in Ostia Antica. The Romans had the habit of almost always writing the age at death of the deceased, sometimes in an obsessive manner—they would write the years, months, and days of life, and sometimes even the number of hours! Naturally, these gravestones are purely indicative, since we do not have the gravestones of all the inhabitants of Ostia. Besides, when the deceased were elderly, their age at death was almost never written (except in rare cases, as we have just seen), since death at an old age was considered a natural event.

A study of six hundred gravestones has come up with an interesting finding. We know that the rate of infant mortality, as in all poor and pre-technological societies, was extremely high. What is surprising is that it wasn't the same for everybody. Under the age of ten, considerably more boys died (43 percent) than girls (34 percent). This may have been the result of greater freedom of movement (and so exposure to danger) for boys than girls. Curiously, the numbers are reversed for ages between twenty and thirty: more women died (25 percent) than men (18 percent). In this case, the difference was owing to deaths in childbirth.

Although not yet analyzed in depth, research on skeletons has produced another interesting finding: in some cases the state of health of the teeth was different depending on whether the skeleton belonged to a master or a slave. This has been found in the case of country villas used as commercial farms, where masters had more cavities than their slaves. This paradox is explained by the master's diet, which was richer in sugars—one of the disadvantages of wealth.

THE EIGHT GREAT PROBLEMS OF ANCIENT ROME
(SAME ONES AS TODAY)

The most annoying problems for the ancient Romans, as Professor Romolo Augusto Staccioli has observed, are incredibly similar to modern Romans (and the inhabitants of all other big cities). In a little less than two thousand years the situation hasn't changed at all. The list is really surprising:

Traffic
Noise and chaos on the streets
Time lost getting around the city
Litter and dirt
Housing shortages and sky-high prices
Building collapses and unsafe buildings
Uncontrolled immigration
Unsafe streets after dark

Like today, as we have seen, getting around town in ancient Rome was a problem; notwithstanding the famous law promulgated by Caesar in 45 BCE that allowed only those vehicles involved in the public administration (which we have already mentioned), and prohibited private vehicle traffic from dawn to dusk. But just as in modern times, in ancient Rome some public officials and certain privileged citizens were allowed to use their own private means of transportation. Even then, in other words, there were official vehicles. Another problem was noise pollution on the streets and alleyways. Here's what Martial has to say about the noise in Rome: "There is no place in Rome where a poor guy can meditate or rest. In the morning, it's the school teachers that don't let you live in peace, at night it's the bakers, throughout the entire day the hammering of the coppersmiths. Here it's the money changer shaking his filthy table piled high with his supply of Neronian coins . . . The goldsmith pounding away with his shiny mallet at Spanish gold . . . The fanatics of the cult of Bellona (a god of war) never stop their chanting, the shipwreck saved by a floating piece of wood never stops telling his story; the little Jew trained by his mother never stops begging: the bleary-eyed match vendor never stops yelling." His lament is echoed by Juvenal who wonders: "Where in Rome is there a house for rent where you can get some sleep? Only people with their own big houses ever get any rest."

Getting around Rome today takes a lot of time even for short distances; the city is congested and paralyzed by automobile traffic. The same was true in the Rome of the Caesars, even though the streets were jammed not with cars but with pedestrians. Some ancient writers complain that they couldn't make it to two appointments on the same morning because the distances they needed to go and the time it took were excessive.

The aliens of the time were a real problem. Juvenal even claimed that the city was already under their control and that the waters from the Oronte river in Syria flowed into the Tiber, "bringing with them language and costumes, flautists, the slanted cords [of the Syrian harp], exotic drums, and girls forced to prostitute themselves near the Circus Maximus." You can't help but see the analogy with contemporary Rome's plague of Slavic and Nigerian prostitution. Just as the railroad stations are the place where you're most likely to encounter immigrants and foreigners today, in ancient Rome it was the area around the main roads coming into the city, the Via Appia from the south and the Via Ostiense from the west. These were the access roads for all the foreigners who came from the eastern shores of the Mediterranean and from Africa. They got off boats in the ports of Brindisi, Pozzuoli, and Ostia and then walked to the capital along these two main roads. Obviously, the arrival of so many strangers (even citizens of Rome attracted by the big city) only drove the cost of housing even higher; costs which we have seen were already four times as expensive than anywhere else on the peninsula. The result was a savage real-estate speculation that made large apartment blocks spring up like mushrooms, tall and hurriedly built with substandard materials. As a consequence, buildings collapsed on a

View of a crowded street. Rome already had a lot of modern problems: chaotic traffic (of pedestrians), vendors' stands blocking the sidewalks.

fairly frequent basis. Juvenal is explicit about this and writes of a city that "is held up for the most part by fragile undersized beams" and claims that "when the administrator plasters over the fissure of an old crack in the wall, he orders us to sleep peacefully but the ruin is still dangling over our heads." The litter and garbage on the streets in certain parts of Rome resembled the situation in certain Middle Eastern cities where you walk on "layers" of all kinds of rubbish, from bottles to discarded legumes: "on one side an old mangy bitch, on the other a pig covered with mud," writes Horace. Finally, the lack of safety on the streets after dark, still a problem today, fortunately, however, not to the same degree as in imperial Rome, where, if what Juvenal writes is true, "you could be considered negligent … if you go out to dinner without having first made a will"!

THE SLAVE MARKET

Meanwhile, we have been roaming around the city, and now we are approaching a piazza. We can see it at the end of the street. It's not all that big, but from all the hustle and bustle that's going on around us, it's easy to imagine that there's some unusual activity taking place there. We make our way through the crowd with increasing difficulty, like when we were at the cattle market. Suddenly, we see a well-dressed man coming towards us, pushing aside anyone who gets in his way. He's short and heavyset, and his manner is brusque and arrogant. Our guess is that he's not a patrician, more likely an ex-slave, now free, and even more aggressive than his former owner. We're surprised to see that he's pulling someone along behind him with a rope. Barely covered by a loincloth is a handsome, young blond-haired man, tall and muscular. The little fat guy jerks his head to look back and yells at him to hurry up, threatening him with a cane, a sort of whip. The younger man could overpower him in a second; the physical disparity between the two is obvious. But he doesn't react; his hands are tied and his face is dejected. He quickens his step in silence and passes right by us. In his eyes there's nothing but resignation and the desire to discover his fate. He is clearly a European barbarian, but it's hard to say which frontier he comes from. Maybe he's from above the Rhine, maybe from beyond the Danube, perhaps from the recently conquered Dacia, who knows. What's certain is that we have understood what's going on in the piazza that we've now entered: it's the slave market.

The world we are about to explore is something foreign to our culture, yet it has been a part of all civilizations, throughout history. From the Chinese to the Aztecs (who had special sectors in their markets reserved for the sale of their enemies to be used in human sacrifice). In Europe, slavery existed before the Roman era and went on for centuries after the fall of Rome, up to the Renaissance and beyond. At a certain point it was abolished with regard to Christians, but it continued to exist for other peoples, like Muslims.

With each step we take, a scene opens up before our eyes and leaves us speechless. The slaves for sale are displayed on a series of raised wooden platforms, arranged in a line like so many fruit stands. But these goods are human. There are men, women, and children. They each have a sign hanging around their neck with their characteristics, almost as though they were bottles of wine or olive oil at the supermarket. With a few, incredibly crude words, the slave traders, the *mangones*, have noted their nationality, their qualities, and even some defects. "Nubian, very strong, doesn't eat much, not a troublemaker"; "Gaul, baker and pastry chef, but able to do any kind of labor, blind in one eye"; or "Learned, speaks Greek, served an important family in the East, ideal for teaching philosophy or for reciting verses at banquets"; and "Daughter of Dacian prince, virgin, useful in the house, excellent bed warmer." How many of these signs tell the truth? The Romans know that you can't trust the *mangones*, because they'll do anything to make money, glossing over defects and hiding "with some artifice everything that's not pleasing to the eye," as Seneca said.

The slaves don't seem to betray their emotions. Any trace of a rebellion, ire, or desperation seems to have vanished from those eyes, framed by red hair or black curls. Yet each of them is the product of a painful tragedy that has brought them here. Now they wait, resigned. Many of them are shrouded in a veil of fear. They know that their former lives are finished forever and that in the span of a few minutes they will take another, perhaps definitive, direction. But what will they become? Will they end up in the home of a patrician as part of the staff of domestic servants? That wouldn't be a bad prospect, because, beyond the probable sexual exploitation, there is the hope of one day being freed, with a lot of advantages if the master is very important. It will be very different if they end up in a shop carrying heavy loads under the command of an ex-slave as their master slave driver. But there's worse. Ending up in a brothel. Born and raised with a certain dignity and social rules, and suddenly you become nothing but a sex object, to be used until it "breaks" or is "worn out" (by exhaustion, disease, or waning of its initial beauty). But there's even worse. Ending up in a quarry or in the country estate of some wealthy patrician. Country slaves, everyone knows, are the ones who live in the worst conditions, with little food, a lot of beatings, exploited right up to the end.

We look on at the trading of these lives as though it were a lottery of life. Moving from one platform to another, we are struck by images that are cruel, inhuman, seen only in cattle markets. On one of the platforms, a slave trader opens the slave's mouth to show his teeth and let his customers sample his breath. Another squeezes the breasts of a woman and caresses her midriff under the morbid gaze of his fat, sweaty client. Still another, in order to demonstrate the strength and good health of the slave he's selling, beats the shoulders and the pectorals of an enormous Teuton, rubbing his thighs and calves.

The words we hear aren't too surprising.

"Look at this handsome lad, he'll last a lifetime."

"He's got an eye infection, I don't want him."

"Turn her around! Let me see her ass!"

"This one will do fine as a replacement for the litter carrier.

You see, he's just the right height and he's blond like all the others."

"I want a brunette. I told you. My master doesn't like these pale blondes."

"He's not expensive; I'm treating you well. These days, Nubians are hard to find."

"This one'll keel over on me after the third amphora. Can't you see how skinny he is?"

"No, not that one. I like this one better. How much does he cost?"

"Take the band off his forehead. There, I was right. He's got a fire-branded F! What did I tell you; he's a fugitive!"

(In Roman times, a recaptured slave was branded on the forehead with *fug*, fugitive, or *fur*, if he was a thief.

We continue our exploration of the piazza, amid the crowd of buyers, sellers, and newly purchased slaves. The slave trade is public and conducted in various places: in the Forum and also in shops. The rules are clear; you have to see the goods, evaluate their quality, and bargain, just as in any market.

Often, the slave markets sell different categories of slaves, depending on the day; one day is for strong slaves suited for heavy labor, the next day is the day for the trades—bakers, cooks, dancers, masseurs, etc.; another day for the sale of boys and girls, ideal for the house and banquets (and other amusements). Then there's the day, or the sector, for the deformed: dwarves, giants, slaves with physical defects, to be used in various ways.

The World of the Slaves
The slave markets are the place where the cosmopolitanism of Rome is most on display. The slaves come from the most remote parts of the Empire, even from beyond its borders, and they belong to a vast range of ethnic groups. It's interesting to note that racism does not exist in the Empire; no one is dis-

criminated against on the basis of color. Discrimination is based on social status: whether you are a citizen of Rome, a foreigner (*peregrinus*), or a slave.

The slave market is highly regulated. The slave traders have to pay for an import-export license and a sales tax on transactions. The traders are generally looked down on by the Romans and are often from the Middle East. But how do they procure the slaves that they sell? In various ways. Some are born slaves. If your mother is a slave, her master can do whatever he wants with you because you are automatically his property. He can keep you or sell you to make a little money. In this sense, Romans who have a lot of slaves have their own "nurseries" that feed the market.

Most slaves, however, were born free, inside or outside the Empire, and then fell into slavery; they are prisoners of war that the Roman State sells to private traders (even in times of peace there is military activity in some part of the Empire and every legion is followed by traders ready to purchase prisoners). A lot of slaves are bought beyond the borders of the Empire by traders from Eastern Europe, Asia, or Africa (just as in more recent centuries, slaves came from black Africa to the rich courts of Arabia and Europe or the mansions and plantations of wealthy Americans). Then there are convicted criminals, unwanted children left in the streets and raised by unscrupulous people who turn them into slaves (a similar fate awaits children kidnapped by criminals or pirates).

Finally, there are also ordinary people who have fallen too deep in debt and have been sold by their creditors to a slave trader. Though, in those cases, the law distinguishes them from proper slaves.

There is also another striking form of slavery that could be called self-enslavement—people who were born free but who are so poor that they sell themselves into slavery.

As we said earlier, there is a big difference between city

slaves (*familia urbana*) and country slaves (*familia rustica*). The former usually suffer less abuse so as not to reduce their value if it should be necessary to sell them. But that's not the case for country slaves. Their lives are incredibly harsh. They are under the command of an ex-slave who manages the property or the agricultural business on behalf of the owner. To his way of thinking, a slave who isn't working isn't producing. So all of his time has to be devoted to work with no time left to rest, relax, or enjoy a little intimacy.

In these veritable concentration camps (from this perspective the villas are forced labor camps; suffice it to say that the lodgings for the slaves are called the *ergastulum* or "lifetime prison"), a slave is not even free to decide to marry. The foreman decides if he can couple and with which partner. In this regard, a slave is not much different than a cow or a dog. Or better, the difference between the slave and an animal is minimal and can be summed up in a few words: a work animal is defined as an *instrumentum semivocalis*, while a slave is an *instrumentum vocalis*. The only difference is speech!

Owning a lot of slaves is a sign of wealth. Private homes owned by average citizens will usually have between five and twelve, never more than twenty. Some patricians, however, own as many as five hundred in the city and maybe two-to-three thousand outside of Rome, on their agricultural estates.

There are also, obviously, public slaves, owned by a city or by the State, and the emperor's slaves. They work in every kind of public activity, for example the public baths, the fire department, food warehouses, the rationing program, and so on, or they are put to work building roads, bridges, and other public works.

Many of these slaves, however, are employed in offices; they're the ones who take care of the public administration and finances. In such cases, the slaves are people who know how to read and write and have at least a basic education. As such, they are treated better than their colleagues who work as farm laborers or stevedores.

All of these slaves keep the Roman economy running. The law does not qualify them as living beings but as things. Their master can do whatever he wants to them, even kill them. At least in one case, their death is immediate. In accordance with an old law, later abolished, if the master is murdered by one of his slaves, all his other slaves are automatically killed because they have shown themselves incapable of protecting him, even

With a few very crude words, the slave traders (mangones) note the slave's nationality, qualities, and defects. In just a few seconds the slave's fate will change forever.

by informing on the murderer. You can imagine, then, what the atmosphere was like in the *familiae* of slaves in every *domus* . . .

Except in a few other cases, the State does not intervene at all in the master-slave relationship. It is a closed world. The master alone decides if he will have a friendly relationship with his slave or one of incredible exploitation. The law will not interfere. To put it another way, it would be like the State intervening to prevent the abuse of a kitchen appliance or a lawn mower. A master can decide to torture, mutilate, or even kill his slaves.

But didn't anybody protest? Many did, like Seneca, or the Stoics, who believed the slaves were human beings, not objects, and should be treated accordingly. Nevertheless, the importance of the slaves is so great for the economy and the finances of the Empire that nobody believes it is possible to do without them. What does happen, in any event, is a gradual improvement of their situation over time.

Although under the Republic their condition was truly extreme, under the Empire over the course of the centuries, the slaves began to acquire not so much rights as "permissions." For example, they could keep for themselves the money they earned on their own to buy their freedom and marry according to the rules of a sort of servile matrimony (although their children would remain slaves forever as the property of the master). Mistreatment would decline and killing by the master would be prohibited. What will not change are more minor practices, such as leasing a slave to a shop, a bakery, or another business in the city to pocket his wages. It's a kind of unearned income that allows even a poor person to survive in Rome. All you need is one or two slaves.

For wealthy masters, on the other hand, there is a form of investment in slaves. You give a sum of money (called a *peculium*) to a particularly talented slave, perhaps buy him a shop and help him start up a business in which he will certainly earn money. The slave obviously has an interest in making the business work well because he will have a better life than his fellow slaves and the respect of his master, and if he succeeds in obtaining his freedom (something quite likely if he has the esteem of his *dominus*) he'll be able to go out on his own and establish a position for himself.

But how can you recognize a slave on the streets of Rome? It's not easy, and this is confirmed by the Greek historian, Appianus. Externally, he looks a lot like a free man. His facial features and ethnic traits are no help in identifying him as a slave, in part because many citizens of Rome are either freed slaves or descendants of ex-slaves. So you have to look at his clothes, usually more modest, and focus on some details. Often slaves have signs around their neck (or even a fixed collar), like we do today with dogs and cats. The sign has their name written on it and, sometimes, the reward that will be paid to whoever returns them to their master.. Archaeologists found a collar in a shop in Ostia (on the Via Diana) that was ready to be put around the neck of a slave and then soldered. On the collar was written: "Hold onto me so I won't be able to escape, I'm running away" (*Tene me ne fugiam, fugio*).

Another medal attached to another bronze collar, which today is part of the collection of the National Roman Museum at the Baths of Diocletian, has an inscription stating that a reward of one *soldus* (a gold coin introduced by Constantine) will be paid to the person returning the slave to his master by the name of Zonino (*Fugi, tene me cum revocaveris me domino meo Zonino accipus soldium*). This slave lived a long time after the era that we are exploring (between 300 and 500 CECE), but the practice remained the same during the entire imperial age.

Making our way out of the slave market, we encounter the tearful gaze of a girl with red hair, being carried off by a man. Fate has been good to her, but she doesn't know it yet. She won't be going to some two-bit brothel but to a well-to-do family who will respect her, within the limits of her social status. Observing her face, her unkempt hair and her little girl's body so cruelly exposed on the platform, we ask ourselves this question: will she ever be able to regain her freedom? Perhaps, if she's lucky.

Actually, many slaves regain their freedom through manumission. It can happen in a number of ways. The master can make it official in a letter, or by way of a will (something very common). Or else, for example, by going to Trajan's Forum, in the Basilica Ulpia, where the ancient *Atrium libertatis* (literally, "the house of liberty") has been transferred, to enroll the slave as a citizen of Rome in the list of the census. In that moment a slave becomes free, acquires Roman citizenship, and automatically comes to enjoy the civil rights of every Roman citizen, that is, the same rights as his master, to whom, however, he is legally bound to provide some days of unpaid labor every year. The master has become his *patron* and these obligations are called *operae* (works).

There's no doubt that in Rome, and throughout the Empire, life is easier for a freed slave than for a free foreigner.

Manumissions are the true lifeblood of Roman society, because they allow for its continual renewal with new cohorts of citizens (strongly motivated to make their way up). Legislation fosters individual manumissions while at the same time impeding mass liberations, for reasons that are easily imagined. A law from the Augustan era introduced the limitation on manumissions by will, establishing a ratio between the number of slaves owned and the number of slaves to be freed, requiring that in any case the number of freed slaves could not be more than one hundred. We know, in fact, that Pliny the Younger, the owner of a thousand or so slaves, freed one hundred of them in his will.

From that moment on, the existence of ex-slaves changes

radically. Often they are fortunate and their lives seem to follow the script of *Dynasty*. We know from the names engraved on gravestones that some old Roman families in economic difficulty were joined in matrimony to these up and coming rich ex-slaves. The former gained in financial stability and thus in power, the latter got the coverage of noble blood, fundamental for their climb up the social ladder.

While we are walking in Trajan's Rome, just a few miles away in Ostia, a shining example of this kind of alliance is being formed. The old family of the Lucilli Gamalae, which has always based its wealth on landholding and agricultural production, has gradually seen its wealth eroded and fade away. In effect, the economy of the city changed suddenly after the construction of a new port built by Trajan: a new, very aggressive rising class emerged, tied to commerce.

So, Publius Lucilius Gamala has decided to take the big step, over the opposition, we can imagine, of the more conservative members of the family. He has united with his enemy. Or better, he has had himself adopted by a certain Cneo Senzius Felice, an immigrant descendant of freed slaves. He's a new man, a real local "tycoon," aiming for a leadership role in politics and business, whose career is skyrocketing. Now both of them have become stronger.

Trying to Understand Roman Slavery
How is it possible that a civilization as refined, developed, and advanced as ancient Rome, devoted to law, sensitive to philosophy, to the beauty of the arts, that has left us masterworks in every sector of human creativity, can conceive and accept slavery, such a cruel system of human relationships? In part, as we have said, the Romans know full well that without the slaves their world would collapse instantly. Roman society, in spite of everything, is a technological society, but still pre-industrial, in the sense that its only source of energy is human muscle and it

has not developed machines that can replace man. So it needs slaves. Anyway, why eliminate the slaves? The cost of their labor is almost nothing (or at worst very little compared to their usefulness) and as a source of energy slavery is theoretically inexhaustible.

To be a slave in imperial Rome is really the worst thing that can happen to you. It is something unknown to us. Sure, in our times we have sex trafficking, like the Slavic or Nigerian prostitutes, or the children who are enslaved by begging, or pedophilia. But these are exceptions and are branded as illegal activities.

Throughout the ancient world, on the other hand, and not only in Rome, slaves are the rule. To understand the plight of a slave in Trajan's Rome we have to try to get into the mind of a Roman of that era. Imagining the life of a domestic animal, like a dog or a cat, may help us get a little closer to the idea. Not so much because we put collars around their necks, but because we have absolute power over their lives. We buy them, sell them, castrate them. We sell their offspring (just like the Romans did with their slaves). It's true that there is a growing movement against animal abuse, and we have even introduced the crime of "mistreatment of animals" with heavy sanctions. But this is something very recent and the fruit of an affluent society (that provides its pets with increasingly sophisticated and costly food and gadgets).

But maybe there is a better example; electric appliances and all the comforts created by technology to make our lives easier. The machines we have in our houses, in fact, carry out the same tasks which in the past were done by servants or slaves. In a certain sense, technology has replaced slaves with robots:

- washing machines have replaced washerwomen
- gas stoves, microwave ovens, toasters, blenders, and electric mixers have replaced cooks and the slaves that stood over burners to prepare food for their masters

- the faucet has eliminated the slave that went to the fountain to fill the water buckets
- bathroom amenities have replaced the slave assigned to bathroom duties
- the refrigerator has replaced the ice man who brought ice to the house
- the dishwasher, the vacuum cleaner, and the carpet beater have replaced the slaves responsible for cleaning the house
- the water heater has taken the place of slaves who heated water in the house or at the public baths
- light bulbs have rendered superfluous the slaves assigned to lighting
- central heating has replaced the slaves responsible for the braziers
- television, radio, and CD and DVD players have replaced the slaves who entertained their masters (lyre players and drummers, mimes, dancers, readers, and verse reciters)
- the typewriter and now the computer have taken the place of scribes and secretaries, like the ones owned, for example, by Pliny the Elder, to whom he dictated his letters and writings, and who read him the texts that he wished to study
- the automobile has replaced the litters and the sedan-chairs (and their porters) and headlights the *lanternarius* (the slave who had to illuminate the road for his *dominus*)
- the hair dryer and the electric hair remover have taken the place of many of the tasks of slaves assigned to personal hygiene and beauty care (*ornatrices*)

And so on.

Of course, many of the tasks listed above were performed by the same slave. But just think of how many electric or mechanical "slaves" each of us has in our home! If you consider five to twelve slaves excessive for the *domus* of an average well-to-do family, take a look at your own situation and you'll see that you too are in line with this average. That's what electric appliances really are, artificial slaves. They are objects that we buy after selecting them in a store (our version of the slave market), that we often use without attention, that we sometimes treat badly when they don't work, while at the same time not giving them much importance. And finally, if they break down or get worn out we throw them away, buying new ones (and complaining about prices). None of us loses any sleep over this.

And in the ancient world it was no different, except that instead of having motors and microchips, their slaves were flesh and blood!

I think this is the best way of getting inside the head of the Romans. Not to justify this practice but to understand it. Some have gone even further and calculated the equivalent in oil of the energy provided by the slaves. It turns out that a bottle of gasoline provides as much energy as fifty slaves pulling a small utility vehicle (like a Smart car) for two hours.

And that's not all. A similar calculation reached the conclusion that electric outlets provide us with the labor equivalent of thirty slaves. Located in various places throughout our homes, these invisible slaves have revolutionized our way of life as never before. And it has all happened basically in the span of just two generations. We don't think about it anymore because we were born into homes that already had electric light. But people who are seventy-five today are the children of a generation who grew up in a way of life not much different from that of past centuries (including the Romans'): oil lamps, carriages, water basins instead of showers and bathtubs, etc.

So we can begin to see how much our society has been transformed by technology: comfort, free time, light, music, etc. are the direct result of technological progress.

So many aspects of our daily lives that we take for granted, or think of as the outcome of social struggle, are actually the by products of available energy sources. Including women's liberation. Without energy and technology, women might still be in the same conditions as their great—grandmothers—almost all illiterate, forced every day to do hard labor in the fields, do the washing by hand, go to the well for water, wash the dishes, cook in the fireplace, do the mending by the light of an oil lamp, give birth to numerous children (because infant mortality was so high), and so on.

One final consideration. Could the Roman system, based on slavery, work today? The answer is no. Not so much because of the laws and rules of civil society, but also for practical reasons. In a social system such as ours, slavery wouldn't be very useful and would probably be counterproductive. Why?

In the first place, because if an entrepreneur wanted to use slaves as the Romans did he would also have to feed them, house them, and provide for their health care. In an era based on flexibility and profit, no entrepreneur would be able to take on such a heavy economic burden for his business. Slavery works only when two conditions are satisfied at the same time: inhuman conditions for the slaves and great wealth and power for their owners. Two features that are characteristic of past societies (even in the relatively recent past, such as the pre-Civil War South) or in contemporary societies dominated by archaic cultures or by extreme poverty and deprivation.

The second reason why slavery could not work today is that it would eliminate so many potential buyers and consumers of products. Since no industrial system can function without large numbers of consumers, if a market is not created by the widespread growth of income the system breaks down. Industrial development requires the end of slavery.

We could, therefore, conclude that one of the big differences between our world and the Roman world is to be found in the system of production, with ours based on technology and the Roman system based on slavery; ours sophisticated and elastic and theirs archaic and rigid. These two systems aren't compatible; you either have one or the other. It is a difference that we too can perceive clearly in the streets we are exploring. Attracted by some shouting, we stop in front of a shop. Right before our eyes, an ex-slave, a *liberto*, is boxing the ears of a young boy, his slave. We don't know what the slave has done, but the barrage of insults that he gets, along with a series of violent kicks, upset us. Nevertheless, the thing that strikes us most, and more deeply, is the total indifference of the passersby. Certainly, there are those who pretend not to notice because they don't want to get involved (as also happens in modern times), but it's more likely that the lack of reaction is dictated by the force of habit. The humiliation and violent abuse of slaves are a normal part of daily life. Probably most of the people walking past behave the same way in their own home.

Fleeting Encounter with a Vestal Novice

For several minutes now, we have been walking through porticos, arches, small piazzas with statues, opening breaches in lines of people waiting to get water from a fountain, or passing short religious processions. People all seem to be heading in the same direction. So let's go with the flow. The part of the city that we're passing through is bordered by the Palatine and Capitoline hills and we know that it leads to the Forum; that explains the direction of movement on the streets.

Now the crowd is starting to enter a long boulevard, lined with very tall buildings, almost as though it were a prehistoric gorge. It's the Vicus Tuscus, named after the ancient inhabitants of the area. The name of this street is famous and anyone can tell you what it is. Curiously, however, it's not written anywhere. Indeed, unlike the modern era, there are no street signs or building numbers. The inhabitants know how to get around because they know the local geography, but a newcomer to the city would find it very difficult to locate a friend or a street without help or some directions to follow ("to find your friend you have to go down to the end of the piazza with such and such a statue, then there's street that'll take you to such and such fountain, across from the fountain there's an entrance to an *insula*, go in and go up the stairs to the fourth floor; that's where he lives"). It may seem surprising, but something of the same sort still happens today in a lot of modern cities, particularly in Japan.

By the way, now we see coming toward us, against the flow, a *tabellarius*, or a mailman, who has to make home deliveries of the letters and documents (actually they are in the form of sealed scrolls and tablets wrapped in cloth) that fill up his bag. He doesn't seem to have any trouble finding his way. In fact, Roman letter carriers know the local territory thoroughly, and especially people's addresses. His name is Primus. He is a *liberto* and seems to be very proud of his occupation, a real jump up the social ladder compared to what he was before, a slave. He will even write it on his tomb, which has been discovered in present-day Vatican City, in the Santa Rosa necropolis for slaves and *liberti*.

The street is getting narrower and narrower and the crowd has become suffocating. People are constantly stepping on our toes or bumping into us. So we decide to turn right down an alley that leads to a parallel street, apparently less congested. Once we've turned into the street we realize that we've become part of a sort of procession. A lot of people are singing religious hymns.

As we walk along, imprisoned by the crowd, we notice that we're passing along the side of a large temple that stands out, immense, against the blue sky. It's a sign that the Forum is very near.

In front of us there's a wagon, one of the very few on the Roman streets during the day. Evidently, it must be authorized. Seeing how the people on the street move out of the way as it passes, we figure there must be someone very important on board. There's even a small procession preceding the wagon, with symbols and musicians; we get a glance of some lictors. It all has the tone of a solemn ceremonial procession. Who can it be? It's impossible to say; the windows are veiled by heavy curtains. Actually, it's a covered wagon, similar to the stagecoaches and carriages that will be on the streets some centuries from now. Only it's not used to transport ordinary people. Its colors, the gilded statues, the garlands of flowers that adorn it indicate to us that it is used as a ceremonial vehicle by someone of the utmost importance in the life of the city.

The covered wagon arrives in a small open space. Right next to it, beyond a high protective wall, emerges the profile of an elegant round temple with a plume of smoke coming out the top. The space between its columns is closed by glass panels. It resembles the top of a lighthouse, an impression reinforced by the flashes of light emitted by the fire burning inside its dark interior. The guards stationed around the temple are another sign that this is an important place in Rome.

The wagon has stopped now. Guards and servants make a corridor with their bodies, keeping bystanders at a distance. The door opens, giving off a fleeting spark of sunlight reflected in a pane of glass (a wagon door outfitted with a glass pane is something rare indeed). The first passenger to get out is an old woman, her head veiled. Then, assisted as she steps out, a minute little girl appears, less than ten years old, moving awkwardly in her oversized clothes.

Suddenly, the mystery is solved. The round temple is the temple of the vestal virgins and the symbols, the gilded sculptures on the wagon, are the symbols of the priestesses. This little girl, assisted by an elderly member of the sacerdotal college, is a novice. She belongs to an important patrician family and has been chosen after a careful selection process, by the *pontifex maximus*, Trajan himself. It was all solemnized some days ago in an important ceremony. This morning the girl left her home for the last time and is now entering the monastery annexed to the temple, to begin one of Rome's most respected spiritual and religious journeys: becoming a vestal priestess.

The crowd that had been following the wagon moves respectfully to the side, and observes the little girl with great deference. Some of the people make broad gestures of a religious nature. Indeed, despite her young age, she is one of the elect who will look after the sacred fire of Rome, a fire on which the fate of the city (and its Empire) symbolically depends, and which burns, without ever going out, inside that round temple.

The life awaiting her will be very much like the life of a cloistered nun. The vestals, in fact, are chosen when they are less than ten years old. They then go through a novitiate of ten years, ten more years of exercising their functions, and ten years teaching new novices. Showered with honors and enveloped by great esteem on the part of all (they even have reserved seating at performances), they have to preside over the most important ceremonies, sacrifices, and rites of Rome. They also have the task of keeping custody over enormously important sacred objects, such as the Palladium, or the wooden image of Pallas Athena from Troy which the Romans believe was brought to their city by Aeneas himself, and which ensures the survival of the Empire.

But, as we know, above all else the vestals have the task of looking after the sacred fire, nurturing it and keeping it from going out. Beyond that, they have to remain virgins throughout the period of their activity (once it has concluded, when they are about forty years old, they can marry if they wish to).

If the fire should go out or if a vestal were to lose her virginity the punishment will be exemplary. Her lover will be whipped to death in the Forum and she will be killed, but without spilling a drop of blood, as the law requires. She will thus be buried alive, with a loaf of bread and a lantern, in an underground cell. A veritable tomb, in a place whose name is quite appropriate: Campus Sceleratus (the Evil Fields).

This little girl who is now disappearing behind the door of the vestals' house is, in short, sacrificing herself for Rome. Beyond that door, a conventual life awaits her in a monastery building endowed with a large interior courtyard. The double order portico that surrounds it is adorned with statues of the most venerable vestals and looks like nothing more than a medieval cloister. This, for the next thirty years, will be her world. The door closes.

CURIOSITY—Brief History of the Forums of Rome

Looking at the splendid marble columns and buildings of the Forum, one cannot help but be struck by their beauty and power. Everyone knows about the Roman Forum and the Imperial Forums, but the details of their history is not so well known, even though it lasted for over a thousand years, going beyond the Roman age. It may be worth going back over it briefly so we can better understand the area that we're about to explore.

Initially, between the tenth and ninth centuries BCE, the Forum was just a swampy, insalubrious area, with a lot of mosquitoes and a small stream, the Velabrum. At that time, it was used to bury the dead bodies of the first inhabitants of Rome, whose cabins were located on the top of the Capitoline and Palatine Hills. Nobody would ever have imagined the way it would be transformed. Some centuries later, the ingenious construction of the Cloaca Maxiumus (great sewer) reclaimed the entire area, channeling away the waters that constantly accumulated in the valley. It was thus possible to pave the area with clay and mark the beginning of its extraordinary history. The city had found the center of its political and religious life but also the fulcrum of its economy, with markets and shops. For centuries, new construction was added, new buildings replacing the previous ones. After the victory over Carthage in 202 BCE, Rome had become the primary beacon of the Mediterranean, and so four basilicas were added and existing temples were restored.

With the end of the Republic, the Forum must have seemed inadequate for a city that by now numbered half a million inhabitants, and for the management of an empire that could be measured in thousands of miles. So Julius Caesar decided to build a new one next to it. This was only the beginning. Under Augustus and other emperors, five more contiguous Forums were built over the span of the next one hundred and fifty years. Today we call them the Imperial Forums to distinguish them from the original Roman Forum. These are the forums of Julius Caesar, Augustus, Peace (built by Vespasian), Nerva, and, the most beautiful, Trajan's Forum.

The whole complex was all built gradually, sacrificing some twenty-two acres of the city, which required the acquisition of buildings, their demolition, and even the tearing down of a hillside that joined the Quirinal and Capitoline hills. A colossal project. Imagine five forums, with their buildings, piazzas, and statues all lined up; you could pass from one to another through the elegant porticos and colonnades that separated them. They constituted, therefore, a single, extraordinary complex, decorated with stuccos, marble, and gilded bronze statues . . . This is where the administration of the Empire had its headquarters, and also its system of justice. This is where the spirit of Rome resided.

The Forums were used throughout the Roman era, until 608, when a column was built in honor of the emperor Foca. That was the last act. Then came the Middle Ages, and the whole area slowly began to disappear under dirt and vegetation, like a ship sinking slowly into the sea. Curiously, its modern aspect, a stretch of ravines, is not due so much to the ravages of the Middle Ages, as much to those of the Renaissance. In the 16th century, Pope Julius II issued the order to exploit the Forums as a quarry for marble and travertine stone to be reutilized in all of the buildings required by his restructuring of Rome. According to witnesses from the time, the temples and monuments were almost all intact! But they were pillaged and razed in the blink of an eye. In the span of just a few dozen days, the buildings that had constituted the heart of the Roman Empire vanished before everyone's eyes.

Many people protested, including Michelangelo and Raphael, but it was no use. Columns, capitals, and marble were carried off to the ovens to be transformed into lime to make the bricks for the new buildings or the mortar that held them together. In the end, it was like the explosion of a cultural atom bomb; all that was left were ruins and shreds of buildings, the ones photographed by millions of tourists today. The area returned to its former use, an area for people to walk in and a pasture for animals, known to everyone as the Campus Vaccinus, or the Cow Pasture.

ARRIVAL AT THE ROMAN FORUM

T he crowd breaks up and, a few at a time, the people get back on their way. The small groups ahead of us all come together to pass under a monumental arch with three openings, built by Augustus. They almost look like three enormous mouths that swallow up, one after another, the small clusters of people—and now it's our turn. The density of the crowd impedes our vision and we can't see what lies beyond the arch. But we can sense, step by step, a steady increase in luminosity. Then, suddenly, there opens up in front of us the great open space of the Roman Forum. It is an extraordinary sight.

The dominant color is a brilliant white that stands out magnificently against the deep blue of the sky. Surrounded by this immensity, we lose our bearings. We try to take in all the details of the piazza, but it's impossible because of the people pushing past us, some of them insulting us. This, then, is the Forum of Rome.

How to describe it? The first example that comes to mind is Saint Mark's square in Venice, framed by its long porticos, with columns in the middle of the piazza topped by statues, the huge buildings, the people crisscrossing every which way.

But there are a lot of differences. First of all, there are no domes in the Forum (like the one atop the Basilica of Saint Mark). In their place, however, are numerous temples lining the piazza like a hedge. They look like a long line of white marble fountains.

Looking at the opposite side of the big square of the Forum, the spectacle is even more majestic.

The impression is that we are admiring a colossal petrified cascade, arranged in descending terraces. The temples, in fact, are built into the slope of the Capitoline Hill, almost as though they were trying to scale it en masse. It looks like a frozen waterfall of Iguaçu, which because of a strange play of perspectives (and meanings) has as its point of departure the two symbolic temples of Rome on top of the Capitoline: the Temple of Juno on the right and the Temple of Jove on the left.

On our left there is a chaotic coming and going of people up and down the broad staircase of a temple: the temple of Castor and Pollux. The crowd is nothing out of the ordinary; this is where exchange rates are fixed, which explains all the traffic of money changers and bankers. But there are also many new dads, as this is where newborns are registered.

A bright-looking boy approaches us. He understands that we are foreigners and he asks if we need some help. He can offer us anything we need. He knows good trial lawyers, places to eat and sleep, even where to find some "company" at a good price. Nothing that interests us, but we ask him if he can guide us through the Forum and he accepts instantly.

We head out into the piazza, walking on a splendid stone pavement of white travertine, polished to a lucid sheen by all the foot traffic. The boy stops to point out a bronze inscription that most people walk over without even noticing it. There's a name on it, L. Naevius Surdinus, the urban magistrate that had this beautiful pavement laid during the reign of Augustus. Something that not many people remember, he says, is that for the whole period of the Republic, this is where the gladiators fought. The Colosseum didn't exist back then. They would build temporary wooden grandstands and people came to watch the fights. Sometimes they even covered the grandstands with canvas to protect people from the sun. The boy is right;

Pliny the Elder describes one of these events, under Julius Caesar, that went down in history almost exclusively because of the suffocating heat. What the boy doesn't know is that seventeen centuries from now, right under where we're standing, archaeologists will discover the underground corridors and even the remains of a wooden elevator used in the games.

While he's talking we notice that behind us, in the middle of the Forum, there are three trees: a grape vine, a fig tree, and an olive tree. They are sacred trees, he says, planted symbolically in the piazza, though some say they sprang up there spontaneously.

Our guided tour continues. We walk by beautiful statues of emperors on horseback standing on high marble pedestals. For the crowd walking through the piazza all of this is normal. In the Roman era, nobody traveled just for tourism; they traveled for work, pilgrimages, or on family business. Nobody travels to see the pyramids, the Parthenon, the Colosseum, or the Roman Forum for pleasure. Nevertheless, you always meet someone in all of these places who's willing to give you a guided tour for a very small fee.

As we come to the far end of the piazza of the Forum, we find ourselves in front of a lot of other temples, on different levels, which the boy describes for us with great care. We won't go into the details.

While our guide is talking, we are struck by other wonders. The boy, in fact, shows us almost distractedly a long terrace that looks out over the piazza. It's a large podium decorated with the prows of captured enemy galleys. These are the *rostra veteran*, or rostrums, and we will learn that it was from right here, leaning against this balustrade, that Marcus Aurelius recited his famous funeral oration for Julius Caesar, featured in so many films. The Forum is a blend of history and architecture.

With the rostrums now behind us, a strange object comes into view: a large gilded column. It shines like a jewel at the feet of the Temple of Saturn. This is the zero point of all the roads that leave from Rome: the *Milarium Aureum* (Golden Milestone). The distances between Rome and all of the major cities of the Empire are carved into its gilded bronze surface. There is no better way to demonstrate the veracity of the saying "all roads lead to Rome," or vice versa, that they leave from Rome.

And that's not all. Just ahead there is an even more symbolic place. The boy points to a small building. "*Umbilicus urbis,*" he says, the umbilicus of the city; that is, the center of Rome. And since Rome is the center of the Empire, that point is the center of the entire Roman world.

But there is also a more sinister side to it. The building is made up of two parts. The upper part is the umbilicus of Rome, the lower part is the *Mundus*, the point in which the world of the living is in contact with the world of the dead by way of a crack in the ground. The boy doesn't want to go near it. According to the Roman calendar, in fact, that door to the underworld is to be opened only three times a year. Those times are thought to be inauspicious, and just yesterday, the door was symbolically closed again. But the boy doesn't trust it. He's worried that there might still be some infernal beings out and about.

We thank him for the tour and give him two copper asses. He walks off happily (he must be content now that the inauspicious days are truly over). We turn back toward the piazza of the Forum. From this higher position we have a magnificent panorama. We look back down on all the monuments and only now are we able to observe better the two enormous buildings that mark the ends of the long sides of the Forum. They are tall and massive, with several levels of arcades and columns, and are topped by a crown of statues that look down on the piazza. What do you suppose they are?

They are the Basilica Aemilia and the Basilica Julia. The term "basilica" might be misleading. These are not temples or places of worship. They are used exclusively for civic purposes. The courts are located here (and, from time to time, other activities are conducted here whether economic or political). But what goes on inside a basilica?

Let's go find out.

Amid the Crowd in the Forum on Our Way to the basilica

Back in the piazza of the Forum, we notice that it never stops filling up with people. It's a living kaleidoscope in constant movement. It really is one of the vital areas of the city. And it's also a social clock. According to Martial, the Forum reaches its maximum crowd capacity around the fifth hour (more or less eleven in the morning). So people often make appointments for when the Forum is half, or three-quarters, full. Habits are so regular that these measurements correspond to an almost exact time.

The Forum is also the daily paper of the Roman era; this is where you hear the news. You'll find people who want to talk politics, others who are upset about the latest taxes, and still others who have the inside dope about job openings in the government. Then there'll be somebody who has a brother serving with a legion who will tell you about the progress of some military campaign, or even a soldier who'll tell you about a battle. Not to mention the upcoming gladiator fights or chariot races, or gossip about famous families in the social limelight. In short, walking through the Forum is like leafing through the pages of a newspaper; there's a business section, a sports page, politics, gossip.

But did newspapers exist in the Roman era? The answer is yes, but not as we know them today. There were the so-called *acta diurnal* (daily record), but these were practically official gazettes, conserved in the government archives. The most interesting and spicy news circulates in the piazza.

There's another striking thing about the piazza: the statues and bas reliefs are colored! Today we're used to seeing them in museums with the natural tone of marble—that is, white. The truth is that the color has faded away over the centuries. If the Romans could view them in our museums, they'd be surprised to see them so pale, like faded T-shirts. The Romans actually paint their statues, and the colors are brilliant: the lips are red, the face pink, the robes blue, red, etc. To be really honest, not being used to it we remain a bit taken aback on seeing this festival of color; the end result is a lot like a naïf painting.

A splendid relief decorating the sides of a rostrum is also vividly colored. But beyond its colors, we are amazed by its message. It shows an event that happened in this very piazza just a few years ago: a tax amnesty! In the presence of Trajan, some servants carry piles of registers on which are recorded the back taxes owed by Roman citizens. They all get burned in the piazza. Imagine the relief of all concerned. What allowed this amnesty, however, was a war. A great campaign whose two phases led to the conquest of a new province, Dacia, with tremendous spoils of gold and silver. This is Rome at the apex of its imperial conquests.

The throng in the piazza is made up of all sorts of people. There are loafers, or people out looking for a dinner invitation. It may seem strange, but in the Rome of the Caesars it's a very widespread activity that begins with scoping out the best places to harpoon a rich guy who might invite you to dinner.

In effect, for a rich man, the piazza of the Roman Forum is one of the best possible stages on which to exhibit his own opulence. And just in this moment we see two litters go by. From one of them dangles a male hand, adorned with eye-grabbing gold rings. A clear message of easy living. The other shows us a different scene. Its curtains are open and inside there's an elegantly dressed man with an aristocratic gaze, his head held high and his eyebrows arched. A secretary, standing at his side, speaks to him with discretion. He is clearly a *nomenclator*, that is, an educated slave, able to remember the names, positions, and interesting gossip concerning the people they encounter. In short, he's a living Rolodex, able to tell you about people you haven't even met but who count in the panorama of imperial Rome or in the world of backroom deals. On hearing the name of one man who is crossing the piazza, the man on the litter jerks to attention and orders his porters to approach him. The litter swerves abruptly and points its prow toward the unknown personality, the encounter-collision is inevitable.

Now within a few feet of his objective, the man in the litter calls the man on foot by name and he comes to a halt, surprised. He tries to remember who that man is who's speaking down to him from the height of his litter. Nothing, he simply can't remember. And it's only natural; the two have never seen each other before. But his position as the new *aquarius* (hydraulic engineer), responsible for the aqueducts in the area at the foot of the present-day Quirinal Hill, will inevitably lead him to get to know this individual better. With gifts, invitations to banquets, and all kinds of pressure tactics, the man in the litter will try to obtain from the emperor, with this man's mediation, the long-sought-after small variation of the water lines so he can have running water in his house.

We make our way toward the Basilica Julia. The long series of brilliant white pillars and arcades make it look like the skeleton of an enormous dinosaur. There's a constant flow of people going up and down its broad staircase. There are only seven steps but they are so wide they look like the marble grandstand of a stadium.

These stairs are the classic meeting place for an appointment before a hearing or a trial. Everywhere you look there are little groups of people huddled together. We can recognize the lawyers by their vaguely aristocratic air and their assistants by the bulging files they carry under one arm. Usually the clients are easily recognized by their attentive gaze and the worried look on their faces. It seems more like a marketplace than a courthouse. Other people are stretched out on the steps, looking listlessly down on the crowd filling up the Forum: they are "witnesses on request"; they'll testify to something in exchange for generous compensation. Others are sitting together in small groups concentrating on something that's happening on the steps; we can figure out from their gestures that some of them are giving advice to the one in the middle while others are even making bets. Our curiosity piqued, we go over to get a better look. Among the witnesses we notice two opponents playing what looks like checkers. The checkerboards, or *tabulae lusoriae*, are engraved in the surface of the steps (a bit of vandalism tolerated for its entertainment value). It's the same scene that can be seen in a lot of parks and piazzas in many modern cities, with people challenging one another at chess.

We continue our climb up the steps. We encounter a man on his way down, cloaked in a striking amethyst-colored toga. Who knows where he got it; it's obviously too big for him. He's thin, with sunken cheeks, and badly tinted black hair; his beady eyes shine with the sly cunning of someone who survives by gaming the system. Right on his heels he's followed (or better, chased) by a group of people. They fire questions at him, pull him by his toga, finally they stop him. So we realize that he's a lawyer and his pursuers are his clients who have just lost a case. They heatedly ask for an explanation. They understand from the tone of his answers and the way he tries to avoid their questions that they've made a mistake by letting him handle their case. He's a total incompetent!

Tempers start to flare. We stop to look and some other people stop to join us. "Look at the plucked chickens," someone near us says under his breath. "Country bumpkins who put their trust in the first lawyer they ran into. And now look at them, the poor devils," another one murmurs. The lawyer breaks away from the crowd and picks up his pace, trying to make a clean getaway. But his pursuers don't give up the chase and the whole group vanishes in the crowd.

He's one of the many "ambulance chasers" who start lurking around the piazza of the Forum before the Basilica opens its doors, looking for clients and cases. The Romans call them *causidici*, or shysters, and those who know Rome well despise them because they are the real sharks of the urban landscape. They're clever at roping in clients and they may even be persuasive speakers, but they're terrible at managing a case. Their greatest ability is convincing their clients, usually people with little or no experience, simple and uneducated. According to the celebrated orator and rhetorician Quintilian, "all they have to sell is their voice." After the initial meeting in the piazza of the Forum, they make an appointment with their victims at the lawyer's house to talk about the case. To impress their clients and deceive them into believing they are well-respected members of the bar, they are ready to use any subterfuge that comes to mind. One still famous example is the shyster who went so far as to place in the atrium of his house a bronze statue of himself on horseback, almost as though he were a consul, in order to be able to boast of his (nonexistent) prestige.

We return to our climb. We're about to enter the world of Roman law and trial practice.

The rooms are enormous; there's a background rumble of voices and shouting that serves as the soundtrack of a chaotic coming and going and milling around. We feel out of place and can't understand where we're supposed to go.

It feels like we've entered a cathedral; the interior is even divided by massive pillars into five long naves. The central nave is the largest and it has an enormously high ceiling, about three stories, with huge windows at the top to illuminate the space below. Thanks to the artful use of light colored marbles on the walls and pillars, the sunlight reflects everywhere, creating a beautiful diffuse lighting.

All of this bears the signature of some of the most famous personalities in the history of Rome. Construction of the basilica was begun by Julius Caesar and completed by Augustus. Under our feet, however, are the remains of Scipio Africanus.

Since the early hours of the morning, the famous *centumvirs* (one hundred men), the corps of judges that operates out of the Basilica Julia, have occupied their place in the main hall, which measures 270 by 60 feet. At this moment, however, some small and medium-sized trials are being held and, to optimize the use of time and space, they are held parallel to each other. To facilitate this, large curtains have been dropped down from above which, together with wooden dividers, subdivide the spacious central nave into four courtrooms. The *cen-*

tumvirs are also divided into four groups. How are trials conducted in ancient Rome? Let's go over and take a peek inside one of the courtrooms.

Two Trials in Ancient Rome

At the end of the room there's a platform where the magistrate who will preside over the hearing has taken his place. Forty-five *centumvirs* sit on either side of him. In front, on wooden benches, sit the parties to the case, together with their friends, relatives, and lawyers. We can barely get a glimpse of the lawyer who is talking now. Between us and the hearing area there is a crowd of onlookers; members of that part of the population that loves to follow the testimony and oral arguments in courtrooms, as though it were a show not to be missed. Just ordinary people; men, women and old people. And there are people behind us, who have found a place to stand wherever possible, even outside of the hearing room, among the pillars of the small naves of the basilica. Or even above us, on a raised floor. Why are all these people here?

For some time now, people in Rome take recourse to the courts for almost any little conflict. Today, for example, in this court the discussion involves the theft of several goats.

In ancient Rome, just as in modern Italy and beyond, the dockets of the trial courts are filled to overflowing. Already in the reign of Vespasian, Suetonius observed, "the trial lists had grown out of all proportion, because pending trials were constantly joined by new ones." Without the measures introduced by Vespasian himself, Suetonius commented, "the entire lives of the litigants would scarcely have been long enough to complete all the trials."

The second modern feature of imperial Roman justice is courtroom spectacle. Just as in our age a lot of violent crime ends up in the pages of our newspapers and on local and even national television news, in ancient Rome public trials drew an audience. And to judge from the overcrowding in these court-rooms, the ratings were high. It might even be more correct to speak not of an audience but of actual spectators.

It's stiflingly hot in this basilica. Just about everybody around us is sweating profusely. And yet nobody wants to leave; they're all glued to this trial. The robbery victim's lawyer is speaking on his client's behalf. He has a very histrionic manner, with broad, theatrical gestures. He looks like an actor in a silent movie. His miming, however, doesn't seem to impress the *centumvirs* on hand. Some of them stare off into space, others talk under their breath, one is pulling the hairs out of his nostrils, another is swaying back and forth perilously, on the verge of falling asleep—which his neighbor has already done, snoring noisily. The chief magistrate is looking at the clouds passing in the windows overhead, squinting one eye to get a clearer look.

Even the onlookers have taken notice of the lawyer's total ineptitude. Many of them are enjoying themselves and have even started to laugh out loud. The only one not laughing is the injured party, a sharp-featured man who comes from outside of Rome, accustomed to work in the fields. When one of the *centumvirs* falls asleep, leaning his head on his neighbor's shoulder, he realizes that it's time to call a halt. Tired of his lawyer's rambling harangue, replete with citations from the great men of history, he gruffly interrupts him, "Not for violence, nor for massacre, nor for poison; I am suing for the loss of three goats! And I submit that my neighbor stole them from me. The judge wants proof but you rail on about the battle of Canne and Mitridate and the false oaths of the Punic fury. You cite Silla, Marius and Mucius with thundering voice and exaggerated gestures. Come on, Postumus, talk about my three goats!" The whole room explodes in uproarious laughter. The lawyer is speechless. The judges are laughing, the elderly one jerks awake, the clouds are forgotten. Maybe this man has saved his trial with this outburst. In a corner, a man is taking notes. Thanks to him, these sentences spoken by a simple farmer and handed down to us will continue to bring a smile.

Suddenly, everyone is surprised by a loud noise followed by long applause and some whistles. In the courtroom next to ours, beyond the heavy curtain and some wooden dividers, a lawyer has scored a major point. Everyone goes quiet. Even the *centumvirs* and the magistrate. The baritone voice of the lawyer in the next courtroom resumes his closing argument. His voice is heavy and beckoning like that of a dramatic actor, and easily transcends the room divider, making it difficult to follow the trial of the three goats.

The people look each other in the eye. Who is he? Nobody knows. Then someone mentions a name. The name of a real prince of the forum, capable of memorable speeches. No one has any doubts; a much juicier trial has begun in the next courtroom. Almost as though the fire alarm had sounded, the crowd starts shuffling and the people in the last few rows start bolting out of the courtroom, trying to make their way into the one next door. The audience has changed channels.

And we follow the crowd too. The courtroom next door is packed. The lawyer is a handsome man—salt-and-pepper hair, a penetrating stare. He has paused to drink a bit of warm water. He launches a severe glance at the *centumvirs* almost as if to judge them, and then another at the hour glass on the table. Each lawyer has a limited time in which to speak. And more precisely, he can ask for as many as six hourglasses; each one lasts twenty minutes, so the total available time is two hours. Naturally, every trial is different; often the judges are indulgent and allow more time, depending on the case and its gravity or interest. It must be said that hearings begin early in the morning and quite often last until sundown.

The lawyer points his finger at a couple, unjustly cheated out of a sizable inheritance. His first words are like rifle shots and they hit everyone hard. He stops, hints at a smile and then walks around, absorbed in thought, almost as though he were searching for just the right words. When he finds them, he turns on his heels and a river of words flows out of his mouth. His eloquence is truly incredible. A glance at one of his collaborators reveals a little trick; his assistant is listening to him with a wax tablet in hand and after each sequence he makes a mark, almost as though he were checking a shopping list.

The lawyer is not improvising at all; he's repeating a speech written beforehand and recalled to memory by way of a mnemonic technique. This, in fact, is the strategy of many great lawyers in the Roman courts: prepare well before the trial.

Some ancient writers speak of dress rehearsals that seemed like proper hearings, with lawyers leaving their offices in a super agitated state, their eyes flashing and their assistants exhausted. In these training sessions, called meditations, much emphasis is given to phrasing, word choice, tone, and pitch of the voice. The sparring partners are usually well-educated slaves. According to Cicero, perhaps the greatest orator of the forum and a master of mnemonic techniques, the great strategy to follow in court hearings consisted of three elements: move, entertain, convince. And create dramatic turns of events. One such turn of events is being conducted right in front of our eyes.

The two hours of speaking time have been abundantly used up. At this point the lawyer rushes toward the couple he's representing, passes them, and starts searching amid the crowd. The judges and the audience are disconcerted. Even his assistants feign shock (but it's all part of the script). Finally, the lawyer re-emerges from the crowd with two little children, a boy and a girl, both frightened. He leads them by the hand, shows them to the judges, and embraces them lovingly. They are the children of the couple, astutely kept in the wings. He now launches into a long speech about their future, about what will become of them when their father and mother are gone—and about how useful their inheritance would be for the future not of mere little children but, he underlines, of two fellow citizens (a reference not lost on the magistrate and the *centumvirs* so tied to the values of Rome).

It's not a new strategy; the lawyer has cleverly made use of a gimmick used more than a century ago by a very illustrious colleague, Sulpicius Galba, a contemporary of Cicero. But the audience doesn't know this. And it is now in their direction that he points the two children, with a theatrical move aimed at breaking the hearts of those who for some time now have been the leading players of Roman courtrooms: the people of the lower classes. He studies their faces, pronounces his last words, and concludes, embracing the two children. An ovation rises up from the crowd and from the audience seated in the courtroom. Applause even arrives from the courtrooms nearby. It seems like the final scene of a play (and actually, in a sense, it is). Even the judges are surprised by the brilliant performance of this man. They had already taken into account that the first few rows of the audience were in fact composed of *laudiceni*, that is, a claque paid to applaud the lawyer (not a rare thing in courtrooms), but they were not expecting such a huge success. Now their judgment will have to take account of the audience's reaction. The lawyer has successfully exercised a bit of psychological pressure that will certainly influence the verdict. And he knows it. Beneath the fake tear now sliding down his cheek is a hidden smile.

The Senate of Rome

Once again, we're back out in the piazza of the Roman Forum and we decide to make our way out of it by heading toward the other basilica, which is opposite us; the Basilica Aemilia, whose portico is more than 320 feet long. Civic activities and trials are held here too. A long time ago there were shops under the portico, but now it's empty. We are attracted by a small-market exhibition of various types of paintings, which occupies two arcades. We're struck by the difference in quality between the frescoes we saw in the *domus* and these very simple, almost infantile works. There is a variety of themes. There's a shepherd, a mythological scene, a portrait of Julius Caesar (which looks nothing like him), a very sketchy view of Rome. But there is a lovely, very realistic painting of a young man. Evidently it is a commissioned portrait. It is not widely known, but sometimes in Roman houses you can see paintings on the walls that depict the owners and their families. None of these paintings have come down to us, but elsewhere, in Egypt, for instance, these portraits are applied to mummies like masks. Today, they provide us with extraordinary snapshots of the inhabitants of the Empire. Who knows how this one ended up here? Maybe the young man died without heirs or relatives who wanted to conserve his portrait, just as a lot of people keep busts of their celebrated ancestors. And that explains how it ended up in the hands of a dealer.

We leave the portico of the Basilica Aemilia and head for the northern sector of the Forum, where in the past the foundations of the Empire were laid and where for centuries Rome's Senators have met: the Curia. And now a large brick building comes into view, with a small portico on the front: the Senate.

Julius Caesar built the Senate. He razed the previous Curia and Comitium to the ground and built this new, imposing building, used throughout the history of Rome.

The Senate's doors are open, and a debate is about to start in a few minutes. It has a beautiful floor with inlays of precious marbles from all over the Empire. Here, one walks upon the Empire. The Senate chamber is very deep, with wide steps on the sides, on which are arranged, in several rows, the senators' high-backed chairs. They are made of wood and all finely carved. The chamber is part *schola cantorum* (chamber choir) and part king's receiving room. The surrounding walls are covered with great marble slabs that make the whole place shine. Who knows how many solemn speeches have been made here; it's impossible to remember them all. Here, in these few dozen square feet, many decisions have been made that have a prominent place in our history books. Few places on the planet have had such a great influence on human history.

A number of the senators are seated at their places, and they're talking to their colleagues who have turned to face them. Some are whispering, others are laughing. We notice some groups that are talking discreetly. The debate is about to start. In the past few days, a number of matters have been considered. Yesterday, for example, there was a discussion of the large soon-to-be completed triumphal arch in Benevento, the departure point of the Via Traiana. But today the item on the agenda is important. Trajan is very far from Rome. In January, he made a triumphal entrance into the city of Antioch, and now he is engaged in combat in Mesopotamia. The news that has reached Rome is excellent; he has completed the conquest of the area with the capture of some important cities: Batnae,

Nisibe, and Ctesiphon, and the legions have acclaimed him with the title of *Parthicus* (Conqueror of the Parthians). The Senate must decide, therefore, how to officialize this title. Actually, since the end of the Republic and the succession of emperors, the role of the Senate has shrunk significantly. The times of the great debates and political conflicts are over. The decisions made nowadays are fairly low-profile, much closer to routine business than to the glorious exchanges of the times prior to Julius Caesar.

A senator makes his entrance through the open doors and nods at the guards who stiffen as he passes. The door at the entrance is made of bronze and it's very tall (the last door of the Roman Senate will be dismantled during the Renaissance and transferred to the Basilica of St. John Lateran, where it can still be admired today).

The elderly senator takes a few steps and is immediately welcomed by some younger colleagues, who walk over to meet him, probably to ask for strategic advice and suggestions to follow in today's debate.

Some assistants apply considerable force to close the door. The Senate chamber gradually fades from our view as though a theater curtain had closed before us. The last image that we see is the senator sitting down, arranging the folds of his toga, and staring at his adversaries severely, from behind his thick white eyebrows. The guards take their positions in front of the door, one hand on their shield and the other on the *pilum*, the javelin.

His sky-blue eyes are set like jewels in his tanned face. They don't budge from the muscular body of his adversary, even now as the two of them are circling each other, looking for an opening. They in turn are being scrutinized by the eyes of thousands of people who, since early this morning, have been observing, cheering, and screaming from the grandstands. The games have begun in the Colosseum. The opening act is the *venationes,* the hunts. Not combat between gladiators, therefore, but between men and animals. The Colosseum, like all the other amphitheaters in the Empire, always follows this same program: *venationes* to open, followed by public executions of criminals, and, finally, in the afternoon, the long-awaited gladiators. The activities of the Colosseum monopolize much of the life of the city, both because of the size of the amphitheater (which holds from 50,000 to 70,000 spectators) and, especially, because of the violent combat that takes place inside it. Like the contest that has just started.

The people in the stands know full well that it will all be over in a matter of minutes. They can see the sweat dripping from the blond curls of the hunter, whose name is Spittara. But the tension is so high in the arena that the crowd has stopped cheering him on. Opposite him, imposing and sure of himself, is one of the great dominators of the arena, Victor. He's not a human being, but demonstrates intelligence in combat equal to any human being. He has beaten numerous hunters, with his cleverness and guile more than with the power of his paws and their razor sharp-claws. Victor, the winner, is a leopard of abnormally large proportions who quickly became a crowd favorite. Once he tripped an adversary by pushing him over the body of another hunter who had fallen to the ground just a few seconds before, then pounced on him and sank his teeth into his neck. Victor, like all the beasts in the Colosseum, is not an animal that attacks from hunger, as is commonly believed. He was captured as a cub, taken to a specialized trainer, and trained to attack, like a pit bull. He was taught where to strike and how to do it. Leopards have this terrible characteristic: when they attack a human, and this still happens in our day, they go straight for the throat, sink their teeth in, and dig into the chest with their powerful paws, shredding the skin. I once had the occasion to speak to a physician in Africa, during a trip there for an archaeological dig, and he confirmed that when they brought him a victim of a lion (who tend only to bite and then shake their prey) he sometimes managed to save him. When they brought him the victim of a leopard, he was dead on arrival.

This wild beast is not guilty, he's a predator. He's just doing what nature taught him to do. But his natural aggression has been amply distorted by his trainers and exploited for entertainment, so that the animal has been turned into a veritable killing machine. Victor has been responsible not only for deaths in the arena but also for the killing of many slaves used as dummies during his training.

Spittara is a skilled hunter in the arena and much admired by women for his handsome physique, but he's not as famous as Victor. The bookmakers have him three to one to lose. Spittara knows it, but he also knows that this may actually be to his advantage. It could help him surprise everyone, even the leopard, with a lightning-fast move. He holds tight to his thick, sharp lance. He has nothing else, no armor, no helmet, and no spear. His only protection is some reinforced cloth leg pads (greaves).

A roar echoes through the arena—the call of a lion that has just come out of a gate to fight against another hunter. That's what Spittara has been expecting and hoping. Victor has been trained very well not to get distracted by the yelling of the crowd or the shouts of his adversaries. But the sudden roar of a lion stimulates his primordial instinct. In the wild, in fact, adult lions kill leopards. It's no more than an instant, a distraction. The leopard suddenly turns his head in the direction of the lion. He barely has time to bring the profile of his fellow feline into focus before he feels himself transfixed, right under his throat, just above his rib cage. In a fraction of a second, he distinctly senses the wide blade penetrating his chest with a piercing pain. He hasn't even heard Spittara's lung-emptying battle cry. The man has launched himself into the attack by squatting down and taking a long stride forward to give more power to the blow, exactly like fencers do to drive home a thrust.

The beast reacts with rage. The leopard bends his enormous neck and tries to bite the lance, but he can't. Then he pounds the lance pole with a powerful blast from one of his paws, almost breaking it off from the blade. Now he manages to bite it and breaks it in two with his teeth. But it's too late; he can feel his strength being sapped. He sees Spittara standing before him, as though waiting for the verdict. If the animal gets a second wind, the hunter, now without his lance, is in bad shape. Maybe they'll give him another one, maybe not. But there'll be no need. In the leopard's inexpressive yellow eyes, Spittara's image begins to cloud over. Blood spews out of the wound and forms a widening puddle on the floor of the arena, between his legs. The blow was delivered perfectly. One last growl, then a death rattle and gurgle caused by the blood gushing into his throat and lungs. The beast gives way and then sprawls to the ground, his jaws half open.

The crowd explodes. A bellowing rumble rises from the stands and shouts out the name of the hunter: "Spittara, Spittara." The Colosseum has a new hero.

CURIOSITY—Animals in the Colosseum

The number of animals killed in the Colosseum and the other amphitheaters of the Empire is enormous. Sometimes the crowd watched as hunters armed with bows and arrows killed deer or gazelles. Sometimes the victims were exotic animals such as ostriches (we know that the emperor Commodus amused himself by cutting their heads off with his sword). In certain cases, the combatants were almost evenly matched: some men dressed as gladiators with a helmet, a shield, and a gladius sword had to try to survive combat against lions, leopards, or bears. The bas-reliefs on columns and temples make it look as though they all fought together, with alternating outcomes. Finally, it was also possible to watch fights between animals; for example, between a bull and an elephant, or other large animals, bound together by chains, while servants stabbed them with pointed poles urging them to fight. Over time, the frequent use in all the major amphitheaters of the Empire of exotic animals like tigers led to a an outright decimation of wild animals in Europe, North Africa, and the Middle East. Many species disappeared, not least because so few of the many that were captured (including crocodiles and rhinos) actually made it to their destination after long journeys on wagons or packed into the holds of ships.

THE IMPERIAL FORUMS, A MARBLE WONDERLAND

We can hear the roar of the crowd even where we are, in the Forum. Some people around us turn to look toward the Colosseum. Its gigantic silhouette, at the far end of the Via Sacra, beyond the Arch of Titus, towers over the area, looming over colonnades and temples. The crowd's chanting of the victor's name reaches our ears but it's distorted, unrecognizable. All we can hear is powerful rhythmic shouting.

Very quickly, those who had paused to glance up at the arena of Rome turn back to their activities, as though nothing had happened. And we get on our way too, leaving the doors of the Senate behind us. The guards had remained impassive at the roar coming from the Colosseum, and even now, as we take our leave, their eyes are fixed in an expressionless stare, imperturbable.

In a little while, we too are going to enter the Colosseum, but first we want to see something unique that's located not too far from here in the Temple of Peace.

The few minutes on foot that separate us from this place will take us through another wonder of Rome: the Imperial Forums.

In fact, Rome doesn't have just one Forum. Julius Caesar, having concluded that the Roman Forum was no longer sufficient, decided to build another one. Naturally, it was named after him: the Forum of Julius Caesar. An obvious demonstration of his power.

His example was followed by Augustus, Vespasian, Nerva, and Trajan. So, over time, a neighborhood of Forums was created, each in communication with the others and with a constant traffic of people. It is a world dominated by luxury, marble, and columns, which expanded the shopping areas available to Romans, as well as the areas dedicated to trade and legal proceedings.

Out of curiosity we follow three men who are arguing vociferously. One of them has a long, aquiline nose, and he's trying everything he can to convince the other two that he's right . . . They are heading in the direction of the Temple of Peace, which is located in the Forum of Vespasian. Entering this huge building is an amazing experience. After walking through a first hall, whose columns are so tall it feels like a grove of sequoias, you come to a great hall, where an entire wall is covered by an enormous map of the city.

This is the famous *forma Urbis*, the plan of the land registry of Rome, which we'll have more to say about later (the version that we know today, whose fragments are conserved in the Capitoline Museums, dates from a later period than the one we are exploring, but it is probable that an analogous model, since lost, already existed under Trajan). It really covers the entire wall. It is a perfect model of the city in a scale of 1 to 240, with the walls of all the houses, the columns, and the fountains engraved and painted red. You can't get up close to it. Beyond a certain point you are stopped by a long railing. Only authorized personnel, equipped with pointers and if necessary tall ladders on wheels, can go near, point to, or touch the *forma Urbis*.

The three men we had seen arguing at the entrance to the building walk over to the model and point to a precise point, and then they turn to an employee sitting behind a desk. The question they are arguing about, we now understand, regards the dimensions and the property limits of a *taberna* that has been put up for sale. Calmly, the employee gives them a chip with a number engraved on it and points to another room where they can ask to consult a parchment copy of the sector they wish to examine. The three disappear down a corridor without ever stopping their argument.

The Temple of Peace also hosts a library on the exploits of Vespasian. Beyond that, it also conserves extraordinary works of art that the emperor brought to Rome from all over the Empire, particularly from the Hellenistic world. This Louvre of the capital also has many masterpieces of painting, which unfortunately have since been lost. The Romans have a great appreciation for this art form and there were a lot of expert critics and collectors, like today. The heart of the Temple of Peace is a room containing a large part of the spoils of war that were brought back from Jerusalem: one well-displayed symbolic object is the famous seven-armed candelabra, the menorah.

We are now outside of the Temple of Peace and we walk back across the sequence of imperial Forums in the opposite direction. There is still one that we haven't seen yet, which inhabitants of Rome consider without a doubt one of the wonders of the Empire. It's the last Forum to be built and it was completed just two years ago. It's Trajan's Forum and its impact is breathtaking. The first thing we see is a vast, curved wall, with a triumphal arch in the middle, topped by a chariot drawn by six horses. This is the entrance to Trajan's Forum.

Several armed guards are standing at attention, so as to underline the solemnity of the place. Through the arch, the immense piazza of the Forum appears before our eyes in all of its majesty: a rectangle 990 feet long and 630 feet wide, covered with great slabs of white and polychrome marbles. We are literally surrounded by one of the most beautiful colonnades in the Roman Empire. It's a long, long portico that runs along the perimeter of the piazza of the Forum—dozens and dozens of deep purple Corinthian columns. And that's not all; atop each column is a sculptured figure—statues almost ten feet high of captured barbarian princes. They are carved in different kinds of gorgeous marble and each statue has a different posture, some with their hair and beard ruffled by the wind. They are defeated Dacian princes. Everything that we see was built and crafted thanks to the enormous booty acquired through the conquest of Dacia (now Romania).

The center of the piazza is dominated by a statue of Trajan on horseback, in gilded bronze. We head toward the large structure that rises up at the other end of the piazza. It feels like we are walking toward the façade of St. Peter's Basilica, and in effect this, too, is a colossal construction: the Basilica Ulpia. Not a temple, therefore, but a building used for civic purposes, as in the other Forums. And what a building!

Everything about it is immense, gilded, princely. On the façade are more statues of barbarian prisoners of war, their hands tied. They form a long line like the line of saints on the colonnade in front of St. Peter's.

We go in. We are penetrating the perimeter of the largest basilica the Romans have built thus far. We feel disoriented by its dimensions, and by the height of the ceilings. Strangely enough, it's empty. For some reason, there are no hearings scheduled today and no other activities either. The only people walking through it are some employees and some curiosity-seekers like us, and the sounds of footsteps and voices re-echo through the interior as if someone were trying to take the measure of the oversized dimensions of the basilica.

It is really impressive: over 560 feet long with two great exedras, or semi-circular spaces, at either end. But what's really stunning is the wilderness of columns that surrounds us; it feels like we're inside a forest. It's impossible to count them all; there are dozens of them, extremely tall, with Corinthian capitals almost as big as small compact cars. They delineate

*Trajan's Forum, One of the Wonders of the Roman Empire.
The Imperial Forums constitute a veritable neighborhood of
Forums, each in communication with the others and with a constant traffic of people. It's a world dominated by luxury, marble,
and columns.*

five naves, and each set of columns is a different color! The ones bordering the central nave are in gray granite from Egypt; the ones along the smaller side naves are of pale green cipolin marble. Everything is decorated. The floor is covered in a checkerboard of marbles, with a geometric design of discs and rectangles with prevailing colors of antique yellow and deep purple. In the central nave there is also an imposing marble frieze representing winged victories. Over our heads are galleries and big windows with powerful rays of sunlight pouring through.

There is a small group of people at the far end of the hall with some praetorian guards forming a security cordon. Who is at the center of that group? The presence of praetorian guards means only one thing: it must be someone very important in the imperial inner circle. But who? The group is looking up at a portion of the coffered ceiling covered with stuccoes. One of them points to a water stain that has altered the colors. Evidently, they're assessing the damage done by water leaks caused by heavy rains.

Now the group moves and starts moving in our direction. The cleated *caligae* sandals of the praetorians echo through the hall and come closer and closer. But there are some other metallic noises too. The gladius swords and daggers clanging against the soldiers' armor. The group passes next to us. In the center, surrounded by secretaries and assistants, there's a small man, with short legs and arms, bald on top of his head, but with thick dark hair on the sides. His features are unmistakably Mediterranean and his voice is calm and sweet. He is Apollodorus of Damascus, the architect who designed the Basilica Ulpia (from Trajan's family name, Ulpius) and this extraordinary Forum. He is an ingenious architect, whose works will mark his era like the works of Brunelleschi and Michelangelo marked theirs. It took him only five years (from 107 to 112) to complete this enormous Forum. But he has also worked on other projects, such as Trajan's markets and baths. It's unfortunate that his relationship with Trajan's successor, Hadrian, will not be nearly so idyllic. On the contrary: Hadrian will send him into exile and in the end he'll have him executed. Meanwhile, the group has disappeared among the columns; the clinking of the praetorians' uniforms gradually fades away and is lost under the echoing footsteps of the people walking through the basilica.

We climb a flight of stairs up to the library. At the top of the stairs we run into a swarm of library staff with papyrus scrolls in hand and slaves pushing carts crammed with files. It looks like the hallway of some government ministry. Through a doorway we catch a glimpse of a long room with rows of shelves and cabinets that look like credenzas. They contain thousands of papyrus scrolls and tablets. The arrangement of the shelves is different from what we're used to; the open spaces don't form rectangles but rhomboids, so the scrolls can't roll sideways but sit one on top of the other like oranges at the market.

Opening a door, we see a balcony that runs around the inside of an inner courtyard. Leaning on the railing, we discover the reason for this curious structure designed by Apollodorus of Damascus. In the center of the courtyard sits the jewel of the entire Forum, placed there at the behest of the emperor himself: Trajan's Column.

It's 100 feet high and is topped by a gilded bronze statue of Trajan (replaced during the Renaissance by a statue of St. Peter, decidedly out of context). The column was erected by placing nineteen blocks of Carrara marble one on top of the other, each weighing thirty-two tons! The interior is hollow and contains a spiral staircase.

But the most impressive part of the column is its exterior, carved with a continuous frieze that spirals the entire length of the column, from the bottom to the top. In all it's 660 feet long and, like a comic strip, it shows the main events of two military campaigns (101 and 105 CE) which led to the annexation of Dacia as a Roman province. A series of frames depicts battles, legions fording rivers, sieges, Trajan making sacrifices to the gods, etc. There are thousands of finely carved, colored figures (especially legionnaires), often with real bronze arms in their hands. These vivid arms and colors will disappear over the centuries and in modern times we will see only a natural marble-colored column with its magnificent bas-reliefs.

We leave Trajan's Forum now to make our way back into the city. Just before leaving behind its gigantic piazza, we happen upon a touching scene: an old man squeezing the hands of a young man and a young woman, who embraces him, making him feel embarrassed. The two young people then fall into a long embrace, with a happiness that is moving, while the old man looks on, content. The three have just come out of a special office located here in Trajan's Forum, where manumissions, or the liberation of slaves, are registered. This old master, in fact, has come here to record the official end of their slavery for his two servants. From now on they will be free and, as in this case, they will be able to marry, something unthinkable when they were the simple property of their master, who decided if and with whom they could couple. Right in front of our eyes, the lives of two young people have changed forever.

CURIOSITY—*Forma Urbis*
the Marble Map of Rome's Land Registry

We know that under Augustus, Rome was subdivided into fourteen regions, the equivalent of the present-day districts of the capital, although their size and borders were much different. Each of these regions had its own administration. It wasn't so easy to simultaneously manage the lives of a million or a million and a half people. We don't know the details of this local government system, but we can easily imagine all of the difficulties. And that's the way it was for centuries. Over two hundred years later, for example, under Emperor Constantine, Rome had 423 streets, 29 large boulevards, 322 major intersections. Can you imagine the huge day to day responsibility of maintaining these streets, ensuring the proper functioning of their fountains that supplied water to the entire population, identifying and punishing unauthorized building, settling border disputes between neighboring businesses, and so on? All of this not only without telephones, computers, and databases but even without paper, pens, and ink.

Roman administrators had a precious instrument for their work. It was the equivalent of the land registry. During the shooting of one of my television programs, we took pictures of some of the sections of the city plan of the time, the famous *forma Urbis*, which reproduces the entire plan of the eternal city at ground level. So it is possible to discover the shape and size of shops, the depth of the colonnades, the tortuous curves of the streets, and even the exact locations of the fountains. We know about several versions of this map, corresponding to different epochs of imperial Rome. Unfortunately, only a few portions and fragments have survived until today, maybe enough to reconstruct a small part of the city. The rest was destroyed in the ovens of the Middle Ages or used to make walls.

But even just examining a few pieces helps us to understand

the richness of daily life in imperial Rome. For this book, I consulted some portions of the map in order to reconstruct my itineraries and my descriptions. Many of our glimpses of life on the streets of Rome are based on the real streets of the *forma Urbis*, and they respect the distances between buildings, the presence of colonnades, the location of shops and even the probable "bars" of the time. The beginning of our story, with that statue in the darkness of the street, reproduces a real section of the center of Rome. All I had to imagine were the features of the statue.

Certainly, some modifications of the city plan inevitably came about over time. Nevertheless, the overall arrangement of the streets and the neighborhoods remained as I have tried to describe it.

Looking at this map, we see that its accuracy is striking, a sign of the great expertise of those who recorded the floor plans of every shop, temple, and building. We have even found some pieces of the map that were discarded because of small errors. All of this helps us appreciate the rigor, almost to the point of fastidiousness, of the Roman authorities in the recording of information, which obviously helped them to exercise greater control over the city and more generally to improve their methods of land management.

RESTROOMS IN ANCIENT ROME

At a certain point in the life of imperial Rome, the city counted some 144 public latrines. And we're about to visit one of them. The latrines are easy to identify. Usually there is quite a lot of movement in the vicinity, like in our railway stations or highway rest stops. And generally, the people going in are in a hurry while the ones coming out seem a lot more relaxed. There are two people in line at the entrance, in front of a wooden counter with a slave behind it. We notice a terra-cotta plate on the countertop and almost immediately we hear the sound of a coin dropping and spinning around on itself. It's clear that you have to pay. But not very much, just a few pennies. Everyone always takes a little time to rummage around on the bottom of their leather bag dangling from their belt (the wallet of the Roman era).

Public latrines are pay toilets and they are managed by tax contractors, called *conductores foricarum*. Curiously, the public latrines gave rise to a Latin expression which is still frequently used in our own time: *pecunia non olet*, or "money doesn't smell." Actually, Vespasian introduced a tax on launderers who used urine in their laundries, collecting it from public latrines. Titus, Vespasian's son, protested this tax, which he felt was excessive and in dubious taste. His father's response was *"pecunia non olet."*

We pass by a narrow stair and then come to a large room, all decorated. There are even niches with statues of divinities. A stream of water cascades down along one wall and above it sits the goddess of Good Fortune, who presides over health and happiness. The stuccos and colors are those of a refined, almost luxurious, decor. But all you have to do is lower your eyes and the panorama changes abruptly: ten or so individuals, of all ages and classes, are seated, intent on explicating their bodily functions. The smell is the unpleasant one of a public toilet, but it doesn't seem to bother these people, who are sitting there as if they were in a waiting room. We discover that this is one of the social hubs of Rome, like the Forum. Some people are chatting, some are buttonholing their neighbor, and one of them attracts everybody's attention by telling a joke. There is even one among them, who, though under no pressure from physiological needs, sits down next to someone whose clothes clearly indicate his status among the well-to-do, and cleverly tries to procure himself an invitation to lunch. Everyone talks, interjects smart remarks, or, hidden from sight, leaves his mark in the form of a graffito. But everyone is careful about what they say or do; informers are everywhere in Rome.

The most amazing thing, or better, the utterly dumbfounding thing, is the total lack of privacy. There are no screens, curtains, or dividers that isolate people from each other. They are all seated on one long marble bench, one next to the other, as though they were waiting for the bus. The Roman concept of privacy is very different from our own and essentially is reserved for the wealthy; those who have the money to isolate themselves and live apart from the common people. In short, having a toilet in the home is a status symbol.

Naturally, none of us would feel relaxed in these places. It should be said, however, that the tunics help a great deal in keeping the private parts covered. Actually, the impression is that everybody is merely sitting down. But sitting on what? There are no toilet seats. The bench is flat, and the people are sitting over cylinder-shaped openings. Underneath the long bench is a deep canal, with running water that carries everything away. The function of these openings is clear. Somewhat less obvious is the function of another opening in the marble, located between the legs; it's a twin opening of the other and it joins it at knee level. What's it for?

We barely have time to ask ourselves the question when a man inadvertently shows us the answer. In the middle of the room there are three tubs filled with water, with a lot of wooden sticks in them. The man reaches out and grabs one of them. We discover in this way that the stick has a sponge attached to one end; it looks almost like a torch. The man sticks the "torch" between his legs and uses the sponge as toilet paper. Not content, he dips it again into the water of a small canal carved into the floor. We hadn't noticed it, it almost seems like an artificial stream, running by everybody's feet. The man thus proceeds in the task of washing himself, similar to the way one uses a bidet. Then, rubbing the sponge on the inside edge of the opening, he detaches the sponge and lets it fall into the sewer. Finally, he puts the stick back in its place, in the marble tub in front of him. During this entire operation, he has never stopped chatting with his neighbor on the bench.

This is the way most of the inhabitants of Rome take care of their bodily needs. As we said earlier, very few Romans have a toilet in their homes. For those who don't want to or can't pay, the solution—at least for the smaller needs—is to be found in the big jars located at street corners or on the side of the street (as can be seen in Pompeii), which are then used by laundries.

Latrines like these are located pretty much all over the city. From the portico of Pompeus to the foyer of the Theater of Balbo. It's really amazing that you can see under the porticos, right in front of the people passing by, a wealthy businessman, a praetorian guard, then a freed slave, a young lawyer, and so on, each taking care of his bodily needs with a totally natural attitude.

A latrine in Rome. Sponges soaked in water are used as toilet paper. The total lack of privacy is striking; people chat, button-hole their neighbors, tell jokes. It's one of the social hubs in Rome, like the Forum and the public baths.

Some latrines are even heated in winter, with an underground central heating system similar to those used in the public baths. That's the case for the latrine located in the heart of the city, between the Roman Forum and the Forum of Julius Caesar. It gets very crowded on cold days.

But where does the solid-waste water end up? The polluted water flows through a complex system of underground pipes, which combine to form a veritable sewer network under the streets and buildings of Rome. Their construction was begun as far back as the sixth century BCE. According to some ancient authors, in certain places the collection pipes are big enough that two hay wagons could pass each other. One famous inspection, conducted by Agrippa, led to considerable improvements in the sewer system during the reign of Augustus. It seems that he even used a boat to inspect some of its segments.

The star of this surprising monument of hydraulic engineering is the Cloaca Maxima, the main sewer of Rome (still partially functioning in modern times). Initially, it was an open-air canal. Then in the Republican era it was covered. It is about half a mile long but it does not run in a straight line due to the constructions located above ground.

The dimensions of the Cloaca Maxima are awesome. In some places it seems like a proper tunnel, more than 15 feet in diameter. Its purpose is to collect not only solid-waste water but also the overflow from the aqueducts, the water discharge from the baths, the fountains and, obviously, rain water.

In this regard, we should mention that the streets of Rome have their characteristic "donkey back" shape to allow the rainwater to wash them and run off to the sides, where it is then swallowed up by drains (an ingenious street cleaning system, therefore, which, surprisingly, is still used today in cities all over the world). The drains are just about everywhere, and they often have the form of a river goddess with a half-open mouth that swallows the rain water. One of these drain covers has become famous all over the world, and is certainly the most photographed one in history: the Mouth of Truth, immortalized in the celebrated film *Roman Holiday* with Gregory Peck and Audrey Hepburn.

The Cloaca Maxima dumps all of its contents into the Tiber, just below the Tiberina Island. And this is where the only problem with this sewer system might show up. When the Tiber is at flood level, its waters rise and run into the Cloaca Maxima, blocking, or better, inverting the sewer flow. In such cases, the sewer water can be pushed back where it came from and start to pour out of the drain covers, gutters, and latrines. Obviously, the sewer system is not sufficient for the entire city of a million or a million and a half residents, so a lot of drains end up in simple septic tanks. These tanks are emptied regularly (we prefer not to imagine the working conditions) and their contents are recycled as fertilizer.

Rome's impressive sewer system, comparable to the kidneys of a human being, is an incredibly sophisticated concept. The ever pragmatic Romans understood right from the start that no great human concentration can exist without an efficient sewer system. And this speaks volumes about a civilization that still had not discovered bacteria but demonstrated its understanding of the fundamental importance of hygiene and cleanliness simply by making the best use of water (something never achieved in the Middle Ages and, even today, not achieved in much of the Third World).

Childbirth in Rome

Her forehead is beaded with sweat. She squeezes her eyes shut with every contraction, and a vein in her throat seems just about to pop under the stress. She's sitting on a high-backed wicker chair, her hands digging like claws into the arms. A scream rings out through the entire house, breaking the tension that has been blocking all activity for hours. The slaves sit motionless in silence in various parts of the *domus*. One of them, a recently purchased man of color, opens his eyes wide and stares at a Middle Eastern colleague who replies with a hint of a reassuring smile, narrowing his eyelids. It's not the first time that the mistress of the house has given birth; nevertheless, there are great expectations. After three girls, everyone in the house is hoping that this time it will be a boy. The master of the house has to have a male heir for his properties and his business.

There's another woman in the room, which has been specially arranged for the birth, along with several trusted maidservants. Her hair is pulled back and she's squatting between the legs of the mistress, giving her some advice on how to breathe. One of her assistants, perhaps her daughter, embraces the expectant mother from behind, pushing her womb downward with each contraction. Some instruments and compresses lie on a nearby table in case of hemorrhaging. The midwife's name is Scribonia Attice and she has come especially from Ostia to help assist at the birth. She was called by a friend of the family, who considers her a genuine guarantee when it comes to important births. The friend himself is a well known *archiatrus*, a sort of chief physician. It must be said that births are almost always presided over by midwives, almost never by male doctors; this is an expression of a sort of old-fashioned modesty, but also of unwillingness on the part of husbands to see another man touching their wives' intimate parts. And it will be that way for a long time to come: the feminine sphere and gynecological medicine will remain in the hands of midwives and female doctors.

The midwife's husband is a surgeon, and he too is at work, in another room of the house. The surgeon's name is Marcus Ulpius Amerimmus. He's about forty years old and well respected. He's now performing a phlebotomy on the leg of the brother of the master of the house. Bloodletting was very much the fashion in the Roman era. The blood is collected in a metal container and then taken away by a slave. As the surgeon dresses the wound in a tight bandage, he turns toward the *archiatrus*, who hasn't taken his eyes off him for a minute; he's the one who taught him this technique. The chief physician observes the dressing, then gives his younger colleague a look of satisfaction, and emits a lapidary phrase, "Life is short, art is long," as though to emphasize that the art of medicine and its techniques are handed down from generation to generation and are passed on by each physician to his disciples.

But let's go back to the delivery room. We're just about there. The expectant mother is at one with the gestatorial chair (so it's called). In the Roman age, childbirth takes place in the sitting position. No epidural anesthesia, no sterilized equipment, only some mild pain relievers when necessary. Throughout the entire classical period (and up until the very recent past) childbirth is a woman's greatest risk. She knows that she may not come out of it alive because of hemorrhaging and infections (whose origin is unknown to the Romans since they are unaware of the existence of bacteria and viruses). Even today, in Africa, one woman in twenty dies in childbirth. In industrialized societies, the statistic is one in 2,800.

"Just one more push," shouts Scribonia Attice. It doesn't take much to get the fourth child out. In just a few seconds, his head with its black hair is already out, but his umbilical cord is wrapped around his neck. An extremely dangerous complication; the baby has suffered from lack of oxygen; the color of the face and body, as it slithers out, is almost maroon. Intuiting the gravity of the situation, the midwife's daughter opens her eyes wide; the baby's not breathing, not moving. And his coloring is not normal. And what's more, it's a boy! How to justify to a father, so anxious for a male heir, a death such as this? He will certainly accuse her and her mother of malpractice. Meanwhile, Scribonia Attice proceeds mechanically. She has obviously gone through the same reasoning and she's going to give it everything she has to try to save the infant. She's taken him by the feet, but he's swinging back and forth like an inanimate rag. She turns him, taps him on the back, first gently and then increasingly forcefully. She has to stimulate the breathing reflex or it will be too late. The mother looks on helplessly at the drama being played out in front of her eyes. She can't even feel the grip of the midwife's daughter anymore, squeezing her too tight with tension. "Save him!" she shouts. She barely finishes the phrase when the newborn is suddenly overtaken by a contortion, seems to gasp, and then emits a violent wail. His little diaphragm contracts rhythmically for the first few breaths, and an influx of burning air enters his minuscule lungs for the first time. His powerful wailing echoes throughout the entire house. The little one is saved. Everyone smiles, even the *dominus*, sitting with some relatives drinking wine. No one knows, nor will they ever know, about the tragedy that nearly came to pass in that bedroom.

The description that we've given is obviously imaginary. But in essence it's quite plausible, because the midwife

Scribonia Attice really lived, and so did her husband, the surgeon Marcus Ulpius Amerimmus. How do we know? Thanks to their tombstones, which have come to light in the necropolis of Portus, near Ostia. Their final resting places were both marked by a slab of terra-cotta, which held a portrait of them at work. When I saw it I was struck by the precision of the scenes represented. Despite their simplicity, they look almost like photographs. The midwife is sitting in front of a woman in childbirth on a gestatorial chair, with an assistant holding her from behind. Exactly what we just saw. The surgeon, on the other hand, is squatting down as he does a bloodletting on a man's leg (unfortunately, the tablet is broken, preventing us from seeing their faces).

These tombs date back to 140 CE, so they are from the same Roman era that we are exploring. Twenty-five years earlier the midwife and the surgeon must have been at the height of their careers. And probably they came to Rome often, called to render their services. I have imagined that this delivery was arranged by the *archiatrus*, the chief physician. Actually, the tomb of this important personality was also discovered not far from the tombs of the other two. His name was Caius Marcius Demetrius. His tomb bears the epitaph "Life is short, art is long." Who knows, maybe it was a phrase he liked to repeat to his disciples.

Will he live to be a citizen of Rome or die in a garbage dump?
Let's go back to the scene of the birth. The *dominus* will now have his male heir, extremely important in a masculinist society like Rome. And we can also imagine what will happen in just a few minutes: they'll wash the baby, cut the umbilical cord, and take him to his father. He will be standing in the middle of the room. His son will be set down on the floor at his feet. At this point, it will only take a few seconds for the fate of the little one to be decided, in accordance with an ancient ritual. If

his father bends down to pick him up and raises him up high before all of his relatives, it will constitute an acknowledgment of his paternity, and the son will be accepted into the family. If, on the other hand, the father remains impassive and does not raise him up, the son will not be accepted into the family.

There are many reasons for this: too many children of the same sex already in the family; too many children to support (especially in poor families); rape; the suspicion that the child is the product of a betrayal or is affected by evident malformations or defects. What will happen at this point? The woman who set the child down on the floor will pick him up and take him away. Very often this will be done by the midwife herself, and many people in ancient Rome consider midwives to be the linchpins in a system of infant trafficking, including exchanges of babies at birth, in order to satisfy the desires of families who are hoping for a boy or a girl. Or for families who have had a child with birth defects.

The fate of unwanted babies is truly terrible. In the best of cases they are placed at certain designated locations on the streets of Rome, the ancient equivalent of Medieval foundling wheels or modern baby hatches, where mothers could safely abandon their newborn children. The Roman historian Festus informs us that near the fruit and vegetable market, the Forum Olitorius, there was a column with precisely this function. Appropriately enough, it was known as the *columna lactaria* because, according to Festus, infants in need of breastfeeding were found there every morning. They are well covered and have identifying marks so that the families of the foundlings will be able to reclaim them in the future. Naturally, in such cases they will have to pay a sum to cover the costs of raising the child.

Paternity was demonstrated through the use of coins or medals cut in half so that the half retained by the family would match perfectly the other half, which was attached to the infant. This system was used for centuries, and it is likely that it was still in use at the time of Trajan.

The peril is that the people who take the child in are free to do whatever they want: if it's a girl, raise her to be a prostitute, if it's a boy, raise him to be a slave or a servant.

In this enormous city, there are even those who have turned the traffic in infants into a profession. Each morning they go around to the designated locations for foundlings, collect them, and sell them for a profit. Some of these traders, just as happens today in India or other poverty-stricken countries, break the infant's legs or blind them so that when they send the children out to beg, passersby will take pity on them and increase the profits of their masters.

But the fate of these unwanted babies can be even worse. As we learn from Seneca, quite often babies who are deformed or premature are smothered to death or drowned. Others, taken secretly to a dump or a little-known side street, are abandoned among the garbage or trash on the street to die of malnutrition or cold or even to be devoured by stray dogs.

But there are also cases of good luck, where foundlings are taken in and raised with love by parents who for one reason or another have no children of their own. And somewhere in Rome on this morning in 115 CE, one such fortunate son may have already found a new home.

12:20 PM

AN ENCOUNTER WITH TACITUS

The street we're walking down, the Argiletum, is on the edge of the most popular part of Rome: the Suburra. Curiously, the Suburra is right next to the Imperial Forums—two extremes, side by side. On one side luxury, precious marble, the symbols of the power and the history of Rome. On the other (just a few yards away) history with a lowercase "h"; a humble world of poverty, where the working classes live. You can see that clearly by the way people are dressed, by the dirt and trash on the street, by the kind of shops, where more economical goods are for sale.

A high wall made of peperino marble, a sort of Berlin Wall, separates the Suburra from the Forum of Augustus. It's a fire wall to protect this important location from possible (and very frequent) fires. When the city of Rome nearly burned to the ground in the famous fire during the reign of Nero, this Forum was saved thanks to this wall, which held back the flames, transforming the Forum into an island; it also saved many of the city's inhabitants.

The street we're on now, even though it's in a poor neighborhood, is also deeply tied to the culture of Rome. This is the street of many bookshops and bookmaking workshops. If you want to find the works of the great Roman writers, from Cicero to Virgil to Martial, this is where you have to come.

A lot of shops have signs outside, and often there are inscriptions etched into the walls on the sides of the entrances.

These shops are generally managed by *liberti* and are known to customers by the names of these former slaves.

So we walk by the rather modest shops of Atrectus and Secundus. Just ahead are those of the Sosi brothers and the Dora family. We notice one especially well-stocked shop, run by the *liberto* Atreccius. It's very large and the walls are covered with bookcases full of literary works. Some are in the form of papyrus scrolls (the *volumnia*), often displayed in protective containers, little pails made of leather and covered by lids (*capsae*). Others are small pocket books with pages made of parchment. And then there are the ubiquitous wooden tablets; every page is a wax "basin" where the text has been written, or, better, etched, using a bronze tip that scratches the surface. (Usually these are short works, such as poems.)

We go in and walk over to one of the shelves. Delicately, we take one of the books off the shelf and try to leaf through it. But as soon as we open it, the pages suddenly unravel, down to the floor. The pages of many works, in fact, are like accordions, that is, the pages are not bound but are composed of a single long strip of folded linen, and they look a little like those booklets of postcards that are sold in our souvenir stores.

The cold stare of an employee strikes us from the other side of the bookshelf. As we put everything back in order, we discover how these books are read. The pages flow in the opposite direction of our books; they go from right to left. A double red line separates the columns of text. Each fold corresponds to one page .

We go out of the store. As we walk along, we see several people coming out of other bookshops carrying rolls of short works. One bookshop looks especially important; it's the Trajan-era equivalent of one of our downtown bookshops. It's owned by Trifone, and its walls are covered with advertisements announcing the sale of volumes by various authors. Outside the shop there is also a litter in waiting, with two soldiers chatting, a sign that there's someone important inside. We stick our heads into the store. Inside, among the bookshelves, we can also see Trifone's printer's room. Gutenberg and his moveable type are still a long way off. Here, everything is done by hand. Rows of scrivener slaves are writing numerous copies of the works, under dictation. They're bent over their desks, a little like medieval monks.

What we're looking at is the last act in the making of a book. First the authors write them in their own homes, then they have them read by friends and acquaintances to check for possible errors or inexactitudes, or even to estimate the impact of their ideas. Pliny the Younger went one step further; he would read his books out loud to small audiences of listeners. According to him, it was during such public readings that he actually made the most important corrections and revisions of the text. Finally, the work is delivered to the human printing presses, where, day after day, under the lantern light, the book takes shape; a true work of craftsmen rather than an industrial product. If we had written this book at the time of Trajan, we would have had to go through this same process.

It's easy to see that the time needed to get a book "into print" in ancient Rome is quite long, but the *liberti* who run these stores have the same market sense of modern publishers and if they think a work is a potential best seller, they suspend all their "production lines" and concentrate the work of all their scrivener slaves on that book.

While we're thinking about all this, we notice a man at the back of the shop who pulls back the curtain separating the shop from the back room and holds it open. He's tall, bald, and bearded, with hollow cheeks and deep-set eyes. It's Trifone, the manager of this bookshop-printer's. As he talks, he holds the curtain open to let his listener past. From the few words we're able to hear, they are discussing the production time of a work the scriveners are already "printing." Evidently, his listener, who still hasn't emerged, is an author. We guess that's he's worried; his work is composed of many volumes and he doesn't want the publishing process to take too long. Trifone tries to soothe him, but he does it with extreme deference; it seems almost like he's taking orders. The author must be a very important celebrity, especially considering the litter and the guards waiting for him at the entrance. Who can it be?

We try to get closer to one of the scrivener slaves, an Egyptian. He's writing a text under the light of a lantern in neat, careful calligraphy. The shadow of his hand and fingers seems to be dancing and almost making pirouettes. Opposite him, on a lectern, is a page of the original manuscript, which he treats with infinite care. At his side, on the bench, are two bound wooden tablets, used to protect the original manuscript pages.

Bowing our heads, we try to read the title of the work— *Annales (Ab excessu Divi Augusti libri)*. It's Tacitus! So, that man with the curly gray hair, with those penetrating green eyes, who is now leaving the store, is the great historian! Not only does he live in the same period that we're exploring but in just a few months, in the year 116, his great work, the *Annals*, will be published. It's the last stage of a long journey through history in which he essentially denounces the evils and decadence of the empire.

We realize that the work is emerging on the page right before our eyes, and that the book that the slave is copying Tacitus's the tenth. It's one of the books that has not come down to us; who knows what's written in it. We remain dumbfounded, motionless. Tacitus turns the corner, bids farewell to Trifone, and climbs into his litter. Only now do we remember that he's not only a great historian but that he has also been a lawyer, quaestor, magistrate, consul, and proconsul. And that explains the escort. The litter begins to move and "floats" through the crowd.

In this same moment, just a few hundred yards away, the last act in the life of a man is about to be played out. It's all going to take place right in front of the eyes of thousands of people, in the middle of the Colosseum.

The Colosseum, Hour of Torment

The guard holds him by one arm and squeezes it tight, almost as though he were afraid he might escape. But where can he go? By now he's imprisoned in a cage, a few yards from the arena of the Colosseum. All around him tens of thousands of people are shouting, laughing, clapping their hands, in an uproar that reaches this cold, dark corridor as a deformed, discordant din. It's as though he were in a gigantic animal trap, with no chance of escape. It would be better to let himself be killed right away with the blade of a sword. But no one's going to do that; on the contrary, he's going to have to die in atrocious pain: he's going to die by being eaten alive! Up to now, his prevailing feeling has been resignation. Even since the judges at his trial had handed down the sentence, everything has followed a precise track, frighteningly well-oiled. He was carried off by the guards, put on a wagon, and led into the cells. Along the way, people insulted him, struck him with stones, spit, even excrement; he's undergone every imaginable outrage. Confusion reigned inside in his head; his brain tried to come to terms with the situation, to find some way out. But it was too late. It was as if some perverse mechanism was driving him toward a precipice, and there was no way he could stop it.

The prisoner knows that humiliation is part of his punishment. He has seen it so many times himself, watching processions of men condemned to death. And he too derided them, threw stones. Now it's his turn. And unfortunately, he knows how it's going to end. He has prepared himself for death these past few days. But now that he's facing it, a feeling of panic is welling up inside his chest, an unbearable mental pain, desperation. He's becoming increasingly short of breath; his face is turning chalk white as the gate of his cage covers his body in a shroud of grated shadows. His only clothing is a kind of rough textured skirt with fringe. The guard senses his emotional state and tightens his grip, smiling. By now he's had a long experience with prisoners condemned to death, and he knows that this is one of the most dangerous moments.

The sentence had been *damnatio ad bestias*. When he heard those words, the world collapsed on the prisoner's shoulders. Yet he should have imagined that it would end like that. Years of exploitation and corruption had given him an audacious sense of impunity. They had made him think he could be stronger than the system that had brought him to Rome from North Africa, present-day Algeria, in chains. For years he had been a slave, and once he'd been freed he'd begun his climb. He had driven numerous people out of house and home, entire families who from one day to the next found themselves living on the street. And he, the usurer, had spared no one. So many times people had come to him to beg for postponements and pity. But he felt a deep sense of pleasure in telling them no. Maybe even for a kind of vendetta. He had become brutal, cynical, and added violence to humiliation; those who didn't pay were beaten, then (with the help of corrupt officials) their goods were confiscated and divided up among his accomplices. The daughters and wives of his victims often had to pay the usurious interest in sexual favors. His power seemed to have no limit; wealth, banquets, important guests. By now he was expecting to make it to the top of Roman society. Then, one morning, it all came suddenly tumbling down.

He'd been done in by just one official who'd spilled the beans. The guards arrived at dawn, carrying torches. They hauled him off to jail, interrogated him, put him on the rack.

Then the first timid witnesses started talking. A lot of people wouldn'tsay anything, out of shame, but a lot of people did. So part of the mountain of evil deeds done by this former slave to the harm of Roman citizens actually came to light. Intolerable behavior. The sentence could not have been otherwise. And now here he is, his knees trembling, a few seconds from the end.

The guard has taken a step back and been replaced by two men covered by a sort of heavy leather athletic suit. Their heads are also covered by a strange, thick leather hood, with a helmet on the inside. They look a bit like Icelandic fishermen. They are specialists in executions, slaves assigned the task of pushing the condemned man toward the wild beasts. Those strange, blood-spattered clothes are their protection; on the inside they are lined with heavy padding, similar to the gloves worn by present-day trainers of guard dogs.

Suddenly, the cage door is thrown open, and a violent thrust sends the prisoner into the arena. Outside, the flash of sunlight instantly blinds him. He grimaces; he can't manage to cover his face because his hands have been tied behind his back. He can barely hear the roar of the crowd. He's viewed this scene at the Colosseum so many times, and he never would have thought that one day the condemned man in the middle of the arena would be him.

The two executioners push him from behind to get him to run. An instant before the cage opened, they looked each other in the eyes and decided to make this type of entrance on the scene—in part to get the attention of the audience and in part to make them laugh. Years of idleness, in fact, have made the *liberto* fat. The sight of this man incapable of running, with his belly swaying back and forth at every step, his eyes wide open, the crazed look on his face, sends a wave of howling laughter through the grandstands, followed by whistles of scorn. Many of the usurer's victims are in the audience. Some of them are cheering, venting years of humiliation; others remain seated in silence.

Now the trio has slowed the pace and they head toward the lion with the imposing dark mane, who turns and stares at them. As chance would have it, he too, like the *liberto*, comes from North Africa. The lion is not new to these meals in the arena. But he seems to delay. An assistant promptly prods him with a long pole. The lion jumps and lets out a roar at this provocation. Prodded again, he heads off with determination toward the prisoner. With each step, his powerful muscles ripple under his skin.

The man can see his end coming to get him. The lions have enormous heads but what makes them really scary are those bright hazelnut-brown eyes that look like they've been injected with flames. There's nothing in those eyes but ruthlessness.

The condemned man screams at the top of his lungs, stiffens, digs his heels into the ground. But the two executioners are stronger than he is. One of them grabs him deftly by his curly hair and pushes his head forward, as though he were baiting the beast. The second one hides behind his back, like someone leaning against a door to keep it from being battered down. In this position, he pushes him forward. He holds him tight by the hands and waits for the impact, his lowered head covered by his hood.

The lion's final steps are increasingly rapid, but what's really striking is the absolute silence of his movements. The condemned man screams and at the last minute closes his eyes and turns his head. The second the lion leaves the ground on his final jump, the audience sinks into a stony silence.

It all happens in a flash. The executioners release him and run away. The flashing white of the lion's teeth. The condemned man feels the hot breath on his face and then he's bowled over by the mass of his predator.

The audience exults. But the spectacle is horrifying. The

lion has sunk his teeth into the skin between the face and neck of his victim. His teeth have penetrated deep, shattering the bones that support the face and nose, and devastating the orbit. In a single bite he has ripped off half the man's face, tearing the skin and biting into his nose, cheek, cheekbone, and eye, which pops out. The man is a monstrous mask of blood; the nearest spectators are stunned at the sight of a man missing half of his face, but still alive, still screaming, still thrashing around on the ground. The lion keeps him pinned down, like a wrestler, his claws digging into his chest and shoulder. And he looks at the crowd, his muzzle red with blood, his jaws half open. He seems to be asking for consent. A new prod from the assistant convinces him to finish the job. It looks as though he's taking out the pain from the prodding on his victim. He grabs him by the neck and shakes him ferociously. The man's body has stopped moving, his neck is broken, his head hangs down to one side in an unnatural position. A few brief spasms of the legs signal the end of his life. Now the lion starts ripping open his guts . . .

CURIOSITY—Death as Spectacle

The spectacle we have just witnessed is the norm in all the cities of the Roman Empire. It makes you wonder if the Romans were a bit inhuman, people often say. In reality, we need to keep a couple of things in mind. First of all, the times. That was life back then. The Etruscans performed human sacrifice. The Celts, so much the fashion in recent times, were in the habit of cutting off the heads of their defeated enemies (even fellow Gauls) and nailing them to the beams of their houses, like hunting trophies. When the enemies were particularly valorous, their heads were impregnated with cedar oil and preserved for generations.

Heads and skulls were displayed on the entrances to villages or in sacred places (as in Entremont). An impressive example can be seen today in Marseilles, in the Borély museum, where a stone architrave of a famous Celtic shrine, found in Roquepertuse in the south of France, is on exhibit. It has a number of niches where heads removed from the tribe's most dangerous enemies were put on display.

Around the same time, the career advancement of Chinese soldiers depended on the number of heads they cut off (for practical reasons, the accomplishment could be proved by presenting two sliced-off ears back at the camp). In Central America, the Aztecs sold enemy slaves to be used in sacrifices. And so on.

The Romans, in short, belonged to a world very different from our own. The Colosseum was the place for public executions, something which continued to exist in our society until very recent times. France had the guillotine, England the gallows. And every time the execution was held in front of a crowd, as a warning. In the Rome of the Papal State, there were several places for public executions, each with its own prescribed method: in the Campo de' Fiori heretics were burned at the stake; in Trastevere, the condemned person's hands were cut off; Castel Sant'Angelo was the place for hangings, quarterings, and decapitations. In Piazza del Popolo executions, which were often included as part of the Mardi Gras celebrations, were conducted in a truly horrifying manner: victims were hammered to death. Starting in 1826, the guillotine became the method of choice, judged to be less inhuman.

To be sure, the Romans did something that no one had ever done before: transform torture into spectacle. If you want to see the modern version of this same phenomenon, all you have to do is watch television programs based on real-life accidents, chase scenes, and murders: suffering (or death) as spectacle, bloodshed to attract an audience.

By extension, the movies and television dramas with violence, death, and shootouts that can now be seen at any hour of the day or night on TV constitute the modern equivalent of the performances in the Colosseum.

But what did those performances consist of? There were a lot of different shows, some of them quite shocking. There were the most simple killings, like the one we've just described. Other times, the condemned men were tied to poles fixed to carts shaped like small chariots and pushed toward the wild animals. The gushing blood depicted in Roman mosaics indicates that these were indeed violent spectacles.

The audience knew that the executions often held some surprises, and that only helped to raise expectations. Sometimes the organizers would set up ingenious stage sets and conduct the execution according to a mythological or historical script, applying the same principle as a *tableau vivant*, or our contemporary living crèches. And so, there's Icarus attempting to fly; the condemned man imitates the unhappy flight and leaps into the void, splattering onto the ground and squirting blood as high as the emperor's box. That's how Suetonius recounts it.

We know of condemned men forced to reenact the feat of Mucius Scaevola, who burned one of his hands in a fire, or others forced to relive the self-emasculation of Attis, or the torture of Ixion who was fixed to a wheel that was set aflame.

Martial recounts, on the other hand, that the inauguration ceremonies for the Colosseum included a show based on the myth of Orpheus, who, desperate over the death of Eurydice, succeeded with his song in calming the wild beasts. The condemned man was placed in the arena surrounded by a theater set of rocks and trees which gradually rose up from the underground (one of the many special effects) together with numerous wild beasts. Unfortunately, Orpheus couldn't manage to placate a bear, and amid the hilarity of the crowd "the singer was torn to pieces by an ingrate bear," as Martial puts it.

Another theatrical execution was inspired by the myth of Prometheus, who gave man the gift of fire and was punished by being chained by the gods to a rock, with an eagle who came regularly to eat his liver. The condemned man was mangled by a bear brought from Caledonia (Scotland).

No less cruel was the fate, during Nero's reign, of a woman who was forced to interpret the myth of the birth of the Minotaur, by impersonating Queen Pasiphae of Crete as she coupled with the bull of Poseidon. We know that this type of public execution was enacted on more than one occasion, notoriously under Titus.

But there were also actors who entertained the public by enacting dangerous exploits with the animals. Rather than criminals condemned to death, they were acrobats who tried to survive the attacks of bears and lions with skill, hiding behind revolving doors (similar to those in hotels) or inside of baskets that rotated around a pole. And there were others who, with the help of a pole, jumped over the bears or climbed onto fragile scaffolds with the beasts circling menacingly underneath.

Among the various forms of the death sentence was the so-called *damnation ad gladium* (condemned to combat)—a truly perverse form of public execution that consisted of putting two condemned men opposite each other, outfitting them with a gladius and ordering them to fight to their death. The winner then had to fight another condemned man, and so on.

Finally, to this gallery of horrors of execution used as entertainment, we must add death by fire.

In these cases, the victims were forced to put on clothes soaked in flammable substances. The objective was to provoke dancing that was then transformed into tragedy. With their clothes on fire, the condemned moved from dance to contortions, dying from burns inflicted by the flames.

Many Christians were killed by the flames under Nero. They were tied at the neck to a stake so they couldn't move, then bundles of resinous branches, made from papyrus and wax, were placed at their feet, and a fire was lighted.

In this regard, it must be noted that, contrary to what has been believed, no Christians were killed at the Colosseum during Nero's persecutions. In fact, the Colosseum didn't exist yet. Nero's executions took place in another location: in his private hippodrome for chariot races. It was located where the Vatican is today. Many Christians were put to their death with all kinds of torture (covered with animal skins and dismembered by dogs, crucified, or burned alive). According to tradition, Saint Peter was killed and buried here too and that's why the basilica dedicated to him was built on this site. Many Christians were persecuted and killed in other eras as well, but we have no news of this happening in the Colosseum. The persecutions took place mainly in amphitheaters scattered throughout the Empire.

FOR LUNCH, A SNACK AT THE BAR

We're back out on the streets of Rome. We've distractedly taken to following three slaves who walk in single file, each carrying an amphora on his back, holding it by the handle on the side. Evidently, they're making deliveries. Despite the heavy weight, they move nimbly through the crowd in the porticos. People step aside to let them pass and we take advantage of their wake to slip in behind them. With this trick, moving through the porticos becomes a lot easier. Off to the side, we can see the open shop doors, the front entrances to the *insulae*, and so on. Suddenly, one of three comes to a halt; he's arrived. It's the entrance to a *caupona*, a hotel. After being recognized by the manager, he vanishes inside. The other two slaves wait for him, putting their amphorae down on the ground to catch their breath. We take a fast look around to see what this Roman era hotel is like. Naturally, here too there are various levels of quality (the equivalent of our star ratings), but essentially what we find is quite familiar.

Like our hotels, for example, this *caupona* has a restaurant on the lower floor and bedrooms on the upper floor. It even has a "garage" (a stable) for the guests' horses. From the street we get a glimpse of four rooms with *triclinium* couches, one of which is in use. Strange at his hour, because a *triclinium* is generally used in the evening for important dinners, and not during the day. Maybe they're celebrating something or maybe it's a working lunch . . . A maidservant comes out of the *triclinium* holding a pitcher and pulls the purple curtain closed, obscuring our view. The diners have thus reclaimed their privacy.

We go back to following our three slaves. We cross an intersection, making use of the typical Roman zebra-stripe pedestrian crossings, large stones placed one after the other across the road. They are essential on rainy days; when the streets are transformed into streams because of the slope (often deliberately engineered so the rainwater will clean the pavement), these rocks allow pedestrians to cross the street without getting their feet wet. Exactly the way you do with rocks arranged in a line across a stream.

When it comes right down to it, the streets we've been walking down remind us of our own; sidewalks and lines of shops on both sides. We notice that the places where there are more people milling around on the sidewalk, and where it's most difficult for the three slaves to get by correspond to taverns. In effect, it's lunchtime, and these places are starting to attract crowds, just as in our own time.

Second stop. This time it's at a wine shop. It consists of a long counter with some amphorae lined up against the wall in a corner and a number of small pitchers hanging in the entrance from a long bronze rod. Wine is served here with simple things to eat on the run. Above all, you eat standing up and quickly. All of this reminds us of something Italians know quite well: our coffee bars. At lunch time, we might get half a sandwich and something to drink. Here, the people order the equivalent: a cup of wine and a focaccia bun. The difference is that we almost always conclude our snack with a cup of coffee; the Romans, no, as it still doesn't exist.

What's striking about this locale is a sort of wooden rack hanging from the ceiling along one wall, with eight amphorae sitting in it. They are the equivalent of the bottles on display behind the bartender in the modern era. The manager removes an empty and, helped by one of our slaves, replaces it with one of the ones they've delivered. As they carry out this operation under the curious eyes of the customers (one of whom, however, remains impassive, his eyes tinged with red and his head swaying a little from the effect of the wine he's been drinking), we notice that the locale has the same dimensions as a normal *taberna*. It's no accident that this type of locale is called a *taberna vinaria*, a term that has come down through the centuries giving rise to our word "tavern," which has exactly the same meaning. Having loaded the empty amphora, the trio now continues on its way, with us right behind. There's one more amphora to deliver. Let's see where it takes us.

We go through the Portico of Livia and come to an intersection. The three slaves stop here. They have arrived at their destination. The corner of the intersection is occupied by a big eating place. It's located in a decidedly strategic spot; it has two entrances, one on each of the converging streets. Unlike the tavern that we've just seen, here you can eat and drink sitting down.

In modern times, you'll hear guides in archaeological sites refer to the ruins of one of these locales with the name of *thermopolium*. In reality, if you ask any Roman to show you a *thermopolium*, he won't understand and his eyes will open wide. Actually, it's a Greek word that no one uses in imperial Rome; the word they use here is *popina*.

A lot of people are eating outside of the locale, sitting at counters lined up along the wall, creating more than a few problems for passersby (exactly what happens today as a result of outdoor tables at bars and restaurants in the center city). The advantage for the owner is that this way he can serve more people and increase his profits. The advantage for the customers is that they can eat while they watch the people and everything else that's happening on the street, as though it were a documentary.

Lunch hour. This is what a Roman popina *looks like, with its typical L-shaped marble counter. The waiters take food and wine from the openings in the counter. A Roman lunch is very simple: eggs, olives, cheese, figs.*

Let's go in and take a look around. Even before we go in we're hit by the smell of the cooking food, which makes our mouth water. Especially the smell of meat cooking together with a little branch of rosemary.

The initial sensation is that of entering one of modern Rome's *osterie,* or *trattorie*, sort of like a diner or a neighborhood bar in America. The room is big and there are a lot of tables with people sitting at them and eating. The patrons include both men and women. Stemming the flow of traffic at the entrance is a long L-shaped counter, faced with slabs of white marble with blue veins.

The short side of the L looks directly out on the street, a little like the counters in our ice-cream shops, and a girl distributes plates and glasses to the lined-up customers. She's very pretty, the owner knows it well, that's why he's put her in that position, to act as a lure for passersby. She works very quickly, and she often takes pitchers and glasses sitting on a sort of small marble stair on the right side of the counter, where it meets the wall. But what really interests the male customers is when the girl bends forward over the counter. That's when they can look down and get a very generous view of her cleavage.

The girl leans forward frequently, not to put on a show, but because in the middle of the counter there's a basin of water that functions as a sink for giving a quick rinse to the plates. A pipe feeds this sink with a stream of water, ensuring a minimum of running water. But, sure enough, there's a lot of stuff floating in that water: leftover food, legumes, oil and grease.

This basin, visible from outside thanks to an arched opening, and the little marble stairs on the counter are typical of almost all the *popinae* throughout the Empire. It is a characteristic of these places that makes them easily recognizable at first glance, even from a distance.

We move on. The counter continues into the interior of the locale and the countertop is interrupted by wide, circular holes. These are access holes for the large round amphorae (*dolia*) incorporated into the counter. What do they contain? Another servant, alongside the girl, inadvertently gives us the answer. With a sort of ladle, he extracts some olives from one of the holes, and from another a kind of polenta or grits made from spelt. He puts them on two different plates and vanishes.

A few seconds later another waiter arrives, and from a third opening he takes out some wine. He fills a pan placed on a small brazier and the end of the counter . . . The wine will be heated and served hot . . . Some drops have spilled on the table during the operation, but they won't be lost, because other "customers" will drink them—flies—and there are lot of them in this place.

We move on again. In a corner we see an oven for baking focaccia buns, bread, and other foods. We take a look around the rest of the locale. There are frescoes on the walls, decorations, and the inevitable graffiti left by customers. The tables and chairs are identical to ours. No *triclinium* couches. It's only in the evening or at banquets that people eat reclining on couches. At lunch, they eat like we do, sitting down. As we look around we don't see any interior courtyards. We know that a lot of *popinae* have them, offering their customers a quieter atmosphere.

This place has various kinds of customers. There's a couple, sitting apart in a corner, talking in low voices and staring at one another intensely. A little farther away a man is eating by himself, detaching the thigh from a roast chicken with exasperating slowness. Behind him are two soldiers laughing and pounding the table with their fists. One of them is missing both upper incisors. Here, next to us, two men and a woman are chatting, waiting for the food they've ordered. A dog is making the rounds of the tables; he must belong to the owner. He has a very important role: eating up the food scraps on the floor.

The lunches are always simple, made up of legumes, hard-boiled eggs, olives, sheep or goat-milk cheese, marinated anchovies, onions, a kebob, grilled fish, some figs. Depending on how much he eats, a Roman will speak of a *ientaculum*, for a light lunch, or a *prandium*, for a more substantial meal.

We notice a curious fresco on one wall. It shows a plate with some legumes on it, a glass with some olives, and two round elements, maybe pomegranates, maybe tambourines or musical instruments similar to plates.

This painting is striking because in the excavations in Ostia archaeologists have found an identical fresco in a *popina*. Many scholars have interpreted it as a sort of "figurative" menu painted on the wall so as to be visible to everyone (like we often see today in fast food places). More likely it is a symbolic rendering of what this kind of place has to offer: food, drink, and good music.

Our attention is attracted by a series of rhythmic sounds; we turn around. At the side of the counter, we see a waiter who is grinding something up with a mortar and pestle. Curious, we go over to have a better look. The wine on the burner isn't there anymore, it's been served hot. Now he's preparing another beverage in high demand at the *popina*: the *piperatum* (or *conditum*). It's made by mixing pepper and some aromatic extracts with honey, wine, and warm water.

The cocktail is ready now and the man pours it into two cups resting on the counter. A waitress picks them up and starts off toward a table occupied by two men. She has long, black eyelashes and long curly hair down around her shoulders. She's got a very Mediterranean charm; big hips and above all, buxom breasts. Having put down the two cups on the wooden table, she's about to move away when one of the customers grabs her by the arm and pulls her closer. The man is strongly built and his head is completely shaved, except for a lock of hair on the back of his neck. That's the distinctive sign of a wrestler. A few words, a wink. It doesn't take much to figure out what this guy wants.

The woman smiles, complicit, but she takes the man's hand off her breast. She throws a glance at the owner, who continues unperturbed with his pile of bills. He looks up just for a second, nods, and then dives back into his calculations. The wrestler gets up and he and the waitress head toward the curtain. As they pull it open, some wooden stairs appear, leading up to the inevitable loft.

Having sex with the waitress in a *popina* is something normal, almost banal. It's not even considered adultery, and that gives us an idea of the social status of the women who work in these places. And not only the waitresses. If the proprietor were a woman, she too would be considered an easy woman by everyone, just as her daughters would be.

Up in the loft, the man hasn't even taken his clothes off. He's pushed the woman against the bed, turned her around, and lifted up her long tunic. The bed creaks and pounds against the wall. The sounds coming from the upper level make the two soldiers smile; their table is very close to the stair. The one with the missing teeth looks up and starts to howl, then breaks into a laugh.

When, in a little while, the man and the woman come back down, the customer will have to pay for his lunch and for the "service." He knows that the price of this "extra" won't be more than eight asses, as much as a small pitcher of wine. Cheap wine.

But what is an as? And what's the value of a sestertius? What can we buy with it?

CURIOSITY—What's a Sestertius Worth?

A lot of people ask that question. The answer is not that simple, because the value of the sestertius changed over the course of the centuries due to repeated currency crises and inflation.

But anyway, let's try to figure it out.

The coins in circulation throughout the Roman Empire are, in order of importance: the aureus (gold); the denarius (silver); the sestertius (bronze); the dupondius (bronze); the as (copper); the semis (copper); and the quandrans, the smallest coin in bronze.

The sestertius, therefore, is a coin of middling value, useful for everyday purchases. Its value relative to the other coins was established by the rigid hierarchy handed down by Augustus in 23 BCE:

1 sestertius = 2 dupondi = 4 asses = 8 semis = 16 quadrans

In addition, if the amount to be spent was considerable, other coins would be used, which corresponded, roughly speaking, to our bank notes with more than one zero:

1 denarius = 4 sestertii
1 aureus = 100 sestertii

At this point, we can try to figure out what you can buy with a sestertius. The secret is to examine the ancient writings and the inscriptions on the walls discovered at archaeological sites (especially Pompeii).

They contain a lot of prices, often expressed in asses, but knowing the relationships between the values of the various coins, it's possible to figure out the real purchasing power of a sestertius for the average consumer.

In contemporary terms, a sestertius is worth about two Euros, or two and a half dollars.

That's its value for the whole first century CE, and we can consider it unchanged in Trajan's Rome, at the beginning of the second century CE (115 CE), a period of economic growth thanks to Trajan's military conquests.

Here are some prices, which, in many cases, correspond surprisingly well to prices in our own time:

1 quart of olive oil = 3 sestertii = $7.50
1 bottle of table wine = 1 sestertius = $2.50
1 bottle of choice Falerno wine = 2 sestertii = $5.00
1 loaf of bread = 1/2 sestertius = $1.25
2.2 pounds of wheat = 1/2 sestertius = $1.25
1 bowl of soup = 1/4 sestertius (1 as) = $0.65
1 admission to the baths = 1/4 sestertius (1 as) = $0.65
1 tunic = 15 sestertii = $37.50
1 donkey = 520 sestertii = $1,300
1 slave = 1,200 - 2,500 sestertii = $3,150 - $6,300

The ancient sources are full of curiosities. We know that an average citizen usually carries thirty sestertii, the equivalent of seventy-five dollars.

Other data give us an idea of the enormous gap between rich and poor. Six sestertii a day are enough to feed three people (a small family), but a wealthy man in Trajan's Rome has to be able to count on, as a minimum, an income of 20,000 sestertii a year (that's fifty-five a day) for his vital necessities.

We'd better not go too much beyond that. Actually, the data from different eras are influenced by the effects of the high inflation and repeated currency crises that plagued the Empire. The most impressive example is the price of wheat. In the first century CE you could buy fifteen pounds of wheat (one modius) for three sestertii. Two centuries later (near the end of the third century), the price was 240 sestertii!

This means that, because of the various crises, the sestertius had depreciated to $1/80$ of its former value, or just about three cents. As a result, its value in our terms had shrunk to about three cents.

Roman coins were always engraved with a profile of the emperor's face (and sometimes the first lady's too). In an age with no television, newspapers, or photographs, coins (along with statues and bas-reliefs) also serve the purpose of letting the emperor's subjects know what he looks like. It is such an effective method that, when a new emperor takes office, the imperial mint goes to work immediately to coin new sestertii, denarii, aurei, etc. The engravers are highly skilled; within hours after the emperor's taking the throne new coins are taken by couriers to the four corners of the Empire. They are proof of the changing of the guard and show the face of the new sovereign.

1:15 – 2:30 PM

EVERYONE TO THE BATHS

After a quick snack, we're back out on the street. Looking up on the Clivus Suburanus, we notice some columns of smoke billowing skyward, immediately dispersed by the wind. They all come from the same place. A fire? Doesn't look like it: it's not a thick column of dense smoke but a lot of thin, uniform columns. They are columns of smoke produced by a large public bath facility.

Come to think of it, all our imagined reconstructions of ancient Rome are "clean." In reality, they are missing an important detail: smoke. The great public bath facilities send up impressive columns of smoke that the air currents dissipate almost immediately. They are the product of colossal boilers working at full rhythm, devouring tons of firewood every day. This too is a bit of data that is often overlooked: the gigantic quantity of firewood needed by a city of over one million inhabitants. Wood used for cooking, for winter heat, for artisan workshops, for cremating the dead, for construction, for carpentry (beds, tables, handles, wagons—wood is ubiquitous, the plastic of the ancient world). Finally, wood is the fuel of the great public baths, ecological monsters that burn trees nonstop, day after day, month after month, year after year—For centuries, almost without interruption.

For us, the smell of burning wood is synonymous with winter, a lighted fireplace, or a cozy restaurant with a wood-fired oven, but for a Roman it has an added significance. It means that nearby there is a place where you can get washed.

We head in the direction of those plumes of smoke. In Rome there are a lot of small public baths (*balnea*), that is, very small *thermae* or hot baths, for washing, but the place we're about to discover is something unique in the whole Roman Empire. It is a true architectural, artistic, and engineering wonder, never seen before in the classical world (or even in human history): the enormous construction known as Trajan's Baths.

Hot baths have been known by the Romans for almost two hundred years. Since, that is, the beginning of the first century BCE, when a wealthy and enterprising business man, a certain Caius Sergius Orata, invented the first hot bath facility. How did these first baths come to be? The people who lived on the slopes of the Phlegraean Fields, just a stone's throw from Vesuvius, had always cured themselves with the steaming vapors of the hot springs. These vapors, which spewed out of the ground at 140° F, were channeled into little rooms, which people went into and sweated a lot (not coincidentally, they were called "sweaters," *laconica*). According to the Romans, these sweat baths expelled the bad humors of disease. Caius Sergius Orata figured out that he could imitate nature by lighting underground furnaces and channeling the heat under floors and inside walls. If you wanted to sweat, you didn't need to be near a hot spring; you could do it anywhere. And so hot baths were born.

Many hot bath facilities were built, some of them by order of the emperors, but the one we're about to visit is the largest in Rome, and the largest ever built up to now (115 CE). Others, even bigger, will come later.

The direction we've chosen takes us straight to the entrance of Trajan's Baths. They are very close to the Colosseum, on the Oppian hill. At the end of the street we can see a tall, vertical building with columns and a roof with large windows. It looks nothing like the monuments we've seen up to now. The closer we get the more we realize that its side walls look endless: they are incredibly long and painted almost pure white. At various points along the walls, buildings rise up on the inside. This mastodonic "Great Wall" is the perimeter wall of Trajan's Baths.

We follow the people filing in. We notice that there are men and women, old people and children, craftsmen and soldiers, wealthy people and slaves. The baths of Rome bring everyone together, without distinction. The impression is the same as walking through one of our railway stations or airports.

The line moves quickly. One by one the people give a coin to a slave, who puts it into a small wooden strongbox. Admission is not free, but it is very affordable: a quadrans. Just to give you an idea of how much that is, a quadrans is worth a quarter of an as and with an as and a half you can buy a flask of wine and a small loaf of bread. So the ticket for the baths is really cheap. Nevertheless, once we're inside, we'll have to pay each time for the various services we request: the bath, the cloakroom, and so on.

The Great Baths of Trajan

Beyond the entrance, the first impression is extraordinary. The entrance opens on to a long portico which frames a wide open space—completely covered with water!

It is an immense pool! It's as though an entire piazza had been flooded. The example of Venice is appropriate here too. Imagine seeing St. Mark's Square entirely covered with water overflowing from the Grand Canal, with the porticos reflected in the mirror of the water. This is the *natatio,* a swimming pool, three feet deep, which usually constitutes one of the obligatory stops on the itinerary of the bath experience. But a lot of people use this place to relax, to chat, or to go for a cool swim in the summer heat. In fact, there are people in the water now, chatting with friends sitting at the base of the columns, or on the edge of the *natatio* with their feet dangling in the water. We pass behind them inside the portico. Together with us are men and women, some dressed, others scantily clad. The reflection of the water projected on the walls seems like veils of light, diaphanous as silk, gliding across the frescoes of the portico and caressing the stuccos. Great statues of painted marble loom above us in niches in the walls.

Inside the big pool, some people are playing in the water, fathers and sons chase one another, patricians surrounded by slaves and clients are engaged in a discussion; nobody is swimming. In fact, in the Roman era almost nobody knows how to swim. Swimming doesn't exist as a sport, nor as an educational activity. Only people who are somehow involved with the sea, rivers, or lakes manage not to drown by using their own personal style of swimming.

We exit the portico and find ourselves in one of the big interior courtyards. We can understand why these baths impress everyone. Normally, a bath facility can be viewed in a single glance; it's a single big building. But Trajan's Baths are so big and extensive that they are not only in front of you but around you. They are the size of a neighborhood! It's the all difference between a small, suburban playground and Disney Land. The analogy is not coincidental because Trajan's Baths are a veritable city of pleasure, relaxation, and amusement, a city within the city.

Walking through the Baths
We're thinking about all this as we walk through the enormous interior spaces of the baths. It almost feels as though we're inside an oversized barracks. In the center stands the imposing bathing complex (with the *calidarium, frigidarium*, etc.), while all around it are gardens, woods, statues, and fountains. Finally, the perimeter wall, which is composed of a single portico topped at each of its four corners by towering half-domes, like the valves of enormous seashells rising up to the sky. They look vaguely like the Sydney Opera House.

The architectural design is surprisingly modern-looking. What are these almost futuristic structures? We walk toward them, trying to find the shortest route amid garden paths, flower beds, groups of people strolling, idling, playing. The only places you can enjoy this type of atmosphere today are the parks of big modern cities, from Villa Borghese in Rome to Central Park in New York, and this gives us further confirmation of the baths' role in urban relaxation and amusement. Someone has even called them the "villas of the people."

As we approach one of the shells, we realize that it's a library. The valve is protected by enormous windows held up by a network of supports. Imagine the Pantheon, with its great dome of hexagonal coffers, its curved marble walls and columns: cut it in half as though you were slicing a big cake. That's what the library looks like. In the center there are large white marble reading tables. There are a lot of people seated at them, consulting the era's most authoritative sources of knowledge. This library contains texts in Latin, while the other one, located opposite us about three hundred yards away in the twin valve, contains works in Greek.

In short, the baths are not only for the pleasures of the body but also those of the mind. Literally, *mens sana in corpore sano*, "a sound mind in a sound body."

A quick glance at the remaining two shells on the perimeter of the piazza shows them to be nympheums or monumental fountains, faced in marble and mosaics, with the water spouting forth from numerous niches arranged in an arc. But where does all this water come from? From an aqueduct and an enormous cistern with a curious name designed by Apollodorus and still visible today: the Seven Rooms. In reality the rooms are nine, but they still amaze any modern visitor. They are huge spaces, tens of yards long, with a lot of openings between one and the next. Their vaulted ceilings are almost as high as a three-story building. The cistern had a total capacity of almost two million gallons of water and it was filled by a designated aqueduct.

We're back out on the garden paths, among the trees. How many people can these baths hold? Modern estimates suggest about three thousand. On seeing these spaces that figure seems perfectly plausible. On one side the perimeter wall shifts from a straight line to a slight curve, transforming itself into a sort of theater with a semicircular grandstand framing an arena. Performances and competitions are held here.

In this Roman world apart, there's a little bit of everything. We pass by some jugglers performing their tricks to the delight of a small crowd, while under the portico we can see people eating (evidently, there are places that serve meals). A young girl leaning against a column is obviously looking for customers. The baths contain many features of the city outside, on a smaller scale. Even the less pleasant ones: we see a man scurrying toward the exit with a tunic and a toga under his arm, clearly stolen.

Tunics and Loin Cloths

Now let's go in and check out the atmosphere in the interior rooms of Trajan's Baths. We head toward the entrance of the large building that rises up in the center of the piazza. Along the crests of its roofs we notice countless small plumes of smoke wafting upward. They're the ones we saw earlier as we were walking the streets. It really does look like a big house with a fire in its initial stages burning inside. Actually, what we're looking at are small vents arranged in a straight line on the roof to dissipate the hot air that heats the central rooms in the baths.

And here we are in the dressing room, or *apodyterium.* At the entrance, we hand over another quadrans to a servant for taking care of our clothes (we've already seen what happens if you leave your tunic and toga unguarded). This won't be the only charge we'll have to pay; we'll need double this amount (half an as) to be admitted into the baths and to wash, and then other sums for other services such as massages, oil, towels, etc. It's surprising that women pay more than men: an as to use the baths! Or maybe the opposite is true, that men pay less because they are more frequent customers. In any event, some customers get in for free: children, soldiers, and slaves.

The dressing room is a large space with colored marble facing and stuccos, and a large mosaic in the middle of the floor with the figure of Triton. A long bench runs all along the walls, where men sit and chat, do up their sandals or fold their clothes. One man is having himself undressed by his slaves as though he were a little boy; he's obviously well off. Above their heads is a line of niches where they can put their bundle of clothes, unless they had already handed them over to the custodian at the entrance.

Do you have to take all your clothes off? Not really; some people keep their tunic (it will keep them warm during exercises in the gym), but there are also those who remain clad in a curious black leather loincloth that makes them look a little like Tarzan. Martial called it a *nigra aluta*. Almost everybody, however, wears a sort of band around their waist, the *subligaculum*.

Around us are all kinds of bodies. There are bald, fat men with pale white skin and a huge spare tires hanging over their linen waistband. Others, on the contrary, are skinny, their collarbones sticking out, with bony shoulders and olive skin. Here, nudity creates no scandal, just as in the locker rooms of all the gyms in the modern world. What's surprising is the crowding of bodies. In our western societies, we're not used to being crammed together like this in lines and especially in dressing rooms. In ancient Rome, interpersonal space, as it's called, is much more like it is in certain countries of the Far East than Western Europe or America. One thing, however, we do notice: this dressing room is only for men. The women, evidently, undress in another room.

Sport and Nudity

Our road continues and takes us to the first stop on our bath itinerary: the gymnasium.

Trajan's Baths have two gymnasiums, and they are both in the open air; two large courtyards surrounded by colonnades. The scene that opens up before our eyes is truly unusual. All around us are people running, jumping, and rolling around on the ground in wrestling matches. The underlying principle of this space is simple: exercise not only helps you to keep in shape but also induces you to sweat, and sweating will be the main purpose of the rooms to follow.

Here we also see for the first time a lot of women. They are playing a sort of volleyball with some men or running after some hoops, exactly like children used to do until just a few decades ago. Each hoop (*trochus*) has metal rings around it that function as an acoustic signal for people to move out of the way.

The ball game is interesting to watch. A cord is stretched between two poles, and the ancestor of beach volleyball is being played right in front of us. There are at least three kinds of balls: one is filled with feathers (*pila paganica*), one with sand (*pila harpasta*), and one with air, probably with little air chambers made from animal skins (*pila follies*). The game obviously changes a lot depending on the type of ball. Seneca describes a game (*ludere datatum*) that's identical to what we call poison ball, where you have to be ready to stop a ball in the air, without letting it fall to the ground, and hit it back immediately.

The Romans also play a sort of handball (*ludere expulsim*), and finally there's the famous *trigon*: three players stand at the corners of a triangle drawn on the ground and throw balls at each other without warning. They have to hit them back with their hands without catching them. Often, two players will both target the third, peppering him with repeated blows. Slaves standing outside the triangle act as ball boys and keep score.

Off in a corner two men are wrestling, watched by a small crowd, cheering them on. Their bodies are covered with oil to make it harder to be held by their opponent. Helping and coaching them are some old veterans of the gym, commonly known as *gymnasiarchs*. As we cross the courtyard, we discover three more women doing exercises with weights made of lead or stone, the *halteres*, shaped like dumbbells. The modernity of this scene is amazing. Their objective is to strengthen their arms and "reinvigorate" their chest.

Some men are watching them, murmuring amused comments to each other. In effect, from time to time during the weightlifting, the torsion of their bodies and the expansion of the thorax exalts their female forms. It also often happens that their thighs and buttocks are uncovered. The women who play ball wear a tunic, while others are in what, for all practical purposes, is a bikini. But the result is the same: their breasts bounce up and down, sway back and forth, pop out, attracting male eyes. The female presence at the baths was at the center of heated debates over the centuries.

Initially (second century BCE), separate itineraries were designed for the two sexes. But as early as Cicero (106-43 BCE), this rule was often not observed, and his barbs about the abandonment of the old rules have gone down in history. We know that, a few years from now, Hadrian will order that the sexes be separated in the baths, with different itineraries or different hours. Women will be able to go to the baths from dawn to 1 PM (the seventh hour), and then it will be the men's turn, from 2 to 9 PM (from the eighth hour to the second night hour). Nevertheless, these restrictions too will never really be respected.

In the era that we're exploring, promiscuity is the norm. Women can choose how they behave; whether to be "traditionalists" or "transgressives" and go to the baths with men. We know that a lot of them will choose, as we will see, the second option.

For decades, there have been a lot of critics who have lamented this "decline in values," from Pliny the Elder to Quintilian, who even calls women *adulteresses* for the mere fact of entering the rooms and the bathing tubs together with men. The scandals are countless. It all seems strikingly similar to the reaction to the spread of topless bathing on modern beaches. It is worth noting, however, that if you go to a gym in Germany today, the male and female dressing rooms are often adjoining and communicating rooms. And in the saunas of many hotels in the Italian region of Alto Adige, not only are all the rooms open to both sexes, even the showers, but it is often prohibited to wear a bathing suit or cover yourself with a towel.

We finish our visit to these gymnasiums of ancient Rome struck once again by the sight of a man training by hitting a sack of flour (or sand) identical to our punching bags, but even more so by two muscular women engaged in a wrestling match.

Before exiting, we notice that several men, having finished their matches and exercises, are standing around chatting while their slaves clean them of the residue of sweat and oil from the massages. First of all, the servants have sprinkled their masters' bodies with fine sand, an excellent way to absorb the oil and sweat (exactly like when we remove oil or grease stains on our clothes with talcum powder). Then they begin using a strigil, a curious instrument that looks like a sickle, but instead of a blade it has a sort of curved gutter pipe that is used to gather up the sweat, oil, and dirt. The slaves skim it over the skin like when you use a spoon to get a glob of jelly off your shirt.

We approach a fat bald man, evidently a wealthy aristocrat, who's having his sweat and oil removed by a servant. The slave's movements are delicate and resemble those of a barber. It really is a strange scene. This patrician is surrounded by a group of slaves and clients who have accompanied him through the baths from the very beginning, assisting him in everything: perfuming him, massaging him, bringing him towels and ointment jars, etc. It almost seems like we're watching Formula I mechanics at a pit stop. Maybe they too will give themselves an ablution or two. If, that is, the patrician leaves them some time when they've finished with him.

Tepidarium and Calidarium

We're now entering the heart of Trajan's Baths. The large building that contains the block of the *tepidarium, calidarium,* and *frigidarium*, rises up in the center of the bath complex and has the same dimensions as a cathedral, with big windows. The first room we come to is the *tepidarium*. It's average size, has a very high ceiling and a moderately warm temperature. A lot of people skip it, since they've already warmed up with some exercise.

The real surprise is the next room, the *calidarium*. Imagine entering a big church, a basilica. Those are the dimensions of this space. You feel tiny, squashed by the monumental scope of the space, by the height of the columns. This *calidarium* is filled with a vapor that creates an atmosphere of unreality, as though someone had extended an impalpable veil to serve as a filter between us and the ceiling, a little like going into a bathroom after someone's taken a shower.

High above, the ceiling vaults are covered with an embroidery of colored stuccos. There are paintings of mythological and heroic scenes, arborescent decorations, geometric shapes. We are able to make out every little detail, even from ground level, thanks to the skilled use of colors, which are few but highly visible: red, blue, yellow, white, green. Big windows with the usual latticework of glass panes let in the sunlight.

We are thus able to intuit an important detail. The entire bath complex is oriented in a way to provide the hot rooms with the greatest exposure to the sun.

Another characteristic feature is the windows. They are large, it's true, but from down here we can see that they are double-paned to ensure better insulation for the *calidarium*. Our gaze moves down the walls over slabs of colorful marble from every corner of the Empire, inserted in a beautiful inlay design. They are precious and rare marbles, like the yellow from Numidia in North Africa or the purple from Phrygia in Asia Minor, which accentuate the feeling of luxury.

Enormous Corinthian capitals carved from white marble top powerful fluted columns of yellow marble. Our gaze, continuing its downward course, finally comes to ground level and runs across an extension of marble and elegant geometries. The floor looks like a gigantic chessboard, formed by large round discs and white squares on a background of pale yellow.

Now it's the ear that takes over from the eye. Our brain only now takes notice of the voices reverberating all around and a continuous thumping on the floor. The thumping comes from the special wooden clogs that a lot of people are wearing. In effect, the floor is scalding hot. Around us a lot people are sitting on marble benches and counters. And they're sweating like mad. Some of them stare at the inlaid pattern on the floor, ignoring the drops of sweat falling from their chins, after streaming down their cheeks and noses. Other people do notice, but they leave the drops free to run down their bodies while, seated, they look up at the vaulted ceiling of the *calidarium*, way up there, immersed in the mist.

Considering the heat, we figure that in the winter people also come to the baths for relief from the cold.

Every now and then some enfeebled men and women emerge from some narrow passages and go and sit down to get their strength back. We try going into one of these passages, which lead to the *laconicum*, the hottest room in the baths, compared to which the *calidarium* feels cool . . . There must be more than one *laconium*, as the one we're looking at is a circular room with a lot of niches where people take turns sitting. Here the temperature is close to 140°F. It's a proper "bath" of hot, dry air.

The heat is generated by the hot air that runs through a cavity in the walls. It's as though dozens of smokestacks were running through the walls. Without some protection, like sandals, clogs, or towels where your skin touches the walls or floor, you could easily be burned.

We can't bear the heat very long, and on returning to the *calidarium*, we almost have the sensation of being hit by a puff of cool air. At this point we start looking for one of the tubs of water. There are three, beautiful, that occupy large niches on the sides of the room. They are the size of the water basins of the fountains in our piazzas and they can hold a lot of people at a time.

As we're going in, the water feels too hot, but, clenching our teeth, we go down a couple of steps. There's a woman sitting opposite us and she smiles on observing our less than athletic entry. She has very elongated dark eyelashes and her hair is pulled back. Her makeup is running from the sweat. It's not until we're used to the heat that we notice that she's semi-nude. She's sitting on an underwater step opposite ours and the water comes up to her midriff, leaving her big breasts uncovered. When she gets up to leave, the light cloth that warps her hips is totally soaked with water and almost transparent. The woman slips on her clogs and wraps herself in a big towel. Then, with a thoroughly feminine stride, she heads for the exit.

What we don't see in this room is the whole invisible mechanism that generates the heat. It's a little like being on the stage of a theater and not seeing all of the equipment that's used to change the sets. In reality, veritable rivers of hot air are circulating all around and underneath us. Under our feet, in fact, there is a human rabbit warren, made up of underground passages used by coughing slaves. They're the ones who, like so many stokers, feed the big wooden furnaces, which serve two purposes: on the one hand, as we have said, they generate the hot air and steam and smoke that go into the labyrinth of cavities in the walls and under the floors, which are raised and held up by miniature columns. But at the same time, some of these furnaces heat the water that goes into the tubs of the *calidarium.*

We get out of the tub and head toward the next room. We pass in front of a gentleman sitting motionless on a bench and talking business with another man. We stop for a second and look at him. There's a certain regality in his gestures, despite the heat and the copious sweat running down his brow.

We recognize him; he's the *dominus* of the house we visited this morning at dawn. He goes to the baths every day. We can see that because the heat doesn't seem to bother him in the least. He comes here, certainly, to wash. But also to talk business. The baths, in fact, are one of those places that combine business and pleasure, exactly like we do today with working lunches. He notices that we're staring at him, pauses, looks at us for a second, flashes a fleeting "noble" smile, and then goes on talking. He's probably mistaken us for one of his many *clientes.*

Enough of the heat, already, now we're going to the *frigidarium*! As we're going out, we run into the woman from the tub, the nearly naked one who, now wrapped in her towel, has stopped to chat with a friend. They both head off in a different direction from ours and skip the *frigidarium* completely. Why? Women are advised not to confront the cold of these rooms and such violent jumps in temperature.

The Big Chill of the Frigidarium

We finally enter the *frigidarium*. It's almost identical to the *calidarium* in its marble and decoration, but there is an obvious difference: it's even bigger and more overwhelming. The monumentality of Rome seems endless and it surprises you everywhere you go.

Just for the sake of example, in the modern era the rooms of the Baths of Diocletian, next to the main train station in Rome, have been turned into a multi-story museum, the national Roman museum, and the *frigidarium* has become a big church: Holy Mary of the Angels. Entering it is truly a moving experience. The marbles haven't been changed; the immense granite columns from Egypt are still the originals. And the windows with their cross vaults faithfully reproduce the volumes that you would have seen on entering the ancient *frigidarium*. It's very easy to close your eyes and imagine that you can see around you patricians, soldiers, and slaves with their voices and the sound of their footsteps. In this incredible theater set you really have the impression of being immersed in the magnificence of the Roman Empire.

Let's take a look at the people in the *frigidarium*. We notice that there's a man in a corner reading a text out loud. He has others in a *capsa*, the leather bucket that contains some papyrus scrolls. He is clearly a secretary slave who is reading to his master. Exactly as the slave of the famous naturalist Pliny the Elder did forty years ago when he accompanied his master to the baths.

It's really true that you can see all the social classes of Rome reunited in these rooms. Curiously, the wealthy, even though they have their own private baths at home, are perhaps the most assiduous users of the public baths. The reason is fairly evident: this is where you meet people, make deals, let yourself be seen with your following of clients. This place is one of the fulcrums of society, where visibility is at its height.

We also know that the emperors always went to the baths, mixing in with the crowd (we don't know, however, just how much they came into contact with the popular classes; probably they were surrounded by their escorts, to avoid being importuned).

We turn around. Everyone's attention is directed toward a group of people standing over a man who has collapsed on the floor after taking a few steps into the *frigidarium*. A man in a tunic, evidently a physician on duty at the baths, runs over to the group. They try to bring him to; then they lift him up and carry him off, taking him to an infirmary somewhere in this "city of the waters." Evidently, the man has had a fainting spell, maybe a heart attack. It's not rare at the baths, with the constant change from hot to cold and vice versa.

We know that many people come here every day. But some really exaggerate and go through the whole itinerary two or three times a day. There are some famous cases. It is said that the emperor Jordanus took five baths a day, and that another emperor, Commodus, the son of Marcus Aurelius, took as many as seven or eight.

Beyond heart attacks, there are also strokes and bones broken in bad falls on the marble, made dangerously slippery by the water and the constant foot traffic.

And in the long run, the baths can also provoke hearing problems. As has probably happened in the case of a man in front of us, on in years but not old, but whom everybody has to talk to in a loud voice, almost shouting. He's in the water, in one of the tubs filled with ice-cold water, with some other friends, and they're throwing a ball around for fun. He had started complaining about a hearing loss in just one ear. After a while the other one started giving him problems too. Now he's on his way to becoming almost completely deaf. The cause will be discovered by anthropologists who will study his bones some nineteen centuries from now, in the modern era.

We also call this "surfer syndrome" (or "sailor syndrome"). It strikes those who are accustomed to spending long periods in cold and humid environments. In our acoustic meatus, that is, our external ear canal, the bones produce an excretion that gradually obstructs the passage. It's as though the ear defends its internal micro-climate by constructing a barrier against the constant insults of cold and humidity. This process, known as "hyperostosis of the acoustic meatus," still afflicts fishermen and lovers of the sea.

In the Roman era more of its victims were men rather than women. Why? The reason, as we have seen, lies in the different itineraries inside the baths. Women, in fact, hardly ever go in to the *frigidarium*, thus avoiding the cold and humidity. And thus also avoiding "bath deafness."

Roman Massages
After the freezing cold of the *frigidarium*, almost everybody jumps into the big swimming pool of the baths, the enormous *natatio* that we saw on the way in; the water must feel really warm. It's really such a relaxing and fun moment. We, however, skip this collective dip in the pool to go directly to the last stop on the bath itinerary: the massage.

The room we discover is furnished with marble tables on which a lot of people are getting a massage, while others are waiting their turn, leaning on columns or against the wall. Some of the flaccid bodies on the marble table tops look awkward and seem like seals lying on the polar ice caps.

What strikes us most in this massage parlor is the difference in the sounds. At the entrance there's s sort of borderline of sounds: in the *frigidarium*, we were immersed in a chaos of

chattering, with shouting and laughter reverberating everywhere. Here, however, all you hear is the tapping of fingers
against the bodies to be massaged, the slapping of hands that
sends waves across the skin, the rubbing of the masseurs'
palms as they rub in the oil.

The faces we see are almost always immersed in thought.
We know that the use of oils is recommended not only for
esthetics and the well-being of the body, but also because it is
believed that they prevent colds. Therefore, an oil massage is
always recommended before leaving the baths, especially in
winter.

The masseurs are public slaves who come from all over the
Empire. They work in silence. Not all of them, however,
belong to the public baths. Here, some customers bring their
own slaves from home. There's one, at the end of the room,
surrounded by slaves. One is massaging him, another is holding, still another hands him towels, and so on. It even gets to
the point where you can see these well-off Romans, just finished with their bath, being carried to their sedan chairs by
their slaves in order to avoid the effort of completing the last
part of the itinerary on foot.

The little bottles of oil can be made of glass or bronze.
There's one shaped like the bust of a slave with the opening
at the top of the head. It has wavy hair, almost curly, and the
almond eyes bely Asiatic origins. A drop of oil slides sinuously down his face. It is an enigmatic face, with strange
beard on its cheeks, but also on the sides of its mouth, both
above and below. On closer look, it isn't a beard; it almost
looks like tribal scars, almost an identifying mark of some
Asian people. Who knows what people it might be (the Huns
had the habit of cutting their faces with knives, leaving highly visible scars like these, but much less elegant, or better,
perfectly monstrous). This object, we know, will end up one
day in the glass case of a museum, with its baggage of infor-

mation on extinct cultures. A hand grasps the handle that serves as a halo around the head of this slave-bottle and carries it away. The massage is over.

CURIOSITY—Building Trajan's Baths

The person who revolutionized the classical concept of the baths was Apollodorus of Damascus, the architect we met at Trajan's Forum. This work of his will serve as a model for all of the great imperial bath complexes that will subsequently be built in Rome and around the Empire, even the famous baths of Caracalla. But in order to build this gigantic complex he needed a large area to raze to the ground in the heart of Rome. How to do this? He got a helping hand from a raging fire that seriously damaged the famous Domus Aurea, Nero's fabulous residence. Apollodorus had everything that was left of its upper floors demolished, leaving only the vaulted rooms of the ground floor, to be used as a "pedestal" for the future baths. But that wasn't enough—he needed more space. So he had entire buildings (public and private) in the adjacent areas torn down and buried, leveling everything that was taller than a certain height (155 feet above sea level). In this way, he obtained a grand platform measuring 1040 feet by 1090 feet on which to build his emperor's baths. Managing to clear twenty-five acres in the middle of a city of more than a million inhabitants was not an easy task and really had something miraculous about it.

In a certain sense, we're grateful to Apollodorus, because, without intending to, he made us an enormous gift: everything that he had interred (the Domus Aurea, the adjacent buildings, etc.) was conserved until the modern era. Archaeologists have been able to uncover part of Nero's palace, including the famous Octagonal Room, where he held his banquets and where, it is said, rose petals rained down from the ceiling. But recent excavations have brought to light new rooms with frescoes representing cities of the Empire and mosaics of grape harvests (the oldest "color" mosaics in ancient Rome), still being studied and restored.

3:00 PM

Entering the Colosseum

It's early afternoon. Many Romans believe this is the best time for the performances at the Colosseum. After the morning hunts, the lunchtime executions, now's the time for the main events on the program: the *munera*, or gladiator fights.

It's difficult to describe the feeling you have in front of the imposing profile of the Colosseum. Today, in the modern era, tourists and residents of Rome are used to its fractured shape. It is a ruin, a wreck, a diminished version of what it once was. Outside, almost half of its most exterior ring is missing and on the inside all that's left is some brick vaulting ribs. You can no longer appreciate the impact of its brilliant white travertine grandstands, the arena floor, the statues in the arcades, the gallery over the last row of seats, way up top. Not to mention, obviously, the atmosphere created by the flags, by the colors of the crowd, the roar of the spectators. Today, all we can admire is the skeleton of this great amphitheater. Yet each year some four million tourists want to see it and go inside it, even at the price of passing up other sights and museums. The cruel fascination of this place has remained intact. But what did it look like back then? Let's try to figure that out.

Our route has been indicated by a baker. "Take the Clivus Pullius. Go beyond the intersection into the Clivus Orbius, and then on the left, where there's a *popina* on the corner, go down the Vicus Sandaliarius; that'll take you straight to the Colosseum. You can't miss it." Then, covered with flour and cleaning his hands with a wet rag, he went back into his shop to bake some more bread.

His directions are perfect. Now we have started down the Vicus Sandaliarius. It's narrow, lined with high-walled buildings. The sudden shade keeps us from seeing very well, but the spectacle is extraordinary. At the end of this urban canyon, in an incredible contrast with the dark buildings, looms an imposing golden structure, lit up by the sun.

As we gradually make our way down the street, the black walls of the buildings that frame it seem to open up like a curtain. That shining structure is an immense statue that towers over the piazza: the gilded bronze statue of Nero, the *Colossus Neronis*. Beyond it, almost as though it were a mountain, appears the Colosseum. Naturally, all we can see is a slice, created by the canyon of the buildings, but it is awesome. It looks like part of the horizon and it's even higher than the surrounding buildings.

We come to the end of the Vicus Sandaliarius and stop in our tracks, amazed. There's the Colosseum, right in front of us, a brilliant white, with its infinite shadowy arcades, the great shields hanging on the walls, the colored ribbons waving in the wind. And, around the top, its thick crown of poles.

It's very different from how we know it. Being intact, it seems much taller.

The statues that we can see in the middle of each of its arcades are extraordinary. They are sculptures of divinities, heroes, legendary and real figures from the history of Rome, even some eagles. They are all colored and almost seem like guards keeping watch. They make us feel as though we're standing before a fortress or a temple. Certainly not a place where performances are held.

The people on the street seem to ignore its presence, accustomed as they are to seeing it there. Yet it is something very recent in the history of Rome. We are in 115 CE, at the moment of Rome's maximum expansion, but the Colosseum was only built thirty-five years ago. Julius Caesar never saw it, nor did Augustus, Tiberius, Claudius, or Nero. It was the emperor Vespasian who decided to build it. And do you know where he built it? Inside of the famous Domus Aureus, the imperial residence built by Nero in the center of the city.

After the famous fire, Nero wanted to build an enormous imperial space for private use. We could almost call it his luxury ranch in the heart of Rome. It included various palaces, gardens, woods with deer, and even a large lake with swans. When Nero died, Vespasian wanted to give this area back to the Romans, and he came up an ingenious and highly symbolic idea: empty out the lake and exploit its empty bottom to build the foundations of the Colosseum, the biggest amphitheater ever built, dedicated to the people of Rome.

The only remaining legacy of Nero's villa in Trajan's Rome is an enormous gilded bronze statue. We're standing at its feet right now. It has an athletic body and heroic nudity. At one time it had Nero's face, but after his death it underwent a radical operation of cosmetic surgery. Now it has the face of the sun god, Helios, with a crown of rays.

Everything we see is the work of a Greek sculptor, Zenodorus. And what work!

The statue is more than 90 feet tall, that is, taller than a ten-story building. The Romans have always known it as the Colossus of Nero. It's curious to think that the name "Colosseum" really comes from the existence of this giant that rose up beside the amphitheater. It's a true nickname that the Romans have attached to it, in place of the official, perhaps too impersonal, name: Flavian Amphitheater. Although, to be honest, the word "Colosseum" would not appear for the first time in written form until the Middle Ages.

A good portion of the buildings around us are related to the Colosseum. They are service buildings, which complement the internal structures of the amphitheater. They include the weapons depot for the gladiators and warehouses for sets and theater props. Probably there are also small zoos for the temporary custody of animals, and also a sort of hospital, where wounds are treated. And then there is a barracks for gladiators, still visible in modern times, outfitted with a lot of cells and a small arena for training. This is the Ludus Magnus, also equipped with an underground tunnel connecting it to the Colosseum. In short, we're talking about a true service area around the amphitheater.

A roar goes up from the crowd inside the Colosseum and a flock of pigeons, who had been perched on the top, take flight. Something has happened in the arena to spark the enthusiasm of the spectators. We start to make our way over there. It's like approaching a glacier rising up from the valley floor. It's glowing white, completely covered in travertine marble.

The Colosseum rises above us over one hundred and fifty feet high. It is divided into four stories. The first three have eighty enormous arcades, containing statues taller than a man. To build it, some 130 million cubic yards of travertine were brought from the Albulae quarries near Tivoli, outside of Rome, on a specially built road, twenty feet wide.

The Colosseum has been standing, as we know, for two thousand years, yet it was built in less than ten! How did they do it? With a trick. Vespasian's engineers repeated an infinite number of times something they knew how to do quite well: the arch. It's as though they had built a number of aqueducts on top of each other. In this way, the weight is distributed perfectly on the ground below.

In short, while the pyramids are full (of stone blocks), the Colosseum itself is hollow, and its skeleton is practically composed of a skillful interweaving of arches. The design was so well conceived and executed that it is still standing, despite the depredations, the pillaging of the Middle Ages, and earthquakes.

As we approach it, we notice one of the stratagems used by the Roman architects. Travertine, in fact, doesn't allow a lot of sculpted detail because it is rich in pores and cavities that make it ill-suited to the execution of small details. So the architects never finished monuments in travertine. And the columns of the Colosseum, for example, are barely "sketched" and have an unfinished look. To please the eye, therefore, you have to look at the structures from a distance and allow yourself to be struck by the mammoth dimensions of the monuments. Less quality but greater quantity, in a certain sense. That's the way it is for the Colosseum, but also for the Theater of Marcellus, etc.

We pick up our pace. There's a constant rumble from the crowd, similar to the sound of the ocean when you're approaching a beach. It's like a wave breaking on itself. The impression you have is that the Colosseum is alive, pulsing with vital energy. It's as though it were shouting to attract us. We walk forward, almost hypnotized. The closer we get, the higher its mass soars into the sky.

Suddenly, some dark clouds pass overhead, dimming the splendor of the marble. Instantly, the Colosseum takes on a gloomier look. From down here it's like a tower of Babel climbing skyward, with its internal roar of people looking on at death. The Colosseum is like no other place on earth.

You don't have to pay for a ticket; entrance is free, although you have to have a kind of invitation, without which you can't get in. It's a card made of bone, and engraved in it are not only the place where you sit in the stands but also the sector and gate through which you are to enter. Over every arcade that opens to the outside there is a number, from I to LXXVI (1-76). Our card has the number LV (55). A ticket taker checks it and we go in.

We are now in a large vaulted corridor. It is illuminated by natural light coming from outside. The vaults are all decorated with painted stuccos. It's a beautiful kaleidoscope of colors, human and mythological figures, geometries and elements of architectural design. It almost feels like we're inside an imperial palace instead of a public building. We can hear shouting, laughter, arguments. In effect, there are a lot of people around us. Beyond a constant flow of spectators, there are vendors selling cushions for the grandstand, or snacks: focaccia, pine nuts, olives, peaches, plums, cherries (whose pits have been found in the sewer pipes by archaeologists).

But there is also another group of characters, typical of the fauna to be found in the bowels of the Colosseum, but also, in a certain sense, very modern: bookmakers. Clusters of people are hovering in the corners. Someone raises a hand, indicating a number. Someone shouts. Somebody else protests that the number is too high. The cluster gets bigger as newcomers come clambering down the steps to wager on the winners of the next round of gladiator fights.

This activity shouldn't be taken lightly. Betting on the fights is one of the essential parts of this show. Just as happens today at boxing matches and horse races, and by now almost for almost every kind of spectator sport. There are champions, challengers—and also, very probably, some fights that are rigged.

Between two pillars, we notice a flight of stairs with people going up. It's our sector. We follow the others. The structures of the Colosseum are really impressive; we can easily figure out how the crowds are able to exit so quickly, thanks to the efficient system of ramps and corridors. Climbing the stairs with us there are only men. This sector is off limits for women.

We can see daylight at the top of the last flight of stairs; it must lead up to the grandstands. The name given to these openings is truly peculiar and it helps us understand the nature of the crowd that flows through them: *vomitoria*.

We're almost there; it's like coming out of a tunnel, and the noise of the crowd keeps getting stronger. It's a rumbling crescendo.

Suddenly, we're outside, in the stands. It's a breathtaking sight. In front of us an artificial valley opens up, wide and deep, like a funnel. It's completely filled with people. There must be from fifty to seventy thousand people, shouting, cheering, gesticulating. They look like human confetti, in every imaginable color. The only comparable image that comes to mind are the circles of Dante's Inferno.

We're pushed forward by a father and son who were behind us on the stairs. We find our seats thanks to the number engraved in the travertine.

The last public execution of the day is now in progress. A man is being chased by a bear. He's managed to free himself from the pole he'd been tied to. This unexpected turn of events delights the crowd. The man zigs and zags, trying to confuse the bear, and then breaks into a sprint toward one of the fences on the edge of the arena. The bear almost nabs him, but the man manages to jump up on the fence, extracting a big cheer from the crowd. He starts climbing the fence, finding his grip and then losing it, getting it back again. He gets to the top. Will he succeed in jumping over it?

The fence is topped by what looks like an elegant white reinforcement, almost like a cylindrical cushion. But right at that point, a step away from safety, the man's escape is interrupted and he starts flailing. He tries repeatedly to get his hands around this plump sausage but each time he falls back. What's going on? On closer inspection, we notice that the cylinder is a roller made of ivory that turns on itself, keeping him from getting a grip on it. It's one of the security systems to prevent escapes by animals or prisoners. He keeps trying, desperately but uselessly. Nevertheless, the bear, standing on his hind legs, can't reach him. The crowd laughs. It looks like a stalemate: the man is motionless, hanging on to the webbing of the fence and to one of the elephant tusks sticking up from the supporting poles. Then he suddenly arches his back, once and then a second time. There are two arrows sticking out of his back. They were shot by guard archers, stationed in their niches. The shots were precise and well-calculated, and they've penetrated a lung. The man loses his grip; one arm dangles. He remains hanging by just one hand. A third arrow sends him falling back down into the arena, accompanied by a roar from the crowd. The bear pounces immediately and kills him with a paw slap. The crowd cheers.

The man next to us is cheering too, and turning to us, the newly arrived, explains that the man was a murderer. He killed a shopkeeper while robbing him of fifteen sestertii. The price of a tunic.

With this last cadaver the executions have concluded for today. Some stagehands lead the bear back into one of the side doors. Others are cleaning the arena, dabbing up the scattered pools of blood. We note with a certain disgust that right underneath us they are picking up the remains of a woman torn to pieces by a lion. They heave her body onto a small cart where it falls into an unseemly clump; a few yards away they pick up an arm, a little farther on a leg, partly mauled. Another stage hand, some distance away, picks up something and walks over to the cart. It looks like a bag. No, he's holding the woman's head by the hair. He tosses it onto the cart as though it were a knapsack. For an instant we see her blond hair fluttering in the air one last time. Even our neighbor grimaces in horror.

The words of Gregory of Nazianzus, who lived in the fourth century CE, capture the atmosphere of these spectacles, where every trace of humanity literally disappears. The scene is engulfed in a sort of frenzy, by a sadistic pleasure that feeds on itself, even though the crowd is made up of ordinary people. The place and the circumstances (a public execution) seem to explain the absence of any moral restraint which, to be sure, most of the people present exercise in their daily lives.

Gregory says, in fact, that if a man saves himself from the wild beasts, the crowd protests, as though they had been deceived and their time wasted; "but when a man's flesh is torn, when he screams and writhes in the dust, their eyes are devoid of pity and they clap their hands with joy when they see spurting blood."

Two acrobats have now appeared in the arena, displaying their skills in some entertaining numbers. But not many people are paying attention. It's a moment of intermission, in fact, and a lot of people are standing up, chatting, while others go to drink some water from the fountains present on each level of the Colosseum, and others go down through the *vomitoria* toward the latrines on the lower level.

We take advantage of the moment to take a more technical look around the Colosseum. A construction conceived from the outset as a place devoted solely to performances.

CURIOSITY—Secrets of the Colosseum

The Colosseum is not round but elliptical, so it can hold more people. Moreover, its grandstands are sloped at an angle of 37°, so every seat has an excellent view. The grandstands are made of blinding white marble but you can't sit just anywhere. A little like in our own stadiums, there are various sectors. The lowest ring, the one closest to the arena, is reserved for VIPs: senators, vestal virgins, priests, magistrates. The next level up is for members of the equestrian order. Still higher, the level for craftsmen, shopkeepers, public guests, etc. Higher up, separated by a walkway lined with niches and statues, "the people" sit in the highest part of the Colosseum. Here, women have a special section reserved for them to avoid, as they say, promiscuity. Finally, there is one last sector, a wooden "peanut gallery" that runs around the entire rim of the Colosseum, it too reserved for regular people. This amphitheater, in short, is something of an upside-down version of the social pyramid of Rome; the lower down you sit the more important your social status.

Among the services available to spectators, aside from the drinking fountains (a hundred or so) located at regular intervals along some internal walkways, there are also some curious surprises, like getting sprayed with perfumed liquids, rosewater, saffron, etc.

An extraordinary feature is the system for covering the Colosseum. The top of the rim has a crown of 240 robust poles, which are the anchors for the same number of long cables that hold up a large central ring, some 400 feet above the ground. Over this suspended web of cables, pieces of cloth, probably made of lightweight linen, are unrolled (like so many carpets), converging at the edge of the center ring. This creates a cover made of long wedges of cloth that protects the crowd from the sun (which during Roman summers can be unbearably hot). In the middle there remains a large round opening, like the roof of the Pantheon, but designed for this temple of entertainment. Considering the dimensions of this veiling, the rings used to pull it into place along the cables, in addition to the ropes and winches, recent estimates put its total weight at 26 tons, or 220 pounds per pole. It shouldn't be surprising, then, that the system was operated by one thousand sailors from the military fleet at Miseno. The covering had to be capable of withstanding the heavy seasonal winds of Rome as well as the strong updrafts that a "basin" full of people like the Colosseum can generate. In this sense, the covered amphitheater is a little like an immense sailboat.

The boat metaphor is also apt for the arena, but in a different way. It's over 80 yards long and about 50 yards wide. As we know, under the sand on the floor of the arena, the Colosseum goes down for another 20 feet or so, with several underground levels. In order to cover the arena with a wooden floor, Roman engineers came up with a system of beams, servings, and ribbing very similar to the hull of a boat. Considering that this wood flooring is also rounded to allow rainwater to run off to the edges, where it is collected by a system of gutters and grates, the example of the overturned boat offers a good image of the arena's durability.

But what's underneath this floor? The very soul of the Colosseum. Like a theater, in fact, the Colosseum has wings, but rather than on the sides, they're under its surface. Accounts have come down to us of dramatic special effects, with fake whales suddenly appearing in the arena and opening their mouths to release fifty bears. In other cases, what slowly emerged on the arena floor were richly decorated theater sets, replete with rocks and trees.

Under the sand and wood, in fact, there are two underground levels, with walkways, stairs and rooms, arms, lion cages, prisoners, etc. Thanks to special inclined planes and winches located in strategic places, it's possible to hoist all kinds of sets and backdrops up and onto the floor of the arena. Special freight elevators also make it possible to bring up gladiators and wild beasts. All of this apparatus allows for some amazing theatrical effects, like for example the simultaneous entrance of "a hundred lions, whose roar was so loud the entire Colosseum crowd was struck dumb."

The presence on these underground levels of firewalls made of peperino marble reveals one of the dangers of these dark rooms, where slaves, prop masters, animal tamers, gladiator trainers, etc., worked away under the flickering light of lanterns.

Initially, these underground levels didn't exist and almost certainly the arena could be flooded to host small naval battles, or shallow-water horse and chariot races.

The organization of the events was always characterized by an iron discipline because that's the only way to carry off such grandiose spectacles, with casts of thousands. In 80 CE, when the Colosseum was inaugurated by Titus, Vespasian's son and successor, 5000 animals were killed in 100 days!

Something a bit closer to us, given the period we're exploring, are the celebrations for Trajan's victory over the Dacians. The Colosseum held performances for 120 straight days, featuring the killing of 11,000 animals and 10,000 gladiators.

Here Come the Gladiators!

Meanwhile, some wagons are being pulled around the perimeter of the arena, with slaves wearing garlands and wreaths of flowers throwing gifts to the crowd: bread, coins, etc.

After a few minutes of excitement over the gifts, everyone is back in their seats in the grandstands, including the senators and the VIPs in the first ring of the Colosseum. The organizer of the program also takes his seat, a patrician belonging to one of the wealthiest families in Rome. Although he holds an office of a fairly high level—he's an *aedile*, or a magistrate who administers public-works programs—he is still at the beginning of his career in public life and he needs more fame and visibility. He's the one who has paid for these games, the sponsor of everything we're going to see (or the *editor,* as the Romans call it). These three days of games in the Colosseum must certainly have cost him a fortune, but on the other hand he's obliged by law to organize these events and he'll undoubtedly get something out of it. He will receive, in fact, official recognition from the Senate and the appreciation of the people, who will support him in his future political, social, and financial career. Popular support that will also carry weight in his relationships with his political adversaries—*Panem et circenses* (bread and circuses), as Juvenal liked to say.

And then there is also a subtle personal pleasure: the opportunity to feel a little like the emperor during these three days, cheered and praised by the crowd as he decides the fate of gladiators, beasts, etc. These games, in short, are an important starting point for his career and they will certainly also be recalled by his descendants. Probably, a new mosaic will be added to his villa on the outskirts of Rome, representing the salient moments of the games with gladiators and condemned prisoners (that's why we so often see such violent mosaics in museums and archaeological sites).

The man is seated on a finely sculpted high-back marble chair. He's rather different than the common image we have of a powerful Roman; he's not fat, bald, and covered with rings. On the contrary, he's tall and athletic looking, with dark hair and blue eyes. Next to him is his wife, very young. She is certainly the daughter of some powerful Roman patrician; a marriage that has opened a lot of doors for him in his brilliant career. They are a couple that ignites gossip, both at the exclusive banquets of the aristocracy and on the noisy landings of the *insulae*.

Behind them, guards stand at attention, the red plumes of their helmets touching the heavy gold-embroidered drapes, barely moved by the breeze.

The crowd starts getting noisy, clapping their hands, almost as though they're calling for their favorite warriors. Now's the time! The man makes a signal with his hand.

On the edges of the arena, some small bands strike up a triumphal march. The Colosseum crowd explodes in a single roar. It's like a sudden thunderclap that the amphitheater amplifies, like a huge echo chamber, sending it rumbling throughout the city.

The doors under the triumphal arch swing open, majestically. A procession emerges, led by two lectors carrying the insignia of the organizer of these games (since the man is an *aedile*, a magistrate without the power to issue the death penalty, the bundles don't have axes). They are followed by musicians with long trumpets (*buccinae*), then a wagon with a big board illustrating the program of fights. It's the equivalent of a mobile billboard. Often the various emperors' triumphal processions that parade through Rome also use wagons with big paintings narrating their victorious battles and conflicts. It's a sort of popularizing of the victor's exploits, in a way that everybody can understand; something between a Sicilian horse cart and a storyteller. Behind it is a man who symbolically carries the palm branch of the victor.

At this point the slaves come out carrying helmets and swords, the instruments of the gladiators. They'll be used in the fights, even though a lot of them are only good for a dress parade.

And finally, there they are: the gladiators. The crowd is delirious. You have to cover your ears to shield them from the noise. For a second, you have the impression that even the Colosseum could collapse under the shouting and the beating feet of tens of thousands of spectators. A look at the crowd and down at the arena shows us the grandest image of the amphitheater, at the moment of maximum enthusiasm. But it is horrifying to think that all this has been achieved solely for the purpose of producing spectacles of death.

It sends chills down your spine to think that the Colosseum's four and a half centuries of activity made it the place on Earth where the most people have died in such a small area. Neither Hiroshima nor Nagasaki produced such a high concentration of death. In this simple arena, hundreds of thousands of people went to their death—according to some estimates, as many as one million!

The calculations are simple, bone chilling. Even if we limit ourselves to the era we are exploring. As we have said, eight years ago, in 107 CE, Trajan staged fights between ten thousand gladiators (almost certainly prisoners of war). Six years ago, in the course of games lasting some 117 days, more than 9,800 gladiators died in the arena. Two years ago, in 113 CE, some 2400 gladiators fought in the arena, although we don't know how many of them were killed. These numbers, as is easily imagined, are the outcome of exceptional events, but they help us understand how easy it was to die in the arena. And they obviously don't include executions of criminals condemned to death.

If we assume a mortality rate of fifty to a hundred people a month, between gladiators and condemned criminals (a very conservative estimate for such a large structure, which, however, takes into account periods of "crisis" over the centuries), the total comes to between 270,000 and half a million people. Some observers believe the figure could be much higher than that, maybe even double.

Sex Symbols and Fighters. Who Are the Gladiators?
The gladiators come to a halt—the crowd is ecstatic—and they make wide gestures with their arms to thank them for the cheering. Then they start warming up, miming sword thrusts and showing off their skills with thunderous blows. Every movement brings a roar from the crowd.

In modern times, only great soccer players or the superstars of music or cinema, can provoke the same kind of excitement. And the same response from women. We know, in fact, that the gladiators are very much "appreciated" by the female audience, not only by the matrons of the people, but even more so by the ladies of the upper classes.

In Pompeii, thanks to some graffiti discovered by archaeologists, we have come to know of a gladiator who was considered the "young girl's torment." What's more, Juvenal tells the story of Eppia, the wife of a senator, who ran off with a famous gladiator named Sergiolus. Their tryst, which today would be a juicy tidbit for the world of tabloid newspapers and paparazzi, was probably the talk of the town, and Juvenal commented with feigned surprise on the gladiator's less than

Adonis-like looks. He had scars all over his body, bags under his eyes, and a dent in the middle of his nose from his helmet. In short, as he wrote, "What women love about gladiators is their sword."

But really who are these gladiators who fight each other in the arena? What are their stories? Each of them has his, or *her,* own story. First of all, there are the slaves, including those sold to the gladiator training schools by their masters to punish them. Then there are prisoners of war condemned to death. After Trajan's conquest of Dacia, where no less than 50,000 prisoners were taken, the arenas of the Roman Empire were probably inundated with masses of tall, bearded, violent combatants, used to splitting the heads of their adversaries with a single blow of the long, curved blades of their swords. Then there were also free men who became gladiators (aside from exceptional cases like the combat between four hundred senators and six hundred knights organized by Nero), for example, a lot of ex-legionnaires who look at it as a sort of occupation, and even some down and out lovers of adventure, or of a paycheck. Sometimes the gladiators include a few women. Even from good families. Today, for example, there are four women who will be fighting each other, in pairs. Female gladiators will be outlawed by the next emperor, Hadrian.

But there are also some desperate cases among the gladiators; ordinary people who have fallen into debt and, not being able to pay the amount they owe, have been sold to the gladiator school by their creditor, who is thus able to get his money back.

There are a lot of gladiator schools, in Italy and throughout the Empire. The most famous and profitable are obviously those owned by the emperor, but there are also others owned by senators, patricians, or simply wealthy investors. The gladiators are trained by the *lanistae,* hated by the people but indispensable for these collective "amusements." The training is brutal; the gladiator's life is almost as hard as that of a shaolin warrior monk. But contrary to the Hollywood myth, they are not without some liberty. From ancient texts and archaeological finds, we know that many gladiators are happily married with children, or else united with companions with whom they share the joys and suffering of this activity (often they are the ones who write the epitaphs on their mate's tombstone).

Many gladiators manage to make it to the end of their careers, perhaps with a number of victories to their credit, like Maximus, who lived in the first century CE, and who piled up some forty victories. These veterans are then offered the *rudis*, a simple wooden gladius that symbolizes the end of their nightmares. From then on they are free never to fight again. And no longer bound to their *lanista*.

Iugula!

The gladiators have now left the arena after their initial introduction and have gone back to the service quarters of the Colosseum. We know that some young attendants are now dressing them in shin-guards (greaves), arm guards, and helmets. The crowd is strangely silent. The entire amphitheater is in the grip of an invisible tension. Everything seems to be moving in slow motion.

There's one thing that has surprised us: none of the gladiators stood before the organizer of the games to shout the famous ritual phrase "*Ave Caesare, morituri te salutant.*" (Hail Caesar, those who are about to die salute you.)

Why not? Because this is another of the many legends that have grown up about the gladiators. None of them actually utters this phrase. It happened only once, decades ago, under Claudius, moments before a *naumachia*, a naval battle. And it also had a tragicomic aspect to it. Claudius responded to this salute with a catchphrase formality, saying, "Perhaps." The result was that everyone interpreted it as an order to set them free and they refused to fight. Claudius had to correct himself and armed soldiers had to be called in to convince them to begin the naval battle.

The sound of trumpets (*tibiae*) and horns (*cornua*) rings out, the equivalent of our drum roll. Suddenly a series of dust spouts rises up from the arena floor of the Colosseum. They look almost like fountains of sand. A loud roar rises up from the crowd. When the dust clears, we can see, as though by a magic spell, the outlines of human bodies. They are the gladiators, who seem to have materialized out of nothing. Actually, they have emerged from the underground levels of the Colosseum, transported by the numerous freight elevators. Their hatches were hidden under the sand of the arena and they were opened suddenly, provoking as many explosions of dust. It's one of the crowd's favorite special effects. The gladiators pair off and immediately start fighting.

There are at least twelve different types of gladiators, some even on horseback or on wagons. But the ones we see now are classic pairs of combatants, the ones most loved by the crowd.

There's a famous *retiarius* (net fighter) who's fighting his traditional enemy, a *secutor* (chaser). The first is armed with the famous net and a trident. The second has a large rectangular shield and an arm guard. But most important he's wearing a strange egg-shaped helmet, with two simple holes for his eyes. The smooth shape of his helmet has been especially crafted to keep his opponent's net from catching on it. And a first throw comes up empty, the net slides over the *secutor* and falls to the ground. The two go on fighting.

Each pair of gladiators is flanked by a pair of judges who are former gladiators. They wear white tunics with two vertical red stripes. And they make sure, a little like the referee at a boxing match, that the fighters respect the rules.

In one case, we can see that they've interrupted the match between two *provocatores* (challengers), armed as legionnaires with a long shield, a gladius, and a helmet with a neck protector. One of the two has lost his shield and they give him time to pick it up.

The crowd is yelling words like *verbera, iugula, ure*, that is, "whip," "slice," "burn." In effect, there are attendants ready to "stimulate" reluctant gladiators with whip lashes or seething hot irons.

Around the edges of the arena the orchestras keep on playing, underlining and accompanying the most salient of the fights, like pianists used to do for silent movies. There's also a woman playing a strange organ; very much like a church organ, with a lot of vertical pipes, but smaller. For the execution of her pieces she has a miniscule podium raised up directly over the wall of the arena.

We notice a curious thing about the gladiators: none of them is wearing armor; they're all fighting bare-chested, contrary to what we're used to seeing in the movies. Only the *provocatores* have breastplates.

Another little known feature of gladiator dress is feathers; many of their helmets are loaded with them, almost like the headdress of an Indian chief. It's a detail that adds a lot to their image, and it's a very old tradition, dating back to well before the Romans, and widespread among warriors of many Italic, Mediterranean, and European ethnicities and cultures. Today, only members of the Italian *bersaglieri* keep light infantry corps up this custom.

A roar from the crowd highlights an important moment: one of the fighters has been wounded. A hoplomachus (two-knife man) has struck a Thracian. Both are equipped with small shields and large protective helmets. Their short swords allow for close combat, but the hoplomachus has an extra weapon: he's armed with a lance that he uses to try and hit his adversaries in their most delicate points, their face and eyes. The Thracian staggers and puts a hand up to the grate of his helmet where his blood is gushing out. The blow was precise. The hoplomachus has now stopped and is waiting. He's turned to the referee and the *editor*, the organizer of the games. The Thracian has raised his left hand with this index finger pointing upward; he's asking for clemency. The crowd rumbles. Some want him to live; others want him to die. The *editor* makes a sign: he's been pardoned. He must have put up a good fight.

A gladiator has many ways to ask for clemency: kneeling, raising his left hand, letting his shield drop, or even standing with his gladius behind his back and offering his chest. At that point, his adversary has to stop. The gladiators, after all, are slaves. They don't have the power to inflict death on a man. The decision rests with the one who paid for the games, the *editor*. And only him. The Thracian is carried off to the applause of the crowd.

But it's not over. There are other fights in the arena and like so many others in the crowd we are gripped by one particularly violent one that's going on in the middle of the oval of sand.

The opponents have two different systems of combat: one slow and one fast, like lightning. You can see that there's more in play here than just the ardor of the fight; the two hate each other. Maybe they already know each other. One is a murmillo (fish man), the other a Thracian. The murmillo is solid as a rock and hides behind a large square shield. He's massive and very strong. He has a greave on his left leg and a big helmet with a protective grate; it looks strangely like a wide-brimmed cowboy hat. His helmet also has a crest of brightly colored feathers. He moves very little; he's like a tank. But as soon as his opponent tries to move in on him he shows him the tapered point of his gladius.

His adversary, a Thracian, is his exact opposite. He's shorter, thin, but incredibly agile. He has a small, rectangular sword, very high greaves, and protective leather bands around his thighs, and he too has a big, grated helmet with a crest of feathers. The detail that allows us to identify him as a Thracian is the head of a hippogriff mounted on the top of his helmet. The hippogriff is a mythological animal, half horse and half griffin, and the Thracian fights in a way inspired by these two animals. He's almost sitting on his knees and he writhes like a snake.

His weapon is the murderous *sicca*, a short sword curved like a sickle. Why? It's well-suited to striking the adversary on the sides, with a murderous thrust to the hips, neck, or legs.

A skilled Thracian is truly a formidable opponent. And the murmillo knows it. He knows he can't commit a single error. The Thracian keeps running back and forth in front of his opponent, stopping and swaying his body, squatting like a cat. Then he suddenly springs forward, jumping onto the murmillo's shield, and tries to strike him on the neck, unleashing a terrible right hook. The murmillo ducks and the blow glances off the top of his helmet, emitting a dry, metallic clang. The crowd explodes, chanting *hoc habet, hoc habet* ("now he strikes him, now he strikes him").

The Thracian jumps down off the shield and backs off a few paces, and the siege starts again. The murmillo looks unfazed. He knows he's fended off a mortal blow, and that he was lucky. The next time he might succumb. Abruptly, he advances toward his opponent, rattling him, but he loses his balance and his shield wavers ever so slightly. The Thracian understands that this is the moment he was waiting for and leaps forward again, climbing onto his enemy's big shield, sure that this time he'll be able to land the winning blow.

But it's a trap. The murmillo has pretended to make a mistake in order to encourage him to leap forward. As the small, nimble gladiator jumps at him, he beats him to it and violently raises his shield, as though it were the sliding door of a garage. The Thracian is surprised; he suddenly finds himself suspended on the shield of his enemy, who's now holding it with both hands. In a fraction of a second, the Thracian is thrown to the ground after a rough flight. The crowd exults at this sudden turnabout. The Thracian tries to pull himself up, but the murmillo, amazingly quick for his size, thrusts his gladius at his side, stopping just short of penetration. The fight is interrupted by the referees. And everyone looks in the direction of the *editor*. He looks over the Colosseum crowd, with a slow, theatrical turn of the head. He can't understand what the people want.

Contrary to what we've been led to believe, the system of thumb up or thumb down is actually not widely used or universal. In this case, for example, nobody uses it. Pleas regarding the fate of the loser are more often made by a voice vote, shouting precise words: *mitte*, that is, "free him," or *iugula*, literally "cut his throat."

The *editor* opts for death. The murmillo turns to his adversary. The Thracian, demonstrating incredible self-control, bares his throat and waits. We're shocked by the courage and professionalism of the gladiators, who show no fear even in the face of death, almost as though it were normal. The murmillo moves his sword closer and then, with a decisive movement, drives it home. The crowd exults. The winner removes his helmet and is immediately rewarded, by young girls running onto the set, with a palm branch, the symbol of victory, and two silver plates filled with gold coins. Other gifts arrive on another tray. With this prize, but above all with the big prize, his life, he walks off toward the exit, amid the acclamation of the entire Colosseum. His spectacular move, performed with perfect timing, has also won over the crowd, who will long remember it. He turns, addresses a last salute to the crowd, and then disappears under the arch of the main door. That's where the winners exit.

And his adversary, the Thracian? He lies there lifeless, in a sea of blood. Some stagehands approach him wearing Charon

He suddenly springs forward, jumping onto the murmillo's shield, and tries to strike him on the neck, unleashing a terrible right hook. The murmillo ducks and the blow glances off the top of his helmet, emitting a dry, metallic clang. The crowd explodes, chanting *hoc habet, hoc habet* ("now he strikes him, now he strikes him").

masks and special clothes. Even their skin is painted a violet color. They harpoon the body with hooks and drag him off with chains, toward the door opposite the victor's door, the *libitinaria*. The door of Libitina, the goddess of death.

It will be brought to a special room, with rounded corners (for easy washing) and it will be stripped of clothes and weapons. If the gladiator is moribund, one of these Charon-masked figures will give him the final mortal blow, with the help of a stiletto.

But it won't end there. Some of the bodies will have some blood drawn from them. The blood of gladiators, in fact, is highly sought after. It's thought to be a cure for various ill-nesses, such as epilepsy, and the sick are urged to drink it or rub it on their bodies. Furthermore, given the physical vigor of the gladiators, it is considered a tonic and a sort of Viagra! There are a lot of people who profit from this sordid com-merce. In the end the bodies will be thrown into common graves, outside the city.

What It's Like to Be a Gladiator

Up to now we've been watching the spectacle of death from the grandstands. But what exactly does it mean to fight in the arena of the Colosseum with a helmet and the cheering crowd? Let's try to imagine it, putting on the helmet of a murmillo who's fighting against a terrible adversary, the retiarius. It was the luck of the draw that has matched them against each other (usually, the retiarius fights another kind of gladiator, called a *secutor*).

In the end it's a matter of tradition. This couple symbolically represents the fisherman, equipped with a net, trident, and dagger, and the fish; the name murmillo (or *mirmillo*) comes from *mormýros*, which means fish in Greek, or from *muraena* (moray eel), which hides among the rocks, ready to unleash its lethal bite (exactly like this type of gladiator, hiding behind his enormous shield).

While the retiarius bases his strategy on constantly circling his adversary, trying to surprise him with his net, the murmillo has a more difficult time of it. He always has to keep his opponent right in front of him. The murmillo's helmet, in fact, allows him to see only to the front and not to the sides. Besides that, the helmet's protective grate reduces his vision even more and makes it hard to breathe. It's very much like a football player's face mask. Imagine what it's like inside there in the middle of a fight; air is in short supply and breathing is tough. Then there's the heat. In the hot sun, the metal gets blistering hot, and passes the heat through to his head. Finally, the weight: a helmet like this weighs about eight pounds. The *secu-tor*'s helmet weighs even more: ten pounds! It's like carrying a boulder on your head.

You're surrounded by shouting, by the inciting cheers of fifty to seventy thousand people, a thunderous rumble that reverberates, incomprehensible, inside your helmet. Not to mention the referee's orders, the shouts and grunts of nearby gladiators, fighting or wounded. One of the toughest obstacles to overcome for a rookie gladiator is the emotion. Fighting in such a hostile and difficult place requires a huge capacity for self-control.

Obviously, we still haven't said anything about the gladiator's own state of mind. He knows that his life is at stake, every second. Just one mistake or one false move and it's over . . . Yet, despite all this, the murmillo named Astyanax keeps his cool. He doesn't lose sight of his opponent, whose fame he knows well, an able and hard-nosed retiarius, named Kalendius. He always keeps him in the center of his face mask, well framed by the borders of his visor. The retiarius circles him, running, and he, like a cornered crab, rotates on himself.

This story is true, the names are real.

The retiarius stops abruptly and coils as if he's about to change direction. But it's a trick; he's preparing to strike.

Without warning, the retiarius unwinds and unleashes his net. In an instant, Astyanax feels something heavy slam down on him, as though someone had jumped on top of him and has a grip on him. Then the rough ribbing of the net appears in front of his face mask. They are specially made nets, certainly not made for fishing, but designed to weigh on a gladiator and hinder his movements. It's a like a death grip, almost as though you were being squeezed by a live beast.

The net also keeps Astyanax's helmet tilted to one side and he has to struggle to keep his head from bending even more. He has to gasp to breathe; it feels like the air is being sucked out of his helmet. Kalendius can hear the deep rasping noise, almost a wheeze, coming from his opponent. But he doesn't attack. Not right away, at least. He knows from experience that it's better to wait a little until his adversary, caught in the net, tries to move and gets himself even more tangled up, or trips. He has to strike in that precise moment. Astyanax feels trapped and just then he recalls the words of his trainer, himself a murmillo and a former gladiator: bend your knees and raise your sword a little. That'll create a sort of low "hut" that will offer fewer openings to the trident of the retiarius. That's what he does, but it's not easy with the net pulling him all to one side.

The first blow of the retiarius is high, aimed to hit between the shoulder and the throat, because he knows that the weight of the net will make the murmillo lower his shield. Astyanax feels a sudden burning sensation in his shoulder. The sharp trident has shot through the webbing of the net like lightning and hit him with a glancing blow. The "low" position suggested by his trainer has saved him. And the armored sleeve that he's wearing has also helped to absorb the blow. The referees don't consider the wound sufficient to interrupt the fight, even though blood is starting to drip from the metal scales of his sleeve.

The crowd notices some reflections of red and exults. But the two fighters don't hear the shouts, they're concentrating too intensely. The retiarius has gone back to circling the murmillo, trying to disorient him. Astyanax continues to keep him framed in his face mask. He knows he's fended off the first attack, but how much longer can he hold out with that weight on his back and his mobility so hindered?

The retiarius adopts another insidious tactic, exploiting his opponent's reduced mobility. He'll fake another high blow so the murmillo raises his shield, and then he'll thrust his trident down low to cut through his opponent's far leg, the one without protective greaves. He begins his strike. As predicted, the murmillo moves his shield, leaving one of his sides exposed. The retiarius rapidly withdraws his trident to strike down low. The murmillo sees him and swerves to the side, a difficult maneuver with his helmet tilted. But it works, the trident misses! And there's a sudden turnabout. Astyanax, the murmillo, guesses that something's not right. The retiarius keeps on thrusting his trident, over and over, moving in and out. For an instant, Astyanax is afraid he's been hit and that he can't feel anything because of the tension, while the retiarius continues to mangle his flesh.

But that's not it. He can feel the net pulling on him from all directions, and he understands. Attempting the "perfect" strike, Kalendius has thrust his trident into the webbing of the net and it's stuck. Now he's entangled in his own net and he's trying desperately to free the trident. But he can't get it out; on the contrary, the more he tries, the worse it gets . . . The fisherman has fallen into his own net. Astyanax understands that this is his chance, maybe the only one he has to save himself. He takes three or four powerful steps backward, dragging the retiarius, who in his rage is thinking only of freeing his trident. Then he fills his lungs with air and throws himself at him with all the strength he can muster. As soon as his shield comes into contact with Kalendius' body, Astyanax sticks him with his gladius. He acts on instinct, calculating his opponent's position from the impact he felt against his shield. Years of training have paid off. The gladius thrusts forward out of the net like a silver-plated claw. The crowd sees a flash of silver and then nothing. The next image, in everyone's eyes is the retiarius lying on the ground, surprise on his face, like a KO'd boxer. He tries to push himself back up with his arms, but he can't do it. The inside of his right thigh has a gaping wound that's gushing blood. The blood is not bright red anymore but dark. A big stain spreads over the arena floor.

Astyanax is ready to strike again, and he's about to; the adrenaline keeps him from feeling the weight of the net. His muscles are now being commanded by his survival instinct, not by his brain. He barely hears one of the referees yelling at him to stop. He stops short, gasping for air. The way the crowd sees it, his head is moving as if he were literally trying to "bite" the air around him. When his breathing is more regular he looks at his adversary on the ground. He still has that treacherous look on his face that he'll never forget for the rest of his life. But there's something else in those eyes; a request, almost an order. The retiarius offers him his dagger. Perhaps in a desperate attempt to ask for clemency. But it's not Astyanax who can decide. Nor the referees, who, their arms outstretched with their thumbs up, ask the *editor* what to do. The verdict is death. Astyanax approaches. His adversary understands now that all is lost and raises his throat. A short breeze moves his hair, almost a final caress of life. Then an unbearably sharp pain and everything goes dark.

This episode was faithfully recorded in a mosaic discovered on the Appian Way and now conserved in the national archaeological museum in Madrid.

But did it always end up that way? In reality, it seems that death in the arena was somewhat less frequent for gladiators than it was for criminals condemned to death or slaves killed in theatrical spectacles or hunts. There were various reasons for this. First of all, because it took a lot of time to train a gladiator, and so losing him quickly meant throwing away years of work. Moreover, gladiators were costly, both to the *lanista* who trained them and to the organizer of the games, who, in the case of death, had to pay a higher price for them. So it's easy to see that it wasn't painless for the organizer to turn his thumb down.

Besides that, we shouldn't forget about the betting business and the fan support enjoyed by many of the champions, who, for obvious reasons, "had" to go on living. In short, especially in the era that we're describing, there were probably fighters who ended their careers with the *missio,* or the salvation of the defeated, while fights *sine missione*, that is, to the death, though they certainly did occur, were relatively less frequent than is commonly believed.

GETTING INVITED TO A BANQUET

L ate afternoon is upon us. What happens now in Rome? The stores are almost all closed by now, and have been since lunchtime. The Forum has emptied out, and everyone's left the basilicas, except for a few servants who are cleaning the floors. In the Senate, the light streaming in from the big overhead windows shines on long rows of empty chairs. People are leaving the baths, strolling slowly, relaxing after their massage. Even the Colosseum crowd is on its way out, after the last fights, the ones most waited for.

At this point, all the inhabitants of Rome and of the Empire are making their way toward the last big appointment of the day: dinner. Why so early?

Essentially for two reasons. In the absence of electricity, it's better to make your activities coincide with the hours of sunlight. In a certain sense, daily life follows the sun; people get up at dawn and go to bed shortly after sunset. Dinner also ends before the sun has completely disappeared. This makes it possible for guests to get back home before the streets become dark and dangerous, even though there are a lot of banquets that go on far into the night (Nero's until midnight and Trimalcione's till dawn).

The second reason is very practical. As we have mentioned, there are three meals in imperial Rome: breakfast (*ientaculum*), lunch (*prandium*), and dinner (*cena*). The first is abundant, the second simple. It's understandable that people start to feel hungry halfway through the afternoon, about nine hours after breakfast. Dinner will satisfy their appetites and allow them to make it through the long night without more food. The dinner hour for Romans, therefore, changes with the seasons: the ninth hour in the warm months, and the eighth hour in the cold ones.

But what do the Romans eat in the evening? We all have the image in mind of the sumptuous banquets we've seen in movies. Is it really like that? Let's find out.

Romans organize banquets quite frequently, a lot more often than we do dinners with friends. It's a habit, or better, almost a social rule (naturally, only for those who can afford it; for the tenants of the *insulae*, it's a very different story).

Instinctively, we tend to think that banquets are organized in order to socialize, relax, and have a good time. That's true, but most of all they're a way to network, see and be seen, show off your comfortable station in life. Often, banquets are public relations dinners, to cultivate good relationships with important people, to negotiate political or business alliances, and so on. In short, more than a dinner, a banquet is what more recent centuries would have called a "salon."

While we've been thinking about all this, we've entered a street illuminated by the oblique light of the afternoon sun. We're under the portico of an *insula*, strangely empty after the morning crush. All the stores are boarded shut.

At the end of the portico we notice some moving figures. The sunlight shining from behind them creates thin golden halos around their black silhouettes. We're able to make out the slaves, from their short tunics, and the master, the *dominus*, with his flowing toga, accompanied by his wife. The couple is getting into two separate litters, assisted by their servants. We get a good look at the man's red hair, almost inflamed by the rays of the sun.

When it's the woman's turn, the light shines through her

long shawl that covers her body. Only silk is this transparent—a true status symbol for wealthy women, to be displayed ostentatiously. On one of her shoulders we glimpse the brief sparkle of a gold pin. The couple is dressed in a decidedly elegant fashion. We have found what we were looking for someone invited to a dinner. All we have to do is follow their litters and we'll discover the secrets of an ancient Roman banquet.

The short procession leaves the portico of the *insula*, almost like two sailboats leaving the dock. The slaves remain standing along the banks of the sidewalk, almost at attention, looking at their departing owners. Then they go back home. Except for one, who stops on the threshold and sits down, the *lanternarius*. He's carrying a blanket, something to eat, and a lantern. He'll wait at the front door of the house until the master returns. And when he sees him, he'll accompany him inside, lighting the way. We leave behind this "custodian of the lighthouse" and follow the two litters.

As we're moving through a fair-sized chunk of the city, we notice that it has changed its look. Its streets have now become the equivalent of the suburban beltways of our big cities. It's rush hour and everyone's on their way home; you can tell by their stride, by the look in their eye.

The beehive of activity that we saw this morning is gone. Even the air has changed. You can smell the odor of burning wood everywhere, a sign that all around us thousands of braziers have been lit to cook food.

In some alleyways, where the air doesn't circulate as well, you can see a light mist and sometimes your eyes even burn a little, a sign that the fires are burning dried animal dung, the so-called "poor folks' wood."

The procession of the litters is led by two men, one with a cane, the other with a lighted lantern. In the back, a man keeps a lookout.

We're there. The little group stops in front of a very elegant front door. The banquet must be here.

The Banquet

We need to clarify something before we enter the *domus* where the banquet is being held. It's not true that the Romans spend a lot of time at the table, between orgies and feasts. That's a myth as mistaken as it is widespread. The Romans are simple people who eat very little; food is associated with sobriety.

Obviously, there are exceptions. Indeed, part of the society manages to grant themselves splendid dinners. We're talking about the minority that commands Rome. It's made up of all those who in some way or other have a piece of the political, commercial, or financial power. So, not only the patrician families and representatives of the senatorial and equestrian orders but also freed men who have made their way up the social ladder.

These dinners, as we have said, are a fundamental social mechanism for the elite. But for the rest of the population, ninety percent of the inhabitants of Rome, dinner is a very simple meal.

The sound of the door knocker echoes through the entrance hall of the *domus* and re-echoes in the great atrium. The front door slave is ready to open. When he pulls open the two sides of the door, he sees before him the two luxurious litters of the guests, sitting on the ground. With great solemnity, arrangements are made for the man and woman's descent to the ground. A stool is set down for them to put their feet on, along with a carpet. With royal slowness, the couple descends from their litters. Once in the atrium, the two of them follow the slave who will show them the way. As in the *domus*, here too the long entrance hall opens onto a pretty atrium with a pool to collect rainwater. But here, everything is much bigger.

This *domus*, in fact, is one of the most spacious in Rome. It is famous for its enormous peristyle, with a long colonnade that frames the garden. In the garden there is a large arbor, several fountains, original bronze Greek and Persian statues, and even a small wood populated by several couples of peacocks.

When they get to the atrium, the two guests hand over their napkins (as etiquette requires) and they're shown to their places. Some of their host's slaves remove their shoes and begin washing their feet with perfumed water. As all of this is happening, the woman observes the *impluvium*, in search of some defect to comment on later with her friends, or of some idea to copy. Between the columns are long red curtains,

Wealthy Romans frequently organize banquets that last six to eight hours. It's a way of being seen, and negotiating political or business alliances. Rather than dinners, these evenings are more like "salons," gladdened by delicacies such as oysters, roast flamingo, and free-flowing wine.

almost all of them tied elegantly like scarves. The surface of the water is adorned by small constellations of rose petals which the air currents have gathered together in chance formations. And also floating in the water are some swan-shaped lanterns, with several flames each that are reflected in the water. It's a very original idea that the woman will try to replicate at her next banquets.

Her husband, on the other hand, is staring into the void. Perhaps he's thinking of something catchy to say to their host, a senator who has asked to see him urgently, even reserving for him the role of the last invited, a privilege which is probably in exchange for some request for financial assistance or political support. Considering his by-now solid position in the Middle Eastern animal trade (which allows him to import rare animals such as tigers and rhinos), it's likely that his host is thinking about organizing some games at the Colosseum, and wants a supply of wild beasts at a favorable price.

The two are invited to continue toward the banquet room. The route is complicated and planned that way, in order to show off to the guests the most important features of the house. As though it were a short guided tour, the two pass in front of the family strongbox, and then the fine mosaic in the home office (the *tablinum*), which also conserves a historic relic: the sword of one of Hannibal's lieutenants, "or perhaps of Hannibal himself," which one of the senator's ancestors picked up on the battlefield at Zama, fighting side by side with Scipio. Each time, the stop is almost imperceptible, the explanation of their guide, the butler slave (*nomenclator*), brief, but his words are well calculated and highly effective. Often in this *domus* there are tables with silver pitchers and plates, skillfully displayed as though in an exhibition of price-less treasures.

The sound of music, at first distant and gradually more intense, signals to the couple that they are nearing the *triclinium*.

Finally, they make their appearance in the famous peristyle, still well lit by the sunlight. They can see all of its celebrated wonders. The woman is struck by the virile beauty of a young boy standing motionless in the middle of the garden. After a few steps, she realizes that it's actually the bronze statue of a Greek hero, with flowing hair, shining silver teeth, and red lips, made of a copper alloy—Without a doubt, a work brought back from Greece by another of the senator's illustrious ancestors.

Having turned the last corner of this private cloister, the *triclinium* finally comes into view. It's on one side of the garden, a room of the house that opens perfectly onto this oasis of green and tranquility, with the statue right in the center of the view. It's really big, with frescoes of mythological scenes, bucolic landscapes, and fake architectures that fill every inch of the walls. There are also a lot of garlands of perfumed, colorful flowers. In the center is a very low, round table, already laid with silver cups and appetizers that the guests have already started nibbling.

The guests are reclining on the famous three couches of the *triclinium*, arranged in a horseshoe around the table. They are a highly elegant azure with large yellow pillows for each place. And they are slightly inclined with the higher side near the table so the person dominates his servings.

The floor mosaic is a classic *triclinium* scene. It reproduces the remains of fish, lobsters, shells, bones—in short, the remains of a banquet symbolically designed on the floor.

A *triclinium* is not only a dining room. Its various parts represent the whole world. The ceiling is the sky, the table with the *triclinium* couches and the guests is the Earth, the floor the world of the dead. Outside the room, in a corner of the colonnade, five musicians are playing some pleasant background music, with flutes, lyres, and tambourines.

At a signal from the butler slave, they intone an almost triumphal motif that accompanies the couple's arrival, as though it were a wedding march. The senator, stretched out on the center couch together with his young wife, raises his hand, showing off a big smile. All of the guests stop talking and look at them. There are both women and men, of various ages. Our guest recognizes, among the other guests, the secretary of the prefect of the city, a key man (even more so than his superior) for obtaining special permits to hold games at the Colosseum. He has a lovely wife, with Nordic features. Her hair is blond but the color might not be real; her hairdo, very much in vogue, and similar to a high "flame," is probably a wig. A chubby woman with black hair, heavy makeup, fleshy lips and a fake mole over her mouth occupies almost half a couch by herself. Her hairdo is striking, even more monumental than the Nordic woman's, a true "papal tiara," replete with gold stars and even some gems. With her short, pointed fingers, she fondles a big gold locket that hangs from her neck.

The *nomenclator*, the butler slave, recites the names of the guests and their titles. Many of them make some sign of approval and delight, more feigned than real.

On a sign from the senator, two servants indicate the places on the *triclinium* reserved for the two new guests. The good news is that the man's place is on the senator's left, the place of honor. The bad news is that he'll be next to the cumbersome mass of that enormous woman. He already imagines the little space he'll have to move, the heat of his neighbor's body and, as if that weren't enough, the exaggerated waves of perfume that she'll be emitting to cover the smell of her sweat. He can sense already that he won't even be able to perceive the smell and the taste of the food.

All things considered, his wife is better off. She'll be lying between a woman with a friendly face and a handsome man whom she'll discover to be the senator's nephew, on leave from the eastern front where he's been fighting with Trajan. He'll have a lot of stories to tell—war stories but also some gossip (which everyone wants to hear).

As soon as they have taken their places, two slaves approach the guests and wash their hands, using water perfumed with rose petals and drying them with beautiful towels of embroidered linen.

What do people talk about at a banquet? It's considered inopportune to talk about political issues. All other subjects, however, are allowed, including jokes and wisecracks, a little like our informal dinners, and also verses of poetry.

The dinner begins with the appearance of a very well-dressed slave, with a pointy white beard. He's an educated slave who was a teacher for the senator's children; now that he is elderly he is used on various occasions to give a touch of culture to the evening, reciting verses in Greek and Latin. Sometimes the verses are famous; sometimes they are personalized compositions, which almost always praise the master and his guests. His accent reveals his Greek origins and his words are accompanied by the lyres of the musicians.

His verses are a signal for the slaves to begin serving the starter, or *gustus*, as it is called.

In an instant, everyone stops listening to the poetry in order to concentrate on the servers, who are arriving with a large tray covered with steaming, plump cones. It looks almost like an array of little volcanoes.

The slave in charge of managing the various courses arches his eyebrows, puffs himself up, and declaims the composition of the starter: "Pig teats stuffed with sea urchins!" The guests are taken aback with satisfaction; it's one of the most renowned and longed-for dishes at capital dinner parties. It combines the sweet taste of pork with the marine flavor of sea urchin eggs. The servers (*ministratores*) put the plates and goblets down on the table.

While the guests start to delight in this delicacy, other slaves go around and fill the goblets with wine. The one that accompanies the starter is always very special; *mulsum*, wine mixed with honey.

A Roman dinner is a little bit like a concert program, with a very specific selection of dishes. All the guests know that the banquet they're going to taste this evening will be memorable. The senator is famous for the refinement and fantasy of his dinners. On other occasions, he has served plentiful portions of oysters, dormouse, and flamingo. But also sow vulva in the form of fish and heron tongue in honey sauce. One time the senator amazed everyone with a massive female boar stuffed with live thrush and surrounded by little bread-paste pigs sucking its milk.

We know that a good banquet can last from six to eight hours. The only thing that approaches it in the modern age are wedding receptions (or farm-family holiday lunches in our grandparents' time). Imagine having to go to a wedding reception two or three times a week. If you're part of the upper crust of Roman society, that's often what you can expect at certain times of the year!

How do they eat all of these courses? With a system that has gone down in history: propped up on their left elbow resting on a pillow. They hold onto their plates with their left hand, while the right is used to bring the food to the mouth. The dinner companions lie next to one another, shoeless, with their bare feet washed.

But isn't it uncomfortable? We might not be able to do it; we're not used to it. Our left arm would fall asleep; after a while back bent in that position, it would start to bother us. Our stomach would fill up fast, giving us a false signal of satiety.

But Romans are used to eating this way. For them it's a sign of elegance and superiority, a general rule of etiquette to be followed rigorously at official or important banquets (just as today good table manners require that we refrain from putting our elbows on the table or holding our fork in our fist like a dagger). At dinners with friends, however, the atmosphere was much more relaxed and informal. People changed positions, shifted from one elbow to another, or both, and turned to speak with people lying behind them. Initially, wives didn't eat lying down but seated on chairs next to their husbands. Not in Trajan's Rome, however. The only ones who still eat sitting down on small stools, next to their father, are children.

A recent study suggests that eating in that position, given the shape of the stomach, would favor digestion. It's an interesting finding, but it may be more logical to suppose that this position is only the fruit of practicality. Lying on your left side, in fact, leaves your right hand, the one we use more often, free. The rest is merely a question of habit.

The first course arrives. It's a huge platter with a lot of lobsters stuffed with caviar. They are arranged along the sides of a volcano of shaved ice. Its crater, shaped like an enormous goblet, holds an enormous quantity of oysters. The role of the belt around this marine volcano is played by moray eels drowned in a hot sauce.

It must be said that such culinary triumphs, decorated in this rather vulgar style, are typical of Roman banquets.

The arrival of this hefty construction, almost three feet high, requires the combined strength of three servants, but it provokes a chorus of admiration.

What will the guests use to eat these various foods? Romans don't know about forks (they're an Italian invention dating from the Renaissance and first used in Florence). The Romans eat everything with the fingers. But after all, as Carcopino says, "that's what the French did all the way up until modern times."

In reality, even though forks don't yet exist, each guest has various kinds of knives and spoons at their disposition, including a ladle (*trulla*), in the classic style, and a smaller spoon similar to a teaspoon for children (*ligula*). Another spoon has a pointed handle (*cochlear*), used above all for emptying eggs and seashells.

We should add, that, precisely because there are no forks, the habitual strategy of Roman cuisine is to serve food cut into small pieces, pre-prepared mouthfuls. That's why just about everywhere you go, even in the taverns, you see a lot of meatballs, kebabs, tidbits and so on. In a certain sense, this tradition has remained unchanged in all those countries where the traditional cuisine still assumes that you eat with your hands, like India, North Africa, etc. When, for example, they serve couscous in a Moroccan home and everyone eats together, seated in a circle on cushions around a single big plate, you can't help but think of the atmosphere of a Roman dinner.

It's clear that eating in this way, your hands immediately get dirty with sauces, condiments, etc. So there is a constant traffic of slaves around the diners' couches who pour perfumed water on their hands from silver pitchers before drying them with an immaculate towel.

Another indispensable implement is toothpicks, which, as we mentioned at the start of the book, have a number of uses. One of them we can see now. One of the guests, a man with a crew cut, is carefully cleaning the interstices of his teeth, using the curved end of his decorated toothpick. Now he switches ends and sticks the other end, outfitted with a little hand inside his ear. After giving the instrument a good, full turn, he pulls it out, gives a distracted glance at what he has collected, picks it off with his fingers, and then rubs them together so it all drops on the floor.

While the guests are listening to an off-color story told by the senator (at the end of which it is obligatory to laugh), the complex machine of the banquet keeps moving forward. One of the slaves distributes the plates for the next course. He is the *structor*, who is like a choreographer of the courses. With millimetric precision, once the joke is finished and the orchestra has struck up again (it too dutifully mute during the master's performance), he has the second course brought in.

The guests still have their mouths full, but they welcome this pleasant turn of events. Making its triumphal entrance is an ornate platter with a yellow sauce of saffron and eggs, an imitation of desert sand, in the center of which are some strange, dark smoking structures. These are camel feet! A true delicacy of Roman cuisine with countless fans at banquets. To tell the truth, rather than camel feet they are dromedary feet, only recently arrived in North Africa, thanks to the invasion of Egypt by the Persian king Cambises. But they have also found a place on the menu of Roman banquets and in Roman recipes.

The Roman palate
This dish that the table companions have begun to enjoy (already the yellow sauce has started running down their wrists) gives us the chance to open up a brief parenthesis on the Roman palate. One of its characteristic features is the constant alternation of sweet (honey) and savory, for both dinner courses and desserts. And sometimes these two tastes are mixed. But the most striking thing is the Romans' predilection for very spicy foods, and their exaggerated use of condiments, aromas, and spices. There's an echo of this cuisine today in Indian and Mediterranean cooking, and that's how the Roman dishes being served at this banquet would have seemed to us. But it would be a mistake to consider Roman cuisine as something far removed from our own. In reality, the basic ingredients are the same ones that we use today.

The dimension that is almost totally lacking in our dishes, however, is the superimposition of tastes. We understand the culinary art as the harmonious combination of different tastes. For the Romans there is also a higher level. If you take one taste or flavor and add it to another one, you will obtain a third absolutely new taste completely different from the first two.

I had this experience when I tasted a *gustus* (starter) re-created by expert "archaeologists" of Roman tastes and culinary customs, who belong to an association with a charming name, Ars Convivialis, specializing in original Roman menus (whose dinners come with an archaeologist who explains each course to you as it is served). Biting into a toasted slice of Roman meal (spelt) bread, coated with a spread of ricotta cheese and garlic, you taste a very distinct flavor. Adding a sip of dry white wine brings to the surface, as though by magic, another flavor, which resembles neither of the previous ones.

With this type of cuisine, cooking is a bit like making music with the numerous components of an orchestra. And one of the best-loved instruments has as a very famous name: *garum*.

What is *garum*? It's the most highly requested sauce at banquets, used like mayonnaise or ketchup. Actually, it would be better to compare it, for its delicacy, to our precious balsamic vinegar. But its origins are totally different. Hearing how *garum* is made may make you grimace. You take the innards of fish (anchovies, mackerel, etc.) or the whole fish, depending on the occasion, and you let it marinate in pickling liquid for several days. The product of this process is then distilled by passing it through various sieves, each of which yields a more refined and costly *garum*. Its odor is anything but appealing, and Apicius, the great gourmet chef of the Roman era, advised doctoring it with smoked laurel or cypress, with honey and fresh must.

But what does *garum* taste like? Re-created today, it's a little thicker than olive oil and it tastes like anchovy paste. If you think of how we use anchovy paste or even anchovies themselves in Italian cooking, you can get an idea of why its salty piquance made the Romans wild about it.

Another characteristic of Roman cuisine is its decided preference for soft foods over crunchy ones (before being roasted, for example, meat is inevitably boiled). The Greeks, who always considered boiled meat a very unsophisticated food, had the habit of referring to the Romans with an unflattering nickname: "boiled meat eaters."

Meat is one of the highlights of Roman cooking. In addition to being skewered and grilled, it is also ground and eaten with various kinds of filling. And so meatballs start showing up on your plate. Or maybe some pig intestines filled with the discarded parts of the animal (innards, gristle, etc.), which remind us of sausages. You'd be surprised to learn that in imperial Rome it was possible to find a kind of sausage very familiar to Italians today: *luganiga* or *lucanica*, as the ancient Romans call it. They make it from ground smoked beef, or pork, mixed with a lot of herbs and spices, such as cumin, pepper, parsley, or savory. The mixture is then enriched with pine nuts and lard. The result is a real delicacy. Another dish that we know well is *foie gras* (goose liver paté), already a prized creation in the Roman era.

The Secrets of the Senator's Cook

The banquet is proceeding amid comments, jokes, riddles, even a small lottery. All accompanied by pleasant background music. But the host of a banquet is obliged to amaze his guests. At the snap of his fingers the orchestra strikes up piece with a strong rhythm featuring the tambourine. All of a sudden, two acrobats appear on one side of the peristyle's colonnade and start performing extraordinary balancing acts and contortions to the delighted applause of the table companions. They are followed by some clowns who get everybody laughing with stories, gags, and circus tricks.

Putting ourselves in the place of the stretched-out diners, the garden seems like a little theater stage with the columns, trees, and statues serving as backdrop and wings. Today, we'd say it looks like the set for a variety show.

In the meantime, however, what's going on in the kitchen?

Who's working in there, and above all, who has prepared all these triumphs of the palate? Let's go in and take a look, leaving the host and his guests laughing at one of the clowns' slapstick routines.

The kitchen is not far away and, as in every *domus*, it's not very spacious. That's why, for this evening, part of the service passageway has also been occupied. The atmosphere is not joyous like the *triclinium*. Here, tension reigns; all the courses have to succeed perfectly and satisfy everybody, especially the master.

Observing one of the servants, we discover that he's finishing up preparations of one of this evening's two roasts. It's a flamingo. As he's putting on the final touches, he's telling one of the senator's grandchildren, who's snuck into the kitchen, the secrets of the preparation. Nobody dares send the child away, obviously, and for us it's a chance to find out the cook's secrets. So we discover that the flamingo has been defeathered, washed, and tied. Then they put it in a deep casserole pot, with lightly salted water. They added dill, a drop of vinegar, and they heated it over a slow-burning fire. When the meat started getting tender, they added some flour to the water, stirring with a ladle so that it would thicken into a nice sauce. At that point they added some spices and, finally, they put it on a big tray, pouring the sauce over it and adding some dates. "This is the recipe of the famous flamingo served at banquets throughout the Empire," the servant continued. "And this is the same way we cook—parrots!" The little boys' eyes spring open in surprise . . .

The flamingo is carried into the table by some servers. We can hear the shouts of amazement all the way in here.

But the tension in the kitchen remains high.

"*Pullus farsilis! Leepus madidus! Patina piscium!*" (stuffed chicken, stewed hare, panful of fish), shouts a slave, behind us, lifting the covers off three casserole pots. These are the reserve dishes, in case the dinner requires more, unplanned, courses.

This planning for the unplanned shows us that the kitchen

is under the command of a real professional of the stove. A *magirus,* as he is referred to in Greek, literally, a "high priest" of cooking. Something like a head chef (*archimagirus*) with his sous-chefs.

In effect, any well-to-do host can rent a cook with his squad at the Forum. But when you enter the kitchen of someone as important as the senator, it's a different story. These great families have their own personal chef, just like they have their own pastry chef and baker.

The senator's chef is famous and now we are watching him give orders to his assistants.

But what are the secrets of this wizard of the palate? The kitchen is in perfect order; everyone's position and movements seem to follow a script learned by heart. We have the impression that we're in some kind of operating room.

One table is laid out with a vast array of herbs and spices: mint, coriander, garlic, celery, cumin, bay leaves. To be sure, they are used to "exult the flavor and blend perfectly with ground meats," as Apicius suggests. But they also serve another function.

In reality, the heavy use of herbs and spices in Roman cooking is indispensable in order to conceal the smell of meat (and fish) that is going bad—an unpleasant consequence (which we have pretty much forgotten) of the lack of refrigeration and preservatives.

As we continue to observe the ingredients, we note the lack of some that are very important for us, for example: tomatoes, potatoes, beans, corn (and therefore, also corn oil), chocolate—all things that will be discovered in the new world, thanks to Columbus. Like turkeys. Mozzarella cheese isn't known either, since it is made from the milk of Asian buffaloes, which still haven't been imported into Italy (it may have been the Longobards who imported them, when they invaded the peninsula in the High Middle Ages). The same thing is true of eggplant, which was brought to Italy in the Middle Ages by the Arabs.

It's curious to think of an Italian cuisine without so many of its characteristic ingredients and dishes.

Since there is no mozzarella and no tomatoes, no one has invented pizza. Spaghetti and the other kinds of pasta still don't exist and will be developed in Italy starting in the Middle Ages (well before Marco Polo's voyage to China, as attested by various documents). Spaghetti is an Italian invention. China will develop its own version, completely independent of spaghetti.

We walk over to the *archimagirus*, the head chef, as he is preparing a truly special dish, requested in order to amaze the master's guests: nightingales with rose petals. Everyone else has moved out of the way; he's the only one working.

He has calculated two birds per person and has put the rose petals in a bit of water to soak. Then, delicately, he coats the birds in honey.

His assistants have prepared the stuffing and he checks it, nodding his head in approval. The paté of ground innards is just right. But it's not enough. The winning card of this dish is what he's about to add to the stuffing. So he starts chopping mint leaves and mountain celery. His delicate knifeblows against the cutting board echo about the room. Then he turns, picks up a marble mortar, and grinds up an abundant mixture of garlic, cloves, pepper, coriander and olive oil.

He adds a clump of aromatic herbs and then, the master's touch, also a drop of *defrutum*, concentrate of grape juice.

At this point the stuffing is ready; he scoops it into each bird, with the addition of a nice plum. He turns to his assistants and orders them to cook the birds over a low flame and, when they are ready, to decorate the plate with the rose petals. If they are served with a nice amphora of Falerno wine, success is guaranteed.

Few of those present know that this is actually a recipe of

Apicius, who lived a couple of generations ago. With this dish he won over the palate of Drusus, son of Tiberius. But this comes as no surprise; the chefs of all the great families always try to take their inspiration from famous, strange, and exotic recipes. And our head chef is a true follower of Apicius. How do we know? From a detail: that touch of *defrutum*, the grape juice concentrate, is a typical culinary trick of the *maestro*.

Another typical trait of Apicius is the rose petals. His dishes are beautifully decorated, even though the decoration is useless, and in this he anticipates by almost two thousand years the tendencies of many modern chefs.

Dinner Table Etiquette

We head back to the *triclinium*. In the meantime, the flamingo has been carried off and replaced by another garish triumph, the second roast. It's so big it has to be carried on a sort of stretcher. A veal calf, boiled and "dressed" with a helmet fixed between its horns. The slave responsible for cutting the meat is wearing an Ajax costume, and uses his sharp sword to prepare the portions of meat for the various table companions.

The calm atmosphere is broken when the fat woman with black hair emits a loud belch that surprises a guest, who immediately spills half a cup of wine on the floor. The senator looks at him and smiles, almost thanking him. The first belch is echoed by another, and then still another. And each time the senator smiles. But what kind of dinner party is this? What do the Romans consider good table manners?

The least one can say is that they're very different from ours. Even an emperor would risk being asked to leave one of our neighborhood restaurants if he behaved himself according to Roman etiquette. Yet, Roman table manners are just what we have seen: they eat with their hands, constantly getting them dirty. Any discarded food is thrown on the floor: bones, lobster shells, clam shells, pig bones, etc., in front of and under the *triclinium* couches. And the belches are countless—and very much appreciated. They are even considered—are you ready for this?—a sign of nobility! Or better, a mark of civility. According to Roman philosophers, belching is a way of following nature's example and so it is considered, really, to be the last word of wisdom.

An echo of this habit has remained in the Arab world and India, where belching is even expected by hosts as a sincere appreciation of the food.

I myself experienced great embarrassment once in North Africa during a dinner at a friend's house. There was an air of expectation, almost as thought the meal had not been to my taste or that something had gone wrong in the preparation of the food. When I gave in to local custom, a general and evident satisfaction spread around the room.

And that's not all. At a banquet like the one we've been observing, even farting is allowed. As vulgar as that might sound, at a high society banquet nobody is scandalized. On the contrary, flatulence was just one step away from being consented at table by law! It appears that the emperor Claudius actually planned to issue a flatulence edict, when he learned that a dinner companion had risked his life by "containing himself" in the emperor's presence.

Continuing our journey through Roman table etiquette, we discover other rules decidedly distant from our own. At a certain point, one of the guests snaps his fingers. A servant approaches him with an elegant blown-glass bedpan and, his toga pulled up, the guest is permitted to "relax," freeing himself of his excess of accumulated liquids.

Much has been said about the habit of vomiting during banquets. The truth of this is hard to establish. Juvenal speaks openly of vomiting on the floor mosaics at the conclusion of banquets, but it's difficult to tell if this was a habit or an accidental consequence of overeating. Seneca, however, is more precise and explains that sometimes the guests got up from the table to go vomit in another room in order to make room in their stomachs for more food.

Finally, there is one Roman habit that strikes us as quite modern: guests are allowed to take food home, wrapping it up in their napkins. In theory, the food is to be given to their servants, but in reality taking the food home gives the master a chance to taste it again the next day. This custom, known as *apophoreta*, is surprisingly similar to the doggy bag, which is such a common and accepted practice in American restaurants (in this case too, in theory the leftovers are meant for the dog, but in practice they are eaten by his owners).

Sweets, Fruits, and . . .
The servants remove the table and sprinkle the floor with sawdust painted red. This is the sign that the main part of the banquet is over. Now begins the part called *secundae mensae*, in which sweets and fruit will be served.

Trays are brought in loaded with little masterpieces of pastry, and a big cake. Martial was right when he said "the bees work only for the pastry chefs of the capital." On seeing the massive quantities of honey used in Roman desserts (but also in wine) one realizes how many beehives and beekeepers were necessary to ensure the supply. In effect, honey was the main sweetener of the Roman age.

The fruit that follows is mostly of apples, grapes, and figs. But ever since the Romans have begun to reach out toward the East, especially now under Trajan, peaches and apricots have begun to make an appearance on banquet tables, and the Romans are wild about them. The word "peach" comes from "Persia," Persian apple (*malum persicum*), and in Rome and certain regions of northern Italy, peaches are still called Persian apples.

One of the guests picks up a fig from a plate, admires it, and exclaims: "*Carthago delenda est*" (Carthage must be destroyed). Then he bites into it. The others approve, smiling. His reference to history is precise and perfectly suited to a period such as this one (not least because everyone knows that the senator is one of Trajan's biggest supporters, and one of the biggest beneficiaries of his conquests). In other situations, it could have been a terrible gaffe. But what is the connection between Roman history and figs?

In 150 BCE, Cato the Elder was very worried about the rebirth of Carthage. One day, he had an idea. He arrived in the Senate with a basket full of fresh figs and said to his colleagues, "When do you think these figs were picked? Well, they were picked just three days ago in Carthage. That's the distance that separates our enemy from our walls." Cato couldn't have imagined a better theatrical effect. The senators were very impressed by the freshness of the figs. It is said that this was the straw that broke the camel's back and the Senate voted in favor of the third Punic war against Carthage, satisfying Cato's desire. His phrase "*Carthago delenda est*" became famous. It's amazing to think how much history there can be behind a simple piece of fruit . . .

Suddenly, the orchestra strikes up a new, very exotic melody, and from both sides of the *triclinium* dancers appear and begin to move about sinuously to the sound of castanets. This kind of dance is known all over Rome. It is typical of the women generically referred to as Gades, that is, from Cadiz, a city in Andalusia. The surprising thing is that even today in this region of Spain it's possible to admire a very famous kind of dance very similar to this one, even in the use of castanets: the flamenco.

The movements of the dancers at Roman banquets are very sensual and at this time of night they open the door to all sorts of possible developments. The image in our heads is that every banquet ends up with an orgy. That's not right. The Romans invite people into their homes for political or social networking, or for public relations, or even more simply just to invite friends to dinner. Just like we do. There is no rule that says the evening has to end up with an orgy. That said, however, sex at the end of a banquet is not an unusual event.

CURIOSITY—Gold on Roman Necks

At this point of the evening, it may be worth leaving the food aside for a moment to concentrate on the table companions' jewelry. This dinner being an occasion for social networking, everyone is showing off their most precious items.

The men are wearing essentially two kinds of jewelry: pins and rings. The rings are big and they look like wedding rings that get thicker and wider on the top of the finger, where a gem or precious stone is set, or else a carnelian with a figure carved in it. Usually it's a mythological figure or the profile of a hero.

These rings are used as seals to be impressed in wax. Sometimes men also wear bracelets, but only rarely.

It's the women who show off the largest quantity of gold; sometimes in an almost ethereal way, with a very thin gold net wrapped around their hair. Other times, with much more ostentation, with flat arm bracelets worn around the biceps or forearm.

The most famous ones have two lion heads or serpents staring each other down with emerald eyes.

The women's earrings are very showy, in the shape of an elongated triangle or a scale, with pearls on the ends. These are the famous *crotalia*, so called because they chime with each step. The variety of these objects is limited only by the goldsmith's imagination.

One of the women at the banquet has a curious large-ringed necklace that flows down her chest and meets between her breasts, like two bandoliers. At banquets you have to show off as much gold as you possibly can. Women's fingers, therefore, are covered by a myriad of rings of various sizes and settings.

We are struck by a ring worn by a very refined woman who has spoken very little. She has a very large and thick ring on her finger. At its center is not a precious stone but a small piece of totally transparent rock crystal that functions almost as a porthole covering an underlying niche. Inside, there is a carved bust, whose features are visible thanks to the lens effect of the crystal and above all to the exceptional work of the jeweler. The bust is a woman, corpulent and no longer in the flower of her youth; in short, a true "matron" whom we guess to be her mother.

In this era, an object like this is the equivalent of those lockets with pictures of children or parents that we often see around the necks of women in the modern age. It's a custom whose roots go back to ancient Rome.

TIME FOR THE *COMMISSATIO*

B elieve it or not, the banquet isn't over yet! Now begins the last part, the *commissatio*. How to define it. In brief, it's like a cheerful game of toasts, which ends very late and almost always with everybody drunk. The amphorae have a label (*pittacium*), which indicates their origin and year. The wine is poured through a strainer into a *krater* (large bowl) and diluted with water. The proportions vary depending on the occasion, but in general the ratio goes from one part water two parts wine to four parts water one part wine. Then the goblets are dipped into the *krater*.

At this point, the host (or a president who has been elected) decides how to drink. Almost always there is a series of goblets to be drunk in one gulp! How? For example, everyone gets in a circle, each drinks a goblet in one gulp and then passes it to the person next to him.

Or else a guest is chosen and the others drink a toast to him by raising (and chugging) a goblet for each letter of his name. Since Roman names are long and compound (in accordance with the *tria nomina* rule of the typical Roman citizen), we can imagine the consequences of this series of toasts.

There are a large variety of wines, from cheap, second-rate wines to ones thought to be really vile concoctions (qualifying in this last category are wines from Marseilles and the Vatican Hill). But there is obviously no lack of excellent wines. According to Pliny the Elder and Horace, the best is Falerno, produced in northern Campania, the region of Naples.

Martial, however, prefers the wine of Albano, coming from the same area south of Rome that today produces the famous wines of the *castelli romani*. Horace completes the list, adding Caleno (a wine for the wealthy), Massico, and Cecubo, produced near Fondi, in the south of Lazio, which he considers "generous and very strong." It's interesting to note that almost all of these wines were bottled for generations in the most beautiful amphorae, made in these very areas, which you can see today in museums. They are amphorae of the Dressel two variety, tall and elegant, with elongated handles and necks. A masterwork of the hands for a masterwork of the palate. How were these wines supposed to be tasted? Horace gives us an idea (claiming that the best Albano was the one that was aged for nine years): you must sip them, he says, together with your lover.

Origins of Roman Cuisine

Rome created the first great European culture of food. It invented the quick snack or refreshment (the forerunner of today's fast food), and it also contributed to the flowering of the first great chefs, establishing the bases of refined Italian cuisine, which for its variety and richness is the most appreciated in the world (even more than French cuisine, whose glaring lack of first courses and almost exclusive use of butter in cooking limit its variety and lightness).

In the Roman world food is much more than a nutrient. The Romans offer food to the gods during rites and sacrifices, and to the dead during libations in their honor, pouring honey and wine into special terra-cotta tubes that run from the tombstone down into the tomb (ending at the height of the face). But in the early years of the history of Rome, things were quite different. People ate essentially a kind of polenta (corn meal) called *puls* with eggs, olives, and fresh, unripened cheese, in addition to lots of legumes and green vegetables. Meat was rare, and there was only pork and chicken. Until the third century BCE, in fact, it was forbidden to slaughter and eat beef cattle, which could only be used for working in the fields and for sacrifices. Afterwards, the conquests of Rome brought new flavors and products to the capital and the era of sumptuous banquets began.

So Roman culinary culture has distant roots, but it grew and developed especially after the second Punic War. From that time on, there is a crescendo in the refinement of Roman food. A little like what happens even today thanks to TV, many chefs were rewarded with success in Roman houses and started writing cookbooks. The most extraordinary cooking manual of the Roman era is without doubt *De re coquinaria*, written by the most famous chef in antiquity, Marcus Gavius Apicius, active under Tiberius. What we have today is a collection of some 468 of his recipes, written three hundred years later by another Roman cook. More than a chef, Apicius was a wealthy Roman bon vivant and passionate food lover, who made good cuisine his reason for living.

It is said that he squandered a fortune hosting festive dinners. He even outfitted a ship to go lobster fishing along the Libyan coast, where the lobsters were supposed to be unusually large and tasty. It was he who renewed Roman cuisine by mixing sweet with savory, a custom that would not survive the Middle Ages. Ambitious and demanding, he became ill with depression. Seneca informs us that he committed suicide by drinking a cup of poison. It seems that he did it thinking he was about to go bankrupt (but he still had ten million sestertii, or about 25 million dollars).

His way of cooking turned the tables of classical cuisine, planting the bases of many modern recipes and trends. Trying to re-create his dishes, however, is very difficult. Like every great wizard of the kitchen, Apicius described his ingredients but not the dosages, and often he left out some of the spices to be added. The only way to achieve the right balance of tastes is by trial and error. But we'll never know just how Apicius did what he did.

Naturally, there were a lot of other great chefs in the Roman era, even some famous names: Cato and Virgil, for example, left us some recipes, and we also know that Cicero liked to cook as a hobby. Even some emperors were cooks, like Vitellius. According to Suetonius, Vitellius invented the famous "Minerva's shield": a veritable explosion of flavors whose ingredients included, among others, flamingo tongues, parrotfish livers, peacock and pheasant brains, and "milk" from a moray eel.

Good eating is not only a sin of gluttony but also a form of civility, and this world of Roman cooking will be lost entirely with the barbarian invasions of the fifth century.

CURIOSITY—Ingredients, Details, and Some Recipes

But apart from the sumptuous banquets of the wealthy, what did Romans eat? Is it true that many of their foods were unappetizing?

Certainly, it is disconcerting to think that fish innards and all the parts of a fish that we usually throw away, salted and left to marinate for days then became, with its pungent flavor, the favorite sauce of ancient Rome, *garum*.

Nevertheless, Roman cuisine was rich with ingredients that represented, so to speak, the keys of a very long gastronomic keyboard that produced symphonies which we too would have appreciated.

Imagine exploring the kitchen cabinets and opening the jars on the shelves. Here are some curiosities that you would find. First, the spices: saffron, pepper, cumin, ginger, cloves, sesame seeds.

Among the "scents" the dominant ones were rosemary, sage, mint, and juniper. They were combined with onions, garlic, walnuts, almonds, plums, and hazelnuts.

There was also a role for dates, raisins, pomegranates, and pine nuts. Obviously, salad greens and legumes were also widely used. It's striking, however, that arugula was considered an aphrodisiac. Some foods had a more important role than they have today: wild asparagus was particularly popular and especially turnips, which played a major role in the cuisine (perhaps because tomatoes and potatoes, which would come to Europe only after Columbus, were still undiscovered).

Another pillar of Roman cooking was cabbage, to which was attributed medical and curative properties. It was cooked exactly as we cook it today.

Other allies of cooks were chickpeas (boiled, salted, or roasted), lentils, and fava beans.

Arbutus berries and black raspberries, fresh or jellied, completed the ingredients of daily cuisine.

Roman bread came in a variety of forms. Beyond hard rolls and pocket bread, we know that there were no fewer than twenty different varieties of bread: from bread seasoned with oil and bread for dipping in wine to bran bread. There was even one kind of bread that was used to make mash for animals.

And what about meat, fish, fruit, and sweets? Here is a brief panorama of these dishes.

Pork was the most widely consumed meat. Suckling pig was a real delicacy in the form of stew or meatballs, cooked over a slow flame. And then, as we have seen, there were also stuffed sow teats, pig jowls, and kebabs. Pig's feet and smoked sausages were also well liked (especially the ones from the famous butchery of Vitalis).

Fish: common fish cost from two to three times as much as meat. There was no lack of choice in the markets: you could buy mullet, dentex, dory, conger eel, tuna, octopus, brill, sole, moray, eel, and sturgeon. Certain big catches of moray or sea bass were even sold at auction.

Mollusks and crustaceans: from stuffed snails to oysters, always a part of starters. Lobsters, shrimp, scampi, and prawns were a big hit, just as they are today.

Birds: all kinds, from flamingos to thrush, cranes to parakeets. Also on the list, especially as an ingredient for starters, were eggs. Already back then, geese were force fed and fattened up with figs, and their livers, like today, were used to make *paté de foie gras* (the Roman name was *ficatum* from *ficus* or fig).

Fruit: missing were bananas, pineapples, and kiwi. For fruit a Roman would have understood what was most commonly served at the table: apples, raisins, dried figs, roast chestnuts. Then came cherries, pears, dates, grapes, pomegranates, quince, walnuts, hazelnuts, almonds, and pine nuts.

Sweets: there were many recipes for sweets. One of the most famous was the "cassata" represented in the frescoes of the villa Oplontis, near Pompeii, and identical to the cassata we eat today, but with a mysterious taste. The most common, but very expensive, sweetener was honey. An alternative was cane sugar, from the Orient, were boiled figs, or cooked must. It was boiled until it looked like a sugary lump, as is done today in some regional cooking.

Sweets for children: one common custom was to use recycled stale bread, cutting it in slices, dipping it in milk and then frying it. Afterwards, honey was spread over it, and its success among the little people was guaranteed.

The Magirus Recommends

Marinated Hare: The hare will be marinated in a sauce to be prepared as follows: finely chop and grind together onion, rue, thyme, and pepper. Add a little *garum*. Take an already cleaned hare and spread the sauce over it, then put it in a roasting pan in the oven. While it's cooking, baste it repeatedly with another sauce, which you have already prepared, of oil, wine, *garum*, onion, rue, pepper, and four dates.

Barley Soup. Mix together peas, chickpeas, and lentils. Boil them all together with barley that's been cleaned and crushed. Pour the mix into a pan and add oil, dill, coriander, fennel, beet greens, mallow, cabbage, and green leeks (all cut in pieces). In another pan, boil the cabbage with fennel seeds, oregano, privet, ferula, or *laserpicium* (a plant from the Cerenaica region of northern Africa, now extinct, whose juice is also used by the Romans for its medicinal qualities). Everything must be finely ground with the addition of *garum*. Mix and add, when you are serving at table, little pieces of cabbage.

Boiled Stuffed Pig. Buy a small pig at the market. Eviscerate it, clean it, and brown it. In the meantime, prepare the stuffing: grind together pepper, oregano, *laserpicium*. Drip some *garum* into it. Cook a sufficient amount of the brain to make the stuffing. Cut some round discs of cooked sausage. Beat some eggs as though you were making an omelet, enriching them with *garum*. Mix everything together and stuff the pig, which you have coated with *garum*. Sew up the pig, put it into a tight basket or in a bag, and emerge it into a culdron of boiling water. When it's cooked and dripped dry, you can serve it.

Parthic Goat. Choose a nice kid goat. Prepare and put in the oven. In the meantime, chop together onion, rue, savory, pepper, *laserpicium* and pitted Damascus plums. Add oil, wine and *garum*. Put it on the fire to cook and when the goat is out of the oven, pour the sauce over it, and serve.

Hypotrimma (salad dressing). Grind some pepper, mint, lovage, raisins, pine nuts, and dates. Add some fresh cheese mixed with honey, vinegar, and cooked must.

Homemade sweets (dulcia domestica). Pit some dates and fill them with ground pepper, walnuts, or pine nuts. Sprinkle them with salt, cook in honey. Serve.

The Evolution of Roman Sexuality

Origins

The Romans were no more free, or perverse, than other peoples. They simply followed different rules and principles, which evolved over time. Initially, Roman society, very rigid and bound to tradition, placed men at the center of everything: *pater familias,* defender of the fatherland, master of the house. The world also revolved around men when it came to sexuality. In addition to their wives, who must always remain faithful (in early times, a betrayed husband could legally kill his wife and her lover), their other partners, whether women or boys, had to procure them pleasure. The only rule to be respected, which will remain unchanged throughout the entire Roman era, is that the person with whom the man has sex outside of matrimony must be of inferior rank, that is, he or she must not be a citizen of Rome like them, but a slave, male or female.

Free Sex, Emancipation of Women, and Divorce

The great change comes with the military conquests in the Greek-Middle Eastern world, starting in the second century BCE. Greek customs are brought to Rome, and morality accepts a new way of experiencing sexuality: "Greek style" homosexuality is allowed, and sexual practices expand. Women too, acquire much greater independence; they can seduce men.

Accompanying these great changes that come from the East are a series of events that have a big impact on the condition of women. This is a subject that has been treated by a number of scholars, most notably Professor Eva Cantarella. The women of the first century CE reach a level of autonomy and freedom that will not be achieved in the modern era until the 1970s. They become economically independent and, most importantly, divorce becomes easier. What accounts for this emancipation of women?

For centuries, the law had allowed women only a theoretical right to inherit goods, property, and money. In reality, their wealth was managed by men (fathers, brothers, husbands). With the famous civil wars of the first century BCE, things changed: in fact, the senators realized that a large portion of the male Roman elite had been killed in these wars and there was, therefore, a real danger that their money and property would end up in the hands of a few unscrupulous men, real dictators like Silla or Julius Caesar. What to do? Turn to the women and allow them the right to inherit personally. And so it was done; the Senate approved these new laws.

The traditional marriage relationship, which placed women under the complete authority of men, also changed. In its place was born a type of union in which the woman was under the (financial) control of her father and no longer of her husband. So, when her father died, the woman automatically inherited lands and money, acquiring economic power and independence. Divorce changed too and became easier. To dissolve the marriage bond it was enough that the man or woman declare before witnesses that he or she no longer wished to be married.

The consequence of all this was the reinforcement of the female position. In case of divorce, the woman, by now the legal owner of money and property, could leave the man and maintain her economic independence.

And so, often the roles are reversed. Men who had married women only for their money risked losing everything only to find themselves on the street.

Obviously, these laws had more of an impact on the elite of Roman society, on the wealthy, than on the rest of the population. Roman law in regard to matrimony and heredity was not, therefore, "equal for all": it favored citizens who were free and wealthy over the others (slaves, freed slaves, foreigners, etc.)

During the three and a half centuries between the first century BCE and the third century CE, a lot of other things changed in male-female relationships. While before, marriages were arranged by their families when the two future spouses were children, now it was sentiment that guided the choice. Often, couples lived together without getting married (there were many types of unions, from formal contracts to simple cohabitation, depending on social standing and the amount of property involved). There was even a severe drop in the birth rate, which Augustus would attempt unsuccessfully to combat with special laws.

It is truly shocking to compare the situation then with what is happening now in Western societies, and particularly in Italy, where the number of marriages is dropping, divorces are rising, and the birth rate is plunging (even though here there are other contributing factors of a practical nature, like the economic difficulties of young couples).

It shouldn't be surprising that this period in the Roman age is characterized by sexual freedom. Sexual practices, in fact, became increasingly more open and permissive, for both men and women, giving rise to all of those behaviors for which the Romans have been famous through the centuries.

Return to More Moderate Habits

Starting with the second half of the third century (around 260 CE), with the first barbaric invasions of the Empire, instability and economic crisis provoked changes throughout Roman society, including the sexual sphere. The couple's great freedom begins to shrink. The two spouses become more united and there is more modesty. A new conjugal code is born, imposing reciprocal fidelity, condemning homosexuality, and establishing the main objective of sexual intercourse as having children. Morality is still pagan, but it is this morality that becomes the fulcrum of Christianity, whose path is opened by Constantine. This new morality becomes a useful instrument for the clergy to use in controlling the faithful by threatening divine punishment. While, on the one hand, the new morality involves everyone and restores to women an important role in the family and in society, on the other hand it is a step back for women in the direction of the oldest Roman traditions, where it had all started: arrive at matrimony still a virgin, remain chaste within the conjugal union, and stay married to your man until death.

9:00 PM

ROMAN SEX

We're back out on the street. By now it's dark out. The sound of the lyre and the tambourines has faded away. All we can hear now from the *domus* is the laughter and singing of the host and his guests, in their cups. Sounds and voices that grow increasingly weaker and distant. The two litters are still waiting outside the *domus*, with the slaves sitting on the sidewalk, chatting. In a little while, as we know, we'll encounter other, much noisier vehicles: the delivery wagons that are already waiting outside the perimeter of the city. Wagons loaded with amphorae, food, lumber, animals, roof tiles, beams, bricks, fabrics, dishes, and pots and pans to be sold. Everything that's needed for Rome to live another day. As though the city filled its tank every night.

Here on the street we also run into other people scurrying on their way to play cards in a gambling den, to meet a lover, or simply go back home without being mugged. Or to go looking for sex. Where? In the *lupanari* (wolves' dens) or brothels. Or in certain areas of the city. In some Roman neighborhoods, it seems as though you were walking down the streets of prostitution in Mumbai, with a line of doorways filled with young girls smiling at you and inviting you in, even from the windows. Elsewhere, the situation is more "street life." In front of the arches of the Circus Maximus, for example, the services of Syrian girls are sold exactly as happens today along modern Rome's suburban roads with girls from Eastern Europe or Nigeria. Sex slaves; nothing has changed.

The brothels, however, can be recognized by the lights hanging outside. Nothing special, just a pair of lanterns with multiple light holes. They're like lighthouses attracting the moths of sex.

Considering the number and intense activity of these *lupanari*, we can easily say that the Romans succeeded in establishing a true "fast food" sex industry. Another modern trait.

As we approach one of these whorehouses, we see three men standing around and chatting. It looks like the scene in front of one of our bars, at night, with customers gathered outside. They're bantering with a woman whose hair is dyed a bizarre color; under the lantern light it looks blue. And it is. She's certainly a prostitute; hair that color (like orange hair) is a distinctive sign. Another sure sign is the way she's dressed. While wealthy women wear multiple robes, prostitutes dress light to facilitate quick sex.

We walk by discreetly. The woman is standing in front of the entrance to the brothel, very simple, and its partly open curtain allows us to see inside. There is a narrow hallway, illuminated by more lanterns hanging from the ceiling. Along the walls are doorways to some small rooms closed by curtains. They must be the cubicles, where sex is performed in exchange for money. We know this because there's a famous brothel in Pompeii. A curtain is pulled to the side and a man comes out, arranging the belt of his tunic. He is followed almost immediately by a woman who leans her hand against the wall. She's naked. Her hair is pulled back in a bun and her features are Mediterranean. Today we would take her for a Turk or a woman from the Middle East. Her build is Junoesque, with wide hips, a prominent belly, and small breasts.

These features tell us a lot about the aesthetic taste of the Romans. The fashion models of our time would certainly be appreciated for their height, their well-proportioned bodies, and their perfect faces; no scars or bags under the eyes (and all their teeth intact). But a Roman would find them too skinny, with little sex appeal compared to a buxom woman.

Throughout the classical period, canons of beauty for the ideal woman for having sex or bringing up children included the "rotundities," exactly what women today want to reduce or eliminate altogether, but which for centuries were considered by men to be a guarantee of fertility, healthy pregnancy, capacity to breast-feed, etc. And therefore a source of attraction. A look at past paintings of nude women is enough to make you realize that this model of the "florid" woman was in vogue right up to the beginnings of the modern age. And even today, the canons of beauty in many third world countries, and even, on the southern rim of the Mediterranean, confirm that this tradition is still alive. It's the higher standard of living in Western countries that has made women's "rotundities" apparently useless. But, on the subconscious level, the Roman ideal of female beauty still persists in the minds of more than a few men.

The woman disappears into a corner for a quick wash. One of the three men starts to go in. It's his turn. But the woman with the blue hair stops him and sticks out her hand, palm up, to ask for payment. The words we hear are surprising. She's reciting a list of names and prices. The names are the names of the girls (Attica, Aneida, Myrtale). Myrtale, the girl we've seen, is a real fellatio specialist. The prices are around two asses, the same as a glass of cheap wine. But for Myrtale she asks for more: four asses. The man smiles, pays, and then takes off his cape and goes in the room. A moment later, Myrtale arrives and rearranges her hair, redoing the knot that her previous client had partially undone in his passion. The woman throws a glance at the two men at the front door, her next customers, then vanishes into the room and pulls the curtain closed. It's obviously a downscale whorehouse, for people of humble extraction.

Brothels are just one aspect of Roman sex. And they're certainly not a novelty; they have existed in every age.

What's really different compared to our own time and other historical periods is the way it's done. For example, why is it that at this very moment, in a *domus* right behind us, a man is having sex with a woman while his wife, in the next room and fully aware of what he is up to, doesn't say anything? And why, in that other *domus* at the end of the street, has a man refused to have oral sex with his wife even though they love each other?

What are the Roman rules of sex? What are their taboos? It's a subject about which there are a lot of inaccurate stereotypes. As we shall see, things are very different from what is usually thought to be the case.

First of all, it's simply not true that the Romans are depraved, base, or immoral, as is sometimes believed. On the contrary, they would judge our sexuality as excessively complicated and loaded down with mental complexes and roles—too many rules about what a man can do and what a woman can do, how adolescent sex should be, what's obscene and what's not, proper heterosexual behavior, and proper homosexual behavior.

A Roman would say that even if we think we are sexually free, in reality our heads are full of prohibitions.

Let's begin with the most important point, the real key to sexuality in the Roman Empire.

For Romans, sex (in whatever form) is a gift of the gods, and particularly of Venus. Therefore, it is right to enjoy it and important to do it; it's one of life's pleasures. And not only. The Romans believe that having healthy children depends on both partners being good at sex.

From this perspective, it is clear that sex is not at all a sin or something perverse. In short, if sex is a blessing from Venus, why criticize or guilt-trip those who practice it?

But be careful. Romans do not preach free sex. They have rules. It's like wine; it too is a gift of the gods. It's not a sin to drink it, but there are social rules that indicate how to drink it and how much. Otherwise, you're put on the index. It's the same for sex. There are rules. But they are different than ours and that's why the way Romans behave in bed seems depraved to us.

We have to force ourselves to forget about our rules for a minute and put ourselves into their world. We might agree with their rules and we might not, but there is a very simple logic to them.

First rule. A free Roman man (understood as the classic *civis romanus*) must always be the dominator in bed. He can have sex with partners of all kinds (men and women) but only if they are his social inferiors: a woman, a female slave, a young male slave.

Second rule: oral sex. The Roman man must "take pleasure" and not "give pleasure." Romans have a real obsession with the mouth. For them it is something noble and sacred. It is a social instrument that is used for talking, calling each other by name, exchanging information, etc., and so it must be pure and immaculate. And, in the Senate, it is a political instrument. As John Clarke, an expert on Roman sexuality, has observed, to accuse a senator of having performed oral sex is tantamount to accusing him of treason by reason of his having "dirtied" his mouth, which has such an important role in his service to the collectivity.

So the person who has an active role in oral sex is scorned, while the person who has a passive role is not. In this regard, it is curious to note that in accordance with the Roman mentality, the Clinton-Lewinsky scandal would not have caused an uproar in ancient Rome, not only because the two of them had, after all, accepted a gift from Venus (and then because a powerful man had had relations with his subordinate, who was, moreover, a woman, something accepted by the social rules) but the one who would have borne the brunt of public opinion would not have been Bill Clinton but Monica Lewinsky because of her "active" role.

To be precise, when it comes to oral sex, the Romans have three taboos, or better, three things that must not happen: that a male Roman citizen should practice oral sex on another man (fellatio); even worse that he should be forced to do it; and finally that he should practice oral sex on a woman (cunnilingus). Famous in this regard is Martial's scathing attack on Coracinus, in which he accuses him of having oral sex with women. We can see, therefore, that accusing a Roman man of being a *fellator* is a grave insult. It is today too, but not in such a violent way.

And group sex, how is that viewed? Not very well, because on such occasions there is too much risk of not respecting the above-mentioned rules and taboos.

Naturally, everything we've said so far is theory, which is not necessarily followed to the letter. In their intimate moments, the Romans do what they want and a lot of them break the rules and the taboos. But the difference is more subtle. No Roman will publicly admit doing these things, because they are unspeakable, if not downright scandalous.

Why is that?

Instinctively, many explanations come to mind: rules as precise as these are also useful to Roman society as a justification of the sexual exploitation of men and women of inferior social rank; to keep women of the higher classes under control; to attack political adversaries. Even today governments, religions, and moral codes prohibit certain sexual practices such as premarital sex, adultery, and homosexuality. Depending on the society and the place, penalties range from jail to the death penalty. It is a form of social control that is very widespread in space and time.

But perhaps there is another explanation. At bottom, these rules serve to conserve the power of the Roman elite. Think about it. Why is it considered adultery to have sex with someone of your own status but not with someone of an inferior status, such as a slave, an ex-slave, etc.? The reason is economic. The birth of an illegitimate child of the same social status might threaten the rights of legitimate children.

Besides, having sex with a slave, maybe even breaking some taboos, automatically protects you from all accusations, because the word of a slave is worthless. All of these rules, therefore, are valid first and foremost for the patricians and the well-to-do. And the other inhabitants of Rome? Almost none of the people that we have met on the streets of Rome have these taboos. For them, sex has many fewer restrictions and remains a wonderful gift of Venus (and Priapus) to be enjoyed with good cheer. It must be remembered, however, that for a large part of the population sex is not chosen but imposed: the slaves, both men and women. In the Roman mentality, every slave and every ex-slave that you meet on the street has suffered or is still suffering the "attentions" of his master. Nobody is scandalized by this; it's normal. Slaves and ex-slaves are all potential sexual toys; it all depends on what their *dominus* decides. Or their *domina*.

Roman Kama Sutra

Many details about the sex lives of the Romans have emerged from graffiti found by archaeologists during excavations, in ancient texts, and on tombstones. For example, how do you say "have sex" in Trajan's Rome? *Fotuere*. It's a term that has remained almost unchanged in its journey down through the centuries and it is still used today, not only in contemporary Italian but also in French, and always in a pejorative sense.

It is striking to note that the male sex organ, indicated with so many nouns and synonyms (*mentula, virga, hasta, penis,* while the female organ, on the other hand, is known as *cunnus*), is also defined as *fascinus,* also the name of the Roman fertility god, whose symbol is an erect penis. The reason is that this word derives from *fas*, "favorable," and the *fascinus* is the dispenser of fertility and thus also of prosperity. For this very reason it is able to drive off bad luck and evil spirits. So that's why you see so many of them around, painted or sculpted on the streets, in craftsmen's workshops and in the houses of the Roman Empire.

But more than anything else, it's the paintings that spark our curiosity and imagination. From the very first excavations in Pompeii, lots of small wall paintings of erotic scenes have been discovered. Many were deliberately destroyed at the moment of discovery because they were thought to be too risqué for the morality of the time. Others were cut out and hidden away in the famous secret cabinet or "cabinet of obscenities," whose collection is mostly on display at the national archaeological museum in Naples. Contrary to what is commonly believed, the buildings where the paintings were found were not brothels but ordinary homes. A painting with erotic scenes was part of the art collection typical of a wealthy family, something refined and noble. A little bit like putting a classical statue of a nude in your house today. Ovid mentions these paintings in wealthy people's homes. Suetonius states that Tiberius had a lot of them in the bedrooms of his residence. An extraordinary find of these paintings was made in Rome in 1879, during the excavations in the gardens of the Palazzo della Farnesina. Archaeologists discovered the remains of a villa that was buried under the silt of the Tiber, which had preserved its frescoes. Only four rooms and two hallways were brought to light, but the remains were attributed to the villa of a very famous couple: Julia, the daughter of Augustus, and her husband. One of the frescoes shows a naked man trying to cajole a woman, clearly dubious, sitting on the side of the bed and still dressed; she even has a veil over her head. In the next painting, the roles are reversed: the now semi-nude woman has been overcome with erotic rapture and embraces the man, who seems taken by surprise. The frescoes also include some servants, perhaps chambermaids, present even in moments of greatest intimacy.

One thing that leaves us a bit disconcerted is that these sex scenes can also be seen by children and young girls. But they are not considered pornography. The Romans speak openly of sex in their everyday lives (they even venerate gods of sex such as Venus and Priapus), and sex is represented not only on the interior walls of houses but also on lanterns and luxurious flatware used with dinner guests. In this case, as we have already said, the aim is not to make a show of something sinful but to evoke the idea of the luxury, the culture, and the wealth present in the house.

Often there is some further significance. Exaggerated scenes of group sex can be useful in fostering a cheerful atmosphere and thus in keeping the evil eye at a distance. In the same way, images of Priapus with an exaggeratedly large phallus are a symbol of wealth and abundance.

These paintings, along with statues and lantern decorations, reveal to us a genuine Kama Sutra of the Roman era. Viewing the glass cases in museums or the frescoes in so many cubicles, atriums, and hallways in the Roman cities of Pompeii and Herculanum allows us to see all of the positions in which sex was practiced in those times.

And so here we have the *mulier equitans*, the woman riding "on horseback." Or a woman on top of the bed on all fours, ready to be had from behind. The Romans called this the pose of the "lioness." And moving right along, the classic position of the "missionary."

The lantern decorations and the paintings also have scenes

of oral sex for the man (*fellatio*), for the woman (*cunnilingus*), and for both, sixty-nine.

Some of the scenes are striking, for example, the sex scene between two women in the missionary position; one of the two is wearing a belt with a fake phallus. In this regard, Seneca the Elder tells us in one of his writings (*Controversiae* I, 2, 23) about a man who caught his wife in bed with another woman and killed them both, after verifying whether the lover was a real man or an "artificial" one. It seems he got off with very light punishment; it was a true crime of honor. Martial also writes of women with male roles, concerned as he was mostly about the prospect of female independence.

And there was no lack of group scenes. In some cases there are two men and one woman, in others two men and two women, outright "tangles" or trains . . . It's clear that some of the participants in these cases can no longer respect the sex taboos of aristocratic Romans. In this sense, the one we might call the "man in the middle," then commonly called with contempt the *cinaedus,* seems to have held a certain appeal for women.

Nor is there a lack of deliberately humorous scenes, like one of a woman having sex in the *equitans* position riding a man while holding dumbbells, or a Cupid who's pushing a man to help him lift up a woman during a rather acrobatic orgasm.

Bisexuals and Gays

And what about homosexuality? For the Romans, being gay is not a problem. It's interesting to note that they don't even have specific words equivalent to our "gay" and "lesbian," and this is an indication of their lack of prejudice.

Today, we proceed by categories: a man and a woman are heterosexual, or homosexual, or bisexual. That's not how it is in Roman society. It is accepted that a Roman citizen, as he wishes, may find beauty and pleasure in a man's body as much as in a woman's body.

But on one essential condition. That if he goes to bed with another man he must have the "active" role, let's say, and not the "passive" one. Furthermore, this object of his desire (because this may actually be the best way to define him) must be of an inferior social rank. These are the rules for male homosexuality.

So nobody will be scandalized when even an emperor, like Hadrian, appears in public with his lover, the famous Antinous, and even ends up deifying him after he dies by drowning in the Nile.

What the Roman mentality does not accept is that a man can freely choose the passive role in a sexual relationship. That is infamous.

Roman men who liked having the passive role were contemptuously known as *cinaedus* or *pathicus*. They even had a different legal status, like prostitutes, gladiators, and actors. They couldn't vote and they couldn't represent themselves at trial.

There is also another feature of Roman homosexuality that leaves us disconcerted: having sex with young boys. For us, it's pedophilia and that's that. For the Romans, no. The only rule to be applied is the (usual) rule of social status, the well-known prohibition of the "passive" role, and, naturally, difference in age.

But where did this custom originate? Between the second and third century BCE, when Rome expanded to reach the Greek and Eastern worlds, Greek customs arrived in the city: from food to medicine, from philosophy to art. And sex. From then on, in imitation of the Greek world, it became almost a fad for wealthy men to have a young boy or a lovely young girl in the house to have sex with. All in the same *domus* where he lived with his wife. In Trajan's Rome, things haven't changed. It's shocking for us, but it must be remembered that, for a Roman, sex is often what happens between two people of unequal rank or between the master and a sex object (a male or female slave).

From that moment on, wealthy Romans developed the habit of purchasing slaves who could also be used, when the need arose, for their own sexual pleasure. Unlike female slaves, male slaves are never purchased specifically for the purpose of being toys for sex. But, according to some scholars, the main role for a good-looking male slave between the ages of twelve and eighteen is almost exclusively to provide their master with sexual satisfaction. Or their mistress. Yes, because for women of the upper classes, wealthy and independent, the same holds true. This explains why slaves and ex-slaves are always looked on with contempt; it is presumed that they have been abused by their masters.

At this point we might ask the question: since there are female prostitutes in imperial Rome, are there also male prostitutes? The answer is yes. It's surprising to find out that they pay taxes on their earnings and they also have holidays, just like their female counterparts. The main difference is that while female prostitutes are almost always slaves, come in all ages, and offer their services at bargain prices, male prostitutes, on the contrary, are usually young and hire themselves out at top-dollar fees. We might well define them as real gigolos of the *haute bourgeoisie*, more for men than women. Many of them have become quite wealthy.

Sometimes the tangle of human and sexual relationships becomes more complex. Some tombs have come to light in Ostia whose tombstones, according to the scholar John Clarke, indicate the existence of proper "love triangles." The writing on one of them says, "Lucius Atilius Artemas and Claudia Apphias dedicate this sarcophagus (or tomb) to Titus Flavius Trophimas, so that the three of them can rest in peace together." In another case, a man named Allius buried Allia Potestas, a slave whom he shared with another man. On her death, the tombstone recites, the two men stopped being friends. Nobody would write such things on their tomb today, making public a type of relationship condemned by the precepts of morality and religion.

The Woman in the Mirror

As we conclude this journey of ours through Roman sexuality, it must be said that, as we have seen, it is a world very different from our own, a world in which everything turns around a single beneficiary: the male citizen of Rome. Nevertheless, thanks to the level of emancipation they have achieved, Roman women (especially wealthy women) are able to carve out a role for themselves and obtain their share of sexual satisfaction. Considering the epoch and the situation in other cultures, civilizations, and ethnicities, that's no small accomplishment. Not least because women will have to wait another two thousand years to find themselves in a comparable situation.

And it is just this kind of atmosphere that now appears before our eyes. The scene is imbued with poetry and love. She is in the flower of her years, beautiful and stretched out on a finely decorated bed, with soft silk sheets. Her man, powerfully built with curly hair, is behind her, united in an intense orgasm. The two look at one another. She turns and embraces him, and caresses him tenderly with her hand. They have no clothes; the only garment, she wears is gold jewelry.

She has bracelets around her ankles, wrists, and arms. A lovely necklace with precious stones and droplets of gold circles her neck and rests on her collarbones. But the most extraordinary piece is a wide mesh gold chain that drops down from her shoulders, covers her nipples, and crosses at her navel before gliding again up her back, like those cartridge belts that used to be worn around the neck. All of this gold confirms that we are in the *domus* of a well-to-do woman. Next to the bed is a brazier burning some resins whose perfume infuses the air throughout the entire room. There is also a little dog for companionship resting on a stool, who seems to be alarmed as he watches the arrival of a mouse getting ready to drink out of his bowl. On the wall is an erotic painting in a shuttered frame so the mistress can open it only for those she wants to see it.

This is the back side of a bronze mirror that belonged to a Roman matron. The owner had herself portrayed with her lover and her gold jewelry. According to the Romans, sex is a gift of Venus.

Yes, the *domina*. Looking at her, we can see that her hair-style is slightly out of fashion. Her long hair is gathered in a bun on the back of her neck and then rises up on her forehead, creating a sort of halo. But isn't this style a little old-fashioned for the era of Trajan? In effect, it was in vogue twenty years or so ago, under the Flavians, and even earlier. We don't have time to finish this thought before a female hand, no longer young, passes in front of us and carries away this sensual image.

What we have seen up to now, in fact, is not a real scene, but the decoration on the back of a bronze mirror. An extraordinary decoration featuring the two lovers with the woman in the center of the scene, emancipated, young, and sensual. The hand that is now holding the mirror, on the contrary, is the hand of a woman on in years. It must be the hand of the owner of this object.

We can't see her face because the mirror is covering it like an eclipse. We take a step to the side and stare at that wrinkled face; the resemblance to the woman in the decoration is amazing. No, it's really her!

As often happens, high society women like to commission decorations for their bronze mirrors. And this *domina* commissioned this one several decades ago, having herself portrayed as she looked then, in the flower of her years. Now, time has passed, that young suitor has lost his curls, he has wrinkles too and he's snoring in his sleep just a few feet away, in one of the cubicles of the sumptuous *domus* in which they have always lived, here on the Esquiline hill.

The woman is looking now at her face reflected in the bronze mirror, looking at her wrinkles, her long white hair that a servant is combing with care. And then she looks at the edge of the mirror, along which runs a frame engraved with all of the symbols of the zodiac. She observes them distractedly: Sagittarius, Capricorn, Aquarius, Pisces . . . Their purpose is to recall the passage of time for those who look at themselves in the mirror. As if to say: enjoy yourself while you're young and beautiful, seize the gift of Venus. *Carpe diem*, as Horace said. The woman's eyes start to smile. She has tasted her best years to the fullest, one by one.

This bronze mirror with a diameter of about 5 inches will be discovered many centuries later by archaeologists working on the Esquiline. Now it is conserved in the Antiquarium of Rome, with inventory number 13,694. An empty number, like so many others. But that mirror reflects a life that tells the story of an entire epoch.

By now, night reigns on the streets of Rome. All we can see are a few "headlights" passing by; lanterns carried by slaves, lighting the way for small groups of people. The other lights that we see, fixed, belong to some typical nighttime businesses, like the brothels, but these are gambling dens. In the roadside inns, the *cauponae,* there are still people playing dice, betting, and losing money. Playing cards still don't exist, but cheaters and brawls certainly do. We are attracted by a sudden barrage of shouting. It's coming from a *caupona.* We can hear stools rolling, pitchers shattering. A woman comes out, screaming. She's probably a prostitute who works at the inn, or maybe the owner, who knows. But her screams are not in vain. She's calling a patrol of *vigiles* that passed by just a minute ago. In a few seconds, these firefighter-cops are inside the joint. We hear more shouting, then suddenly silence. At almost the same time two *vigiles* come out of the inn holding a man, they've got his arm turned behind his back. But he goes on struggling and protesting. Nothing can keep him still until he's pummeled by a sudden onslaught of cudgel blows. Followed by some kicks. Here the police don't mess around. We'd best be on our way.

Drunks in the taverns, murderers in the darkness, the nighttime perils of the streets of Rome are really everywhere. And they can even come from above. It's not only falling urine you have to look out for. You can also be hit by heavy objects thrown from windows, like broken pottery, stools, and other now useless things (just as it was once the custom on New Year's Eve in certain Italian cities). It's against the law, but it happens rather frequently.

On some streets we can see the profiles of slaves assigned to street cleaning. They work under torch light; the night (and dusk) is the best time to clear the streets of garbage. During the day, there is so much traffic it's practically impossible.

The Ritual for Scaring Off Evil Spirits

We enter a side street. In this nocturnal silence, a strange litany catches our attention. We try to make out its point of origin; it seems like it's coming from the first floor of a building. The wood shutter of a window is ajar; a faint slice of light shines out from behind it. We walk over to it in silence and put our eye up to a crack in the rotten wood. What we see is a scene as curious as it is ageless.

Under the feeble light of some lanterns a man is conducting a ritual to drive off the spirits of the dead. The Romans are very superstitious. They believe that the shades of dead family members (that is, their ghosts), called Mani, continue to circulate in the houses of their children and grandchildren. If you are able to ingratiate yourself with them with rituals and offerings, they can help the living, protecting them in their daily activities. Otherwise, they can transform themselves into wicked creatures, called *larvae* or *lemurs*, which appear at night or in your sleep. Sometimes it's necessary to perform actual purification rituals in the middle of the night.

What we are seeing corresponds amazingly well to a description of these rituals left to us by Ovid. The man has gotten out of bed and is walking around the room in his bare feet. In total silence, he snaps his fingers well over his head. Then he purifies his hands by washing them in a basin of spring water—an uncorrupted water that he had to buy at a high price from a sly merchant.

On the table, next to the water basin, is a plate of black beans. It's his offering to the shades of the dead. To show them that the beans aren't poisoned, he picks up a handful and puts them in his mouth. Then, without turning around, he takes them back in his hand and throws them one at a time over his shoulder, repeating each time the phrase that attracts our attention: "I throw these beans and with them I free myself and my loved ones." You must never turn around. In theory, the souls of the dead, behind the back of the living man, pick up the beans and nourish themselves, at least symbolically. Given the hour and given how sleepy he is, the words are pretty garbled, but still comprehensible.

Then comes the last part of the ritual. The man puts his hands back in the water basin and asks nine times that the souls of the departed leave his home. He does it while banging bronze plates against each other. In the end, he stops, gasping, in silence. All he has to do is turn around to check if the shades have gone. He hesitates a minute, uncertain, then he turns with a jolt and stares at the room around him. His face relaxes into a smile. It looks like the ritual worked.

12 MIDNIGHT

A LAST EMBRACE

By now, there's no one left on the streets but us. All around us, Rome is asleep. Some in their luxurious cubicles, wrapped in covers. Others on a humble bed of straw on the upper floors of the *insulae*. Still others on the floor, in the hallway of their master's *domus*.

Ahead of us is a wide street lined with shops on both sides. At this time of night they're shut with heavy wooden boards inserted in the sidewalk and fastened with sturdy bolt locks. Raising our glance we notice that all we can see around us are the profiles of the *insulae* rising up to the stars. It almost seems that we're standing on the floor of a dark canyon with a star-filled canopy overhead.

As we walk down the street, there is an unreal silence. A silence broken only by the sound of the water flowing in a neighborhood fountain, just a few yards away. The sound of the falling water is our only company.

Curious, this silence. More than curious, it's rare. Here we are, right in the heart of a city of a million and a half inhabitants. Usually, the middle of the night is the time for deliveries to stores and workshops, with the clamor of iron wagon wheels turning on the stone pavement, men shouting, horses neighing, the inevitable imprecations . . . And it's those noises that we can now hear, off in the distance, coming from another street. They are echoed by a barking dog. Rome never sleeps.

In front of us, there's a fork in the road. And right in the middle of the intersection we notice an unknown human figure who's watching us, in silence. The figure is standing straight, in a long white gown and with the arms half open, as though to welcome and embrace us. Our curiosity aroused, we move a few steps closer. Now we can see who it is. And we can see that she is not looking at us.

Her eyes are staring off into the distance, like someone lost in contemplation. The pale moonlight reveals a soft countenance, milky white, with just a hint of a smile. She has a ribbon around her forehead and her hair is up, but a few disobedient strands have broken loose and lie on her shoulders. A sudden puff of wind raises a cloud of dust around her, but her hair doesn't move. Nor could it; it's made of marble. Just as her bare arms are made of marble, as well as the hundreds of folds in her gown. The sculptor who crafted her used one of the world's most precious marbles, fixing in stone the likeness of one of the Romans' most revered divinities: *Mater Matuta* (the Great Mother), "the mother of good auspices," the goddess of fertility, of the beginning, and of dawn.

And so concludes our day in the life of imperial Rome. An ordinary day, almost two thousand years ago.

ACKNOWLEDGEMENTS

I would like to thank Professor Romolo Augusto Staccioli, a great expert on the daily life of ancient Rome, for his attentive reading of the book, and for the precious advice and suggestions he has given me over the years. His works and his descriptions of life as it was lived two thousand years ago sparked my interest in the Roman world.

My gratitude also goes to Professor Antonio De Simone, who introduced me to and made me love Pompeii, the best place in the world to discover the secrets of the daily lives of ancient Romans.

Obviously, these pages would never have existed without the work of all those who, over the span of several generations, have brought to light the details of life in Rome. My thoughts go out above all to all those archaeologists who have helped me during site visits, inviting me to share the details and curiosities of their discoveries and answering the countless questions that I've asked them.

I am also grateful to Gabriella Ungarelli and Alberto Gelsumini, of Mondadori, who have believed in this project from the beginning, following its inception and development with keen interest. I want to thank Luca Tarlazzi for his masterful "photograms" of daily life in Rome, so perfect it seems he must have walked the streets of ancient Rome with his sketchbook, and Gaetano Capasso, for his precise and suggestive computer-graphic reconstructions.

Finally, I want to thank my wife, Monica, for the infinite

patience she has always had in the face of my enthusiasm and my stories about ancient Rome, every time I came back from filming or visiting an archaeological site or finished reading the umpteenth study on the life of the Romans.

BIBLIOGRAPHY

AA. VV, *Roma Antica*, Vol. 1-6, Istituto Geografico De Agostini, Novara, 2003.

Amato, F., 2004. *La cucina di Roma Antica*. Rome: Newton & Compton.

Aries, Ph., and Duby, G., 1985. *Histoire de la vie privée I. De l'Empire Romain à l'an mil*. Paris: Editions du Seuil.

Augenti, D., 2001. *Spettacoli del Colosseo,*. Rome: L' "Erma" di Bretschneider, Roma, 2001.

Bertrandy, F., Ferries, M., and Sartre-Fauriat, A., 2002. *La ville de Rome de César à Comode*. Paris: Editions Ellipses, 2002.

Carcopino, J., 1939. *La vie quitidienne à Rome à l'apogée de l'Empire*. Paris: Librairie Hachette.

Ciarallo, A. and De Carolis, E. (eds.). 1999. *Homo Faber*. Milan: Electa.

Clarke, J. R., 2003. *Roman Sex*. New York: Harry N. Abrams.

Croom, A. T., 2000. *Roman Clothing and Fashion*. Stroud: Tempus Publishing.

De La Bedoyere, G., 2000. *Voices of imperial Rome*. Stroud: Tempus Publishing.

Drinkwater, J. F., Drummond, A., and Freeman, C., 1993.*The World of the Romans*. Oxford: Andromeda.

Dupont, F., and Eloi, T., 2001. *L'érotisme masculin dans la Rome antique*. Paris: Editions Belin.

Friggeri, R., 2001. *La collezione epigrafica del Museo Nazionale Romano, alle terme di Diocleziano*. Milan: Mondatori-Electa.

Garbucci, A.(ed.), 1999. *Il Colosseo*. Milan: Electa.

Giardina, A., 1985. *L'uomo romano*. Rome-Baria: Gius. Laterza & Figli.

Guidobaldi, P., 2005. *Il Foro Romano*. Milan: Mondadori Electa.

Houston, M. G., 2003. *Ancient Greek, Roman, & Byzantine Costume*. New York: Dover Publications.

Jacques, A., 1985. *Etre mèdecin à Rome*. Paris: Les Belles Lettres., Paris, 1985.

La Rocca, E. A., De Vos, M. and A., 1994. *Pompeii* Milan: Mondadori.

Moscati, S. (ed.), 1993. *Vita quotidiana nell'Italia antica,* Vol I-II. Milan: Mondadori.

Paoli, E., 1962. *Vita romana*. Florence: Le Monnier.

Pavolini, C., 1986. *La vita quotidiana ad Ostia*. Rome-Bari: Gius. Laterza & Figli.

Peché, V., and Vendries, C., 2001. *Musique et spectacles dans la Rome Antique et dans l'Occident*. Paris: Errance., 2001.

Puccini-Delbey, G., 2007. *La vie sexuelle à Rome*. Paris: Editions Tallandier.

Robert, J., 1999. *Rome*. Paris: Les Belles Lettres.

Scheid, J., and Jacques, F., 1990. *Rome et l'intégration de l'Empire*. Paris: Presse universitaires de France.

Staccioli, R. A., 1986. *Guida di Roma Antica*. Milan: RCS Rizzoli Libri.

Staccioli, R. A., 1996. *Italia di ieri Italia di oggi*. Rome: Archeoroma.

Staccioli, R. A., 2000. *Guida insolita ai luoghi, ai monumenti e alle curiosità di Roma antica*. Rome: Newton Compton.

Staccioli, R. A., 2001. *Vivere a Roma 2000 anni fa*. Rome: Archeoroma.

Staccioli, R. A., 2005. *La città che chiamiamo Roma*. Rome: Archeoroma.

Staccioli, R. A., 2004. *Cedamus patria, ossia fuggire da Roma*, in *Strenna dei Romanisti*. Rome, 21 Aprile 2004.

Weeber, K., 2000. *Alltag im Alten Rom: ein Lexikon.* Düsseldorf: Artemis & Winkler Verlag.